LITTLE SISTERS OF MURDER

The Library Lady saw it first. Standing a little behind the moving door, it took Glinda a little longer. The Library Lady cried out. Glinda just stared. Maybe it was all too bizarre to accept at first glance.

"Oh, dear," the Library Lady said. "Oh dear, oh dear, oh dear."

Out there in the storeroom, there was no water except for a few dark spots of damp that trailed along the carpet from the outer door. There were no green baize cardboard tables, either, which was what had been in there the last time Glinda looked. As far as Glinda could tell, the storeroom was empty, except for the body of Brigit Ann Reilly stretched out across the floor . . . and the snakes.

Glinda would have rushed in to see if the girl was all right, but she couldn't.

Brigit Ann Reilly was covered with hissing, snapping, spitting water moccasins, and water moccasins were very poisonous snakes. . . .

Also by Jane Haddam

A GREAT DAY
FOR
THE DEADLY

❖

Jane Haddam

BANTAM BOOKS
NEW YORK · TORONTO · LONDON · SYDNEY · AUCKLAND

A GREAT DAY FOR THE DEADLY

A Bantam Crime Line Book / March 1992

CRIME LINE and the portrayal of a boxed "cl" are trademarks of Bantam Books, a division of Bantam Doubleday Dell Publishing Group, Inc.

ISBN 0-553-29388-5

Published simultaneously in the United States and Canada

Bantam Books are published by Bantam Books, a division of Bantam Doubleday Dell Publishing Group, Inc. Its trademark, consisting of the words "Bantam Books" and the portrayal of a rooster, is Registered in U.S. Patent and Trademark Office and in other countries. Marca Registrada. Bantam Books, 666 Fifth Avenue, New York, New York 10103.

PRINTED IN THE UNITED STATES OF AMERICA

RAD   0 9 8 7 6 5 4 3 2 1

Prologue

❖

Thursday, February 21

There was a big maple on the front lawn of St. Ignatius Loyola Parochial School, covered with papier-mâché leprechauns and painted-plastic glitter-encrusted shamrocks. Brigit Ann Reilly passed it every day on her walk from the Motherhouse of the Sisters of Divine Grace to the Maryville Public Library. Sometimes she thought the tree was pretty, a perfect example of the simple faith of children. Sometimes she thought it was wrong, because it replaced the sacred symbols of Christianity with representations of a lot of pagan superstitions. Mostly she didn't notice it at all. Brigit Ann Reilly was very self-conscious about her walks. She was only eighteen years old, just out of high school, and she had arrived in Maryville to enter the convent just this past September. Before coming, she had watched a dozen movies about girls who decided to become nuns and read a handful of books put out by the Church on the same subject. She hadn't even begun to be prepared for what it was like. She had imagined herself in a habit more times than she could remember. She hadn't realized how exposed it would make her feel to actually wear one. A postulant's habit wasn't much—a long-sleeved black dress that reached to the bottom of the calves; a caplike French babushka—but it was enough to make Brigit feel that everyone must be staring at her. Especially today. On top of being naturally shy and more than a little self-involved, Brigit was one of those people who are pathologically self-conscious in guilt. She was supposed to go directly from St. Mary of the Hill to the library. St. Mary of the Hill was on one end of Delaney Street, at the top of the highest rise in town. The library was at the other end. It was a straight shot, without detours or side issues, right through the center of town. Brigit went down the hill with books to return and a list of books needed. She came up again with whatever Glinda Daniels could find of what was on the list. It was, as Sister Scholastica always said, a position of trust and a test of religious obedience. Brigit had been very obedient for most of the past six months. Today, she was getting ready to make an excursion of her own.

It was ten o'clock on the morning of Thursday, February 21. On this day of any other year, the landscape would have been frozen solid, full of snow and grit. This far north in New York State, edging up toward the banks of the St. Lawrence Seaway, February was a hard month. This year, for some reason no one could tell, there had been an unprecedented thaw. On Valentine's Day the temperature had risen to fifty-two degrees. Three days later, the rain had started, washing away what was left of another big rock candy winter. Today the temperature was nearly sixty and the rain a thick curtain threatening to bring flood. Brigit wore a simple shawl over the shoulders of her habit and carried an umbrella to keep the rain off her head.

"Good morning, Mr. O'Brien," she sang out, when she got to the shoe store, just half a block past Iggy Loy. The shoe store was worse than the school, in terms of Irish decorations. Its window was hung with green paper streamers studded with buttons that said "Erin Go Bragh." Brigit didn't know what "Erin Go Bragh" meant, but she did know that Sister Scholastica hated it. Sister Scholastica was Mistress of Postulants. She always said there ought to be a murder mystery out there called *Erin Go Bang*. Brigit skidded to a stop at the shoe store's door and said, "You shouldn't be standing out in the rain without a hat, Mr. O'Brien. You'll catch a cold."

"I never catch colds," Jack O'Brien said. Then he rubbed the rain off the top of his bald head with the flat of his hand and sighed. "Never mind. That's the kind of thing I used to say when I was twenty-two. These days, I'd be glad to go back to sixty-two."

"I never think of you as old," Brigit said virtuously.

"Hunh. Must be why you're going to be a holy nun. Excess of charity. What are you doing out in weather like this?"

"What I always do. Going to the library."

"Well, the good Sister Scholastica must not have looked out her window this morning. Assuming she's got windows. Don't you realize, child, there's going to be a flood."

"Is there really?"

O'Brien shrugged. "Not a big one. Not like the disaster we had in '53. But if the rain keeps on coming down like this, I'd expect the streets along the river to be underwater by three this afternoon."

Brigit turned in the direction of the river, invisible behind block after block of solid two-story frame buildings, stores, and houses that made up the center of town. She had never been down by the river. The only times she was allowed into town from the Motherhouse were on her library trips and her literacy days, Wednesdays, when she and half a dozen other postulants and novices were bussed over to St. Andrew's parish to teach reading to adults. Literacy days were Brigit's first experience of Doing Good to the Poor. That, like entering the convent, had turned out to be not at all what Brigit expected. Sometimes Brigit wondered if there was something wrong with her. Her best friend among the postulants, Neila Connelly, never seemed to have the same kinds of trouble. Neila never seemed to have any kind of trouble. Neila just . . . floated.

Brigit turned her head away from the river, thinking she might be giving herself away—although that was silly—and smiled at Jack O'Brien again. "Sister Scholastica was probably just excited," she said. "About Margaret Finney. You know."

"Margaret Finney?"

"The founder of our Order. She was beatified last week."

"Ah," Jack O'Brien said.

"If she actually gets all the way to being canonized,

she'll be the first Irish-American saint. You wouldn't believe the kind of fuss that's going on up at the house. We're even having our parents up for St. Patrick's Day and putting on a program."

"What kind of a program would that be? Nuns dancing?"

"Some of us," Brigit said. "Mostly it's going to be postulants and novices singing and giving speeches. You can come if you want. The whole town's going to be invited for after the parade. I'm going to speak on 'The Snake in Irish Myth and Legend' and 'The History of the Immigrants National Bank.'"

"Two speeches?"

"Everybody's giving two speeches. We have to. Sister Scholastica is always saying how they wouldn't have had to in her day because there were a hundred girls in her postulant class. Can you imagine that? A hundred."

"Yes, well," Jack O'Brien said, "the good Sister's right about that. There aren't nearly enough vocations these days. People are too selfish."

"Maybe there aren't as many people."

Jack O'Brien cocked a single eyebrow. "That's a kind of selfishness, too. 'I'd rather have a new TV set than raise another child.' Or are you one of those people who thinks the ban on birth control ought to go?"

"To tell you the truth, I never think about it."

"Yes," Jack O'Brien said. "Maybe that's natural. In the old days, nuns never thought about birth control." He rubbed the top of his head again, and sighed again, and looked back through the door of his store. It was empty and likely to stay that way, with the weather this bad. Brigit could practically see him making up his mind to close up and go home. "Listen," he told her, "you get back up the hill from the library, you tell the good Sister how bad it is down here, all right?"

"All right."

"The nuns have always been good for this town. In '53 the lady who's now your Reverend Mother General came right down to Hibernia Street in that big flowing habit they used to wear and hauled sandbags with her own two hands. The old Reverend Mother General opened the doors of the convent to anybody who needed shelter and half the town was up there before midnight. Caused a terrible fuss. Had to have something or the other reconsecrated."

Brigit shifted uneasily under her umbrella. It really was raining very hard. The air itself was saturated, thick with wet. Brigit could feel the damp chill under her habit and inside her shoes.

"Well," she said, "I'd better get going. Sister fusses so much when I get back too late."

"Sister ought to fuss when you're back late. It's a form of protection."

"I'm eighteen years old, Mr. O'Brien. I can take care of myself."

"Hunh. Well. You try to do that for the rest of the day. I think I'll pack it in and see how my Mary is getting along. You sure you don't need an escort?"

"Positive."

Jack O'Brien nodded, turned, and went back into his store.

Out on the sidewalk, Brigit Ann Reilly bit her lip, looked at the rain streaming past the edges of her umbrella, and wondered if she ought to go through with what she had agreed to do. Her sense of local geography was weak, so she couldn't be sure, but she thought the place she was supposed to be going to was down near the river. If the river really was flooding, then what? She turned in the direction of the library and started to move, slowly, sloshing along the pavement as if she were wading in surf.

All around her, Maryville, New York—founded by Irish immigrants just after the Civil War and sustained by them for more than a 125 years since—was getting ready for St. Patrick's Day. It was getting ready in ways that had nothing to do with the conscious will of the people living in it, too. There were so many deliberate things—like the polished '57 Chevy Stu Morrissey kept on the roof of his body shop on Corrigan Street, wrapped now in green ribbons and sporting a larger-than-life-size leprechaun at the wheel—but what struck Brigit were the undeliberate ones. The rain and the thaw had done their work. Grass was sprouting in thick emerald green carpets on all the lawns. At the library, the border made of a deeper green plant Brigit didn't know the name of had gone wild. It was at least half an inch taller than the grass beside it, and thick, and very dark. It reminded Brigit of a dust ruffle. She stared at it for a moment and shook her head.

If she had any sense, she would go right down to the bottom of the hill and in through the library doors, get her job done, and then go right on home. That was what she owed Sister Mary Scholastica and the Sisters of Divine Grace and the Catholic Church. It was called religious obedience and she had made a promise to practice it all the way back in September. The problem was, she no longer knew what religious anything meant any more. Ever since she had entered the convent, religion had been falling apart on her. Neila Connelly was always telling her it was a very bad sign, that it meant she had no vocation, but Brigit didn't like to think that. She was one of those girls who had "always" wanted to be a nun, the way other girls "always" wanted to be mothers or ballet dancers or models. She couldn't imagine herself doing anything else.

There was an old-fashioned lamppost at the intersection to Londonderry Street, where she would have to turn if she wanted to go on her extracurricular errand. It had been left standing by the town as a gesture to the "history" of Maryville, and festooned with green satin ribbons with gold harps and mock shillelaghs at their hearts. The ribbons were drooping in the rain and the harps were losing their gold. Brigit stopped beside the mess and looked first toward the library and then down Londonderry Street. Londonderry Street seemed to stretch out into fog and blackness, mysterious.

When she had set out from the Motherhouse this morning, Brigit had had a whole set of rationalizations. Her errand was important, maybe even a matter of life and death. Her errand would hurt nobody and take nothing away from the Sisters of Divine Grace. There wasn't any reason not to bend the rules a little to help a friend. Now it struck her with particular force that it wasn't the errand she was desperate to carry out, but the person who had asked her to do it that she was desperate to keep as a friend. Like most girls her age, Brigit would never have admitted to anyone that she was unsophisticated or naive—but she was both. She had grown up in a small town in New Hampshire where the rest of the population had been made up of people exactly like herself, except that some of them had been Protestants. Before coming to Maryville, she had never met an atheist or a Jew, never mind a really rich person or a really poor person or someone from an entirely different culture. Maryville hardly seemed the place to throw her into contact with things like that, but it had. In the process, it had taught her something that disturbed her greatly. In Maryville, all the things that weren't supposed to matter—beauty and money, surface brilliance and superficial shine—actually did.

Brigit looked at the lamppost again, and then at the library. The plant border down there looked an even darker green than it had a moment ago. She turned away and looked down Londonderry Street again. The choice seemed so plain. The library was safety and submission. Londonderry Street was adventure and risk. It couldn't have been plainer if it had shown up in her senior year psychology book back at North Frederickson High.

She shifted the umbrella to her other, not yet sweated hand, and made the turn. Even if she didn't have a million other reasons to be doing what she was doing, she had this: If she went to the library, she would have to pick up books on snakes. Brigit Ann Reilly hated snakes.

They hissed.

[2]

"What I don't think you realize is what the scope of this thing will be," Don Bollander said. "I don't think you have the faintest idea. Of course, it could turn out to be nothing, but it doesn't have to be. It could turn out to be—Lourdes."

Lourdes, Miriam Bailey thought, and then: If it were forty years ago, I'd call for my smelling salts. Since it was not forty years ago, she picked up her twenty-two-carat gold Tiffany T-pen and sucked at the tip of it as if it were a cigarette. She had quit smoking back in 1966, and since then she had sucked on a variety of objects, all of them expensive. She took that thought and held on to it for a moment, smiling secretly to herself. She could think of a perfectly filthy interpretation of a line like that, and one that would, in her case, be true. Miriam Bailey was sixty-two years old. Three days after her sixtieth birthday, she had been married for the first time. Her husband's name was Joshua Malley. He was very poor; very beautiful; and very, very young. He also cost as much to maintain as an eighty-four-foot sloop.

There was a twenty-two-carat gold Tiffany letter opener lying on her green felt desk blotter. Unlike the T-pen, which had been given to her by her only real lover before she married Josh, it had belonged to her father. It might have belonged to her grandfather. Miriam was always stumbling over the gaps in her knowledge of what had gone on down here, at the office, in the years when she was being forced to be a girl. Sometimes she looked up at the portrait of her father on the north wall and lectured him about it. He should have realized she would never marry the kind of man who could take over the Bank. Even back in the forties, when women never ran banks, she had intended to run this one.

Don Bollander was hopping from one foot to the other, aware that he didn't have her full attention, impatient. Miriam found herself thinking idly that, in the end, she had been forced to be a girl on a permanent basis, at least in the minor matters. Since she'd moved in to the president's office, she'd worn makeup and very good suits from Chanel and had her hair done. Since the fashion in women's bodies had shifted in the mid-sixties, she had made sure she was always exceptionally thin. It was too bad she never wanted to retire. There were days when all she wanted was to sit down in front of a table full of hot fudge sundaes and eat.

Don Bollander had passed beyond foot shifting to hopping. He was getting positively apoplectic. Miriam sat forward, took a deep breath, and dragged herself into the present. Don Bollander's present.

"All right," she said. "Lourdes."

Don Bollander looked hurt. He was a tall, abstemious-looking man who always wore a very bad toupee. When he looked hurt, his lips swelled.

"I'm only trying to look out for the interests of the company," he said. "The company has a lot invested in local real estate."

"I own half the town. Say what you mean."

"I am saying what I mean," Don said. "Do you know anything about the process by which people are made saints in the Catholic Church?"

"I know a little." Miriam knew a lot. She had attended parochial school right here in Maryville, then the Convent of the Sacred Heart in Noroton, then Manhattanville in the days when it was still a Catholic college. Her early life had been a paradigm of the proper upbringing for a rich Catholic girl.

"The thing is," Don Bollander told her, "now that Margaret Finney has been beatified, the nuns on the hill there will probably begin running a campaign to collect evidence of miracles that have occurred because of Margaret Finney's intercession. That's what they have to have to get Margaret Finney canonized. Evidence of miracles after her death."

"Yes, Don, I know."

"Well, think about it. Miracles. Here. Pilgrims. The

town full of people even in the winter. It could be—a
bonanza."

"A bonanza," Miriam repeated.

"Of course. We just have to manage the publicity.
We could get our people in New York right on it. The
Sisters would probably welcome the help."

"Help, Don? What kind of help do you want us to
give them?"

"I told you. Publicity help. And maybe other kinds.
Maybe we could build a shrine on one of the properties
we own out on Clare Avenue or Diamond Place. God
only knows we aren't doing anything with the stuff out
there anyway. It's falling down."

"It's probably being washed out to sea, at the
moment. Look at this rain."

"I wasn't talking about the rain." Now Don looked
not only hurt, but angry. He always got angry when his
more ridiculous ideas weren't taken seriously. "I've been
working on this all night, Miriam. I really have. It's not
a stupid way to go about things. This is going to make the
news around here any minute now. It's going to be all
over this part of New York State."

Miriam hauled herself out of her chair, walked to
her window, and looked out at the rain. It was ten
minutes after ten in the morning. Two stories below her,
sheltered under the broad black expanse of a nunly
umbrella, one of the postulants from St. Mary of the Hill
was making her way along Londonderry Street. Miriam
knew it was a postulant because of the shoes and the
ankles. Nuns and postulants and novices all wore the
same shoes, but only postulants showed their ankles.
Miriam wondered who it was and what she was doing
here. The Sisters of Divine Grace were a very conservative order. You rarely saw any of them wandering
around town on their own.

Miriam raised her head a little and looked into the
parking lot across the street. She owned that parking lot,
just as she owned every building on this block, but she
wasn't interested in the condition of it or the business it
was doing. She had a maintenance department to keep

track of the condition and an accounting office to keep track of the business. What she wanted to see was whether the bright red Jaguar XKE was still parked along the east wall, which it was. She didn't expect it to be there for long. When she asked herself if she expected Josh to be with her for long, she didn't come up with an answer. The proposition should have been straightforward. It made her a little crazy that it wasn't. Josh was a young man without skills and without prospects. He had his body and his docility to sell, and he could get a good price for it or a bad. Miriam thought she had given him a very good price for it, and that that should be enough. Millions of young women had made the same bargain over the centuries and managed to keep up their end of it. Why should it be any different for men?

Out on Londonderry Street, the postulant was slipping out of sight in the direction of the river. Across the way at the edge of the parking lot, the back door to Madigan's Dry Goods swung open and let out a slight figure in a bright blue slicker. Her name was Ann-Harriet Severan and she had hair almost as brightly red as the slicker was blue. Miriam knew that even though the hair was invisible under a thick plastic rain hat, just as she knew that Ann-Harriet wore size seven narrow shoes and size twelve dresses. It was all contained in the private detective's report she had commissioned over a month ago. Ann-Harriet stopped at the side of the Jaguar, fumbled in her pockets, and came up with the key. For a moment, she seemed to be frozen in contemplation, maybe of the postulant still making her way in the rain out of Miriam's sight. Whatever it was didn't hold her attention long. Ann-Harriet shook her head, rubbed the key dry on the lining of her slicker, and then opened the Jaguar up. Seconds later, the exhaust began to belch white smoke and the windshield wipers began to sweep and pulse. The Jaguar had cost $92,528, not including tax. Miriam had bought it for Josh on his last birthday. She had bought him other things during their time together, including a menagerie that had once held a lion and now kept an eclectic collection that ranged from a llama to snakes, but Josh had shown no inclination to share that with Ann-Harriet Severan.

Miriam turned away from the window, went back to her desk and sat down. "Don," she said, "do you know what it takes to get a miracle accepted by the Catholic Church?"

"What it takes? Why should it take anything? I thought the Church *wanted* miracles."

"I don't know if it does or not," Miriam said. "In a case like this, where there is a chance of canonization, once a miracle has been claimed, Rome will send an investigator. Rome may send several. One or more than one, it doesn't matter, because if there's more than one, they'll be clones. Priests, of course, and very well educated priests. Priests who don't believe in miracles."

"I didn't think that was allowed," Don said stiffly. "Priests who don't believe in miracles."

"All Catholics are required to believe in the miracles attributed to Christ and his apostles in the Gospels and any other miracles directly asserted in Scripture. Beyond that, they aren't required to believe in miracles at all. The Church doesn't declare miracles to be authentic. It merely declares that belief in the miraculous nature of certain events is not contrary to reason— meaning they've investigated the event and can explain it in no other way—and not contrary to faith. That's it. Not real, just not contrary."

"But Lourdes—"

"What about Lourdes? The Church has declared three specific healings to be 'not immediately explicable in any other way' and belief in the intercession of Mary in those cases and in the appearance of Mary to Bernadette to be 'not contrary to faith.' Just three, Don, in over a hundred years. And any Catholic who wants to is free to think that even those three are a lot of superstitious bunk and that Bernadette herself was an hysterical girl who was seeing things that weren't there."

"I don't see—"

"I do." Miriam hauled herself to her feet again, she

didn't know why. Ever since she had been absolutely sure of the affair between Josh and Ann-Harriet Severan, she had been restless. It bothered her, because the only other time she had ever been restless in the same way was when she was waiting for her father to die. Then she had had a perfectly sensible reason to be restless. Only after her father's death had she been able to make her move to take control of the Bank. The old chauvinist fool would never have allowed it. If he'd realized what she'd intended to do, he would never have left her the stock that made it possible for her to do it. This thing with Josh was an entirely different matter. If he proved unsatisfactory he could always be fired—meaning divorced. If a boy toy was really what she required at this stage in her life, she could always find another one. She had picked Josh up in a bar in Corfu. Greece was a good place for things like that.

She went back to the window, looked down into the empty parking lot, and frowned. She had to get control of herself. She was beginning to think like an Irish-woman, and that could end in blood.

"Don," she said, "pay attention. I remember the campaign to have Elizabeth Ann Seton canonized."

"And?"

"And you want to push but you don't want to push too hard. Pushing too hard holds things up. Like with this business in Yugoslavia. There's been too much publicity. Rome is dragging its feet."

"Having Margaret Finney declared a saint would be very good for the town," Don said.

"Yes," Miriam said, "I agree with you. It would also be very good for the Sisters, and we all owe a great deal to the Sisters. Just—go easy, will you please? Try not to jinx this thing."

"Jinx it," Don repeated. He looked disapproving, with his mouth clamped into a thin line, but he often looked that way when there was nothing wrong with him but a little indigestion. Maybe he had indigestion all the time. He was a holdover from that interim time between her father's death and her successful coup, and she had only kept him on because he was accommodating. In fact, he seemed to have no sense of what a job description should entail at all. No matter what she asked him to do—no matter how bizarre or how unrelated to work—he did it.

She went back to her desk again, and sat down again, and rubbed her face with her hands. She was pacing, like the heroine of a bad forties "women's" picture.

"On your way out, tell Julie to tell Kevin Hale I'm going out for a couple of hours. We were supposed to have a meeting about that glitch in the computer system we haven't got straightened out yet."

"Are you sure it is a glitch in the computer system? I was thinking about it last week, you know. It just might be that what we've got here is a theft."

"It certainly looks like a theft," Miriam sighed, "a really clumsy theft. The mistake sticks out a mile. Still, with the bank examiners coming in on the fifth, we've got to keep on top of it. I hate to put off this meeting, but there's something I have to do. Just tell Julie to tell Kevin I'll be gone and I'll get back to him when I can."

"All right. But I hear rumors, Miriam. I hear that that mistake can be traced straight back to Ann-Harriet Severan's desk."

"It can't be traced back to anybody's desk at the moment."

"If you say so. But you're much too trusting, Miriam. That's the problem with women in business. They don't know what kind of absolute moral cesspools most people really are."

Absolute moral cesspools, Miriam thought, closing her eyes as Don went out the door. She just wished that most people were absolute moral cesspools. It would make them far more interesting than what they really were, which was not much of anything. It amazed her sometimes, just how wishy-washy and unimpressive people could be.

She got her thermos of tea out of her bottom left hand drawer and stood up to stuff it into the deep pocket of her cashmere coat. She had a good five minutes or so before she had to leave. She decided to use the time to think herself into another place, or maybe another century. A place where a woman, betrayed by a man as Josh had betrayed her, would resort to murder as a matter of course.

There had probably never been such a place or such a century, but Miriam always wished there were.

[3]

Samuel Xavier Harrigan was an Irishman who had been raised in Scotland, educated in England, and brought to the pinnacle of his career in places like Borneo. He had built his precut cedar log house halfway up an Adirondack mountain on the west side of Maryville because he wanted to spend his free time in a place where there was snow. At least that was what he told people, especially media people. When the silly, skinny girls came out from *Time* and *TV Guide*, he couldn't help himself. Samuel Xavier Harrigan had a reputation as a wild man. He was big and his white hair was shaggy, although not particularly long. He had a sheepskin lined winter jacket and a thick-timbred baritone voice that tended to roar. He had once eaten roast grubs with chicory and chives on the Public Broadcasting System. He could have told them he came up here to commune with the spirits of reincarnated squirrels and gotten them to believe.

The truth was somewhat more prosaic. Years ago, when Sam had been nothing more than a decently respected herpetologist with enormous stage presence and an even more enormous appetite for a good time, his best friend from Oxford had come up here to teach at one of the local universities. He had also come up here to die. This was back in 1980, before anybody really knew what AIDS was, but AIDS was what James had—and once Sam did know something about it, he wasn't particularly surprised. James had always put the lie to the Oxford stereotype of the homosexual as effete.

James had always been a rip, and he remained a rip until very nearly the end. In the meantime, Sam built the house, kept him company, and tried to write a book. James always said Sam would have been perfect if he could get over this thing about wanting to go to bed with girls.

After James was gone, Sam could have moved onto something more—well—suitable, but he hadn't wanted to. James died in 1984, and by then Sam was already on PBS, cooking wild dandelion greens over an open fire in the Scottish highlands. *The Fearless Epicure* had been born and was about to go into a growth spurt. In 1985, the schedule would include wild goat with thistles in Albania, buffalo in a prairie grass shell in Montana, and stewed carpenter ants in Mozambique. Summer of Love Productions, the company that funded him, didn't care what Sam did as long as he didn't cook anything that was endangered. He just kept on getting wilder and wilder, farther and farther out, until he got tired for the season and decided to come home. Every once in a while he thought about moving, and then he thought how stupid that would be. The Rocky Mountains were full of people who did the kind of thing he did. So were New Mexico and southern California. So, God help him, was Jackson Hole, Wyoming. Sometimes it seemed like the Adirondack Mountains were the only place in America that hadn't been invaded by television. Sam Harrigan definitely wanted to stay in America. He thought his reasons were too complicated to explain to Americans, but he wanted to stay.

At eleven o'clock on the morning of Thursday, February 21, he wanted to get dry. He had been sitting on his screened porch since seven thirty, watching the rain come down and no one at all come out of the little house halfway down the hill. He had been worried about his animals. Most of them hibernated and their schedules had been thrown way off by this false spring. His red panda was agitated and tearful. His lizards were jumpy and upset. His snakes seemed to have disappeared. He was worried about the little house down the hill, too, and the person who lived there. It was much too late for nobody to have come out. Worst of all, for the last ten minutes he'd had his ear glued to the telephone. Charlie Wicklow was calling up from Boston, steamed up in that underpowered WASP way of his about something or other. Charlie Wicklow was Sam's agent.

"All I want from you," Charlie was saying, "is a promise that you'll at least not offend anybody. Especially not the Cardinal Archbishop of Colchester. And especially not in public in front of half the town of Maryville."

"I don't know the Cardinal Archbishop of Colechester," Sam said reasonably. "Maryville is used to me. Is that the back door?"

"What?"

"Nothing." As it turned out, it *was* nothing. Sam was sitting watching the little house down the hill. He'd thought for a moment that he'd seen movement there, finally, after a thoroughly dead day. It bothered him. She always left for work between seven thirty and eight, Monday through Friday, without fail. He didn't know what she did at night—he didn't watch her at night—but whatever it was it never kept her out to the next day. Or it hadn't, until now. Sam rubbed his knuckles against the stubble on his chin and fretted. Maybe she'd found a man she wanted to see. Maybe she'd decided to move in with him. Why hadn't he made his move before this, when he still had a chance?

"Sam?" Charlie said.

"Sorry."

"You ought to be sorry," Charlie said. "You're not listening to a word I say. This is important."

"In case I meet the Cardinal Archbishop of Colchester."

"For Christ's sake. Sam, let me start again from the beginning, all right? Maybe, if I repeat it one more time, you'll retain enough of it so that we can discuss it. Do you remember my saying that you'd received an invitation to attend a reception on St. Patrick's Day at the sisterhouse of the—"

"Motherhouse."

"What?"

"Motherhouse," Sam repeated. "Not sisterhouse. A Motherhouse is the first and principal house of a religious order. I take it I've been invited up to St. Mary of the Hill."

"The Sisters of Divine Grace," Charlie said.

"Same difference. What do they want me up there for?"

"I think they're putting on some kind of program. There's going to be a Mass. 'Celebrated' by John Cardinal O'Bannion. That's what it says here. 'Celebrated.'"

"That's what it would say, Charlie. That's how it's said."

"Yes, well, that wouldn't have got to me. Even the Cardinal Archbishop wouldn't have gotten to me necessarily. It's what this reception thing is for. Those nuns are going to have a saint."

"What?"

"Listen to this, Sam. 'On the occasion of the beatification of the Blessed Margaret Finney, a Mass of petition for her successful canonization.' Doesn't that mean that they're going to have a saint?"

There was a pack of cigarettes lying on the low picnic-style rough pine coffee table, torn open on one corner and shedding flecks of tobacco. Sam picked them up, extracted one, and lit it with a wooden kitchen match. He had wooden-handled kitchen matches all over the house and kerosene lamps to go with them, because his electricity up here was provided by his own private generator and something was always going wrong with it. He took a deep drag and exhaled and stared through his screen. There was still no movement at the little house, but something hopeful had occurred to him. Her car was a bright red two-door Saab. It was parked just where it belonged, halfway up her drive.

He took another drag on his cigarette, stared at the porch ceiling and sighed. It really was a mess out there today. Maybe she had decided to call in sick so she wouldn't have to go out into the wet. Maybe she really was sick, and he ought to go down there and rescue her.

He imagined her lying curled up on the carpet in her living room, burning up with fever, only half-conscious. He didn't even know if she had a carpet in her living room. He only knew her name because of an accident. He was either insane or regressing to an adolescent state. This was the way he had fallen in love for the first time, when he was fourteen, with little Ginnie MacIver. Little Ginnie MacIver had had a head full of bubble bath and a size thirty-eight chest.

Sam took yet another drag, blew yet another stream of smoke into the sodden air, and chucked the burning butt into the tin ashtray he kept on the plant shelf. Charlie Wicklow was babbling on and on, on and on. Sam didn't want to listen to him. Charlie Wicklow was a Protestant, and like all Protestants he was going to end up giving Sam a headache. This was true even though Sam hadn't been inside a Catholic Church for over twenty-five years.

"Charlie," Sam said, "calm down a minute. Why did that invitation come to you?"

"Your invitations always come to me," Charlie said. "At least, they do when they're from somebody you don't know."

"Right. They come here when they're from somebody I do know."

"I don't get it."

"It's just this, Charlie. I don't know any of the Sisters of Divine Grace on a first-name basis, to put it both awkwardly and inaccurately, but I do know them. They send a pair to knock on my door twice a year collecting for their missions, and I give to their missions, too, to the tune of four or five hundred dollars a visit—"

"That must be why you got invited."

"Maybe so, Charlie, but the point is, if they want to invite me to this reception, why don't they just send another pair up to deliver the invitation? They love coming up here. They stand around and sniff and try to figure out what I'm making in the kitchen."

"What are you making in the kitchen?"

"Usually popcorn. Charlie, take a look at that invitation you've got and tell me—"

But for once, Charlie didn't have to be told. He was rustling papers. He was coughing and heaving and hemming and hawing. Finally, he got back on the line and said,

"The invitation didn't actually come from the Sisters of Divine Grace. It's for a reception at the Motherhouse of the Sisters of Divine Grace, but the invitation itself is from the Cardinal's office."

"Ah."

"What do you mean, 'ah.'"

"I mean you've got to hold on for a second. There's something I want to do."

The something Sam wanted to do was get closer to the screen. He could have done that with the phone in his hand, but then he would have been distracted by Charlie's nattering. There was movement at the little house down the hill at last. The front door had been flung open and slammed shut. The drive had been possessed by a swirling storm of beige raincoat and wide-legged dark blue pants. She always dressed like that, in pants with legs so wide they might as well have been culottes and tight little shells topped by oversize jackets that flowed almost to her knees. She had straight blond hair blunt cut to her shoulders and across her forehead that reminded Sam of Mary from the folk song group from the sixties. She was five feet four and maybe a hundred and forty-five pounds. Like most American women with the kind of figure Sam liked, she probably thought she was fat.

She got to her car, dropped her keys, managed to pick them up without ruining her clothes in a mud puddle, and let herself into her car. Seconds later, smoke began to pump out of her exhaust pipe. Sam leaned sideways and grabbed his telescope. He had never done that before—he didn't spy on her, for God's sake; that wasn't what the telescope was for—but today he was worried. The road to the bottom of the hill was narrow and twisting and hardly safe for a vehicle meant to cruise on city streets. He should have gone down and offered her a lift this morning. It would have been a good way to get himself introduced.

"Forty-two," he said out loud. "Maybe forty-five."

He had been holding the phone again. Charlie said, "What?"

"Never mind," Sam said. He thought he'd been saying it all morning. "I just want you to realize, before you go accepting that invitation, that the Sisters may have no idea they're giving a reception."

"What are you talking about?"

"I'm talking about Cardinal Archbishops and Princes of the Church. Especially enthusiastic ones, and John O'Bannion certainly is one of those."

"Are you saying you *won't* go?"

"No, Charlie, I'm not saying I won't go. I'm just saying you should let me check this thing out a little. Let me find out what the Sisters really want. I don't care what John O'Bannion really wants. I don't have to live with John O'Bannion."

"But—"

"Trust me."

The hesitation on the other end of the line was like a physical entity. Charlie didn't trust him, and Sam didn't blame him. Sam knew he had never been particularly trustworthy. Finally, though, Charlie sighed, and Sam knew he had won the point, at least for the moment.

"All right," Charlie said. "But Sam, this thing has a deadline on it. March 1. Get back to me before then or I'll accept in your name and stick you with it."

"Right."

"I mean it, Sam."

"I said right."

"You never take me seriously," Charlie said.

There was a sharp click in Sam's ear—sharp enough to make Sam wince—and then the phone went to dial tone. Sam put the receiver back in the cradle and sighed. He had been hanging onto the telescope for the whole of his last series of exchanges with Charlie, but it hadn't done much good. Between the rain and the bright green budding caused by the thaw that had allowed the rain and the crazy way Maryville went about celebrating St. Patrick's Day, Sam had been able to keep her car in sight only sporadically. He kept getting fuzzed out by pouring water or blocked by leaves and plastic decorations. He hadn't trained the telescope on the hill below him before. Now that he had, he seriously wondered if the people of Maryville took drugs in preparation for their celebration of the seventeenth. They seemed to have swarmed up here and stuck plastic shamrocks and little ceramic shillelaghs to every branch.

At the very bottom of the hill, the bright red Saab shot out of the trees, turned left onto Londonderry Street and raced out of sight. Sam kept the telescope trained on the place where she had disappeared, thinking. He hadn't realized how good it was, how clearly he could see what was down there. His picture of Londonderry Street and Clare Avenue and Diamond Place was so clear, he could have been watching them on television. He watched a garbage truck rumble down Clare Avenue on its way to the warehouse on the river. He followed a pair of old men moving from store window to store window on this lower end of Londonderry Street. Then he saw a very curious thing. The buildings on Diamond Place were all abandoned. Sometimes in the summer they were claimed by drifters and by bums, but in the winter they were always empty. Up here it didn't do to try to live without central heat. Since Diamond Place didn't lead anywhere, it was possible for that short street to go months at a time without any human presence. Now, though, it quite definitely had one. Sam saw her turn off Clare Avenue and head up toward the worst of the abandoned buildings, the ones at the end whose front walls seemed to be coming down. Sam recognized her clothes, too. She was one of those nuns-in-training from the Sisters of Divine Grace, a postulant, with a long black dress and a black thing on her head that wasn't exactly a veil. She was walking swiftly, as if she knew where she was going, and so intently she seemed not to notice the rain. When she got to the barrier of the dead end, she stopped, looked closely at the buildings on either side of her, and nodded at one. Then she climbed its steps, opened its door, and disappeared.

I wonder if the other nuns know what she's doing, Sam thought. They're crazy if they let her go into a place like that by herself. He had half a mind to pick up the phone again and call someone at the Motherhouse, to let them know what was going on. Then he told himself he was being nosy, and he hated nosy people. Nuns had to be trained to deal with all kinds of places and all kinds of people. They were supposed to help the poor. What he'd just seen could have been some kind of educational exercise.

He turned the telescope away from Diamond Place and tried to fix it on the library, where She worked. He couldn't do it. The library was deep into the valley, on one of the lowest plots of land in town. The best he could do was catch a flash of the dark green border of its lawn. He folded the telescope up, sat back, and found his cigarette burned to a cylinder of ash in his ashtray.

Glinda Daniels. That was her name. Glinda Daniels. Sam wondered if her mother had been obsessed with the movie or the book, if she'd been named for the Good Witch of the North or of the South. He refused to believe that her mother had been obsessed with Billie Burke.

[4]

For Father Michael Doherty, rain in February was the worst kind of news. It was bad enough for being impossible. It never got warm enough for rain up here in February. Even his most freshly arrived parishioner knew it. Even his old established stalwarts were beginning to revert. Father Michael knew what they were doing every time he turned his back: coming together in groups, speaking not so much in Spanish as in the jungle dialects most of them had been born into, talking about the evil eye. Michael Doherty knew something about the staying power of superstitions that had been given to you in childhood. "Michael," his mother had always told him, "if you throw the bread away without kissing it, God will see. God will let you starve." Michael Doherty had a degree in biology from Georgetown, a degree in theology from Notre Dame, and an M.D. from the Albert Einstein College of Medicine. He had been in Korea as a medic and come to the priesthood late, after a disastrous marriage that had ended in the death of his wife by drunk driving. He was a tall, spare, ruthlessly logical man of sixty-five—and he never threw bread away without kissing it first.

The other reason rain in February was such a bad idea was that it caused so much sickness. Michael hadn't thought of that in advance—whatever for?—but now that it had happened he could see it made sense. St. Andrew's Parish stretched itself across the dead end of Beckner Street, off Clare Avenue just above Diamond Place. On either side of it, marching back toward town, were four- and five-story tenements. Since Clare Avenue was now entirely commercial and Diamond Place was deserted, the people in the tenements on Beckner made up all of Michael's parish. There were more of them than Michael would have thought, if he hadn't lived here. They had a tendency to catch cold. Michael supposed that was perfectly natural. They were used to temperatures that grew very hot instead of very cold, and that changed gradually instead of on the spur of the moment. Their bodies were probably on circuit overload, trying to figure out how to deal with the change of planet.

It was now eleven thirty on the morning of Thursday, February 21, and the weather showed no signs of returning to normal. If anything, it looked about to get more strange. Michael hadn't been in Maryville for the flood of 1953, but he'd seen enough flooding in his life. He knew the signs. All morning he had been pacing back and forth in his small office off of St. Andrew's vestibule, trying to get a glimpse of the river or some sensible weather news on WKPZ. His view was blocked by the disintegrating brownstones on Diamond Place and WKPZ was having a Beach Boys bonanza. Downstairs in the basement, his clinic was open for business, as it was every morning except Sunday. On Sunday, it was open after twelve o'clock Mass, all afternoon.

There was a knock on his door—unnecessary, because the door was open; very necessary, because, as Michael had learned, these people were passionately polite—and Michael said "come in" to Hernandito Guerrez. Hernandito was the boy Michael was sponsoring for Georgetown, premed, in the hopes of seeing him go off to medical school in time. He should have been in school, but Michael had had sense enough not to tell him so today. Leonardo Evangelista, Michael's prime candidate for the priesthood, was here now, too. They would both stay until they were sure their mothers and fathers and aunts and uncles and cousins and neighbors were no longer in any kind of immediate trouble. It was the kind of thing Michael made himself remember in the dark hours of Saturday night, when he had patched up four knife wounds to ship to the county hospital and fielded three calls from the medical examiner's office, all asking him to do courtesy autopsies on possible drug ODs.

Hernandito came in, looked around pityingly—the office always looked like an explosion in a paper factory—and said, "I think you better come downstairs now, Father. Senora Diaz is very bad."

"You mean Señora Diaz is getting hysterical," Michael said. "I'll come down, Hernandito, but you know as well as I do that she's just scared to death. I can't do anything about that."

"Maybe the baby is coming early."

"The baby isn't due for two months and she isn't contracting. I know. I checked not more than ten minutes ago. Is Sister with her?"

Hernandito's lips pressed into a thin line. "Sister is perhaps not the best choice. Someone who is more competent might be a better idea. Someone like that might give Señora Diaz more confidence."

There was a green enameled pen on Michael's desk with "MY BOSS IS A JEWISH CARPENTER" written down the side of it in gold. Michael picked it up and resisted the urge to bite into it. "Sister" was Sister Mary Gabriel from the Sisters of Divine Grace up the hill, and she was perfectly competent. She was a first-rate obstetrical nurse and a qualified midwife. The problem was that she was also relatively young and very pretty. None of these people believed that young and pretty women could do much of anything besides have sex and tantrums.

"Look," Michael said, "forget Señora Diaz for a moment. I've made a call into town about the rain."

"Yes, Father?"

"Mostly it was like asking a politician for his position on the budget, but I did manage to get something done. We're going to move this operation to higher ground for the moment. Up to Iggy Loy."

Hernandito looked momentarily confused. Then the connections were made, and he smiled slightly. He would never have called St. Andrew's "St. Andy's." He would have considered it insulting.

"If we're going to move the clinic to higher ground, Father, maybe we should move everything. Everybody, I mean. Of course, most of the women are in our basement anyway—"

"Most of the children are down there, too. What's left on the street? A few old men?"

"Also the Estevan family that owns the market."

"All right. You could get some of the boys together and go door to door. We've got the van—bless Sam Harrigan—and we can get another one from St. Mary's. I've talked to Reverend Mother General."

"Reverend Mother General is a competent woman," Hernandito said.

Reverend Mother General was seventy-eight years old and a cross between Queen Elizabeth I and Medusa. Michael had no idea what she looked like, because he'd never dared look her in the face. Like everybody else, he was afraid of her on principle.

"I got hold of somebody else," he said. "Glinda."

"Ah," Hernandito said.

"It's a good thing I did get hold of her. She'd overslept her alarm clock. Anyway, she has to go in to work, but she'll meet us at Iggy Loy around three o'clock with blankets and food and a few other things. Sometimes I think I ought to get her together with Sam Harrigan and see what comes of it."

Hernandito was offended. "Sam Harrigan is a television star," he protested. "He would not want something so old as Miss Daniels."

"No? Well, Hernandito, you're very young."

"I'm old enough," Hernandito said. "You're a priest, Father. There are things you don't understand."

"Trust me, Hernandito, they don't let you enter the priesthood if you don't understand *that*." Michael stretched his legs and back, looked out the window again, shook his head. "It gets worse by the minute. I can't understand it. Are you ready to brave the land of the green and the home of the shamrock up there?"

"Of course I am," Hernandito said. "I like St. Patrick's Day. I march with the Fife and Drum Corps."

"That's right, you do. I'd forgotten."

"We've all made a decision about this, Father. All of us here. There were two ways we could go. We could ignore them all up there, or we could join the party. Joining the party had certain advantages."

"Green beer?"

"A future. Someday there will be enough of us here, we will have a celebration for St. Rose of Lima. Since we have always helped them, they will have to help us. No?"

"It's beyond me. All right, Hernandito, go find some friends and get going, door to door, don't miss one. Father Fitzsimmons up at Iggy Loy doesn't think there's going to be a real problem, but we shouldn't take any chances. The last thing we want to do is come back here in a day or two to find out some little old lady has drowned."

"I know every little old lady on the block."

"Keep a list," Michael said. "Oh, and when you get downstairs, send Sister Gabriel up. Old Señora Sanchez is going to need an insulin shot and she sure as hell isn't going to give it to herself."

"Should a priest say *hell*, Father?"

"It depends on where he is, who he's with, and what he intends to accomplish. Go, Hernandito."

"I'm going."

He was, too. The next thing Michael saw was his retreating back, making the sharp turn that led down the rickety stairs to the basement. Michael looked down at the papers on his desk, decided that most of them were useless, incomprehensible and out of date, and ignored them. He sat down instead, swiveling so that he could stare out at the rain.

Years ago, during those long dark months just before he turned forty, when he had first begun to think he might be called to be a priest, he had imagined himself as a kind of clone of the priests he had known when he was growing up. Big men with big voices, they had ruled over little fiefdoms of good Catholic families. Irish-American and working class themselves, they had preached the Word of God in a world where Irish-American and working class was all there seemed to be. There were people now who said that parishes like that had disappeared, but Michael knew it wasn't true. Iggy Loy was just like that, and Father Fitzsimmons, fifteen years Michael's junior, always seemed to Michael to be an older man out of an unquiet past. Michael wondered sometimes if he was suppressing a wish to be posted to a place like that. In some ways he thought it would be nice: a place where he wouldn't have to run a clinic every day, or, God help him, do autopsies as a "courtesy" to his people and the ME's office; a place where violence would come down to bare fists after too much beer; a place where men would work too much and women would clean too much and everybody would eat too much until the day when a combination of bad habits and the genetic bad luck of the Irish produced the expected heart attacks. Oh, yes, there was something very pleasant in the thought of all that kind of thing, and in the thought of saying Mass for people who spoke his language and had lived his past. On the other hand, there was also something inestimably boring.

He got out of his chair, and stretched again, and looked out his window again. He had to get going. Fitzsimmons might be right. There might be no flood in the long run. Even Fitzsimmons didn't think Michael ought to be taking chances. Michael leaned against the window glass, squinted out, and cursed to purgatory the idiot who had built an art deco replica of the St. George campanile right in his line of sight. What kind of neighborhood had this been all those years ago, when it was first put up?

He was about to give it all up when he saw it, what he would later think of as The Strange Thing. She was coming down Beckner Street from the direction of Clare Avenue, seemingly headed for the parish church. Michael had never seen her before, but he knew what she was. With the long black dress and that tight sided black head covering, there was only one thing she could be, a postulant from the Motherhouse up the hill. Michael found himself feeling caught, half-paralyzed. One of the things he had been intending to do was to call back Reverend Mother General and tell her he would need those vans after all. Now he wondered if he had to. Maybe she had misunderstood him and sent the vans as soon as they'd hung up earlier. On the other hand, maybe this postulant had nothing to do with vans. Postulants and novices from the Sisters of Divine Grace came down here every Wednesday to teach literacy classes and tutor high-school students who were having trouble with their work. Michael never saw them, because Wednesday was when he went out to visit the prison and then stopped in at the county hospital on his way back to town. Maybe this postulant was one of those, and she was here on some errand about books or writing supplies.

The idiocy of this idea—the stupidity of thinking that any of the nuns up there would send a child out into this storm just to check on something that could as easily have been checked on by phone—struck him at the same

time that he lost sight of the girl. She had been walking
rapidly, holding the umbrella stiffly, directly over her
head, and she had passed out of his range. She was too
close now to be seen unless he stood on the church's
front steps. He turned away from the window, left the
office and strode out into the vestibule. All of a sudden
he had taken a positive dislike to this entire situation.
There was something about her being out there like that
alone that made him cold. He wanted to get hold of her
and give her a talking to.

The church's front doors were great double oaken
things with cast-iron handles instead of knobs. Michael
grabbed both the handles at once and swung both the
doors inward, feeling his biceps ache the way they had
when he'd been twenty-odd and in boot camp. Then he
stepped out into the rain, and stopped.

To the left of him, Hernandito and a half dozen
other boys were huddled together under the plastic
awning of Number 36, apparently getting ready for their
apartment-to-apartment search. To the front of him,
Beckner Street shot through the rain to Clare Avenue,
empty. To the right of him, the steps to Number 37 were
empty. For a moment, Michael thought he saw something black fluttering in the crack between Number 37's
door and the frame it hadn't quite been shut into, but
that might have been imagination, or wind. The storm
was getting worse and there was a great deal of wind.

What bothered Father Michael Doherty was that
the postulant he'd been watching for he didn't know how
long had disappeared, completely, as if he'd made her
up.

[5]

"If I were you, young man," Reverend Mother
General was saying, "I would sit very still in my chair
and listen very carefully to what I was about to hear. I am
going to repeat myself exactly once more. Try to get it
through your thick head that Cardinal Archbishops may

come and Cardinal Archbishops may go, but I will be here forever."

Standing at the front of the small classroom directly across the hall from Reverend Mother General's open office door, Sister Mary Scholastica got the almost irresistible urge to chuck her lesson, abdicate her responsibilities, sit down on the nearest desk and tell her postulants, "You want to know how to be a nun? Well, listen to that, there. That's a nun. That's a real nun. Not one of these wimpy little political angels that keep showing up on television." Actually, she might as well have done just that. Since Reverend Mother General had started to get thoroughly exasperated, Scholastica certainly hadn't gotten any teaching done. First, she'd found herself thanking God that the young man involved—probably in his forties and at least a monsignor—was fifty miles away in the relative safety of the Chancery in Colchester. Then she'd started to wonder what was the matter. Reverend Mother General was a dragon, but she didn't usually chomp at the bit in her eagerness to tear the Cardinal Archbishop into certified Irish confetti. Reverend Mother General knew how to pick her spots. Finally, Scholastica began to worry about what she had been worrying about all morning, because as soon as her mind began to stray from whatever task was at hand that was what she did. It was now quarter to twelve on the morning of Thursday, February 21, and the schedule was not being adhered to. Scholastica was teaching her class on Principles of Interior Silence, just the way she was supposed to be according to the agenda Sister Alice Marie had drawn up in September. Out there in front of her, crammed into the tiny desks that had been designed for large college lecture halls, twenty-one of her twenty-two postulants were listening to it. And that, of course, was the problem. There were twenty-one. There were supposed to be twenty-two. Brigit Ann Reilly was missing.

Missing.

Across the hall, Reverend Mother General was reading someone the riot act. From the tone of her

voice, it was probably John Cardinal O'Bannion himself.
Scholastica tucked stray wisps of hair under the edge of
her veil and wondered what it was she was supposed to
do in a situation like this. It wasn't as if she'd done
anything wrong. Somebody had to go to the library
every day. Scholastica had thought it would be a good
idea to send Brigit, because Brigit was getting claustro-
phobic. Some postulants were like that. Scholastica had
been like that herself. Postulants were young and newly
away from home and lonely and not entirely sure they
should have gotten themselves into all this. You had to
be careful with them or you ended up destroying their
vocations before God had had a chance to test them.
Still, one of the things Scholastica was supposed to
determine was who among the postulants was responsi-
ble and who was not. What did Brigit's disappearance
say about that? Did it matter that Brigit had been going
to the library, without incident, every day except Sunday since the first of the year?

There was a sharp click from the other side of the
hall, the sound of a phone being not quite slammed,
because Reverend Mother General never slammed
phones. Across the classroom, postulants giggled, hiding
their mouths behind their hands. Scholastica shook her
head at them and smiled.

"Don't laugh," she said, "wait until you're out on
mission somewhere and your bishop decides he wants
you to teach catechism standing on your head. Bishops
may be our shepherds, but they're also crazy, and they
get crazier the higher up the hierarchy they get. When
you run into one who's gone entirely off his nut, you're
going to wish you had Reverend Mother's talent for—
argumentation."

"Argumentation," someone repeated in the back of
the room. There were more giggles, and a few of the
girls covered their faces entirely, so they wouldn't be too
obvious in their mirth. Scholastica had no idea why. She
was hardly the gorgon Postulant Mistress of legend.
She scanned the faces before her and came to a halt at

the one with no amusement in it at all: Neila Connelly, Brigit Ann Reilly's best friend. Neila was worried, too.

Scholastica was standing reasonably near the door. She leaned over, opened it wide, and stared across the hall at Reverend Mother General's office. Hanging over the transom there was a bouquet of papier-mâché leprechauns sent up by the children at Iggy Loy. Taped to the wall next to the door was a shamrock cut out of white construction paper and plastered over with green glitter. There weren't supposed to be any secular ornaments in that part of the convent considered part of the cloister—which this was—but somehow the rule always seemed to get relaxed around St. Patrick's Day.

Reverend Mother General had got up from behind her chair and gone to stand at her window. Scholastica could just see the back of her, stiff and straight and still as a wooden doll.

"Just a minute," Scholastica said to her postulants. "I want to talk to Reverend Mother now that she has a minute. Why don't the bunch of you look at chapter five in the Merton again and we'll discuss it when I get back."

"Can we talk?" Cara Fenster asked.

"Yes," Scholastica said. "Quietly. If you get loud enough for Sister Alice Marie to come in here, we'll all be in trouble."

There was an outbreak of giggling again. Scholastica smiled indulgently at the pack of them, nodded encouragingly to the ever-more-worried Neila Connelly, and took off across the hall. Scholastica knew what Neila was thinking. The same thought had been bothering her. Brigit hadn't been very happy here the last few months. That happened—girls came up and found out they just weren't suited to the life—but when it did it was supposed to be hedged about by custom and ritual. There were things to be done and said and promised and performed when a girl left before the end of formation. The Order liked to keep in touch with girls like that. It even ran a kind of alumnae organization. Every once in a while, though, a girl would let her unhappiness get too deep and the pressure build up too high. Then one day,

in the middle of everything, she would just snap. Snap,
crackle, pop, Scholastica thought. A mile's walk down to
Exit 56 on Route 144. A thumb in the air. A ride to
Colchester. Gone.

Reverend Mother General had opened her window
and was leaning out, into the rain. Scholastica knocked
sharply on the open door and waited for her to turn
around.

"Oh, Sister," Reverend Mother General said, when
she did, "one of the people I wanted to see. Are you in
the middle of a class?"

"A formation class, Reverend Mother, yes."

"Sister Alice Marie is rehearsing the novices for the
folk singing. Maybe I can send one of your postulants to
get her. I'm afraid we're going to have a very disrupted
day."

"Your day has already been disrupted, Reverend
Mother. I heard you on the phone to the Chancery."

"What? Oh. That. You know, Sister, the finances of
this Order would be in a good deal worse shape than
they are if John O'Bannion wasn't such a pigheaded,
arrogant old Irishman."

"Is that what he is?"

"Don't be ridiculous. You've known him most of
your life. You know he is. Do you know what he pulled
this time?"

"No, Reverend Mother."

"Well, I'll tell you. He decided that he had a
wonderful idea. Margaret Finney had been beatified.
He was going to come up here on St. Pat's and say a Mass
of petition for her canonization, give one of his great day
for the Irish speeches and watch the town parade. It was
the perfect time, the absolutely perfect time, for us to
throw a party."

Scholastica was confused. "We are throwing a party,
Reverend Mother. I had the postulants making posters
about it all yesterday afternoon. We're inviting their
parents and the whole town."

"I know that," Reverend Mother said, "and you
know that, but John didn't know it. He didn't bother to

call and ask, either. He just had that assistant of his send invitations to forty people. Do you know what that means?"

"No, Reverend Mother. But it shouldn't be any problem. The plans we've worked out will accommodate—"

"I'm sure they will, Sister. I'm sure you've all been very efficient. There is absolutely no reason to tell the Archbishop about that. I've got him feeling thoroughly guilty. The Archdiocese is going to pay for the food."

"Ah," Scholastica said.

"Exactly," Reverend Mother General said. "Now I've got more immediate matters on my mind. Have you looked out the window lately?"

Technically, outside of Reverend Mother General's office, there wasn't much in the way of windows to look out of in this part of the Motherhouse. There were openings in the walls with glass in them, but they looked onto the courtyard and were sheltered by trellises and hanging vines. The hanging vines were of so venerable an age that their twisted stems were thick and matted enough to cut off any access to the sun, even in winter when they were denuded of leaves. At the moment, they weren't even denuded of leaves. The thaw had been a kind of false spring.

"I stick my head out every once in a while," Scholastica said cautiously. "It's raining very hard."

"It may be doing something worse than that. Were you alive in 1953?"

"No, Reverend Mother, as a matter of fact, I wasn't."

"Of course, you weren't," Reverend Mother General said. "You're only thirty-six. Well, I was not only alive, I was assistant to the Mistress of Novices in this house—that was in the days when we needed assistants. Anyway, there was a flood. You may have heard about it."

"I have, Reverend Mother. I've heard it was horrible."

"It was. Now, I'm not saying that what's going on

out there is going to be as bad as that, but there was a lot of snow and ice on the ground before the thaw, and now we've got all this rain and the river is rising. I've had a call from Father Doherty down at St. Andrew's. They're going to evacuate the whole neighborhood up to Iggy Loy as soon as possible. They need our vans."

"Yes, of course, Reverend Mother."

"They probably need our new gymnasium as well," Reverend Mother General said. "Oh, what we couldn't have done with that in '53. We ended up putting cots and mattresses in the hallways of the cloister and the whole house had to be prayed over right and left when the waters receded. Silliest thing I ever heard of in my life. Don't ever let anyone tell you that Vatican Two was an unqualified disaster. It wasn't. Have you ever been part of a disaster relief team before?"

"No, Reverend Mother."

"Sister Alice Marie has. She'll know what to do. Go find her and get her up here, and in the meantime assign one of your postulants to monitor the weather reports. Uh—good grief, I'm becoming disorganized. Are you standing there like that for some reason, Sister? I thought I just asked you to go."

"Yes," Scholastica said. "Yes, you did. The thing is—"

"What?"

Sister Scholastica had spent most of her life dealing with people like Reverend Mother General. She had wanted to be one from the time she was six or seven years old. She had certainly long gotten over the inclination to be intimidated by sharp eyes, black habits, and spines as straight as executioner's swords.

What was making it hard for her to speak was this: Less than ten minutes ago, she had been worried (and slightly annoyed) at the possibility that Brigit Ann Reilly might have done a bolt. She had called Jack O'Brien first at his shop and then at home. She had found out that Brigit had stopped in to say hello at just the usual time. Then she had called Glinda Daniels at the library and found out that Brigit hadn't been there at all, although

Glinda wouldn't have seen her if she had been. Glinda had overslept. Scholastica had talked to the young woman who had been at the check-out desk in Glinda's place. At that point, she had had to admit it. It really did look as if Brigit had run away. She had disappeared so completely, into nowhere and never been.

Now it looked like something else might be going on, something Scholastica was having a far harder time admitting to. She seemed to have sent one of her postulants out into dangerous weather, and that could mean—anything.

Scholastica thought of feet slipping on mud, heads cracking on pavement, bodies sucked down into swelling waters—and told herself she was crazy. She still had no reason at all to think that Brigit Ann Reilly had done anything but take off for parts unknown.

On the other hand, before she told Reverend Mother General about it, she did ask Reverend Mother General to sit down.

[6]

It was one o'clock by the time Glinda Daniels managed to get her life put together well enough to be operating at anything near her ordinary efficiency, and by then it was obvious that all she had left to be efficient about was leaving. The one weather report she'd heard on her racing drive into work had dismissed the possibility of another flood out of hand. Forty-five minutes later, as sirens and church bells began to ring noon all over town, the storm had kicked into double time. Glinda had seen weather like this once or twice in her life, but never in Maryville. It might have been like this here during the last flood, but Glinda didn't remember. She had been only two years old at the time, and asleep. What this reminded her of was the kind of storm they used to get before the tornadoes came when she was at the University of Nebraska, picking up her master's degree in French. Glinda Daniels had a bachelor's degree in archaeology from Bryn Mawr, a master's degree in French from Nebraska, a master's degree in Far East Asian Languages (Chinese and Cambodian) from Michigan, a master's degree in classics from Columbia, and a doctorate in library science from Simmons College. She and Father Doherty had a standing joke that they got on so well together because they were the only people they knew who had spent so much of their lives in school.

At the moment, she didn't want to joke about anything. The weather out there had gone from bad to impossible to positively dangerous. She wanted to lock up, get out and make her way up to Iggy Loy. She could have done it, too, except for the fact that the library wasn't empty. She had sent Shelley and Carl, her full-time paid assistants, home at once—almost as soon as she'd walked through the door. They had gone, too. Like most people with jobs they weren't particularly interested in, they were happier than not to be sent home from work. She had sent old Tommy Douver up to Iggy Loy, assuming that he'd been evicted from another rented room. Since he was drunk and that was the only reason he came into the library anyway, it was a safe assumption. She hadn't had any patrons to send anywhere. The general population of Maryville had been up, awake and nervous long before she had. A lot of them had been in town during the flood of 1953, and the rest had heard the stories. No, it wasn't any of these usual categories of people who were giving Glinda trouble. It was that puzzle of puzzles, confusion of confusions, The Library Lady.

Glinda had packed away everything on the checkout desk except for the rubber stamp. She had even put her extensive notes on what the library was doing to celebrate St. Pat's and honor the Blessed Margaret Finney in her tote bag, so she could carry them up the hill and be sure they weren't ruined. Now she put the stamp in the desk's center drawer and slammed the drawer shut. The Library Lady was Mrs. Barbara Keel, and technically she should be called a Community

Volunteer. Like the other Community Volunteers, she was supposed to walk around the library putting abandoned books into a cart, make posters, decorate for holidays, and generally do the million and one pieces of small work the paid staff didn't have time for in these days of not enough paid staff. Like the other Community Volunteers, she was old, well over sixty, possibly over seventy. Unlike the other Community Volunteers, she was something of a character. That was why the children had nicknamed her The Library Lady.

"I know it's none of my business," The Library Lady was saying, "and I know it's a new day and age and all of that, but I still think it wasn't right. I mean, right there in the woman's own bank. Do you think that makes sense, a woman owning a bank?"

"I don't know," Glinda said. The truth of it was, she didn't have the faintest idea what Barbara was talking about. She never did. She picked up her keys and started for the stacks. There were a set of closets back there that had to be checked and locked, and a storeroom with doors to both the inside and the out. She cast a quick glance at the great sheets of plate glass that made up the doors and windows of the library's front entrance. They were covered with shamrocks cut from white construction paper and dusted with green glitter and paste, the work of the half dozen four-year-olds who came every week to Story Hour. Glinda wondered if she should take them down and put them in her tote bag to preserve them, and decided against it. There were too many of them and there wasn't enough time.

"The thing is," The Library Lady said, "I don't know what to do about it. In the old days I would have told Father and that would have taken care of it. I suppose I could tell Father now. It's just that Father Fitzsimmons is so—young."

Father Fitzsimmons was forty-six, but Glinda knew what the woman meant. There was a touch of naïveté about him that was disconcerting at times. Glinda got to the back of the stacks and the first of the closets and opened up to check. It was full of Story Hour supplies and green metal folding chairs, folded up. Glinda shut the door again and went for her keys.

"What were you doing in the bank on a Thursday?" she asked The Library Lady. "What were you doing in a bank at all? I thought Father Doherty got it all straightened out for you, having your check direct deposited."

"Oh, he did, Miss Daniels, he did. I suppose I could tell Father Doherty about this. He wouldn't be shocked. But it's not his parish, then, is it?"

"I suppose not."

"I was putting in a little check from my daughter in Albany. She sent me twenty-five dollars. Did I tell you about my daughter in Albany?"

"Yes," Glinda said, "you did." Actually, Glinda knew The Library Lady's daughter in Albany. They had graduated in the same class from St. Margaret's Academy. It was Glinda's personal opinion, and the opinion of practically everyone else in town, that Jennifer Keel was a world-class shit. That was the only explanation anyone had for why Jennifer would let her mother live alone in Maryville on Social Security and unpredictably scattered twenty-five-dollar checks, while Jennifer played Up and Coming Legislative Aide in Albany with a Maserati and a closet full of Ralph Lauren Polo. Glinda got to the second closet, checked it out—it was full of clear plastic dust jacket covers, enough to last a million years or more—and went on down the line.

"You should have told one of us you had the check," Glinda said. "We'd have gone to the bank for you."

"Oh, I know you would have, dear, you're all very nice, but I didn't have anything to do this morning and I like to walk. And I don't think those boys would bother me in broad daylight, do you?"

Yes, as a matter of fact, Glinda did. It wasn't the time or place to say so. "It's been terrible weather out there all morning," she said instead. "It wasn't such a good idea to go out when you could catch a cold."

"But I was going to go out anyway. I was going to come here."

"Well, in a few moments you're going to go up to

Iggy Loy with me and you're going to stay there. I think there's going to be another flood."

"Flood," The Library Lady said.

Glinda made it to the third closet, stared in despair at a jumbled mess of rags and old pieces of wood, wondered what in God's name they had ever been of any use to anyone for, and then wondered at how long it had been since she had locked up herself. Of course, the truth was, it hadn't been long at all. It was just that she didn't usually open the closets before she locked them, to see if water had gotten in and done any damage.

"The thing is," The Library Lady said again, "it was a terrible day to be at the bank. There were so many people there. Maybe they were trying to get in out of the rain. And there was so much confusion. People throwing boxes back and forth and up and down."

"Boxes?"

"Yes, dear, you know. For St. Patrick's Day. The bank always puts up that little exhibit, you know, the history of the Immigrants National Bank, the pictures and the little balsa-wood houses that show what the town was like in 1875 or whenever it was. They were doing that today. They were bringing the boxes up from the basement and bringing them down again. It was very distracting."

"I'm sure it would be."

"That was how I saw them," The Library Lady said, "Miss Severan and Mr. Malley. Wriggling."

"Wriggling," Glinda said. She was peering into closet number four. It was full of books that had been donated for the library's annual used-book sale. She locked it up and began moving toward the storeroom. "What do you mean, wriggling?"

"Well, they did have all their clothes on, dear. There was that. But they were wriggling."

"Wriggling how?"

"It was in the back hall near the officers' desks. Behind that, I mean. Do you know that hall? There's a ladies' room there."

"Is there?"

"Yes, there is. It's very convenient. The lines were very long, you see, so I went down to powder my nose. And I was thinking about things, you know, and not paying attention. So when I came out I turned right instead of left."

"And?"

"And they were wriggling," The Library Lady said positively. "I saw them as soon as I got to the corner. The hall turns there in the back, you see. I was so preoccupied, I nearly bumped into the wall. But there they were. Wedged front to back in a wooden crate in the utility room they have back there, and him with his hand on her, um, well. Yes. Now, I know, Miss Daniels, I know that everybody in town knows that those two have been going at it for six months, and I know that means Miss Bailey must know too, I mean Mrs. Malley, it's funny how you never think of her as Mrs. Malley, but that's not the point, is it? I mean the point is—"

"Wait," Glinda said.

"Is something wrong, dear?"

Something was very definitely wrong. Glinda was standing right in front of the storeroom door. She had the key to it in her hand, because unlike the closets the storeroom was usually kept locked. It had a thick metal door that had been padded with acoustic insulation, too, which made what she had been hearing, right through The Library Lady's babblings, even worse.

"Listen," she said. "Listen hard. Water."

The Library Lady had come up right behind her and was now standing at the storeroom door. "That doesn't sound like water," she said. "That sounds like someone hissing."

"Don't be silly," Glinda said. "There's nobody in there hissing."

"I'm just telling you what it sounds like," The Library Lady said.

Glinda rubbed the side of her face in agitation. All she could think of was the outside door, breached somehow, pushed open by the storm or left open by someone's carelessness, letting in a thick puddle of filthy wet to ruin the carpet. The vision was so awful, she was having a hard time making herself act.

"Be careful what you pray for," she told The Library Lady. "Last night I was praying for an adventure in my life."

"Well, dear," The Library Lady said, "I think God is smart enough to understand you really meant a man."

Glinda jammed her key into the lock and turned. On that note, she was no longer primarily worried about water damage in the storeroom. She was worried about having to spend just long enough with The Library Lady to turn homicidal. The key stuck and she rattled it. The key to the storeroom always stuck. It drove her nuts. She got the thing to turn and pulled the door open.

The Library Lady saw it first, because she was standing on the side where the gap widened. Standing a little behind the moving door, it took Glinda a little longer. The Library Lady cried out. Glinda just stared. Maybe it was all too bizarre to accept at first glance.

"Oh, dear," The Library Lady said. "Oh dear, oh dear, oh dear."

"Go back toward the front doors," Glinda told her. "Go back now. Run."

The Library Lady didn't run. She might not have been able to. For a second or two, Glinda thought she was going to have to push the old woman to get her to move at all. Then The Library Lady gave a shuffle and a cough and started to back slowly away.

"Don't you touch those things," she told Glinda. "Don't you touch them."

"I won't," Glinda promised her.

She meant to keep that promise, too. Out there in the storeroom, there was no water except for a few dark spots of damp that trailed along the carpet from the outer door. There were no green baize cardboard tables, either, which was what had been in there the last time Glinda looked. As far as Glinda could tell, the storeroom was empty, except for the body of Brigit Ann Reilly stretched out across the floor—

—and the snakes.

It was the snakes that changed everything.

Glinda would have rushed in to see if the girl was all right, or if there was anything she could do to help, but she couldn't. She couldn't for the same reason that The Library Lady had taken direction for once and retreated to the library's front doors.

Brigit Ann Reilly was covered with hissing, snapping, spitting water moccasins, and water moccasins were very poisonous snakes.

Part One

Thursday, February 28

—

Sunday, March 3

One

❖

[1]

When Gregor Demarkian first heard about the death of Brigit Ann Reilly, he was standing in the lobby of the Hilton Hotel in New York City, wondering what he was going to do about his shoes. It was one o'clock on the afternoon of Thursday, February 28, a cold, gray, bitter day with too much wind, and Gregor had just come from four solid hours of listening to a lecture on VICAP. VICAP was the Violent Criminals Apprehension Something, Gregor couldn't remember what. It was also a computer program, devised and implemented to help the FBI's Behavioral Sciences Department help state and local police forces find wandering serial killers. Before his retirement, Gregor had been head of the FBI's Behavioral Sciences Department. In fact, he had been the man who set it up. He had also been the man who had argued, time and time again, for a computer system like VICAP. Standing by the long wall of plate glass windows that looked out on a curving drive that connected to a street whose name he couldn't remember, Gregor tried counting all the bureaucratic reasons he had been given for why he couldn't have one. It was amazing, really, what bureaucrats would tell you when they knew you wanted something from them. It went beyond lying and got tangled in a form of occupational pathology. It got worse when there was true and undeniable need for whatever you were asking for. Those were the last days of the career of Theodore Robert Bundy, with the papers full of stories about college girls killed in their sorority-house beds. Congress and the American people had been all primed to spend money—to do anything—to protect the country from repeat performances. Gregor had gone to the attorney general's office and got—what? He couldn't really remember. Something silly. Something along the lines of "we-can't-ask-Congress-for-that-this-year-because-we-asked-them-for-brass-spittoons-last-year." Something like that, when Bundy had left a dozen dead that anyone knew about and the not-quite-formed Behavioral Sciences Department had files on half a dozen cases from Texas to Maine that looked like they were working themselves up into the same damn thing.

Of course, Gregor thought now, the political climate had changed since then. He wasn't sure exactly how—he wasn't very good at politics—but he thought it had something to do with who was spending money for what where. That was a safe guess, because it almost always had something to do with who was spending money for what where. Maybe Ronald Reagan had been a law-and-order president and he hadn't noticed it. George Bush had gone to war in the Persian Gulf and he would never have noticed that, either, except that Donna Moradanyan had put a yellow ribbon on his apartment door. He looked down at his shoes again and sighed. Almost everyone who was attending the conference on VICAP—ex-Bureau agents, crime writers, newspaper reporters, local police officers—was staying at the Hilton, but the conference itself was being held across town at a small hotel the Bureau had favored since early in the reign of J. Edgar Hoover. Unfortunately, the hotel hadn't done any maintenance since early in the reign of J. Edgar Hoover. The place was falling apart, and the pack of them had to troop over there every day anyway, getting their shoes full of grit and slush. The present director had probably gone to the attorney general's office to ask for the Hilton and been told it couldn't be done. The Department of Redundancy Department had got themselves into the Hilton just last year.

Gregor heard heavy footsteps on carpet and turned, to find Dave Herder bounding up from the direction of one of the bars. That wasn't where Dave was supposed to have gone, but Dave was Dave. Gregor didn't put a lot of effort into making him make sense. He did think it was a good thing the lobby was so empty. He didn't like Dave sneaking up on him.

"Where's Schatzy?" Dave said. "I told him where you were. Had to be half an hour ago. Said he was coming right out."

"You haven't been gone for half an hour," Gregor told him.

"I've been gone long enough. I ran into Schatzy. I told you that. God, but I'm hungry. You think that thing they've got is going to work?"

"It depends on what you mean by work."

"Catch psychos." Dave shrugged. He was a small man with very little hair. He had once been the best agent the Bureau had for kidnapping detail. Like all the best agents the Bureau had for anything, he had burned out early, dropping into retirement five years younger than the mandatory age of fifty-five and taking a position at the John Jay College of Criminal Justice in Manhattan. Gregor had dropped into retirement before the mandatory age himself—well before the extended mandatory age, which he would have been allowed because he was by then in administration. He had blamed his leaving on the painful and protracted death of his wife, but he knew that that was only half true. He wondered what Dave blamed his leaving on.

"Come back to earth," Dave said. "God, that was a disgusting demonstration. Did they get those pictures from your old department?"

"Those were computer graphics. They probably got the pictures they copied them from from my old department."

Dave shook his head. "I don't think I could have

stood it. Getting up every morning to one more set of
blood stains on the wall. I heard from Jim Fitzroy that
you'd gone private, too, and done a whole stack of
murder cases—"

"I haven't gone private," Gregor said, "and I've
hardly done a whole stack of anything—"

"Jim said he saw a story about you in *The Philadel-
phia Inquirer* that called you the 'Armenian-American
Hercule Poirot.' I didn't know you were Armenian-
American."

"I've always thought of myself as just American.
Here comes Schatzy."

"If I'd just spent ten years of my life chasing guys
who chopped up their girlfriends for spare parts, I
wouldn't go private and do murder cases. I wouldn't go
private and do anything. I'd get a job with IBM."

"Here comes Schatzy," Gregor said again, a little
desperately. Dave got like this—he always got like
this—it was some kind of reaction to all those years
sitting alone in cars on stakeouts. What was worse, it was
always on the mark. That was the other half of the truth
of Gregor's leaving. He had been unable to face one
more set of blood stains on the wall, especially with
Elizabeth gone. He didn't want to think about it. It
brought it all back much too vividly.

Unlike Dave, Schatzy was a big man, not as big as
Gregor himself, but recognizably outsize. He was chug-
ging along toward them from the dark center interior of
the hotel lobby, carrying a magazine under his arm and
looking both pleased and distracted. His full name was
Bernard Isaac Schatz, and for the first ten years of his
career, he'd been the only Jewish agent the Bureau had.
Gregor hadn't seen him for a decade before this conference. He hadn't heard that Schatzy had been assigned to
bank robbery and hated it. He hadn't heard that Schatzy
had quit the Bureau and gone into business manufactur-
ing gourmet pizzas. He had no idea what Schatzy was
doing at this conference or why he had been invited. In
the reunion atmosphere of the conference room, it
hadn't seemed to matter.

Schatzy had taken the magazine out from under his arm and begun to wave it at them. Gregor caught a full-color cover picture of a cobra with its tongue in the air, with a small black-and-white inset beside it of a teenager with slightly buck teeth. Schatzy waved the magazine again and it all became a blur.

"Got it," Schatzy said. "You can always count on *People* to give you what you want. It only happened last Thursday, too."

"What only happened last Thursday?" Gregor asked.

"The murder," Schatzy said.

"Oh, God," Dave said, staring at the ceiling. "Let's get off this and find a restaurant, can't we? I've spent all morning talking about murder."

"This is a good one." Schatzy unrolled the magazine and shook his head. "That's a cobra they've got here and it wasn't a cobra at all. It was a water moccasin, or ten water moccasins to be precise, and that was weird enough because it was Upstate New York and water moccasins aren't native to Upstate New York. Copperheads are native to Upstate New York. You in Boy Scouts, Gregor? You learn all that stuff about snakes when you went to camp?"

"I learned all that stuff about snakes at Quantico," Gregor said. "I took both the poisons courses. And I have never been to camp."

"I was the first Jewish Eagle Scout in the history of scouting in Dade County, Florida. Can you imagine growing up Jewish in Dade County, Florida, when I grew up in Dade County, Florida? It must have been terrible. I can hardly remember any of it."

"I grew up WASP in Marblehead, Massachusetts," Dave said. "I can hardly remember any of it, either. Adolesence is terrible."

"How is it murder if the girl was bitten by snakes?" Gregor asked. "Did someone deliberately plant them in her bed?"

Schatzy grinned. "She wasn't in her bed. She was in a storeroom at the public library, nobody knows why.

And nobody knows where the snakes came from, either. That's the best part. Pack of water moccasins all over the body, water moccasins not native to the state, hissing and snapping and the first thing that hits the Medical Examiner when they get them off her is that, of course, she hasn't died of snake venom—"

"Wait," Gregor said. "Hibernating. Why weren't the snakes hibernating?"

"There'd been a thaw," Schatzy said. "This was in Upstate New York last week, I told you. Haven't you been listening to the news? They had a thaw up there went to sixty degrees on Valentine's Day and didn't cool off for eight or nine days, all the way up near the Seaway, melted everything and caused a lot of flooding—"

"I see," Gregor said. He did see. He was just glad that Schatzy wanted to talk instead of to listen, because he was a little embarrassed by the fact that he had not seen before. The flooding near the Seaway had been major news, major enough so that Gregor had heard about it. The problem was, he didn't much like news. He, therefore, rarely read or listened to it. The depth of his ignorance of current events was astonishing.

Schatzy was not in the mood to pursue it. "Right," he was saying, "well. It was up there. In this town called Maryville. Body discovered with snakes crawling all over it, weirdest thing you ever saw, but like I said, she's not dead from snake venom. They puff up—"

"Oh, for God's sake," Dave said.

"Well, they do, Dave, they do. And she didn't. So as soon as they could see her face, they knew that wasn't what she died from. But there she was, dead. And there were the snakes, they couldn't let them just slither away and terrorize the local populace—"

"They wouldn't have terrorized the local populace for long," Gregor pointed out. "The weather had to have gotten back to normal eventually. They'd have frozen to death."

"The weather did get back to normal eventually," Dave said. "It's back to normal now. They have pictures of it on the TV news. It looks like an ice cube up there."

Schatzy had paged through the magazine until he came to the story. Like all the major crime stories in *People*, it was spread across two pages and illustrated with photographs in black and white. The two thin columns of text crammed in on either side of the fold looked feeble and anemic under the black heaviness of the headlines. "MYSTERY," one of those headlines read, and then, "THE STRANGE STORY OF THE SNAKES AND THE NUN." Gregor stopped at that word, *nun*, and looked back at the picture of the girl who had died. *Girl* was the operative word. She looked barely old enough to vote. She certainly didn't look like a nun.

"They won't have anything I wouldn't be able to get from the papers," Schatzy said, "but they'll have interviews. I love the interviews. I love crime stories in *People*. They're like reading Ellery Queen and Agatha Christie."

"Gregor's been a crime story in *People*," Dave said. "Gregor's been more than one."

"Tell me about this business with the nun," Gregor said. "What do they mean when they say that she was a nun?"

"Oh, that. That's just an exaggeration." Schatzy flicked his fingers at the offending word. "She wasn't a nun, exactly. She was one of those girls who wants to be and goes to a convent to train to be one—"

"A novice?" Gregor tried. "A postulant?"

"A postulant, Gregor, that's it. This Maryville place has a local convent, one of the kind where girls go to learn to be nuns—"

"A Motherhouse," Gregor said politely. "Or a provincial house."

"Yeah. Like that. Anyway, that's where she was living. In this convent with the Sisters of Divine Grace. I don't know, Gregor. When I was growing up, nuns had sensible names, like Benedictines or Augustinians or Sisters of Charity. What's a name like that supposed to mean, Sisters of Divine Grace?"

"I don't know."

"Schatzy, look at what you've done," Dave said.

"You've got him upset. For God's sake. Just because you spent your career reading financial statements doesn't mean the rest of us did. The rest of us are tired of this kind of thing, I mean."

"Are you?" Schatzy asked Gregor. "Tired of this kind of thing?"

"Not exactly," Gregor said. "Why don't you let me borrow your magazine for a minute. I want to go to the men's room. I'll meet you in the restaurant in a couple of minutes."

"Talk about something else," Dave said. "Talk about this girl he's seeing. Woman. I don't know what to call her. Young enough to be his daughter, from what I can tell."

Gregor tucked the magazine into the pocket of his coat. "She is young enough to be my daughter, and I'm not 'seeing' her, as you put it. I have a much too well developed sense of self-preservation. I'll see you two in a couple of minutes, all right?"

"All right," Schatzy said.

"She has a strange name," Dave persisted, too brightly. "Dennis or Hennis or Lennis or something."

"Bennis," Gregor told him. "Bennis Hannaford. They've got her books in the same newsstand where Schatzy probably bought this magazine. I'll see the two of you *later*."

Dave started to babble again, but Gregor had already turned his back and begun making his way toward the interior of the hotel. Behind him, he could hear wind whistle every time one of the glass doors were opened or shut. He passed the reception desk and noted in a distracted way that someone had put out a few forlorn decorations, a leprechaun sitting on a pot of gold and a stand-up cardboard shamrock for St. Patrick's Day. What was it about some people that they couldn't let a holiday pass without gearing themselves up to celebrate another one?

What was it about some people that they couldn't leave well enough alone? Dave Herder meant well—he always meant well—but he couldn't take a hint. Gregor didn't mind talking about murder. As long as the murder in question wasn't a serial one or in some other way the obvious work of a psychopath, it could even be interesting. He did mind talking about Bennis Hannaford, and about everyone else he knew back on Cavanaugh Street in Philadelphia. At least, he minded this weekend.

The men's room was near a bank of pay phones, in a wide empty space in the lobby paneled in blond wood and carpeted in green. Gregor pushed himself through the swinging door with the copy of *People* rolled up in his hand as if he were about to swat a fly with it. The problem with talking about Bennis—or Donna Moradanyan, or Father Tibor Kasparian, or George Tekamanian, or Lida Arkmajian, or any of the rest of them—wasn't that he missed them. He always missed them when he was away from them. The problem was that at the moment he felt that they'd abandoned him.

[2]

Of course, in reality, Gregor Demarkian had not been abandoned at all. When he was being sensible, he knew this. What he was feeling was a mass and mix of things. Before Elizabeth had died, he had been what he now had to admit was a pretty popular Bureau type: The man so dedicated to his work he hadn't known anything else existed. In his case, he had known Elizabeth existed, but she had taken care of everything else for them. She had kept in touch with their families. She had arranged for his mother's funeral and for his nieces' birthday presents and for the anniversary liturgies to be sung for the repose of his father's soul. There were Bureau agents who had no emotional lives at all. Gregor had one, but the one he had was Elizabeth—and until she was gone he hadn't realized how important it all was to him. It had been strange, waking up on the morning after he buried her, staring the end of his leave of absence in the face and knowing he didn't want to go back. It had been even stranger, weeks later, with his resignation accepted and his life at loose ends, realizing he was going to have to pull himself together and give himself a reason for existing.

He had gone back to Cavanaugh Street on a whim, as a self-consciously deliberate first step in the direction of getting himself reoriented to normal life. He had been born and brought up on Cavanaugh Street in the days when it had been little more than Philadelphia's Armenian-American immigrant ghetto. With everything that had gone on in the central cities in the years since he'd left, he'd expected to return to nothing at all, to rubble and crack houses, to dirt and prostitution. Instead, he'd found a refurbished street full of people he'd known all his life, the tenements bought up and remodeled as floor-through condominiums or single-family town houses, the church decked out with every conceivable embellishment that would be allowed by an Armenian bishop. It had been a revelation, and he had bought an apartment almost without thinking about it. He'd settled in without knowing what he was going to do. Fortunately for the kind of man he had let himself become, he had not had to do much. Like Elizabeth, they had given him the life he wasn't able to put together for himself.

The men's room had a little anteroom, with chairs and sinks and a long, low counter for doing God knew what. There were also mirrors. Gregor sat down in one of the chairs and opened Schatzy's copy of *People* magazine. There was a picture of the corpse, taken from above, while it was lying on a morgue slab. *People* was the only magazine on earth better than *The National Enquirer* at getting a picture of a dead body. Gregor stared at the face of Brigit Ann Reilly and wished the picture were in color. Black and white blurred too many details.

"Taxine," Gregor muttered to himself. "Coniine. Lobeline. Some kind of vegetable alkaloid. I wonder where she got it from."

He looked through the scant text for some sign of an answer, but found none. The story was continued on the next page, so he turned and found nothing there, either. When the case was solved, *People* would run a five- or ten-page extravaganza and explain the whole thing, but at this point in the investigation they were only interested in titillating. Gregor looked over the pictures on this third page and found a couple he recognized: John Cardinal O'Bannion, and a young woman in a not very modified nun's habit identified as "Sister Mary Scholastica, Mistress of Postulants and Brigit Ann Reilly's religious superior in the Sisters of Divine Grace." Gregor had known her as Sister Scholastica Burke. At the time, she had been principal of St. Agnes's Parish School in Colchester, New York, and Gregor had been in Colchester looking into a little matter for the Cardinal Archbishop. Gregor ran his finger down the column of type and came up with a paragraph that read,

> According to Sister Scholastica, Brigit was a model postulant. "Postulants often have trouble with religious obedience, but Brigit never seemed to," Sister Scholastica said. "She was always very conscientious about everything she did. I don't know what she could have been doing in that storeroom so late in the day."

Gregor slapped the magazine shut, rolled it up, and stuffed it in his pocket. That was the kind of thing people always said in the wake of a violent death. From what he had known of Sister Scholastica, he would have expected better. He wondered if Bennis was at home right this moment, reading this copy of *People* and coming to the same conclusions. He didn't suppose she was. The last he'd seen of Bennis, she'd been six weeks into her new novel, holed up in her apartment the way doughboys in World War I had holed up in foxholes, every piece of furniture covered with Post-It notes about rogue trolls, enchanted castles, singing unicorns, and damsels more distressing than distressed. She hadn't been out in the air since the middle of January, and she swore she wasn't coming out until she had a draft. Since Bennis's drafts generally ran seven or eight hundred pages of elite type, Gregor expected Ararat to be shipping in restaurant meals for some time to come.

Still, what Bennis was doing to him—and he couldn't help thinking of it like that; as something she was doing to him—was better than what the rest of them had done. That was why he was feeling so abandoned, illogical though it might be. The rest of them had virtually *disappeared*. Father Tibor had gone back to Independence College to teach another course. Lida Arkmajian and Hannah Krekorian had taken Donna Moradanyan and her infant son to Lida's house in Boca Raton. Even old George Tekamanian was in the Bahamas, floating around on a cruise ship with his grandson Martin, his grandson Martin's wife, and his three great-grandchildren.

The truth of it was simple: In the year and a half since Gregor had been back on Cavanaugh Street, he had learned to rely on these people as completely as he had ever relied on Elizabeth. When they stepped out of his life even temporarily, he felt as if he'd had the foundation knocked out from under him. It was something he was going to have to do something about someday. He just didn't want someday to be today. Or ever.

He went over to one of the sinks and washed his hands, just to feel that he had done something practical in the men's room, instead of just hiding from Dave Herder's prattle. Then he made his way back into the lobby. There were three restaurants on this level—or accessible from this level as far as Gregor knew, but the only one Dave and Schatzy would be in was at the back, on the other side of the building from the wall of glass doors. Gregor passed the baggage check and the check-in desk and was making his way along the wall opposite the guest services desk when he heard his name called out.

"Mr. Demarkian?" the high feminine voice said. "Mr. Demarkian, please? If you have a minute?"

Gregor looked over to the guest services desk and saw a small woman—tiny, really—jumping up and down behind the counter. While he watched, she pushed herself up against the counter with her hands and called again.

"Mr. Demarkian?"

"I'm coming." He walked across the hall until he came to her, and smiled. She had let herself down from her perch and was looking a little sweaty and flustered.

"Oh, Mr. Demarkian," she said, "you don't know what we've been through. We didn't know where you were, you see."

"Of course you didn't," Gregor said. "Why should you?"

"That's what I said," the woman told him in a confidential voice, "but you just can't get away with saying that kind of thing when you're talking to the Archdiocese of New York. Oh, I'm sorry. That's what this is about. We have a message for you from the Archdiocese of New York."

"A message."

"Just a minute." The tiny woman rushed to the back, made her way along a row of severely high-tech–looking pigeonholes, and came up with a large manila envelope. It wasn't what Gregor would have called a message, but it was from the Archdiocese of New York. The letterhead was big and bold enough to read all the way across at the counter where he was standing.

"Here," the tiny woman said, thrusting the thing at him. "It came in about two hours ago, and right after it did we got a phone call, and you wouldn't believe how insistent they were. It's stamped all over with urgent, too. They must have a crisis on their hands."

If they did, Gregor didn't see what it would have to do with him. He didn't know anybody at the Archdiocese of New York. He opened the envelope and peered inside. Inside there was another envelope, a padded mailer, with a note taped to its side. Gregor pulled the mailer out and read the note.

"This arrived this morning from Cardinal O'Bannion," the note said. *"He has impressed on us that the matter is urgent."*

"The matter is urgent," Gregor said out loud.

"What?" the tiny woman asked him.

"Never mind," Gregor said. "Thank you. I'll take care of this now."

"I'd find a phone if I were you," the woman said. "They really were very, very insistent."

"I'm sure they were." Gregor hardly blamed them. Cardinal O'Bannion was a very insistent man. From what he'd heard, Cardinal O'Connor could be a very insistent man, too. If John O'Bannion was really intent on getting in touch with Gregor Demarkian—and the effort involved to track Gregor down at the Hilton suggested he was—the clerks at the Archdiocese had probably been driven absolutely crazy since the message came in.

Right now, though, Gregor was not going to go racing for the phone. He was going to sit down with Dave and Schatzy and have a nice substantial lunch, punctuated by conversation first about murderers and maniacs they had known, and then—as was inevitable during any social contact among Bureau agents above a certain age—about the late, vociferously unlamented J. Edgar. By then, Gregor thought he would have calmed himself down enough not to sound too inappropriately happy on the phone.

There was certainly nothing to be happy about in the death of Brigit Ann Reilly, but Gregor was happy nonetheless. Ever since he'd realized that the murder Schatzy was talking about had taken place on O'Bannion's turf, he'd been a little surprised that he hadn't heard from the Cardinal. Gregor knew how John O'Bannion's mind worked. You found yourself an expert you could trust, and you stuck with him.

Besides, with Bennis working and everybody else away, a little murder case would come as a welcome relief.

It had to be better than hanging around New York City in miserable weather, listening to the worst kind of mentally rigid Bureau administrator blithering on about what a wonderful tool they had in this computer program they hadn't yet learned how to run.

Two

[1]

There were people who said that John Cardinal O'Bannion was a Neanderthal, a throwback to the days when Catholics were supposed to "pray, pay, and obey." Those were the people who concentrated on his politics—1930's liberal; now labeled conservative—and his theology, which was definitely of the Absolute Moral Norms variety. There were other people who said he was a wizard. The Archdiocese of Colchester had been a mess when he had been sent in to take it over. Vocations to the priesthood had dried up. Half a dozen orders of nuns, exasperated at his predecessor's high-handedness and his death grip on a dollar, had withdrawn from the parochial school system. The vast majority of the laity was in open rebellion, half in an attempt to be more Catholic than Rome, the other half in an attempt to be God knew what. There were rumors of Love Feasts for the Goddess being held in fields of daisies from the banks of the Seaway to Syracuse. Of course the Cardinal had to be a hard-liner on morality and the liturgy, these people said. That was the only way to bring the little people back into the fold. The little people were always so impressed with pomp and circumstance, and so respectful of authority—as long as it behaved like authority. What the little people wanted more than anything else was not to be forced to think.

To Gregor Demarkian, what John Cardinal O'Bannion was was an original, a big coarse man who had come late to his vocation, an ex-longshoreman who could still talk like a longshoreman, a kind of warrior priest. He was also a passionate Catholic. Many of his contemporaries from the seminary—and hordes of up-and-coming younger men—had replaced their belief in the historical reality of the Resurrection with a vague idea of "spiritual" and "symbolic" rising from the dead, just the way they had replaced their belief in individual sin with a furious opposition to "sinful systems." O'Bannion was adamantly in favor of the traditional interpretations of both. "The point of Christianity," he once told the 3,000 assembled members of the Association of Catholic Psychotherapists of New York State, "is not to make us more emotionally stable people, more psychologically aware people, more fulfilled people, more self-actualizing people. It is certainly not to promote our 'human growth' or to make us better adjusted and more 'accepting' of our natures. The point of Christianity, ladies and gentlemen, is this: that approximately two thousand years ago in Palestine a man who to all intents and purposes had been dead and buried for three days raised Himself up and appeared in His risen body to the people who had loved him and others, and that He did these things *in fact*, and because He did these things *in fact*, we are obligated to listen to what He had to say and to try to follow it, whether what He had to say is what we want to hear or not."

Gregor could just imagine what the Association of Catholic Psychotherapists of New York State had thought of that. He didn't have to imagine what certain other people had thought of it. Reactions to that speech had appeared in everything from the *Saturday Evening Post* to the *New Republic*. The more populist press had tended to approve of it, in a vague and uncomprehending way, because they also tended to approve of God in general and to disapprove of psychotherapists. The "intellectual" press had been furious. Gregor was neither a religious man nor a moralist. He had no strong ideas one way or the other about the existence of God or the philosophical advisability of engaging in acts of promiscuous fornication. He thought O'Bannion had simply stated the obvious, the absolute bottom-line core definition of Christianity, without which Christianity would not exist. The irrationality of the literate press's attacks on O'Bannion had startled him.

The irrationality of the literate press's reactions to the death of Brigit Ann Reilly had startled him, too. It was now ten o'clock on the morning of Friday, March 1, and Gregor was standing in the anteroom to the Cardinal's office in the Chancery in Colchester, rocking restlessly back and forth on his feet and smiling nervously every once in a while at the Benedictine nun in full habit who served as the Cardinal's secretary. The nun was perfectly pleasant and even friendly, but Gregor wasn't used to nuns. All that black and white and unnatural calm made him nervous. He was also very tired. He had opened the Cardinal's envelope yesterday afternoon as soon as he'd got back up to his room from lunch. He had read through it carefully, called the Cardinal, agreed to come up to Colchester and go on to Maryville, and then gone out and bought every newspaper, newsmagazine, and tabloid with a story about the murder in it. The reading proved to be irresistible. He had expected to get at least eight hours of solid sleep before he had to go to the train station in the morning. He had gotten less than five, and those sprawled out across crumbled newsprint while still wearing a suit. He had told himself he would doze on the Amtrak trip upstate. Instead, he had reread the report in *Time* and skimmed through the long quasi-editorial in *The Nation*, looking for God only knew what. It wasn't that any of these pieces contained essential information about the murder itself. Reading them, Gregor wasn't sure the press had any information beyond what had been given out the day the body was found—and that wasn't much. If he wanted details, he had the Cardinal's report to look through. It contained just about anything he could have expected to get, considering the fact that he was attached to no official policing force anywhere in the country. If Gregor Demarkian had formed distinct impressions of the Cardinal Archbishop, the Cardinal Archbishop had formed distinct impressions of him. At least, the Cardinal Archbishop had remembered that Gregor liked his information organized, exhaustive, electic, and typed.

What was fascinating to Gregor about the press accounts of the death of Brigit Ann Reilly—especially the ones in the prestige weeklies—was their tone. From *Time* to the *New Republic*, from *Newsweek* to *The Nation*, the editorial voice seemed to be a cross between the grimly prissy schoolmarm of nineteenth-century fiction and the hell-and-brimstone preacher. Father Tibor back on Cavanaugh Street was always telling Gregor that the American press was hysterically hostile to religion, but Gregor had never listened to him. Tibor was a refugee from Soviet Armenia. He had lived with real-life persecution for so long, he was entitled to one or two conspiracy theories. Now Gregor thought he owed Tibor at least a mental apology. These stories were so bizarre, to call them anti-Catholic was to give them too much credit. The *New Republic* seemed to imply that there was something about "the rigid morality of traditional Catholicism" that led inevitably to violent death. *Time* quoted Charles Curran (briefly) and Richard Mac-Brien (at length) on the psychological health of women who joined religious orders that still wore close to full habit. The consensus between them seemed to be that these women were not psychologically healthy at all. Then there was *Newsweek*, which presented a perfectly bewildering article that seemed to imply that there was some connection between this murder and the Church's response to AIDS. At one point, it even managed to imply that the Church's traditional stand on homosexual practice had *caused* AIDS. What any of this had to do with the matter at hand—the brutal murder of an eighteen-year-old girl in the storeroom of a public library in Upstate New York—Gregor didn't know, but then the writers of the articles didn't seem to know either. They didn't seem to know much of anything, except that they really, really, really didn't like the Catholic Church.

The buzzer on the nun's desk rang and stopped and rang again in jerky impatient spurts. The sound started suddenly and continued violently, making Gregor jump. The nun looked at the intercom, blinked, and pushed a lever. The sound was shut off.

"He'll be right in, Your Eminence," she said at the box, not bothering to hear what the Cardinal Archbishop might want to say. Then she switched the intercom off and turned to Gregor. "Do you like reading *Time* magazine?" she asked him.

Gregor looked down at his hands. He was still carrying *Time*. He had *Newsweek* stuffed into one of the pockets of his coat. "I don't read it very often," he told her. "This week it had an article about the, uh—"

"About the murder in it," Sister finished for him. "Yes, I see. My order is Primitive Observance, you know. According to our Rule, we aren't allowed to read secular magazines."

"Do you want to?"

"To tell the truth, I tried it, when I first came to work for the Cardinal. I had to ask permission of my Superior and go through no end of trouble, and then— well, then I found it very depressing. The only thing I found more depressing was television." She hesitated. "I have read one or two again over the past week. Since the murder."

"You'd have got more information eavesdropping at the Cardinal's keyhole."

"I don't have to eavesdrop at the Cardinal's keyhole," Sister said, "the Cardinal tells me far more than I want to know already. But I am worried about him, Mr. Demarkian. He's been very upset. He's been—brooding about all that, from last year."

"Do you think that's surprising, Sister?"

"No. No, I don't think it's surprising. I don't think it's healthy, either. And then there are those Sisters. The Sisters of Divine Grace."

"What about the Sisters of Divine Grace?"

The old nun looked uncomfortable. "I really don't mean to be critical," she said miserably. "I understand that things have changed since I entered the convent, and besides, an active order is different from a contemplative one. That's what my order is, contemplative. Under ordinary circumstances, I would never have left the confines of our monastery in Connecticut."

Gregor grinned. "When I was here last year, what I heard is that the Cardinal insisted."

"Yes, he did. The Cardinal does have a tendency to insist." Sister moved things around on her desk, biting her lip. "I know," she said slowly, "that it takes a very different path of formation to fit a young woman for work in an active order than it would for life in a contemplative one. In an active order, you can't treat your postulants like hothouse flowers. You're going to send them off to teach religion in East St. Louis. And if SDG was a really modern order—you know, one of the ones where the Sisters don't wear habits and do wear makeup and spend their time agitating for female ordination— well, maybe I could have understood it. As things go, I can't understand it. Mr. Demarkian, what was that girl doing, walking around by herself in the middle of the morning when—"

The buzzer went off again, insanely this time, as if the Cardinal were sitting in his office, pounding on his button with a balled fist. Even Sister jumped this time, a polite little body hop that was nothing at all like Gregor's large-scale clumsy jerk. Sister got control of herself almost at once, and leaned over to push the lever again.

"It will only be a moment, Your Eminence," she said. "Mr. Demarkian is just on his way in."

She released the lever and looked up at Gregor in embarrassment. "You'd better go in," she told him. "Maybe we can talk again on your way out. His Eminence really has been very upset lately."

"Maybe I can calm him down," Gregor said.

Sister shot him a look of such pure skepticism, it could only have been managed by a nun.

"On the day someone calms the Cardinal Archbishop down," Sister said, "the Pope will fire every member of the Curia and restaff the Vatican with Lutherans. Go talk to the man before he has an attack of apoplexy and I get stuck being the one to get him to the hospital."

[2]

Sister wasn't the first person who had told Gregor about the Cardinal's long continued problems with "all that happened here last year." Gregor had heard the same from several people, including from Father Tibor, who had had lunch with O'Bannion in Philadelphia only three months before.

"The man looks as if he is in the middle of a breakdown, Krekor," Tibor had said. "I am very worried. You have met John. You know he is not a man likely to have breakdowns."

Gregor did know exactly that. He found it hard even to imagine John Cardinal O'Bannion in the middle of a breakdown. That big man with his bass voice, his thick body, his air of being able to charge right into the middle of any situation and fix it, by sheer energy. How does somebody like that break down? The answer presented itself as soon as Gregor walked into the Cardinal's office. John O'Bannion was sitting in the swivel chair behind his massive oak desk, smoking a cigar and trying to read a piece of paper through the fumes. It was a characteristic pose and should have had a characteristic effect. Instead of being impressed—and on the verge of overwhelmed—Gregor found himself feeling suddenly, desperately sorry for the man. The ruddy, broken-veined complexion of a man who enjoyed himself too completely and too often was gone, replaced by skin as dry as paper and the color of new ash. The bright blue eyes seemed to be dulled and drowning beneath a wash of yellow film. For the first time in the four or five years since Gregor had become aware of him, the Cardinal looked old.

Gregor shut the office door behind him, walked over to the chair at the side of O'Bannion's desk and sat down. "Stop pretending to work, Your Eminence. You can't see anything through all that smoke anyway. Tibor's worried about you."

"Tibor's worried about everybody." O'Bannion put the paper down. "Tibor's a saint. Hello, Gregor. I hope you don't mind my saying that I was praying never to have to see your face again."

"Let's just say I'm willing to take it in the spirit in which it is intended."

"Good," O'Bannion said. "To tell you the truth, I don't have the energy to be socially politic these days."

"Did you ever?"

"No," O'Bannion said, "but I did make an effort when I was living in Rome. Do you want some coffee? Sister's not modern. She keeps telling me she'd be happy to make me some."

"That's all right, I drank too much coffee on the train." Gregor shifted in his seat and tapped his fingers against the Cardinal's desk. O'Bannion looked so ill, Gregor was having a hard time looking directly at him. "Your Eminence," he said, after a while, "I know you don't take well to advice, but—"

"But I should get away somewhere and get some rest?" O'Bannion raised his eyes to the ceiling. "Everybody's always telling me I should get away and get some rest. What they really mean is that I should go see a shrink and get over feeling guilty about all that last year. I went up there, you know. Checked in. Maybe satisfied my curiosity."

"And?" Gregor sat very still.

"And," the Cardinal said, "our friend is catatonic. Absolutely not home. And likely to stay that way. Whether that's a fitting punishment for murdering three people, I don't know."

"In this case, I think we could let it go."

"In this case, I don't want to let it go. Never mind, Gregor. In spite of all the fussing people are doing over me these days, my present condition is not the result of torturing myself with guilt over what happened last year. In the first place, I have jaundice—"

"Oh, for God's sake."

"Don't take the Lord's name in vain in the office, Gregor. It upsets Sister. And before you go off half-cocked, the jaundice is a side effect of gallstones and I am having both the jaundice and the gallstones seen to. I'm not a complete idiot. I will admit, however, that I haven't been getting much sleep."

"You never did get much," Gregor said. "Is the insomnia of the moment caused by the death of Brigit Ann Reilly?"

The Cardinal hesitated. "Partially. I have, of course, had the Reillys here quite a bit over the past week. That was necessary, under the circumstances. But it's not so much the murder, Gregor, as it is what's going on around the murder. You read the material I sent you?"

"Twice. The girl died from coniine poisoning, that was obvious. I was wondering if you'd had any trouble with the police, over whether you could legitimately call it murder."

"I never have any trouble with the police," the Cardinal said blandly, "especially when the chief is named Pete Donovan. But no, on the question of murder, suicide, or accident, there was never any doubt. The dose she took was massive. She would have to have taken it within half an hour or forty-five minutes before she died, unless we're going to assume she stood on the lawn of the library munching decorative border leaves for Heaven only knows how long—there's hemlock in the library border; that might not be in the report—anyway, unless we're going to assume that, we're going to be stuck with the fact that someone must have fed it to her. Deliberately."

"What about accident?" Gregor asked. "Somewhere in that report you sent me there was mention of a man named Sam Harrigan—"

"The Fearless Epicure?" John O'Bannion grinned. "I know Sam. He's been The Fearless Epicure for a long time now. He wouldn't have been if he hadn't been able to recognize hemlock and had sense enough not to eat it."

"True," Gregor said, "but he's probably some kind of local celebrity. There are probably a few dozen houses in town with copies of his cookbooks in them. Somebody might have—no, that won't work, will it? If somebody had cooked up hemlock greens and fed them to Brigit Ann Reilly innocently, there would be somebody else either dead or very sick."

"Exactly."

"I wonder if that means the murder was premeditated," Gregor said. He shook his head. "It's impossible to tell from this vantage point. You'd think making a decoction from hemlock would take planning, assuming that was how the coniine was obtained, but once you think about it you realize it wouldn't, necessarily. You said there was a hemlock border around the library's lawn. Somebody could have simply grabbed a handful and made some tea—"

"It's not just around the library," the Cardinal said. "It's everywhere. If there's one thing I've learned since Brigit Ann Reilly died, it's that hemlock is an extremely common plant in this part of the United States. There's hemlock in the window boxes outside the second floor offices of the local bank. There's hemlock in Mrs. Ramirez's flower garden down in the Hispanic section of town. There's even hemlock at the convent, growing wild and being treated as a weed at the edge of their property where it fronts the road. Before this death, I'd always thought of hemlock as something native only to ancient Greece."

"So that leaves only the snakes," Gregor said, "where they came from, what they were doing on the body. I put a call in to a friend of mine last night. I'm supposed to call him back when I get to Maryville. He knows something about snakes."

"Does he really? Does he know that these had had the poison glands, sacs, whatever they are—at any rate, they'd been rendered harmless."

"Had they?"

"Oh, yes," the Cardinal said. "That's one of the things we managed to keep out of the papers—we did really well on this one. We managed to keep almost everything out of the papers. I don't know how long that will last. But you realize, once you know that the snakes were harmless, you must know—"

"Somebody's pets," Gregor sighed.

"Exactly," the Cardinal said again. Then he got to his feet and began to make his way across his office, to the far side of the room where he kept his two personal filing cabinets. Gregor had always wondered what he actually kept in those cabinets. He had seen the Cardinal retrieve files from them, but the drawers always looked half empty. Now the Cardinal retrieved a pair of files from the top drawer of the cabinet on the right, and that drawer looked as empty as the others Gregor had seen the year before.

"As to the snakes," the Cardinal said as he lumbered his way back to the desk and sat down again, "I suggest that when you get to Maryville, you ask Sam Harrigan about those. I'm not saying they belonged to him, but he did start his career as a herpetologist, and he is somewhat whacked. You'll see. Right now, let me tell you about these."

"What are those?"

"Round seven trillion, eight billion, six million nine hundred eighty thousand three hundred sixty-six in a war game called Reformation and Counter-Reformation. You'd think people would get tired of this sort of anti-Catholic posturing, but they never do. It's like an addiction. Have you heard about the beatification of Margaret Finney?"

"I'm not even sure I know what a beatification is," Gregor said.

The Cardinal waved this away. "I could go into a lot of technical detail, but what it really amounts to is that beatification is the first official step on the road to official canonization in the Catholic Church. Margaret Finney was the foundress of the Sisters of Divine Grace—"

"I see," Gregor said. "So this is good for them. That

their foundress would be on the way to being canonized."

"Well, yes, Gregor," the Cardinal said, "but it didn't
fall on them out of the air. It almost never does.
Somebody usually has to bring a case for the person to be
beatified—to bring a case to Rome. Some religious
orders mount entire campaigns, and even with the
campaigns it can take decades, sometimes even centuries, before anything official happens. The Sisters up in
Maryville had been working on this for a long time, since
before the present Reverend Mother General was a
postulant. And the Sisters founded that town, by the
way. The first thing in it was their Motherhouse. All of
Maryville has been very, very involved in this effort to
have Margaret Finney canonized—which, by the way, if
it happens, will make her the first Irish immigrant ever
to be made a saint. And Maryville to this day is very,
very Irish."

"And?"

"Take a look at this." The Cardinal passed the
thicker of the two folders across the desk, and Gregor
took it. "These started coming just after the announce-
ment was made, that Margaret Finney had been beatified. That was just before Brigit Ann Reilly died. It got
quite a bit of play in the local papers up here, for obvious
reasons, the beatification, I mean. We haven't told
anyone about these. Take a look."

Gregor flipped open the folder and found what he
had half expected to see, considering the way the
Cardinal was talking. The folder was stuffed with anonymous letters, carefully paper-clipped to the envelopes
they had come in. Most of them were written on cheap
notepaper with blotchy pen or crayon. Gregor read
through one or two and flinched.

"This is quite a stack," he said, trying to hand the
folder back to the Cardinal. "Didn't you tell me the last
time I was here that you had a problem with sort of
redneck anti-Catholic feeling in the rural towns out
here?"

"Oh, yes," the Cardinal said, paying no attention to

Gregor's offer of the folder. "If that's all I had, I wouldn't be worried. Unfortunately, I've got something more. Look at this one now. This is what came after Brigit Ann Reilly was killed."

The second folder was nearly flat. Gregor took it from the Cardinal's hand and opened it up. It contained only one letter, and although that letter was anonymous, it was not written on cheap notepaper and it was not written in crayon. It had been produced on a letter-quality computer printer on cockle finish heavyweight bond.

I FED HER POISON AND I DRESSED HER IN SNAKES AND I TOOK HER MIRACULOUS MEDAL FOR A SOUVENIR. SHE'S ONLY THE FIRST AND ONLY A WARNING. WAIT AND SEE.

Gregor put the letter back in the folder, very carefully. "I take it that's accurate, about the Miraculous Medal?"

"Oh, yes."

"And it hasn't appeared in the press?"

"Oh, no."

"Is this the only letter from the same source?"

This time, the Cardinal did take the first folder back, to flip through it. He found what he was looking for and handed it across to Gregor, being careful not to dislodge the envelope attached to it.

"Except for it being composed on a computer, I never thought it was any different from any of the others. Maybe I gave half a thought to what it might mean, to be saddled with an intelligent fanatic bigot for once."

"Mmm," Gregor said, and then read: THE CATHOLIC CHURCH IS THE SYPHILITIC WHORE THAT IS POISONING THE WORLD. IF SHE DOESN'T WATCH OUT, THE WORLD WILL TURN ON HER IN SELF-DEFENSE AND START TO POISON BACK. He handed the letter back to the Cardinal. "The writer is literate," he said, "and Catholic. He or she wouldn't have called the Church 'she' otherwise."

"I know," the Cardinal sighed. Then he forced

himself to stand and walk over to his window, making his body move when it so obviously wanted only to sit still. Why he did that, Gregor didn't know, but he seemed to need to. He leaned against the window glass and made a face at the gray weather outside. "It would be nice," he said, "if it turned out that these letters were not written by a psychopath who was giving me a warning before embarking on a career of stranger-to-stranger mayhem. It would be nice if it turned out that the person who wrote these letters had nothing to do with the death of Brigit Ann Reilly. What do you think my chances are of having this work out like that?"

"Better than fifty-fifty," Gregor said positively.

"You're an optimist," the Cardinal told him. "Would you mind sending those things off to whoever might be able to do something about them—trace them, test them, whatever?"

"I wouldn't mind, Your Eminence. It would be the easiest thing in the world."

"I'm glad you think so," the Cardinal said. "Now go up to Maryville for me. That won't be the easiest thing in the world."

Gregor Demarkian didn't need the Cardinal to tell him that. Even before he'd seen those anonymous letters, he knew the Cardinal had another world-class mess on his hands. Somehow, the fact that it was also a mess on Gregor Demarkian's hands seemed, to Gregor, to be entirely natural.

Gregor often thought it was a good thing he hadn't been born Catholic. He had far too great an inclination to accommodate the princes of the Church as it was. If he were Catholic, he'd have an obligation to accommodate them—and he'd probably never get a full night's sleep again.

Three

❖

[1]

There was an antique grandfather clock along the west wall of the main room of the Maryville Public Library, and when it rang six o'clock that Friday night of March 1, Glinda Daniels felt she'd won a victory. In fact, she felt she'd won two. Getting through the week that followed the death of Brigit Ann Reilly hadn't been easy. There had been a million and one everyday details to attend to, most of them the result of water damage caused by the flood. Insurance companies to call, replacement carpets to be inspected and priced, St. Patrick's Day decorations to be cleaned or remade and hung: Glinda would have been going out of her mind with work even if she hadn't started feeling sick and dizzy every time she had to pass in front of the storeroom door. That was her first victory, that it all got done, in spite of how she felt or how little sleep she'd had. She had been getting very little sleep, and not much rest when she was awake, either. Her head always seemed to be full of dreams, and the dreams followed her. Sometimes, unavoidably back there in that corner of the room, Glinda thought she could hear them, hissing and snapping, getting ready to strike. It was like the only other time she had ever been forced to live through something awful, the other time that she never thought of anymore because it made her head ache. It *followed* her—there was no other way to describe it—but when she thought about telling other people, she felt struck dumb.

Her second victory had to do with the state of the library itself at six o'clock this Friday night. It had been a big week for library patronage. It might have been so even without the death, because in spite of what Cardinal O'Bannion had told Gregor Demarkian, the news of the beatification of Margaret Finney had not "got a big play" in Maryville before the flood. The Colchester media had made a fuss about it, but the local media hadn't had a clue. The local paper had been bought out five years ago by a chain based in North Carolina, and their present hand-picked, specially shipped-in editor-in-chief didn't know a beatification from a banana split. Then there had been the flood and the murder and the snakes. With one thing and another, it wasn't until the day before yesterday that the paper had got around to mentioning it, and then the inevitable had happened. There were a lot of lost souls out there, the kind of people who watched the *700 Club* but not the TV news, the kind of people who pored through the back pages of the papers for messages from God. They were the spiritual cousins of the people who drove thousands of miles to visit the Shrine of the Blessed Taco, and this week they were visiting her library.

Of course, most of the strange people who had wandered into the library this week weren't in the least interested in the beatification of Margaret Finney. They were following a blood scent to its source—and Glinda thought it a victory within a victory that she had managed not to kill one of them. They slid along the edges of the main room's walls, trying the doors to the closets. They came up to her and asked questions so blatant and gory, even the police hadn't thought of them. They made her skin crawl. For a while there, Glinda thought she was going to be stuck with them, doing involuntary overtime on Friday night. It seemed grudging to call it only a victory, that she could look out the glass wall of her office now and see nobody in the place at all, except Sam Harrigan standing at the check-out desk with a book in his hand. Sam Harrigan often made Glinda Daniels nervous—had, in fact, been making her especially nervous over the past few weeks—but not because he was the kind of jerk who thought of murder as a spectator sport. He just made her nervous, that was all.

Glinda got her camel's hair coat from the coat rack in the office's far left corner, slung it over her arm, and headed out to the desk. Her purse was right there, under the counter next to the extra cards for the check-out pockets. Sam heard her coming and shifted on his feet, standing up a little straighter.

"There you are," he said. "You were wandering around in there so long, I was afraid you'd taken ill."

"I'm fine," Glinda said, and didn't say: *You ought to know, because you could look through the glass at everything I did.* Sam had been in and out a lot in the past week—he'd even formally introduced himself and asked her to call him "Sam"—and in that time Glinda had learned something about him she never would have guessed. Sam Harrigan was a socially awkward man. She would have thought he had too much experience for that, what with doing a television show and going on book tours and having movie stars wander in and out of his house, but there it was. Every time he tried to talk to her, he seemed to lose any sense of what he ought to do with his hands.

Glinda put her coat down across the check-out desk and took the book out of his hand. It was called *Edible Fungi of North America*, and she couldn't believe he needed it. She couldn't believe he didn't own it. She opened its back cover, took out its card, and went searching through the center drawer for her date stamp.

"So," she said, "you were saying. You were listening to the radio on your way into town—"

Sam shifted on his feet again. "I was listening to 'Golden Oldies Rock and Roll,' to tell you the truth. That's how you know you're living in a small town, when they interrupt 'Peppermint Twist' for a press conference by a Cardinal Archbishop. I was speechless."

"It's a Colchester station," Glinda said drily, "and it's owned by Catholics. For all you know, the Archdiocese has a piece of it."

"I try to know as little as possible about the Archdiocese," Sam said. "It's like St. Patrick's Day. Ever since those idiots got caught down in Queens, trying to supply arms to the Irish Republican Army, all I do for St. Pat's is contribute to the mission fund when the Sisters come calling and go down and watch the parade. Anyway, they interrupted 'Peppermint Twist.' And there I was, listening to this man sound even more embarrassed than I would have been, saying nothing at all."

"This man meaning Gregor Demarkian," Glinda said.

"Exactly. My impression was, the Cardinal got him in front of the microphones very much against his will. But he's coming here anyway. I don't think that was against his will. I suppose it might have been."

"I wish I'd had the radio on in the office," Glinda said. "I was so wrapped up in things here, so worried I wouldn't get those terrible people out the door in time—"

"You never have to worry about that," Sam said. "If they give you any problem, you just call me up. I'll get them out of here in no time."

"You'll get me fired," Glinda said. She looked down at the book in her hand. It was duly stamped and ready to go, but Sam didn't seem to have noticed. She closed the cover and pushed it away from her. "I just wish I'd heard it, that's all," she told him. "I mean, you read so much about the man. He's always in the magazines, and the cases he handles—" Glinda shrugged. "I don't know. I would have liked to hear his voice."

"Well," Sam said reasonably, the Scots burr becoming just a little thicker, the way it always did when he thought he was about to utter the obvious, "you'll find out soon enough, won't you? He'll be here any day now. Tomorrow."

"I know," Glinda said, "but then he'll be investigating. He'll be—someone not to trust."

Sam looked down at the book, saw that it was closed, and pulled it toward him. Then he looked at the ceiling. He couldn't look her in the face without blushing. That had been true since the first day he'd come in to talk to her. Glinda found it—endearing.

She opened the center drawer again, checked a lot of things that didn't need checking, and closed it. Then she got her keys out of her pocket and said, "Well. I guess I'd better be going. Any minute now, somebody's going to come by and see the lights, and I'm going to be stuck here half the night."

"You could always refuse to let them in."

"I could," Glinda agreed, "but doing that kind of thing makes me feel guilty. Thank you for coming and telling me about Demarkian, though. I think it makes me feel better that he's coming."

"Why?"

"I don't know. Maybe just because it's all been so strange, with the way I found her and then all the people in town who keep saying they've seen her. It's been like a UFO incident or something."

Sam looked surprised. "Have you had more of those people? The ones who say they saw her?"

"Like you?" Glinda asked him.

Sam shrugged. "I came up front the next day and told Pete Donovan everything I saw through my little telescope. It's been a week now. You'd think that sort of thing would be over."

"I think it's a form of mass hysteria." Glinda sighed. "It's like those people who write in to *The Weekly World News* about how they've seen JFK or Elvis. I had two today. Don Bollander said he'd seen Brigit in the bank the day she died, and Mrs. Murchison swore she'd seen her down on Diamond Place. What Mrs. Murchison was doing down on Diamond Place, I don't know."

"Smoking marijuana?" Sam suggested.

"Mrs. Murchison is sixty-four years old and goes to

the funerals of people she doesn't know. I'm sorry, Sam. I really do have to be getting out of here."

"Do you have anyplace in particular to go?"

"What?"

"Do you have anyplace in particular to go?"

Glinda had been bent over at the waist, locking the drawers of the check-out desk. She didn't usually do this, although according to the rules set down by the Town Governing Board, she was supposed to. She was only doing it now to give Sam Harrigan a graceful way to leave. Except that it seemed he didn't want a graceful way to leave. She stood up and looked at him.

"Excuse me," she said.

Sam Harrigan had stopped shifting on his feet. "The thing is," he told her, "I know your car's out of commission—"

"That's right, it broke down last night right here in the parking lot. I had to have Earl Forrester come pick it up and give me a ride home. But how did you—"

"It's a small town," Sam said vaguely. He was staring at the ceiling again. "Anyway, if you've got someplace to go tonight and someone to see that's one thing, but if you're just looking to take the bus up the hill, well, it's a cold night. And it's dark. And it's right on my way. Your house is, I mean."

"You know where I live?"

"I pass you all the time. When you're shoveling snow in your driveway." Sam tried looking at the floor. "All I'm trying to say is, it is on my way, it wouldn't be any trouble for me to give you a lift, and Mack's Steak House is on the way, too, and it's almost dinnertime—do you know what I really want to say?"

"No," Glinda said, dazed. "I haven't the faintest idea."

"Well," Sam Harrigan told her, staring her straight in the eye, "I'll tell you. I think it's a bloody damn shame when a man gets to my age without knowing how to keep his dignity when he's asking a woman for a date."

A date.

There was a chair pushed up against the check-out

desk counter, a tall barstool sort of chair the assistants used on busy days. Glinda leaned against it, feeling weak.

As far as she was concerned, either Sam Harrigan had lost his mind, or she had.

[2]

It was fifteen minutes before eight o'clock, and Miriam Bailey was sitting at the vanity table in her private dressing room in the house on Huntington Avenue, getting dressed for dinner. She wasn't getting dressed for any ordinary dinner. On the nights when she and Josh stayed home and played at domestic bliss—which was most nights—she wore flowing hostess caftans and wedge-heeled sandals. Even on the nights when she was having one or two people over from the bank, she stuck to good wool slacks and four-ply cashmere sweaters. Tonight she was wearing a high-necked Christian Dior cocktail dress that had belonged to her mother and her best pearls. Josh, who was sitting in the stylized ice cream parlor chair against the wall behind her, was wearing his custom dinner clothes from Brooks Brothers, the first thing she had bought him after she'd brought him back to the States. In her mirror, he looked not only young but perfect, physically flawless, untouched by time. He reminded her of the pictures she had seen, preserved in sepia in the Manhattanville College library, of college dance troupes of the 1900s, except that he was male.

Miriam Bailey had never been interested in disguising her age. She didn't make up to conceal, but to acquiesce. It was easier to make an effort to look like everyone else than to fight the battles of eccentricity. To that end she applied a thin film of foundation and reached for the blusher. In her head, Miriam Bailey went on calling blusher "rouge."

"What I want you to understand," she told Josh, ignoring his mutinous cross-armed pose and concentrating on her own face in the mirror, "is that no matter how exciting or amusing it might seem to you, to just about anybody else it's going to sound suspicious. Of course, I know you well enough to trust you." She caught the reflection of his startled jerk and smiled to herself, biting her lip so it wouldn't show. "You do have to realize," she went on, "that to most of the people in this town you're an unknown quantity, and they aren't used to unknown quantities."

"I don't see what was so damn suspicious about it," Josh said. "I was just walking down by the levy."

"At eleven o'clock in the morning on the day of the flood."

"Why not? Miriam, I think you're crazy. People saw her all over town that day. What difference is one more going to make? And besides, she wasn't killed down by the levy. She was killed in the library."

"She also wasn't seen alive after eleven o'clock." Miriam put down the rouge. She wasn't sure if what she'd just said was actually true. She didn't know when the last time had been that anyone but her killer had seen Brigit Ann Reilly alive. Fortunately, she could be sure Josh didn't know, either. She picked up her eyebrow pencil and bent over to look more closely into the glass. "I wish you'd give some consideration," she said, "to the kind of trouble you get into when you go off half-cocked like this. I wish you'd learn to think. Remember all the fuss we had when you came tearing back from Colchester with your glove compartment full of crack—"

"It wasn't crack, Miriam. It was first-class cocaine."

"It was illegal, whatever it was. And I don't mind your having it, I've told you that. I don't really care what you do as long as you give me what I want."

"I always give you what you want."

"Let's just say that's another subject. Right now, what I want you to do is promise me you won't mention this at dinner tonight. I don't say you have to keep it a secret forever, but at least don't mention it at dinner tonight."

"But I want to mention it at dinner tonight. I mean, for God's sake, Miriam, I've got to have something to talk about. Those people look right through me."

"Those people don't know what to think about the fact that you married me," Miriam said. "They're very nice people, Josh, really. You can talk to them about religion, or art, or—"

"Why don't I talk to them about sex, Miriam? At least that's something I know something about."

Miriam threw her eyebrow pencil down on the table and turned around in her seat. Looked at straightforwardly and more or less up close, Josh wasn't really that perfect. It wouldn't be too long before gravity began to tug at the corners of his eyes. Miriam Bailey didn't care what anybody said. She didn't find older men "distinguished," merely older. She wanted no part of them. For the moment, however, Josh was young and necessary to her. She crossed her arms over the back of her chair, rested her chin on them and said, "Josh, try to make sense, please. You were with me when I listened to the news tonight. You must have heard what was said about the Cardinal sending that man Demarkian."

"So what?"

"So he's a famous expert on murder. He's been called in to consult on cases all over the country. The Cardinal's sending him here can only mean one thing."

"What?" Josh asked suspiciously.

"That the Cardinal wants this thing settled his way," Miriam said definitely. "Trust me, Josh. I've known the man for many years. I know what he's like. The last thing O'Bannion wants is for someone who's respected in one of his parishes, or some little old lady, or whatever, anyway, the last thing he wants is a solution that can tie the Church to this mess. Now here you are, saying you were walking on the levy at eleven o'clock on the morning of the flood—it must have been pouring rain by then, for goodness sake—and you saw Brigit Ann Reilly walking around with a box in her hand—"

"It wasn't a box. It was a paper grocery bag."

"Whatever it was. Add all that to the fact that I knew her—"

"You did?"

"Of course I did," Miriam said, "she volunteered in the literacy program. I didn't know her well, but I knew her to speak to. I know all the volunteers. They'll say you knew her, too, you know, and you won't be able to prove otherwise. You're setting yourself up to be the perfect suspect. The Cardinal couldn't have done better if he'd invented you himself."

Josh raised his hands to his face and rubbed distractedly, a sure sign that he was thinking. Miriam didn't know if that was a good sign or a bad one. Josh thinking was always a loose cannon. She turned back to the mirror and picked up her small bottle of what she thought of as "that white stuff you put on under your eyes and pretend it makes the wrinkles go away." Behind her, Josh had risen out of his chair and begun to pace.

"Let me get this straight," he said. "I've got to be worried about this Demarkian man, not because I actually did anything, but because I'm a stranger in town, and also because I was taking a walk and also because—because what, Miriam? Why would I have wanted to kill some little nun?"

"Maybe you didn't have a reason," Miriam said. "That's what Demarkian did, years ago, for the Federal Bureau of Investigation. He tracked serial killers. You know the sort of person I mean."

"Yes," Josh said. "I know."

"You'd be a perfect candidate for that, too," Miriam said. "Believe me, I know what I'm talking about. You'd be very easy to pin something on. Especially once they found out—"

"Once they found out what?"

If makeup was supposed to do something for your face—instead of just sitting on it—then Miriam didn't see any reason to go on putting more on hers. Nothing short of plastic surgery could do any more for her than had already been done. She wondered why she had never gone in for plastic surgery and then dismissed the idea. It wasn't her kind of thing. Even knowing half the women who would be at dinner tonight had had a tuck here and a lift there didn't matter. That conventional she just didn't want to get. Maybe that was because, unlike most of the other women she knew, she had never relied on her "attractiveness" for much of anything.

She got up out of her chair and shook out her dress, watching its folds shimmer and shake in the mirror. Then she walked over to where Josh was standing and put her hand on his jacket. As soon as she touched him, he stiffened, in every place but the right one. She had her leg pressed against his groin, so she knew. It had been a long time since he'd been able to work up any enthusiasm for his side of this particular bargain. It had been a long time since she really cared. Maybe the nuns who had taught her in school had been right. Maybe there was something about sex no woman really wanted to know on the morning after.

Josh had stepped back, closer to the wall. He caught her looking at him and flushed, embarrassed. "Sorry," he said. "I didn't mean anything. It's just that we don't have time."

"Of course we don't," Miriam said.

"I'd have to get dressed all over again," Josh said. "I'd never get downstairs for cocktails. You wouldn't either. I'd ruin your hair."

"You would do that, yes."

"You don't have to be like this," Josh said. "You don't have to go all sour on me just because it's practically eight o'clock and you're having a party. I don't see why you always have to blame it all on me. It's your committee to—committee to—"

"Committee to advance the cause of the canonization of Margaret Finney," Miriam recited dutifully.

"Well, then," Josh said.

Well, then, Miriam thought. And then she drifted away from him, out of the dressing room and into the bedroom proper, to the big bow window overlooking the back lawns. The back lawns were covered with snow and ice, white and daunting, as frozen as the rest of the town since the waters had receded and the temperature dropped. She really couldn't see anything down there, not in a way that let her recognize it. The gazebo was a huddle of wrought iron near the snow-piled fountain. The menagerie was a single ball of light.

She felt Josh come up behind her and put a hand on her shoulder, tentatively, as an act of propitiation. She shrugged him off and started to laugh.

"Oh, dear," she said. "I wonder how many people in this town realize that what you've got down there is some kind of God-forsaken zoo."

[3]

Pete Donovan had always considered himself a good police officer. He was young and he was raw. He wasn't as educated as cops got these days in cities like New York and Chicago. He didn't have the kind of experience he would have needed to cope with a major suburb like Greenwich or Bryn Mawr. Still, for Maryville, he was a good police officer. He knew the town. He knew its people. Most of all, he knew how to use his common sense. That was how you got through the day in a place like Maryville, as a police officer or anything else. You remembered that Mrs. Cander's son Jimmy always did like to steal chickens and that Stevie Hall went in for starting fights and that the old ladies down at the Lutheran Benevolent Society were still seeing Communists under their beds, and you took it from there.

It was now nine thirty on the worst Friday night Pete Donovan had ever had to live through—worse even than that Friday night two years ago when Father Doherty had decided to bust head down by the river and clean up the gangs there once and for all—and all Pete could think of was that he really shouldn't go home. No matter how tired he was, no matter how crazy the day had been, he had an obligation to stay at the station and see the night through. Just why he felt this way, he couldn't say. He had gone home on the night Brigit Ann

Reilly died. He'd even gone to sleep. Today, nothing much of anything had happened except—craziness.

He looked around the "station" and saw what he always saw, a large open room with a waist-high swinging rail used to divide it into two parts. On his side of the rail were the six desks of the six men, including himself, who made up the police force. On the other side of the rail there were chairs and benches and a desk and radio set for their secretary-dispatcher, Linda Erthe. Linda came in at six and stayed the night, since in the experience of the town of Maryville it was at night when she was really necessary.

Linda was sitting with her back to him, working on a crossword puzzle. The radio was silent but unlikely to stay that way. Pete had just sent Davie Burnham down to St. Andrew's to check on Father Doherty and his clinic, and that always brought in trouble in the long run. Pete cleared his throat and said, "Linda?"

"If you're going to have another nervous breakdown about those calls you've been getting, I don't want to hear about it," Linda said. "It's just mass hysteria. It'll go away by itself in a day or two."

"Yesterday, you were telling me the sightings were mass hysteria," Pete said. "You know, the people who said they'd seen Brigit wandering around town the day she died. All fifty six of them or however many there were."

"Well, that was mass hysteria."

"So this is mass hysteria, too? Do you know how many bodies I went looking for today that weren't there? Six. Six, Linda, it was crazy. I had three of those little postulants in this morning swearing they'd seen a corpse in the hedge outside the library."

"Postulants," Linda frowned. "Well, religious types aren't too stable, if you know what I mean."

Pete thought she was a brave woman to say that in Maryville, where the Cardinal had spies. "Mark Yasborough always seemed stable enough to me," he said. "Good farmer. Nice farm. He said he saw one at the side of Eight eighty-six, frozen stiff in the snow."

"Cabin fever," Linda dismissed it. "He's under a lot of strain anyway. That wife of his has just about had it with Maryville, New York. I heard her talking down to the Camelot the other night. She wants to go back to New York City and I don't blame her a bit."

"Yeah," Pete said. "I see what you mean. Marrying a woman from New York City and bringing her back here isn't too stable."

"It's nuts," Linda said, "and if you ask me, marrying a woman from here and expecting her to stay here is just as nuts. Did I tell you about that? Frank and I had a fight."

"You're always having fights."

"This was our final fight. I promise you. Our absolute last. I don't know what he thinks I'm going to college for. The last thing I want to do is to stick around here after I graduate."

"What're you going to do instead?"

"Go to the city. They've got lots of jobs for social workers in the city."

"Mmm," Pete said. He couldn't imagine Linda Erthe as a social worker. Her life was a bigger mess than the lives of most bag ladies, and the bag ladies had excuses Linda didn't have. Pete Donovan had always thought he'd feel better about Linda if she just took drugs.

He swiveled his chair around to look at the papers on his desk, decided there was nothing there he really had to be concerned about, and swiveled back to Linda again. He wished Davie or Hal or Willie or one of the other boys was in, but there it was. That was why his mother kept telling him he ought to get married. Your buddies were never around when you needed them. Pete cleared his throat and said, "Still. There's a difference. I've been thinking about it all day. A difference in tone, sort of."

"I haven't the least idea what you're getting at."

"The two kinds of reports," Pete insisted. "These today have been just crazy. And, of course, last week I was thinking the same thing about the people who were saying they'd seen Brigit wandering around on her own in town. But those other reports didn't feel the same."

"What's that supposed to mean?" Linda asked. "You've changed your mind? You think those reports were real?"

"I don't know. Let's just say I'm glad I didn't leave them out of my report to the Cardinal."

"You left them in?" Linda was shocked. "You're going to get crucified. You're going to be the laughing-stock of the St. Lawrence Seaway."

"No, I'm not," Pete said. "We're not that far north. And besides—"

"Besides what?"

Pete didn't want to tell her besides. Linda Erthe was nobody to go confiding in. She was certainly no one to tell about his nervousness on the subject of the Great Demarkian, Master Detective. Ever since the Cardinal had called to say that Demarkian was coming down, Pete had been in a sweat.

Now he swiveled in his chair again and pushed his papers around again and listened to the phone ring. He watched Linda pick up, speak into the receiver for a while and grimace.

"You can take this call if you want," she said, punching in the hold button on her set. "It's Mrs. MacBrac out near the flats. She said she found a body in the hay and now it's gone, but you can—"

"Never mind," Pete said. "Just tell her I'm out on a call."

Four

❖

[1]

For Gregor Demarkian, arriving at the Motherhouse of the Sisters of Divine Grace was something of a
revelation. He didn't know what he'd expected a Motherhouse to look like—college Gothic, maybe, with spires
and turrets—but it wasn't this redbrick, sensible structure that reminded him so strongly of a public elementary school. Nor, in his imaginings, had it been so
profusely decorated. The Motherhouse occupied the
highest piece of ground in town and its gate used
Delaney Street like an extended private drive. That gate
was covered with shamrocks made of silk and as big as
wedding cakes. What's more, the shamrocks must have
been dusted. There was no snow on them at all, in spite
of the fact that the rest of the landscape was crusted and
hard and sparkling white in the sun. Then there was the
drive that led from the gate to the Motherhouse door.
Gregor was fairly sure it had to be deep Lent. It was that
time in the Orthodox calendar, and the two calendars did
overlap. John Cardinal O'Bannion hated secular decorations during Easter and Lent. He had a passionate
repugnance to fluffy pink bunnies, fuzzy yellow chicks,
and representations of smiling buttercups in chocolate
and icing. Maybe he felt differently about secular decorations that happened to be Irish. The drive was lined
with them. There were tiny leprechauns nestled around

the glass balls of the lamps, large gilt harps on lawn stakes pounded into the frozen ground, pots of gold made out of cardboard, and Styrofoam balls attached to decorative bricks along the drive's edge.

Like the town of Maryville below it, the Mother-house of the Sisters of Divine Grace seemed to be in the grips of a St. Patrick's Day mania—or at least the outside of it did. Gregor had breezed up to the Motherhouse's front door in the car John Cardinal O'Bannion had provided for the purpose. Like all the cars O'Bannion provided, it was nondescript and in questionable working order, but it came with a driver. This was a good thing, because although Gregor had a license he couldn't really drive. Being driven had the advantage of keeping him out of trouble—Bennis Hannaford once said that putting Gregor behind the wheel of a car was like making a solemn vow to God Almighty that you would do everything possible to get a ticket—but it had an added advantage as well, and that was that he could pay attention to his surroundings. In a way, his impressions of Maryville, driving through, had been as startled as his first impressions of the Motherhouse. He had expected a much smaller town, and a much less diverse one. For some reason, he'd thought Maryville was a farming community in the process of metamorphosis into a suburb. He'd got the suburban part without trouble. The route coming in had passed through acres of neat midsize colonial houses on neat midsize one-acre lots. By now he was sure Maryville had never been a farming community. On the other side of town from the neat midsized colonial houses there was a river and along that river there were buildings that bore the unmistakable stamp of warehouses, abandoned and otherwise. Of course, Maryville was very close to the St. Lawrence Seaway, even if it wasn't on the St. Lawrence River itself. Gregor didn't know why that information had failed to penetrate, but it had. And yet—

And *yet*.

If Gregor had had to put a name to his malady, it would have been information overload. When the Cardinal commissioned a report, he commissioned a *report*, not the usual police officialese outline that might or might not tell you what you wanted to know. With the Cardinal's reports, if someone had seen something or heard something or just thought something, it was there. If there was some bit of background you might need, it was there, too. Last night, Gregor had plowed his way through "a few extra things" the Cardinal had handed him at the Chancery, and those included a history of the local Immigrants National Bank, complete with a biography of its present owner-president and the Cardinal's personal opinion of every part of the operation. (*"Miriam runs a good business. Much better than her father did. Holds the mortgage on the Motherhouse and all the other Church property in town when we need them to be mortgaged and she's always been good about them, too. Surprised she didn't invite you to stay at her house. Usually does that with visiting celebrities and she knows you're coming, I told her myself. Let me tell you, though, I'm counting on Miriam. All this mess the banks have got into. Miriam was telling me just the other day that they're starting to do spot audits, the Feds are, and the Immigrants is due March the fifth. Miriam says she's going to show these WASP nellies how to run a bank. Of course, there is the little problem of her husband . . ."*) Then there had been chapter and verse on Margaret Finney, the Maryville Public Library. (*"Miriam gave the money for the new building. Glinda Daniels has been librarian forever."*) And the Maryville Volunteer Fire Department (*hopeless*). By the time he finished reading them all, Gregor felt as if he'd lived in town forever, but always underground. He knew about everything conceptually, but nothing in terms of personality.

Still, if the overwhelming amount of local information had been difficult to take, the witness reports that skirted the murder of Brigit Ann Reilly had been worse. Just getting the times right had been enough to give Gregor a headache. Pete Donovan had included the statement of anyone anywhere who claimed to have seen Brigit Ann Reilly on the day she died, and there were a lot of them. Gregor had managed to whittle this list down to a very short one that he was sure he could trust:

10:00	Brigit leaves Motherhouse
10:06	Brigit talks to Jack O'Brien on Delaney Street
11:15	Brigit spotted near river by Sam Harrigan using telescope
1:00	Brigit found under snakes by Glinda Daniels in library storeroom

Reading carefully, Gregor thought those were the reports he could trust absolutely. The problem was, he couldn't really dismiss the others. He hated to admit it, but they just didn't sound crazy enough. They also tended to take place during that crucial two hours between the time Sam Harrigan had seen Brigit walking and the time Glinda Daniels had found her body, or in the hour between the time Jack O'Brien had talked to her and the time Sam had seen her. There were such great big spaces of time. She could have been doing anything or been anywhere. Maybe Mrs. Moira Monohan had seen her walking up Londonderry Street at 12:17. Maybe Mr. Thomas Reeve had seen her on the levee at just about 11:00. Their reports got a little shot of credibility from the fact that they, like the others, failed to see her anywhere at all between 10:30 and 10:55. For that half hour at least, mass hypnosis had ceased to exist in Maryville.

Half an hour, between ten thirty and eleven. Half an hour. It nagged at him. It was just the kind of thing he was supposed to be good at—working through timetables, seeing the hidden patterns in random occurrences. He didn't believe that that half hour was insignificant. It stood out too baldly to be that. He just couldn't figure out what it meant.

That was the kind of thing that was driving him crazy, keeping him awake, burning him out. Last night, when it had finally begun to get to him, he had reached for the phone to call Bennis and stopped. Bennis was in the middle of her draft, or near the end of it, or something. She wasn't talking to anyone who couldn't qualify for the Distressed Damsels Union. She had her phone off the hook. He had put his own phone back into its cradle with what felt like desolation. He wasn't used to being cut off from Bennis like this. He didn't like it. God only knew what was going to happen to him if she up and married somebody.

[2]

Now it was ten o'clock on the morning of Saturday, March 2, and Gregor was standing in the Motherhouse's front foyer, out of the cold and away from the relentless Irish mania that accompanied what was apparently Maryville's favorite holiday. The Motherhouse foyer was bare of decoration of any kind, except for a large crucifix that hung on the wall facing the front door and a square oversize portrait in oils of a gentle-faced woman with thick eyebrows and fierce black eyes. This, Gregor thought, was probably the Blessed Margaret Finney, and she looked like a woman and a half. He looked around some more. The floor at his feet was black and white checkerboard marble and very clean. The walls around him and the ceiling above him were both plain, sane white. It was a relief to be away from all that green madness—and from his nattering wondering about why there was so much of it. Everybody in town couldn't be Irish or of Irish descent. Those people he had seen down near the warehouses had definitely been Hispanic of some kind—and they had been decorated, too, right to the point of wearing shamrocks on the lapels of their coats. It was enough to make him think he'd swallowed something he shouldn't.

At his side, Sister Mary Scholastica—née Kathleen Burke and a familiar face from Gregor's stay in Colchester—was just shutting the front door and shaking the cold out of her habit. She was an extraordinarily tall woman with bright red hair that kept escaping from her veil, and Gregor thought she was not behaving naturally. He could think of a hundred conversations they should have been having at just this time. There was the one about everything that had happened in Colchester— months ago, the people who had died and the person who had killed them, and how she felt about that now and how she was coping. There was the one about Brigit Ann Reilly, a girl who had been in her charge, and how she felt about *that*. Gregor found herself wondering if nuns weren't allowed to talk about their emotions to laypeople—or even to show them. He could think of nothing else that would explain her manner, efficient and automatic and as cold as ice.

"The Cardinal," Sister Scholastica was saying, as she kicked at the bottom of the door the way people did when weather stripping made a corner stick, "has already been on the phone to Pete Donovan. Pete Donovan is our chief of police, which you probably already know. I can't believe the Cardinal wouldn't have told you. At any rate, you won't have any of the trouble you may have had other places. Pete had no objection to your being called in."

"That's good," Gregor said blandly. In fact, it was imperative. He had never had to work against the wishes of a local police department. He wasn't sure he would agree to work if a local department was against him. God only knew it would make an investigation practically impossible. "What about you?" he asked her. "Do you have any objections to my being called in?"

"Of course not." Scholastica looked startled. She had finished with the door and was now looking around the foyer, as if she were trying to remember something she had forgotten. "If you really want to know the truth," she said, "it was my idea. Calling you in, I mean. The Cardinal had thought of it—"

"It seemed to me like a natural for the Cardinal."

"It was. But before he called us about it, I mentioned it to Reverend Mother General. That was the day after it happened, a little over a week ago. I just kept looking at the whole situation and thinking—"

"What?"

If Scholastica hadn't been a nun, she would have shrugged. It was Gregor's experience that nuns—or at least the old-fashioned kind—didn't shrug when you expected them to. Instead, she turned to the right and headed for the doors there, obviously expecting Gregor to follow. The soles of her shoes were rubber and her feet were soundless on the marble, but she still made noise as she moved. She had a ring of keys at her waist that jangled.

"I don't know what kind of information you've gotten from the Cardinal," she said, "but we got a great deal of it right away. Maybe that was because Reverend Mother General did the expected thing for once and called the Chancery immediately."

"Immediately when?" Gregor asked.

"Immediately period," Scholastica said. "As soon as Pete Donovan called us. We're supposed to call the Chancery for any death, really, even when a retired Sister of ninety-seven passes away in her sleep, but with that sort of thing we often take a day or two while we get ourselves organized. With an accident of any kind—"

"Did you think it was an accident?" Gregor asked her. "In the beginning?"

"In the beginning, we didn't know what it was," Scholastica admitted. "When Pete called it was still early, maybe two o'clock at the latest, and he didn't really know what had happened either. That was when he still thought the cause of death was going to be the snakes and he was beside himself. I mean, we all knew the snakes probably belonged to Sam—"

"Did you?"

Scholastica blushed a little. "Well, we didn't tell the press, if that's what you mean. We wouldn't. We got so sick of them hanging around, amusing themselves—oh, never mind. Their behavior was deplorable. And word came from the Cardinal in no time at all that he didn't really want to have anything get out, so we—managed."

"Better than I would have thought possible," Gregor said.

"Yes. Well. In the old days, the Church was a great teacher of discipline. Anyway, I think everybody thought they were probably Sam's snakes because he's had stuff like that up there before, it drives the old nellies at the Town Governing Board wild, but then they could have been Josh Malley's—"

"Who's Josh Malley?"

Scholastica shot him a strangely amused look. "Josh Malley is the twenty-five-year-old husband of our sixty-something-year-old local bank president. From what I hear—I was in Colchester at the time—she brought him back from Corfu a couple of years ago and has been doing the Lord only knows what with him since. It's been very strange, really. When people have midlife crises—I suppose this would have been an end of life crisis—when they have these crises they usually change, don't they? They start wearing silly clothes and have plastic surgery and tell all their friends they'd rather be called Kiki from here on out. Well, Miriam didn't do that. She's always been a solid, sensible woman and she's still a solid, sensible woman. She just has Josh."

"And what does Josh have to do with snakes?"

"Oh," Scholastica said, "well. She's always buying him toys, Miriam is, and one of the things she bought him is a menagerie. It's a small zoo, really. She had a lion in it for a while—a very small lion, mind you—but the Governing Board went absolutely nuts and she had to give it away. The menagerie has snakes in it."

"Water moccasins?"

"I don't know."

"Hmm," Gregor said again.

They had passed through a short empty corridor that opened onto nothing, with doors at the front and back like the lock of a canal. Scholastica opened the far set of doors and motioned him through, into another short corridor with more signs of life. This corridor had doors in its walls and crucifixes on them, each crucifix accompanied by a Bible verse in elegant calligraphic

script. Gregor leaned close to one and found Hebrews
13:12–15: *Jesus died outside the gate*. It was, after all,
Lent.

Scholastica led him through another set of doors,
then around a corner. Gregor thought the Motherhouse
hadn't looked this big when he was still outside it. It
hadn't looked this complicated, either. He let Scholastica
take him where she wanted to and forced himself not to
try to make sense of it just yet. He could do that later,
with pen and paper and Sister's advice on how to make
a map.

"Anyway," Scholastica said, "if the snakes had belonged to Josh we would have been happy to let the
world know about it, but we couldn't be sure because
Sam wasn't talking. And in the beginning we didn't know
at all, of course. We just thought Brigit had drowned."

"Was that likely?" Gregor asked.

"After Pete called, no," Scholastica said. "He did
tell Reverend Mother about the snakes. I mean before
that, when she was missing and we didn't know where
she was. The rain really was terrible, and there was
flooding down at St. Andrew's. We were helping out by
packing up canned goods and getting our gym ready to
take anybody Iggy Loy couldn't handle—"

"Iggy Loy?"

"St. Ignatius Loyola Church. It's right down the hill
on Delaney but not too far down. It was high enough up
to escape any water damage, and we knew it would be.
And I know the library is just on the other end of
Delaney Street and I know it's not far—"

"This is the library where she was supposed to be
going."

"There's only the one," Scholastica said. "Brigit
went every day. We're all supposed to have one or two
little practical chores to do around the house, and that
was hers. I thought it was a good idea, but—"

"But Brigit was a flake?"

"I wouldn't say flake, exactly." Scholastica looked
uncomfortable. "Mr. Demarkian, part of me wants to say
that Brigit was nothing particularly special. There were
always girls like Brigit in postulant classes, immature

girls, borderline cases. Before I became Postulant Mistress, I didn't realize how hard it would be to decide whether to keep them or not. The actual decision is supposed to rest with Alice Marie—Sister Alice Marie is Mistress of Novices—in consultation with Reverend Mother, but in practice it comes down to me. And I just have a hard time making up my mind."

They had come to the end of the corridor they had turned the corner into. They were now presented with turns to the right and to the left. The place felt like a maze, turning in on itself, folding up like an accordion. It made Gregor dizzy.

In front of him, Sister Mary Scholastica had come to a stop, turning neither one way nor the other. Now she swung around and faced him for the first time since she had let him through the door. Her face was pale and taut, but there was still no real expression in it. Gregor cast his mind back to last year in Colchester and tried to get some take on this. Had Scholastica been so stoic and expressionless then? Had she been so tense? What was wrong with her? Gregor had come prepared to deal with human emotions. He always did, because he knew too well that if he didn't they would get in the way. That was one of the things the Bureau had taught him, on kidnapping detail especially. Taught or not, he really didn't have a talent for this sort of thing. He was always being thrown by the unexpected.

Scholastica had wrapped her arms around her waist and hunched her shoulders forward. She was still staring at him intently, as if she expected him to give her the answer to a question she hadn't asked.

"Brigit Ann Reilly," she said, with a trace of coming explosion in her voice, "was not that common type, the girl too immature to be in the convent. She was immature enough, mind you, but that wasn't what was wrong with her, as far as a religious order was concerned. As far as I was concerned. She was a perfectly ordinary girl from a perfectly ordinary family in New Hampshire. I'm not trying to imply that there was something odd about her background, because I don't believe there was. I think she would have made a perfectly marvelous wife and mother in the ditzy *I Married Joan* mold, or a competent private secretary to someone whose schedule wasn't too complicated. She wasn't very bright and she wasn't very stupid. She wasn't very imaginative and she wasn't very bad. She was just utterly and incurably undisciplined."

"Undisciplined?" Gregor demanded.

Scholastica turned away from him and went to the left. She was walking quickly now, with an abrupt and decisive step Gregor remembered from nuns he had run across in his childhood. She pushed open yet another set of swinging wooden doors, held yet another one open for him to pass through, and then continued on their way, oblivious of anything but her own words and her own forward motion.

There seemed to be one more set of doors to pass through. Gregor assumed there was only one more, because he couldn't imagine Scholastica slamming the palms of her hands into doors like that time after time without getting hurt. He caught the swing of the door himself as he came through, just in case she had forgotten what she was doing besides talking.

"Brigit Ann Reilly," she was saying, "was the kind of girl who had enthusiasms. She was ready to canonize the postman one week, because of the beautiful things he had said to her when she'd met him on the doorstep while he was delivering the mail. She saw secrets everywhere. Undistinguished people whom she liked had secret lives, according to her. Secret religious lives. She was addicted to falling in calf love—nonsexual calf love, I want to make myself clear—with a different person every week and then"—Scholastica threw up her hands—"I don't know how to explain this to you, really. I don't know— Oh, Mr. Demarkian, the whole thing is such a mess, I don't know where to start talking about it, never mind explaining it."

"I do," Gregor said. "Brigit Ann Reilly was a girl who liked secrets. Other people's secrets."

"But not *blackmail* secrets," Scholastica said. "She

didn't like to know discreditable things about people. I'd have known how to deal with that. I'd have thrown her right out of here as soon as it became clear. What Brigit liked was thinking that someone she was infatuated with had the stigmata and wasn't telling anyone."

"And was that happening, Sister? Did someone she knew have the stigmata on the day Brigit Ann Reilly died?"

They had come to a dead stop again, this time in front of broad door with a window cut into its top half. There was a brass crucifix hanging just under the window. Gregor looked at the walls around him and saw a few unobtrusive homages to St. Pat's. There was more balance here than Gregor had seen in any other part of the convent—but he didn't know that balance was the business convents were into. Scholastica went to the door with the crucifix on it, opened it up and looked inside. Then she pushed the door all the way open and wedged a rubber doorstop underneath it with her foot. The office beyond it was empty, and obviously the sanctuary of the order's Reverend Mother General. There was a full-size poster-photographed copy of the portrait in the foyer on the far wall, surrounded by photographs of two dozen or so other women in the same pose: an order geneaology of Reverend Mothers General.

"Reverend Mother General must be off somewhere with Mr. Donovan," Scholastica said. "She's got him up here, you know, just to talk to you. You can sit down in the meantime, if you want. She won't mind having you in here."

"You were telling me about the stigmata," Gregor prompted gently.

Scholastica flushed. "I didn't necessarily mean the stigmata in particular. Although I've got to admit, that was exactly the kind of thing Brigit went in for. She said in Recreation once that if she got to have just one wish granted it would be to have a vision of the Virgin, and if it hadn't been the first week I'd have thrown her out for that. That kind of thing is a form of hysteria. What I'm trying to say is, all that last week before she died, she'd been—strange in a way I recognized."

"Strange the way she was strange when she formed one of these infatuations," Gregor translated.

"Exactly," Scholastica said. "Only it was different, this time, because I don't think she was fixed on anyone I know. She certainly wasn't fixed on anyone in the convent. I would have found out who it was if she had been."

"Was she fixed on someone she met on her walks to the library? Is that what you mean?"

"I don't know, Mr. Demarkian. I didn't know what to think about it all even before Brigit died. I will say I hope she wasn't fixed on Glinda Daniels because Glinda—"

"Glinda what?"

"I'm going to leave you in Reverend Mother's office now," Scholastica said. "She'll be along in a minute. Just make yourself comfortable."

"Sister—"

But Sister had backed up, out of the door, and then proceeded to do something Gregor had never known anyone but a nun to be able to do: She had truly and undeniably disappeared. Gregor looked up and down the corridor and saw no one, only open doors that revealed small empty classrooms. He looked into Reverend Mother General's office and wondered how she managed to keep it so very neat. His own desk at home was a holocaust, and Tibor's was worse than that. The only pieces out of place in this room were the letters and the single small package at the edge of Reverend Mother's desk, and Gregor found himself resenting the Sister who had put them there, carelessly, without regard to the fastidiousness that marked the rest of this space.

It was the kind of thought that was calculated to make him think he was getting old. He sat down in the only chair that looked like it could accommodate him and settled in to wait.

[3]

Fifteen minutes later, Gregor Demarkian was still sitting in his chair and still waiting. He was going over and over the things Scholastica had told him. He had a feeling that the jumbled account actually meant something, both more and less than she had intended to tell him. The things she had stressed did not seem so important, but one or two of the things she had said in passing did. He tried to put it together with his knowledge that Brigit Ann Reilly had died of coniine poisoning—of hemlock, really—and came up with mostly mush.

He was just consoling himself with the idea that what he had was at least promising mush when he heard a step in the hallway. He had gotten up by then and begun to pace. He stopped in the center of the room and looked through the door at the small woman paused in its frame. She was very small indeed, and very old, but in spite of the fact that she wore the same abbreviated habit Scholastica did, she had all the authority of the women in the pictures behind him who were wearing full robes. This, Gregor thought, must be Reverend Mother General. He started toward her with his hand outstretched, and then stopped.

Reverend Mother General wasn't looking at him, even though he was human and large and taking up a good deal of space in her office. She was looking at her desk, and when Gregor looked too he understood why. The small package that had been lying under the envelopes was no longer where he had first found it, but further along the desk top near the brass base for the pen and pencil set. What was more, it was moving.

Gregor stepped up to the desk, picked the package up, and shook it close to his ear. He could hear the bump and shudder of something trying to get out. He brought the package down and turned to Reverend Mother General.

"Do you mind?" he said. "There's something alive in there."

"Is it safe for you to open it?"

"Relatively safe," Gregor said. "I suppose if it's a rabid bat, I'll be in for a lot of pain with the series injections, but I don't think it's that."

"No," Reverend Mother General agreed, "I don't think it's that, either. The other ones had had their poison glands removed, did you know that?"

"Yes, Reverend Mother. The Cardinal told me."

"Well, if that's what this is, let's just hope it's got its glands removed, too. Go ahead. Open it."

Gregor returned his attention to the box. It had been taped shut at both ends and along its seams, and it was small. He had a big hand and it would just fit across it, without jutting out at either end. He found the letter opener on Reverend Mother General's desk and used that, cutting along a fold that looked weak but wasn't. It took him a good minute of hacking to get it undone.

"Here we go," he said, when he got a slit carved in the tape. He started to pull back the flap and felt Reverend Mother General move closer to him. He gave her points for that. Gregor Demarkian had never been a man who liked wimpiness in women. He got the flap all the way back and reached for the tabs inside.

What happened next happened so fast he almost didn't see it. There was a snake inside the package, but it wasn't a water moccasin, rendered harmless or otherwise. It was a garden variety black snake, about a foot and a half long. With the box closed it had been coiled. As soon as the tabs came open, it lunged as if to strike—even though black snakes don't strike. What it did do was to shoot itself out of the box. For a split second, it seemed suspended in air. Then it was on the floor and headed in the direction of the open door. Reverend Mother jumped away from it instinctively. Gregor just watched it go. Then he looked down at the package in his hand and the floor beyond it and saw what he had missed in the excitement of the snake.

It was a piece of paper about twelve inches long and

six inches wide. It must have been wrapped up in a tube around the snake inside the box and fallen out when the snake escaped. It was now lying face up on the floor. Gregor recognized the printing—it was the same letter-quality computer typeface of the anonymous letters in John O'Bannion's file. The graphics were new. They were also very, very graphic. Gregor had no trouble at all recognizing them for what they were, which was not very abstract abstractions of the female genitalia.

NUNS OPEN THEIR LEGS AND PUMP FOR PRIESTS

the printing said, and then:

ALL WHORES DESERVE TO DIE.

Reverend Mother General looked down at the paper, picked up her skirts, and walked over it. Then she sat down behind her desk and said, "I'd better get Alice Marie down here to set the novices looking for that reptile. We can't have it wandering around the convent no matter how harmless it is."

Five

❖

[1]

Sister Mary Scholastica had entered her order well after Vatican II had changed it. Unlike Sister Alice Marie, or Reverend Mother General, she had never worn full habit or begged her soup after Chapter of Faults or recited the Little Office in Latin. To say she was a thoroughly modern nun, however, was not quite accurate. Some of her postulants would be thoroughly modern nuns. No matter how carefully she trained them, they would come out of formation thinking that all this ritual stuff was a little silly and that it might make more sense if Sisters wore lay clothes and were much more open about the way the convent was run. Scholastica was of a generation that believed—and was encouraged to believe—that what went on in a convent was the concern of the Sisters who lived there, and no one else. If there was a crisis of suitably apocalyptic proportions, Reverend Mother General might decide to call the Chancery, or even the Congregation for Clergy and Religious in Rome. Laypeople were simply out of bounds. You didn't tell laypeople anything, not even what the convent served for lunch. You certainly didn't ask their help in a matter that should have been between you and your superiors. From the moment that Sister Mary Scholastica had first mentioned her doubts about Brigit Ann Reilly's vocation to Gregor Demarkian, she had been feeling guilty. From the first moment afterward when she'd had a chance to think, she'd been feeling worse: like a traitor.

When Scholastica left Gregor Demarkian in Reverend Mother General's office, she went down the north spine of the main Motherhouse wing, around another corner, and out into the courtyard. It was a cold day and she wasn't wearing a cape, but she didn't mind it much. She crossed the courtyard and let herself into the building on the other side. Just inside that door there was both a corridor and a staircase. She had intended to go up to the cloister floor, where she had a "room"—a cell, really— with walls made of muslin curtains and a bed with a gray metal frame. She wanted to be alone and out of sight with a desperate intensity she hadn't experienced since adolescence. That was how she remembered coming to the knowledge of her vocation—not a blinding vision of light in church or the voice of the Blessed Virgin Mary in a dream, but afternoon after afternoon followed by night after night of sitting on her bed at home, thinking it out and not being able to shake the idea. Since then, she had read a lot of words about mysticism. She had even read the words of the mystics themselves, like Teresa of Avila and Catherine of Siena. She knew that people were granted perfect pictures of heaven and hell, sights and sounds the rest of the world wasn't privy to. She also knew she was not one of these people. If she had any direct experience of God at all, it was with a God of silence.

She changed her mind about going up to the cloister at the last minute. Maybe she was too guilty to want to spend time with God. It would be just her luck to have the only true vision of her life when she was feeling barely worth the trouble of calling by name. Maybe she was just too restless. It could be torture, sitting on your bed in a muslin-walled room when what you really wanted to do with yourself was pace. Scholastica looked up the stairs for only a moment and then pushed through the swinging doors onto the classroom corridor.

Back when Scholastica was a postulant, classes were held on Saturdays at the Motherhouse, both for Sisters in formation and for the professed. Sisters in formation got a sixth day of convent drill: practice in custody of the eyes, rehearsal for chapel rituals, and explications of the theories and theologies behind interior silence and the habit scapular. Professed Sisters studied for continuing education credits if they were certified teachers and for pleasure or penance if they were not. Today, no one at all was studying, at least not on this corridor. The doors to the small classrooms were all open and the rooms and corridor were both filled with girls—girls in black dresses and black babushkas, girls in black dresses and white veils, girls in black dresses and white veils with a band of black at the hem. Postulants, canonical novices, senior novices: Scholastica looked at them all, scrubbing floors and polishing doors and cleaning windows, and sighed. She still liked the old custom better. There was something spiritually satisfying about it that could never be fulfilled with soap and water.

Down at the far end of the corridor, near the door that led to the outside, Sister Alice Marie was sitting on a high stool, reading aloud from the *Introduction to the Devout Life* by St. Francis de Sales. Whether any of the postulants or novices was actually listening was moot. From what Scholastica could remember, in her own days of being read to she hadn't listened much.

Scholastica went up to Alice Marie, tugged on her sleeve, and gestured with her head when Alice Marie looked up. Alice Marie nodded and called out for Sister Josepha to come up to read for her. Scholastica watched as impassively as she could as Sister Josepha came up, a pale wisp of a girl for whom even the modified habit looked too heavy. The band of black on the hem of her veil testified to the fact that she was a senior novice, not a canonical one. The sappy look on Alice Marie's face testified to the fact that Josepha was one of the stars of her class. Scholastica let it ride. If Josepha had been one of her postulants, Scholastica would have been seriously considering the possibility of sending her home.

Alice Marie released the stool to Sister Josepha and motioned Scholastica across the hall, into the only classroom that was empty. It was also the only classroom that was entirely clean. Closing the door behind her,

Scholastica noticed that the desks had been buffed to a high hard sheen, as if they were decorative pieces instead of useful ones.

"I'm glad you came," Alice Marie said. "I was sitting out there, droning along about the practice of the presence of God or whatever it was, wondering how it was coming along. Did you talk to him?"

Scholastica sighed. "Oh, I definitely talked to him. I talked to him too much. You'd think after nearly twenty years of practicing silence, interior and exterior silence, you'd think after all that, I'd be able to keep my mouth shut."

"It's only been eighteen years," Alice Marie said.

"Same difference." Scholastica had been standing against the door. Now she moved into the room and sat down at one of the desks. It was too small for her, but it was too small for everybody. Scholastica sometimes wondered if these desks had been misplaced from one of the order's elementary schools.

"I told him all the things we agreed to tell him," she said after a while. "I told him all about Brigit going out and wandering around. I told him all about getting the call from Pete Donovan."

"Did you tell him about the phantom corpses?"

"I didn't even think of it," Scholastica said. "I don't want to. It makes us sound so strange. I don't know, Alice Marie, I just talked and talked and talked. About me, about us, about Brigit. I don't know if I made much of anything like sense."

Alice Marie looked suddenly uneasy—worse than uneasy, really, green around the gills—and Scholastica didn't blame her. A year ago, Alice Marie had been Mistress of Postulants under old Sister Mary Jerome. Then Jerome had had a stroke and Reverend Mother General, who had always said she believed that Alice Marie didn't have what it took to be a Novice Mistress, had had a change of heart. Now Alice Marie's first year as Mistress of Novices was barely half over, and everything was going wrong.

In the old days, Sisters who couldn't contain their nervousness were taught to fold their arms together within the sleeves of their habits and grab onto their wrists. Alice Marie, having been trained under the old dispensation, did that now.

"Scholastica," she said, "when I came down this morning, down to this corridor, it was just going six o'clock. I know because I heard the Angelus bell ring. I'd left my Office down here and I wanted to pick it up." She shot Scholastica an embarrassed look. "You're probably modern enough to think I'm silly, but I don't feel right about not reading my Office, even when I'm praying in community and I can just chant along with the rest of you."

"I prefer to read it, too. What does that have to do with anything?"

"Nothing, really. I came down here, I came into the classroom across the hall from this one, I got my book and I came out again. It was when I came out again that I saw it."

"Saw what?"

Alice Marie put her hand in her habit pocket and came out with a small wadded piece of cardboard. "That was stuck in the door at the end of this corridor. Just under the latch. Open it up."

Scholastica opened it up. It was a square from the side of a box of generic laundry detergent, and that could mean only one thing. As long as there were postulants at the Motherhouse, only postulants did laundry. They were supervised by old Sister Anthony James, but she would never stick a piece of cardboard in one of the Motherhouse's side doors. If she wanted to leave the building after it was locked up, she'd ask Reverend Mother General to use the override key. Scholastica handed the cardboard back.

"Somebody was trying to get out," she said.

"Exactly," Alice Marie said.

"Do you think they managed?"

Alice Marie gave a vigorous shake of her head. "They couldn't have. The security system doesn't work like that. If whoever it was had managed to get this cardboard stuck in the latch, the open latch would have set off every alarm in the building as soon as Reverend Mother pulled the lock-up switch."

"And if that hadn't done it, opening the door would have," Scholastica said. "Except I don't have to worry about an open door. You're right. The latch would do it. You think the cardboard was put in the door last night?"

"Yesterday, yes," Alice Marie said.

"It was crazy," Scholastica said. "Whoever had such an idea? It's knee-deep in snow out there. Nobody could have got out without getting drenched in the process and then she'd have been caught. I mean, even if she'd managed to get her clothes down to the laundry bins as soon as she came back in and before anyone saw her there would be her shoes—"

Alice Marie seemed about to make some protest about the shoes, but just then there was a knock on the door and the creaking sound of a knob that needed to be oiled turning in its socket. A moment later, a postulant named Leah Brady opened the door and stuck in her head, looking scared out of her mind.

"Sister?" she said, looking first at Alice Marie and then at Scholastica. She settled on Alice Marie with something like resolution and said "Sister" again. "Sister Josepha said to tell you you're being buzzed for," she went on. "She said you're being buzzed for a lot and it's Reverend Mother General and it's probably urgent."

"That Demarkian person probably wants to talk to me," Alice Marie said. She still had the cardboard in her hand, flattened out now, big enough to cover her palm. She balled it up and threw it in the wastebasket. "I'll come along," she told Leah Brady. "I want to go upstairs for a moment anyway. Tell Sister Josepha I'll be right out."

"Yes, Sister."

Leah Brady retreated. Alice Marie waited until she had closed the door before she said, "Obviously we can't tell Reverend Mother about this now. We're going to be in enough trouble over Brigit once it all comes out, and it is going to all come out, sooner or later. The only thing I can say, Sister, is that you have to find out—"

"I'll find out," Sister Scholastica said. "You'd better go now. If Reverend Mother really is calling you, she's going to be impatient."

"Because Reverend Mother is already impatient?" Alice Marie asked. "I wouldn't say that. I think Reverend Mother is a Living Rule."

"Of course she is," Scholastica said and then stood stock-still while Alice Marie glided out of the room and into the corridor. As soon as the older Sister was well and truly gone, Scholastica cast her eyes to Heaven and uttered a little prayer. Then she promised every saint she could think of to make a novena to the Blessed Mother on the subject of that piece of cardboard as soon as she got the chance.

Sister Scholastica didn't have to find out who had put that cardboard in the latch.

Sister Scholastica already knew.

[2]

For Father Michael Doherty, the weekend had started at eight P.M. on Friday night, when a boy named Juan José Cortez had been knifed five times in the chest on the corner of Clare Avenue and Diamond Place. Juan José Cortez was fourteen years old, and from the reports of the boys who had been with him, his attacker wasn't much older. His attacker was also Anglo, which figured. There wasn't much violence in Maryville, but what there was always took place on Clare and Diamond and Beckner and always crossed ethnic lines. It might have crossed racial lines, too, except that the local black population was solidly middle class and much too sensible. Father Doherty got called out because of Juan's mother, who, like most of the mothers in the neighborhood, preferred the ministrations of her priest to the arcane aloofness of the county hospital doctors. Michael had arrived at the hospital to find Juan in miraculously good shape, due to the apparent fact that the Anglo who had stuck him had no strength at all in his arms. He had checked Juan's wounds personally—so he could tell Juan's mother he had—and started to go home, when the ambulance brought in another face he knew. That one belonged to Carmen Esposito, and the agony that rippled through it had been caused not by human brutality but by unhuman whim. Carmen Esposito had one of the apartments in the building three doors down from the church on the church's right hand side, and like all the apartments in that building hers had a defective gas stove. She was trying to light one burner when the one beside it started to leak. It didn't leak enough to cause an explosion, but it did leak enough to cause a fire. The fire caught at her sleeve and the next thing she knew she was covered with flame. When Michael first saw her in the emergency room, she looked boiled. He'd stayed most of the night with her. For one thing, she was afraid. For another, he was a qualified physician, although not a burn specialist, and he could help her. For a third, his mere presence tended to get his people better and more prompt care than they would have received at any other time. It was as if the doctors at county hospital didn't think the Hispanic population of Maryville was very important, but believed that their priest had secret ties to John Cardinal O'Bannion's Chancery.

It was now eleven o'clock on Saturday morning, and Michael was tired. In fact, he was exhausted. After he'd finally seen Carmen settled and as comfortable as she was going to get, he'd gone downstairs to take another stab at going home and run into a traffic accident instead. The traffic accident had been a four-car pileup. His people—Dona and Maritsio Dominguez—had been in the third car to hit the knot. They had been prepared and not badly hurt. The occupants of the other cars, however, were almost all also Catholic, and Michael couldn't see his way to abandoning them just because they were not his parishioners. Besides, he had taken pains to get himself affiliated with county hospital. When the rest of the staff saw him there in the middle of an emergency, they expected him to help out.

He should have insisted on getting back in time to say the seven o'clock Mass. He should have at least have insisted on getting back in time to say the ten. By ten, his clinic was supposed to have been open for four hours. Instead, he had let himself be talked into extra duty after extra duty. The duties had been both medical and clerical. He had finished with them less than fifte minutes ago. He was now finally stumbling home, and the last thing he needed was this insistent old woman who had camped herself on the church's steps, holding a brown paper bag full of the Lord only knew what and talking a mile a minute in a Hispanic dialect he couldn't begin to understand.

"From Number Thirty-seven," the old woman said, on one of her rare excursions into English. "This is who I am. From Number Thirty-seven."

"From Number Thirty-seven," Michael said. "Yes, mother, I understand. But I must go into the church now. I am late."

Hernandito was standing on the top of the church steps, waiting for him. Hernandito's arms were folded across his chest and his mouth was set into a line. "I'm glad you decided to come back," he said. "We all thought you'd taken off for Miami."

"I took off for the hospital," Michael said. "It was Friday night."

"It is Saturday morning."

"From Number Thirty-seven," the old woman said again. "From the first floor above the street. From the back."

Michael Doherty was a naturally courteous man. He made it a point to be even more courteous with his parishioners, who came from a culture of civility and who were touchy about their honor. He didn't want to put this old woman off or to offend her, but he didn't know what to do with her. It was obvious that she wasn't in any of the usual kinds of trouble. She was stiff with age but not ailing. Her back was strong and her skin was a good healthy color, in spite of the fact that she was forty pounds overweight and probably fried everything she ate. Her eyes were clear and without cataracts. None of her bones was broken and none of her muscles had snapped. When Michael got to the top of the church steps and the door, she was right behind him. She was as quick as a girl of sixteen, if not as nimble. He held the door open for her and motioned her in ahead of him, even though he knew it wasn't expected of him. She would have thought it perfectly proper for her priest to precede her. When she had disappeared into the vestibule, Michael turned to Hernandito and asked, "Do you know her? Is she from the neighborhood? I can't understand her Spanish—"

"That's Señora Gretz from Two-D in Thirty-seven," Hernandito said. "You don't have time to talk to her now. The clinic—"

"Is in full swing and is barely being held together by Sister Mary Gabriel."

"It's Sister Marietta this time. There will also be Mass? The women are disturbed—"

"There will be Mass at twelve o'clock," Michael told him. "I'll apologize in my homily. Isn't Gretz an unusual name for someone from Central America?"

"There are many people with names like that in Central America. You do not have time—"

"I'm going to have to make time, Hernandito. The woman obviously wants something. She's not going to go away until she gets it."

The woman was standing on the other side of the vestibule, staring at them both. Michael got the uncomfortable feeling that she understood more English than she spoke. He covered his embarrassment and his exhaustion both by shooing her in the direction of the small side hall that led to his office. To get there they had to pass the stairs that led to the basement. Michael could hear the familiar sounds of the clinic: the crying of babies, the squabbling of children, the firm high voice of a nun saying, "Yes, Mrs. Gomez, I understand that you usually get a prescription for your piles, but I'm trying to tell you it will be much simpler and much cheaper to use—" Today, the nun was saying all that in Spanish. Michael was impressed.

He let them all into his office, threw a stack of papers off a chair, and offered the chair to Señora Gretz. She sat down with the brown paper bag still clutched firmly to her bosom. If he hadn't just been told differently by both Señora Gretz and Hernandito, he would have wondered if she were a bag lady.

Inspiration struck him, and Michael said, "Excuse

me, mother, but you have not been evicted from your apartment? You have not been forced out of your home?"

Michael Doherty's Spanish was Spanish-from-Spain and ferociously formal. He had learned it out of a book and never spoke it except here—and here only rarely. He had no talent for languages. Now he found himself repeating the thought every way he could, just to make sure she understood, but she was shaking her head vigorously.

"I am Señora Gretz," she said, "from Number Thirty-seven. From the back."

"Yes," Michael said, "you told me so."

Señora Gretz looked at him long and hard. Then she turned to Hernandito and let out a stream of virulent Spanish that made the boy blush.

"She is committing blasphemy left, right, and center," Hernandito said, when she gave him a chance to say anything. "She wants me to tell you she doesn't believe in God. And that she is a Communist. And that she will not be—" Hernandito groped for the English word and failed to find it. He tried a few in formal Spanish instead.

"Evangelized," Michael said finally. "I see. She doesn't want to be evangelized. Tell her it is my personal opinion that the entire world is an act of evangelization."

Hernandito looked skeptical. "You want to argue theology with this one? I know this one. She's crazy. On the day of the flood, she kept saying she was going to go to the roof instead of being evacuated. To protect her property."

"Her property? I thought she was a Communist."

"With Señora Gretz, all she means by Communist is that she hates the Pope."

Señora Gretz was getting restless in her chair. Now she pounded on the arm of it and let loose with another stream of Spanish.

"She says that on the day of the flood she was brought not to the parish on the hill—she means Iggy Loy, Father—not there but to the house of the nuns," Hernandito said. "She says she was put in a large room where the nuns play games. I think she means the gymnasium. She says that while she was there she was having much trouble with her arthritis."

"Where does she have arthritis?" Michael asked.

Hernandito asked and the old woman flexed her hands—but her hands weren't gnarled or stiff. They showed no signs of arthritis at all. Michael pointed this out.

"I told you she was crazy," Hernandito said.

"Ask her again," Michael told him. "Maybe she misunderstood you. Ask her where she has her arthritis. For Heaven's sake, Hernandito, maybe we can get her in to the clinic and give her a little relief."

Hernandito hesitated, turned back to the woman, and asked the question again. Then he turned back to Michael. Michael wouldn't have thought that so simple a question would have taken so long to answer, but Señora Gretz had responded with one of her monologues. He was stuck with it.

At least, he thought he was going to be stuck with it. Hernandito was opening his mouth to speak, taking in a big reservoir of air. Michael was resigning himself to another secondhand lecture on the virtues of anti-Papism. Suddenly, Hernandito looked at the ceiling, looked at the floor, wiped his mouth against the back of his hand and coughed.

"Father Michael," he said, "this is very strange."

"So tell me."

"Father Michael," he said, "she says that while she was there she went walking around, because she will not let the Sisters tell her where she must go or not go, and she went into what she says is a church. It much have been the chapel. And when she went in there she saw near the front a nun—"

"Well, of course she saw a nun," Michael said in exasperation. The telephone on his desk rang and he picked it up automatically. He was still concentrating on what Hernandito was saying. Nine times out of ten, even on weekends, a ringing phone meant nothing in particular. People in the neighborhood wanted to know what times he was hearing confessions on Saturday, what times he would be available to give instructions to

godparents on Thursday, when the church would be free
for weddings in June. This time, though, he not only had
an emergency, he had just the emergency he wanted.

"This is Sister Marietta," the phone said in his ear,
"there's a woman down here named Señora Diaz who's in
the middle of delivering what I think is a seventh-month
infant. I think you'd better—"

"Call the ambulance," Michael said. "I'll be there
right away. Are you a midwife?"

"Sister Gabriel is a midwife. I'm just an ordinary
nurse. Will you hurry?"

"Yes." Michael hung up the phone and started to get
his things together to go out again. He was going to miss
saying Mass again at twelve o'clock, but he knew Señora
Diaz. If he didn't at least go to the hospital with her she
would transcend hysteria and enter the realm of the
psychotic break.

"I'll be back as soon as I can," he told Hernandito.
"Hold the fort while I'm gone. Tell—what's she doing
now?"

Michael didn't know if he'd forgotten about the
woman in his office because he didn't consider her
important or because he didn't want to have to deal with
her. In a way, it didn't matter. He had forgotten her, as
soon as he had the chance. Now, turning toward the door
and in a hurry to get out, she was blocking his path. If
she had been simply sitting in her seat, the way she had
been when he'd picked up the phone, he might have
gone right past her, blindly. Instead, she was standing
up, waving her hands in the air.

"What's she trying to get at?" Michael demanded.

Hernandito sighed. "She says the nun she saw was
no ordinary nun," he said. "She says this nun was in a
long dress with white around her face like in the old
days, and you couldn't see her hair. And this nun came
up and touched her."

"And?"

"And now," Hernandito said, "she has no more
arthritis at all."

Six

❖

From time to time over the years, Gregor Demarkian had amused himself by reading novels that were
supposed to be about the FBI. It always shocked him
how inaccurate they were. It wasn't mistakes in procedure he minded. Procedure was like a Paris couturier. It
changed its silhouette from year to year. It changed its
preferences in colors and fabrics from region to region,
too, although it often wasn't supposed to. What surprised Gregor was how often popular novelists insisted
on turning the Bureau into a spy organization. In the
fifties, it had perhaps been understandable. With the
Cold War going full blast and the country seeing sabo-
teurs under every mulberry bush, there had even been
a television program that turned the Bureau into a spy
organization. What was wrong with writers of more
recent books, he didn't know. He liked the ones by
Thomas Harris. As for the others, they were all the
same. Agents prowled through the back alleys of urban
slums in impeccable Brooks Brothers suits, infiltrating
gangs of drug runners. Agents glided through those
temples of vulgar luxury called Las Vegas casinos in
impeccable Brooks Brothers suits, infiltrating the Mafia.
Agents sat in the ranks at meetings of the Patriot's
League in impeccable Brooks Brothers suits, infiltrating
the lunatic right. Agents did everything, in fact, except

what they actually did do, which was mundane police work applied to cases under federal jurisdiction or with interstate implications. As to where they got all those impeccable Brooks Brothers suits, Gregor couldn't imagine. In his twenty years with the Bureau, Gregor had only known one agent who owned a Brooks Brothers suit, and that had been a gift from the man's father-in-law. The suit had ended up getting ruined when the agent it belonged to had been pushed off a cabin cruiser into the San Francisco Bay in 1967, victim of a practical joke by three other agents whose sartorial preferences ran toward what could be purchased at Sears.

Reverend Mother General had left her office soon after the snake had, making a single phone call first and looking agitated all the time. Gregor waited politely until she was gone and then got down to what he had been trained to do. The fact that he was not actually authorized to do it in this case didn't matter. Either the Cardinal had been telling the strict truth, unadorned by flights of wishful thinking, and Gregor *was* authorized to do what he was doing, but hadn't heard it from Pete Donovan yet—or the Cardinal was talking straight through his hat. If that was the case, it wouldn't be the first time. As long as Gregor was on Church property, though, it was the Cardinal's version of reality that would apply. He got the handkerchief out of his pocket, draped it across the palm of his right hand to serve as a shield, and went to work.

The Cardinal's driver had taken Gregor's luggage into town, to a place called St. Mary's Inn, where Gregor was supposed to be staying but which he hadn't seen yet. Knowing the Cardinal, Gregor had had the good sense to keep his papers out of his suitcases and tucked into the inside jacket pocket of his suit instead. He didn't have the crime report there—when the Cardinal delivered a report, it had all the verbal economy of a novel by Robert Ludlum—but he did have his notes. What was more important, he had very good photocopies of the anonymous letters the Cardinal had received. He wished he'd had a chance to ask Reverend Mother

General if the piece of filth that had landed on her desk today had been the first. If it wasn't, Gregor hoped she'd had the sense to hold on to the others.

He picked up today's missive, computer graphics genitalia and all, by the upper-right-hand corner. He picked it up with the tips of his thumb and the first finger of his hand, and with both these tips covered by his handkerchief. Then he held the letter up to the light coming from Reverend Mother General's office window. In a way, the precautions he was taking were both useless and silly. Anonymous letters almost never came complete with fingerprints. Either their writer was smart and used gloves—or stupid and used disorganization. It was remarkable how smudged prints could get when their provider was manic and mentally out of control. Then there was the question of watermarks and other identifying signs on the paper itself. That sort of thing was bad enough on a traditional anonymous letter, because a traditional anonymous letter was either printed on cheap mass-produced notepaper or assembled from letters cut out of newspapers on construction paper or newsprint. There was no way to trace any of that except back to the manufacturer, and all the manufacturer could tell you was how many millions of pounds of the stuff he had shipped to how many different states. Gregor didn't know much about computers, but he had a feeling that they were going to make matters worse. For one thing, they always did. For another, Gregor remembered hearing a lecture on the computer explosion at the Bureau once. The man who'd given it had claimed that thousands of pounds of perforated computer paper were being sold across the country every *day*—and that had been in 1978.

With the light from the window streaming through it, the page looked flimsy and slightly oiled, as if whoever else had touched it had been sweating at the time. That could have been good news—body oils produced prints—except that the oiled smudges were much too big and had probably been smeared. Gregor put the page back on Reverend Mother General's desk and took one of the Cardinal's letters from his jacket pocket. There was no point in holding that one up to the light. It was only a copy, and a copy on photocopy paper, not computer paper, at that. He laid it down on Reverend Mother General's desk next to her own letter and stood back to contemplate the two.

"Same printer," Gregor said to himself, half out loud. Then he wondered how much difference that made. Computer printers were not like typewriters. Typewriters were eccentric. They took on individual characteristics in no time at all. Computer printers came with daisy wheels that could be changed at will, and that were discarded as soon as they showed any signs of wear or idiosyncrasy. What was worse, fresh daisy wheels produced printing identical to that produced by other fresh daisy wheels of the same type, so that two letters could look as if they'd been produced on the same machine when they had been written on two different machines twenty miles apart. Then there was the terminal factor: Just because two letters had been printed on the same printer didn't mean they had been written by the same person. That was true of typewriters, too, of course, but computers made the problem harder to solve. With typewriters, you were at least sure that, for two people to have used the machine, two people had to have been *at* the machine. Large organizations with sophisticated computer setups, though, had terminals that could be plugged into their central printers from dozens of different locations and several miles away. Two letters printed by the same printer might have been composed by two different people, neither of whom worked anywhere near each other or the location of the printer itself. Gregor was getting the surreal feeling that investigating these anonymous letters was hopeless and that investigating anonymous letters was going to go on being hopeless forever more. Once the masses were thoroughly plugged into the system, anyone who wanted to could send nasty messages to anyone anywhere and be impossible to stop, in spite of the fact that those messages might be ruining lives, causing divorces, putting an end to international peace—

"I'm overdramatizing," Gregor said. This time he must have said it more than half out loud, because it elicited a response. Although Gregor was facing the desk, he was still turned slightly away from the door. His line of sight was toward the window and the sun that seemed so strong and bright outside it. The cough he heard came from behind him. It didn't sound like anything that could have been produced by Reverend Mother General.

He had picked up one of the anonymous letters while he'd been ruminating on the death by computer of Civilization As We Know It. He put it down again.

"It won't do you any good to worry about it," the voice of the cough said, deep and now unmistakably masculine. "Only way we ever catch these people, we pick them up for something else and find copies of the letters on their kitchen table. And we do pick them up for something else. Almost always."

Gregor would have liked to dispute this observation—there was a great deal about it to dispute—but he was caught by the sight of the man who filled Reverend Mother General's office door. Gregor Demarkian was a physically large male. He was over six feet tall. He wasn't exactly fat, but he had a layer of middle-aged padding on him. He also had a pair of naturally broad shoulders that made him look a little too wild in the formality of suits. The man in the doorway was a giant. His body filled the door frame from side to side. His head came so close to the top of the door's frame, Gregor almost thought he was going to have to duck when he came inside. He was at least six feet ten, and he had bulk to match, fat and muscle both. He was such an apparition, Gregor found himself stepping back instead of going forward to meet him.

Either the giant didn't notice, or he was used to that kind of reaction. He marched into the office—not having to duck when he came through the door after all—and held out his massive hand.

"You must be Gregor Demarkian," he said. "The Cardinal's told me all about you. I'm very glad to meet you. I'm Pete Donovan."

Pete Donovan's voice was a good deep bass. It bounced from window to wall to ceiling like a Roman candle released indoors and made the windowpanes shake.

[2]

Later, Gregor Demarkian would look back on the first fifteen minutes he spent with Pete Donovan as one of the most highly efficient, well-organized introduction sessions he had ever had with a local police officer. Maybe because Gregor still thought in Bureau terms— the efficient is the dry, the well-organized is the linearly logical—it didn't seem that way at the time. Pete Donovan shook his hand in great, ligament-wrenching arcs. Then he walked over to the desk, looked down at the two anonymous letters Gregor had laid out against it, and grunted. Then he retreated to a corner, to prop himself up against a wall. Gregor thought that was very sensible. There were chairs in Reverend Mother General's office, but Pete Donovan didn't look like he would fit in any of them. There was the desktop to sit on, but the desk's legs didn't look like they could hold Pete Donovan's weight. Gregor was awed. Donovan was a young man, a good twenty years or more younger than Gregor himself. Middle-aged spread was still in the future.

Instead of getting into all that—which he didn't want to do and which wouldn't have been polite in any case—Gregor sat down on the chair he had been occupying when Reverend Mother General opened her package and stretched out his legs.

"I wasn't exactly worrying about it," he said. "I was just annoyed by it. What happened to Reverend Mother General?"

"She went off with a lot of other nuns to look for a

snake. Do I have that right? With this nasty letter she got, there was a snake?"

"A black snake," Gregor said. "Not very big. Not dangerous at all."

"I know black snakes." Donovan rubbed the back of his neck. "Which one was it? The letter she got?"

For a moment, Gregor didn't know what Donovan was talking about. Then he realized that the policeman couldn't have any idea which of the letters on the desk belonged to Reverend Mother General. It could have been either or both. Gregor cocked his head and asked,

"Why do you assume it was one or the other? Why not both?"

"Because Reverend Mother General always says exactly what she means and what she said was that she got *a* nasty piece of mail. If she'd got two, she would have said two."

Of course, there were other possibilities. Neither of the letters on the desk might be the one received by Reverend Mother General. Gregor could have substituted two others, for purposes of his own. Reverend Mother General could have taken the real letter with her and palmed off a fake on Gregor. A million and one things could have happened, most of them improbable, but all of them possible given the limitations of what Donovan knew. If Donovan had been an agent, Gregor would have given him a lecture about it.

In spite of the fact that Donovan was so young, however, he was neither an agent-in-training nor Gregor's immediate subordinate in a Bureau operation. Gregor was simply unused to dealing with young law-enforcement officers in any other way. He was going to have to squelch his impulse to instruct. Donovan was being cooperative, probably because the Cardinal had asked him to be. Gregor didn't want to jeopardize that.

He got out of his chair—he was so restless—and picked up the box the letter and the snake had come in. It had fallen to the floor in the confusion and been kicked—by Reverend Mother General or himself, Gregor didn't know—slightly under the desk. Gregor turned it over in his hands and said, "The postmark is Maryville. The postmarks on the Cardinal's letters have been Maryville, too. Did you know the Cardinal was getting these things?"

"No," Pete Donovan said, "but I wouldn't be surprised. Things have been—a little weird around here lately."

Gregor chucked the box onto the desk. "What about Reverend Mother General?" he said. "Has she gotten any more of these things?"

Pete Donovan shrugged. "As far as I know, no. At least, she hasn't come to me about them. That doesn't mean she hasn't gotten them."

"You sound as if you think she must have."

"Maybe I do. Like I said, things have been a little weird around here lately. St. Mary Magdalen's out in Borum Ridge was vandalized about a month ago. Borum Ridge is on the western end of town. Whoever got in there took the crucifix off the wall behind the altar and hacked it into wood chips with an ax. Then they smashed a lot of windows and defecated on the altar. They must have made a racket fit to wake the dead, but Father Testaverdi was away for the week and there wasn't anyone to hear them."

Gregor considered this. "That kind of thing is usually kids, isn't it? Kids pretending to be Satanists or kids getting drunk or stoned and out of control."

"Sometimes." Donovan conceded the point grudgingly. "The problem is," he went on, "this isn't your big city or your bedroom suburb. We've grown a bit. We even have our own version of a low-rent district, complete with Spanish bodegas and knife fights once or twice a month on Friday nights. But even the low-rent district is *small*."

"I don't see what you're getting at."

"What I'm getting at is, we all know each other." Pete Donovan sighed. "Hell, I know every one of the Spanish kids by face and name except for maybe one or two who moved in in the last week or so. I'm not saying I'd recognize everybody who lives in town. It's a bigger town than that. But it's not a much bigger town than that. If someone's desecrating altars and sending nuns—which one did you say it was?"

"This one." Gregor picked up the letter with the picture on it and handed it over.

"Wonderful," Donovan said. He studied the letter for a protracted moment and then leaned over to throw it back down on the desk. He was actually tall enough to do that while keeping one foot bent against the wall. "Now I've got someone sending dirty pictures to a nun. This is all I'm going to need. The Cardinal is going to be livid when he hears about this."

"The Cardinal is fifty miles away in Colchester."

"The Cardinal might as well be hiding under my bed."

Donovan pushed himself away from the wall and began to pace, back and forth, between the office door and the window.

"Listen," he said, "I've lived in this place, in Maryville, all my life, except for four years I spent in the army. I even went to college at St. Francis of the Snows just outside town and I commuted there. I *know* this place. I *know* these people. And I know something else. I know that no outside agitator has moved into the area recently. I know there aren't any strangers lurking in the bushes. The only strangers we get are the ones who immigrate from Central America and none of them is desecrating churches or—did I tell you what happened at Iggy Loy the week before the flood?"

"No," Gregor said. As usual when he was on an errand for the Cardinal, there seemed to be a lot of things no one had told him. "All I've really discussed with anyone is the murder of Brigit Ann Reilly," he told Donovan now. "The Cardinal has been receiving anonymous letters, yes, and he's concerned about them, but not so concerned about them as he is about the death."

"Does he think the two things are connected?"

"You know the Cardinal. He thinks everything is connected."

"I think everything is connected," Pete Donovan

said. "I didn't know anything about any anonymous letters so I haven't had a chance to work them into the theory, but give me time. What happened up at Iggy Loy, that's—"

"St. Ignatius Loyola Church," Gregor said. "Sister Scholastica told me."

"Yeah. Well, Iggy Loy is the closest church. The nuns would be in that parish if they were in any parish, which they aren't because they're a Motherhouse. There's a lot of traffic between here and there. The nuns run the parish school and the CCD program—that's Confraternity of Christian Doctrine, catechism for children who don't go to parochial school. So there's always one nun or the other over there for something."

"Always nuns?" Gregor asked. "Not nuns and postulants and novices?"

"They send everybody everywhere these days," Pete Donovan said, shooting Gregor the desperate glance Gregor had come to think of, over the years, as the mark of a sensible man defeated by Vatican II. Gregor thought it was interesting to see it in a man so young. If Pete Donovan was nostalgic for the old Church, it was a Church he had known only as legend. He cleared his throat a little and said, "It doesn't really matter who they send, for this, because none of the nuns ever saw it because Father Fitzsimmons made sure they didn't. Do you get the feeling that everybody is protecting everybody else around here and nobody is doing anybody any damn good at all?"

"Slightly," Gregor said drily.

"Yeah," Pete Donovan said. "Well, what happened over at Iggy Loy was that the choir robes got torn up. And I do mean torn up. Somebody ripped them apart with his bare hands. Somebody or somebodies. The robes are kept in a dressing room up in the choir loft, along with extra hymn books and arrangements sheets for the organ. Father Fitzsimmons went up there to see if he could find the words to 'Lord of the Dance,' or something and there it was, shreds of cloth all over the place—"

"Did you see it?" Gregor asked. "Were you called in?"

"Oh, yes. The unofficial policy in the Archdiocese is to downplay acts of anti-Catholicism as much as possible. As long as nobody was hurt and nothing drastic happened—desecrating the altar at St. Mary Magdalen was something drastic—anyway, as long as those two conditions are met the incidents usually don't get reported except to the Cardinal. Sometimes the Cardinal will report them to me, but by that time the scene will have been contaminated—"

"Or obliterated," Gregor said. "You sound as if you think this choir robe thing wouldn't ordinarily have been considered drastic enough to have been reported directly to the police."

"It wouldn't have. Somebody went over to St. Bonaventure's School in Kataband, broke all the windows and spray painted 'John Paul Two sucks dick' on the front doors and the first the police over there heard of it was three days later when the insurance company called. I mean, Mr. Demarkian, I consider myself a good Catholic. I even consider myself a loyal Catholic. I even believe in forbearance and all the rest of it. I still think the Cardinal's attitude to this is nuts."

"What happened at Iggy Loy?" Gregor asked. "Why did Father—Fitzsimmons, was it?—why did Father Fitzsimmons call you in?"

"Because Father Fitzsimmons thinks the Cardinal's attitude to this is nuts." Pete Donovan sighed. "The Cardinal's got clout, though. Father Fitzsimmons didn't let me do anything about it except check it out. It didn't make the news, either. Now that's something I think is a mistake. If the Cardinal wants to stop this stuff, he should make sure all the incidents get on the news. That turns people against the vandals."

It would turn some people against the vandals, Gregor thought. The problem was, it would turn others into vandals. It would be a tough judgment call, but Gregor thought he could see the Cardinal's point. The sort of bigot who resorted to vandalism was the sort who might eventually resort to violence. The sort of bigot who was attracted by vandalism was even more likely to end up bashing in somebody's head. Gregor had seen it a million times in cases he'd handled for the Bureau, especially cases involving outbreaks of anti-Semitism. He didn't know what it was about religion, but it inflamed the passions of a certain kind of malevolent idiot worse than anything else.

"Tell me why you think it's all connected," he said to Pete Donovan. "Tell me what you think is going on."

But Pete Donovan was shaking his head. "It would take forever and I'd sound like I was babbling," he said, "which doesn't mean I won't babble but does mean I won't babble now. The Cardinal sent you down here to look into the death of Brigit Ann Reilly."

"Right," Gregor said.

"Well, Mr. Demarkian, I told him he could. In fact, I was ecstatic when I heard the news. I figured I'd finally found my savior. Would you like to know why?"

Actually, given the tone of Donovan's voice, Gregor wasn't sure he would. He said sure anyway and sat back to wait. Donovan stopped his pacing and retreated to the wall again, closer to the window this time, so he could look out. His blond hair was cut very short and very high on his neck. The style made his head look much too short for his body.

"There was the desecration at St. Mary Magdalen," Donovan said, "and the business with the choir robes and the death of Brigit Ann Reilly—the murder of Brigit Ann Reilly, because it couldn't have been anything else. Now there's these letters that the Cardinal's been receiving and not telling anybody about and maybe Reverend Mother General, too. All of this connected to something or somebody in Maryville, am I right?"

"Yes," Gregor said, "you're right."

"Well," Pete Donovan said, "I know everything and everyone connected to Maryville. Or I think I do, and that's worse. I can't investigate this thing. I'm too involved with the people involved with it."

"You could have called in the state police."

"I'm neither a masochist nor a damn fool." Donovan pushed off from the wall decisively this time and headed for the door. "Come on. Let's go find Reverend Mother General and have a talk about anonymous letters. Then maybe you and I can get together in private and have a talk about Brigit Ann Reilly. Then maybe we can start to get something done."

Pete Donovan was out in the hall before he'd finished talking, trailing words behind him like a smoker's mist. Gregor Demarkian hauled himself up and followed.

Donovan's plan of action wasn't necessarily the best possible plan of action, but it was the only one. Gregor was relieved that someone had finally handed him one.

[3]

Less than three minutes later, walking too quickly across the courtyard with his overcoat still lying on the chair in Reverend Mother General's office, Gregor started to revise his opinion of Donovan's plan of action. He started to revise his opinion of Donovan. He was cold and the convent felt deserted. Donovan kept saying something about the Divine Office and regular hours for community prayer. Gregor's familiarity with the particulars of convent life was minimal—really nonexistent—but the impression he got was that Reverend Mother General and the rest of the nuns were off on nunly business that was going to take a while. Whatever he and Donovan were going to do, it wasn't going to be talking to Reverend Mother General in the immediate future. In the light of all this, Gregor thought Donovan could have let him go back to get his coat. At least.

They were almost all the way across the courtyard to the far door when that door swung open and a small girl came barreling out, wearing the black dress and strange envelopelike black cap Gregor had learned to identify—even after so short a time with the photographs of Brigit Ann Reilly for company—as the uniform of the postulants in the Sisters of Divine Grace. The girl got two or three feet into the courtyard and stopped. Her eyes got wide. Her mouth dropped open. She looked Pete Donovan straight in the face and said,

"It's you. Somebody already called you."

"Somebody called me about what?" Donovan said.

Since Donovan had stopped, Gregor was finally able to catch up with him. He drew up next to the small girl and looked into her plain, sensible, square little face.

"I thought I must have been the first one to find it," she said simply. "I thought if somebody else had found it, they would have left somebody to guard it, but they didn't, so I had to be the first one."

"The first one what?" Donovan asked desperately.

"The first one to find the body," the small girl said.

Then she looked straight up into Gregor Demarkian's eyes, smiled one of the sweetest smiles he had ever seen, and passed out.

Part Two

❖

One

❖

[1]

The body had once belonged to a man named Don Bollander, and the girl who had told them about him was a postulant named Neila Connelly. Gregor Demarkian managed to get those two facts established before Pete Donovan's foot soldiers arrived, carrying the plastic bags and cosmetic brushes that served them instead of a mobile crime unit. In the hurrying urgency of their search after Neila Connelly had been revived—Pete Donovan scooping snow off the top of the trellis and rubbing it in her face—Gregor had been on automatic pilot. He had been so thoroughly involved in doing what he was trained to do, he had forgotten to pay attention to the particulars of his circumstances. It was almost an hour later before it struck him: just how small a town Maryville was. No mobile crime unit, no municipal lab, a force of less than a dozen men: Gregor had worked in places that small before, but usually with the Bureau, and therefore, usually with the Bureau to fall back on. The only case he'd ever handled on his own in a place where he couldn't count on accurate, nearly instantaneous lab work had been last Halloween at a small college in Pennsylvania. He wasn't sure he had enjoyed the experience. In the Bureau, he had been famous for "thinking" instead of "investigating." In a large organization where everybody needed something to distin-

guish them, that hadn't been a bad distinction to have.
The "investigating" types had been all around him, after
all. He had only had to ask to get something done. He
had never been fool enough to think he didn't need the
techies.

When Pete Donovan got Neila Connelly revived,
she sat up, rubbed at the sides of her face and started to
cry. Donovan knew her name the way he knew the
names of most of the postulants, because they volunteered in the literacy program down in St. Andrew's
Parish and the police department did a lot of drug
education down there at the same time. He kept calling
her name, over and over again, first as if that ought to be
enough to wake her up and then as if it ought to be
enough to calm her down. Neila, in the meantime, was
sore. In the movies, people who faint collapse in graceful
heaps. In real life, they either go over like boards or
smash into the floor like rag dolls stuffed with glass.
Neila had been a rag-doll type. Donovan had caught her
before she hit the slate paving of the courtyard, but she
was bruised and hurt and bewildered and scared to
death. Gregor and Pete got her propped up on a bench
and moved away for a consultation.

"Do you know this name she keeps saying?" Gregor
asked. "Don Bollander? Does that make any sense to
you?"

"If you're asking if I know who it is, I know who it
is," Donovan answered. "If you're asking if it makes any
sense, that's something else again."

"What's that supposed to mean?"

"Mr. Donovan?" Neila Connelly said.

Both Gregor and Donovan turned around at once.
In the few seconds since they'd left her, Neila Connelly
had begun to return to life. Her eyes had grown
brighter, although not exactly bright. Her back was
straighter. Even the fabric of her black postulant's dress
seemed to have more spring in it. She was still scared
out of her mind, but she was functioning.

Gregor and Donovan looked at each other, nodded

to each other, and went back to the bench where Neila was still sitting.

"We were just giving you time to get your act together," Donovan said. "This is Gregor Demarkian. He—"

"I know who he is," Neila said. "I saw him on television last night, at the Cardinal's press conference. Reverend Mother General made us watch."

Gregor noted with some amusement that Neila Connelly thought it was perfectly natural that the Cardinal's press conference was something she would have to be "made" to watch. Then he wondered why Reverend Mother General had made them watch it. To assure them that something serious was being done about the death of Brigit Ann Reilly? To frighten those of them who might have information into giving it up? Gregor had been in Reverend Mother General's presence for less than a quarter of an hour, but he had taken his impressions. That was one formidable—and ferociously well organized—old lady.

On the bench, Neila Connelly was squirming and shifting. "I went to the infirmary to get an aspirin," she told them. "I've been feeling terrible all day, hot and tired. Not bad enough to skip work but—bad. So I thought I'd get an aspirin and it would make me feel better."

"Is that where you think you found this—where you think you found Don?" Pete Donovan asked.

Neila Connelly made a sharp impatient gesture in the air, so much like one of Father Tibor's that Gregor was startled. Maybe it was a form of all-purpose ethnic sign language. Maybe Neila had picked it up from her cousins in Ireland or the oldest woman on her street.

"I don't think I found Don Bollander," she was saying, "and I don't think I found a body, either. I know it was Don Bollander because I saw his face, and I know it was a body because I—I touched it."

"In the infirmary?" Pete Donovan insisted.

Neila shook her head. "I didn't do anything in the infirmary, really. Sister Hilga was already gone. I really am feeling bad today. Out of synch. The bell for chapel must have rung and I didn't notice it. When I got to the infirmary it was empty and Sister Hilga was gone and we're not allowed to take medication without permission, not even an aspirin. So I decided to come downstairs."

"To go to chapel," Gregor said, trying to get this strange sequence worked out. "If you were late for chapel than it stands to reason that once you realized it you must have gone to chapel."

"That's right." Staring up at him, Neila's eyes were large and round and green, beautiful eyes in a face that had nothing else beautiful in it. "They make a royal fuss around here when you're late for things, especially prayers, because prayers are supposed to be the point. And I'm never late, so when I saw nobody at the infirmary desk and then I looked out into the hall and there was nobody on the corridor—I suppose I should have noticed that before but I just—"

"You were feeling bad," Pete Donovan said.

"Exactly. Anyway, I started downstairs. Sister Scholastica is always telling us not to cross the courtyard without our capes in this weather, but the courtyard is a shortcut and I was in a hurry. You're not supposed to be in a hurry, either, not ever. And now I'm sitting out here and I'm not even cold. I don't know what's going on."

"Tell me where this infirmary is," Gregor said. He was hoping that in getting Neila to talk about the geography of the Motherhouse, he might also get her to talk about the location of the body. He couldn't understand why Pete Donovan wasn't more anxious to establish that fact. What worried Gregor was what he thought should be obvious to everybody, Neila Connelly included. Neila was not a doctor, a nurse, or a paramedic. In spite of her protestations, if there was a body, that body was not necessarily dead.

Neila had left her bench and advanced into the courtyard. She pointed upward and said, "Those windows there, next to the long thin ones that go to the staircase. That's the infirmary."

"And the staircase is just beside it," Gregor said.

"The doors are side by side, except that the staircase door is a fire door that swings, instead of the kind with a knob in it. There's another one, another fire door, at the bottom. It's right across from that one I came out of. It goes to the front lawn."

"All right," Gregor said, "so you came through that door. Was it open?"

"It's never open. We're not even allowed to prop it open. It's supposed to serve as a firebreak."

"Fine. So. You went through it and down the stairs—"

"And when I was halfway down, when I got to the turn and the landing, I saw the door to the utility room standing open. There's a room on the first floor right at the bottom of those stairs with a big industrial sink in it and mops and pails and things for cleaning. Anyway, that's not left open, either. Sister Alice Marie says if you leave that door open, the kittens get in there and eat the cleaning fluids and kill themselves. And there are always kittens around here. There are like five cats and they're always getting pregnant."

Pete Donovan cleared his throat. "Neila," he said, "if you could just—not that I'm trying to hurry you or anything—"

Neila shot him an exasperated look. "You think I'm lying," she said. "You think I'm like Bernadette and Amanda and whoever else went tromping down to your office this week, getting the vapors and making up stories that didn't have anything to do with anything."

"I don't think—"

Neila turned back to Gregor. "When I saw the utility room door open, I thought I was in luck. I'd thought I'd been wrong about missing the bell. The corridor being empty wasn't so unusual, really. There's a lot of work to do around here. It was Sister Hilga being gone that really made up my mind. So when I saw the door open, I thought Sister Hilga had just gone down to wash something up or to fetch a broom or a mop or

something. And I could have my aspirin and I wouldn't
be in trouble."

"What others who went tromping down to Mr.
Donovan's office?" Gregor asked her.

But Neila ignored him, as Donovan ignored him. "I
got to the bottom of the stairs," Neila said, "and it was
then it hit me that the light in the utility room was off.
Sister Hilga wouldn't be standing around in there in the
dark. Somebody must have gone in and then forgotten to
close up. I was going to leave it and run to chapel the
way I had been, but then I decided I couldn't. I mean,
I really do like kittens. If one of them had died it would
have been my fault and I would have felt guilty for a
week. So I thought it only made sense to close up before
I came out."

"Right," Gregor said. "So you—"

"I went in and turned on the light," Neila told him,
"to make sure one of the kittens wasn't already in there.
I didn't want to trap one."

"Of course not," Donovan said soothingly.

Neila went on as if he hadn't spoken. "The light
switch is right inside the door, and when I got it on I was
looking at the floor. That's where the kittens would be
likely to be. On the floor. They're very small, the six we
have now. So I was staring around at the linoleum for I
don't know how long before I saw it."

"Saw what?" Gregor asked.

"Saw the leg," Neila told him. "It was sticking
straight up out of the sink. It was like a flag. It *is* like a
flag. And then I went to the sink and looked down into
it and there he was, Don Bollander from the bank, with
his leg as stiff as a maypole and his face—his face—"

Neila blanched and looked away, at the snow-
covered stones that paved the courtyard, at the bench
she was sitting on.

"I'm very cold," she said tearfully. "Suddenly I'm
very cold. I want to go inside."

"Of course, you can go inside," Pete Donovan told
her.

"I don't want you," Neila said. "I want somebody I

can trust. I want somebody who isn't making fun of me."

"Christ on a crutch," Pete Donovan said.

Gregor kneeled down against the bench next to where Neila was sitting and took her chin gently in his hand. The fainting episode had been shock, phase one, the immediate response. This was shock, phase two, the delayed one. He knew the signs all too well, the sudden pallor, the opaqueness of the eyes. The girl needed either the traditional sweet brandy or something more to the point, like a large glass of orange juice or a chocolate malt.

"Listen to me," Gregor said. "I'm going to go look now at your utility room—you did say it was just inside that door you came out of?"

"Yes," Neila said. "Yes, it is."

"Fine. What I want you to do is to go and find Reverend Mother General. Go and find her right away. You can take Mr. Donovan with you."

"I don't want Mr. Donovan with me."

"You should have someone. You really aren't feeling well. It's obvious. I don't want you to get lost and faint again."

"I won't faint," Neila Connelly said. "I never faint."

"Mr. Donovan will make sure you don't faint," Gregor said. Then he stood up and turned to Pete Donovan, hovering over him like Thor in a temper.

"You can't just go barging around the convent on your own," Donovan said. "And you don't understand—"

"I understand how to get to this utility room, unless she's left out a book of map information. Go take her to Reverend Mother General."

"But for Christ's sake—"

Gregor didn't even pretend to be listening any more. He turned his back to Donovan and Neila Connelly and went striding toward the door Neila had come out of, a twin of the door they had so recently come out of themselves when they ran into her. It's not so complicated, Gregor thought. It just seems that way when you're inside and being led around from one corridor to another. It's basically just a square. If there really was a body—a corpse and not a sick man; a corpse and not a fantasy—he would have to get Reverend Mother General to give him a floor plan.

He plunged through the outer door into inner darkness, paused to catch his breath, caught the light and stopped breathing. The light was coming through an open door in the opposite wall, streaming into the corridor in a sharp-edged shaft. That didn't surprise him. The door was where Neila had said the utility room door would be. The light could have been the one she said she'd turned on. She hadn't said anything about turning it off.

The surprising thing was the person, standing at the edge of the door with her arms folded across her chest and a look of incredulity on her face.

Sister Mary Scholastica.

[2]

"His name was Don Bollander and he was Miriam Bailey's assistant at the bank," Sister Scholastica said later, when Gregor had her sitting down on the floor outside the utility room. It was less than five minutes since he had found her, but it felt as if it had been forever. He had made her sit down just in case. She had been in mild shock when he first saw her. He didn't want to take any chances. Still, she was no Neila Connelly. She was older, better trained, and more experienced. She had seen a man die in front of her eyes last year in Colchester, New York. Even without all that she would have held up better. She simply had more backbone than Neila Connelly ever would.

Gregor was leaning over the sink, trying to find out everything he could without touching anything. The sink was not really a sink at all but a laundry tub, which explained how a body had gotten into it. Listening to Neila Connelly out in the courtyard, Gregor had imagined a stuffing and folding operation it would have taken a trash compactor to complete. He didn't have to worry that their blithering conversation in the cold had cost this man his life, either. Gregor had thought at the time that Neila's description sounded like rigor mortis. It would take a doctor and a good forsenic laboratory to be sure, but Gregor's guess was that Don Bollander had been dead for at least half a day.

"I don't suppose there's any chance it isn't murder," Scholastica said. "Not with him stuffed into the laundry sink that way."

"It's hard to tell much of anything with him this way," Gregor said. "Would there have been any reason for him to have been in this room?"

"Good heavens no. I don't know if you realize it or not, but you're in a restricted area of the Motherhouse. There aren't supposed to be any seculars in this part."

"Is that religious?" Gregor asked. "Have I just done something on the order of desecrating an altar—"

"No, no. Of course not. It would have been a more serious transgression before Vatican Two, but sometimes I think everything was a more serious transgression before Vatican Two. No, my point is, he wouldn't have been anywhere near here unless he'd had a good reason, and I can't think of a reason he might have had."

"He could have been meeting somebody."

"He would have met her in one of the reception rooms. If you mean he could have been having a clandestine meeting, it would have been safer to hold it off Motherhouse grounds. He had the perfect setup. I did tell you he was Don Bollander from the bank."

"You did. You just didn't tell me what that meant."

Gregor was leaning far over the laundry sink now, the only position from which he could stare Don Bollander straight in the face. He had told Scholastica that it was hard to tell anything about this death under these circumstances, but that wasn't quite true. Coniine killed by paralyzing the lungs. There was a blue tinge to the face, faint but unmistakable. Of course, it might have been one of a number of other vegetable alkaloids. Their effects were often quite similar. Because there was already one person dead from coniine, though, Gregor thought he was justified in guessing death by coniine here. In his experience, amateur murderers picked a method they found comfortable and stuck to it.

He backed away from the body and looked around the room. There was a shelf about the sink filled with laundry detergents and white plastic bottles of cleaning materials. There were more white plastic bottles on the floor, lined up against the window. Gregor didn't think Don Bollander could have been brought in through the window. He'd examined every inch of visible skin and he hadn't come up with a single bruise. It was possible that all the bruising had occurred under Bollander's clothes, but it wasn't likely. It was also possible that Bollander had been alive and ambulatory when he arrived at the utility room, but that wasn't likely, either. Alive wasn't impossible. Coniine was a tricky poison. Symptoms almost always started within half an hour. Death was more erratic. Depending on a number of factors—how much coniine the victim had eaten; how much other food the victim had eaten immediately before that; state of health; state of mind; height, weight, and age—death could arrive anywhere from half an hour to five hours later. What made coniine particularly nasty was that death was inevitable a long time before that. Coniine was one of those poisons whose antidote had to be delivered next to immediately after the poison was ingested. It was the kind of poison that grew roots.

He backed away from it all and stuck his head into the hall. "You were telling me about Don Bollander," he said to Scholastica. "You should keep talking. Do you have a notebook?"

Scholastica shoved her hands into one of her pockets and came up with a palm-size notebook and a ballpoint pen. "It's part of the uniform. Do you want me to write something down?"

"A reminder to the medical examiner. I want to know the location and the temporal origin of any bruises found anywhere on the body, no matter how small."

"Temporal origin?"

"Whether they were made before or after death."

"Oh."

"Tell me about Don Bollander."

"Well," Scholastica said. "Well. You know who Miriam Bailey is. We talked about that before. Do you know about Ann-Harriet Severan?"

"No."

"Ann-Harriet works at the bank. As some kind of minor officer. She's very pretty and very volatile, one of those people who go off their nuts at the first sign of trouble, which is interesting because she's always in trouble, because Ann-Harriet is having an affair with Josh—you remember Josh?"

"I remember."

"Miriam must know," Scholastica said. "The two of them are very clumsy about it all. Anyway, that's the kind of assistant Don Bollander was. He dealt with whatever had to be dealt with, and if that meant keeping Ann-Harriet in line, then he did it. And that wouldn't have been easy, either, because Ann-Harriet is a consummate—well, it's tacky to use a word like this in habit, but there really is only one word and that's—"

"Bitch."

"Exactly. The postulants don't like Miriam Bailey much, but they really detest Ann-Harriet Severan. She's always saying things, making fun of them, if you know what I mean. But anyway, Don. Don got a little promotion just about the time Miriam decided to come back to town as a rich old lady with a very young husband."

"So what did Don Bollander have to do with that?"

Scholastica smiled. "I said he was her assistant. What he really was was her flack catcher. He was totally useless as a banker. In all the time since I've been connected to Maryville, since I've entered the convent, I don't think I've ever heard of him doing any banking work at all."

"What did he do?"

"He ran interference. He took care of things that would waste her time. Miriam has a very definite idea of what is and what isn't a waste of her time. She thinks she has to do community work, as she puts it. Otherwise the bank doesn't look good. She funds the literacy program at St. Andrew's and she makes an appearance there every year. Don does—did the grub work. He looked after the paper. He sent the checks she signed. He ordered books when the program needed books and refreshments when the program was going to have a party. Then Margaret Finney was beatified, and Miriam wanted to start a lay committee for—I don't remember what she called it. She wanted to support the canonization effort. It's impossible to explain to people like Miriam that things just aren't the way they used to be. Canonization isn't that kind of adversarial process it was before Vatican II—"

"Back up," Gregor said. He had been listening for sounds in the courtyard or the hall. It seemed to him to be a monstrous amount of time since he had left Pete Donovan and Neila Connelly at the bench, instructing them to get Reverend Mother General and bring her back to him. It shouldn't be taking this long to find the Motherhouse's most important and visible nun. He ran his hands through his hair in irritation.

"I wish I knew what was keeping them," he said. "This is insane. We ought to have forensic people up here."

Sister Scholastica shrugged. "The bell had rung for chapel. It's just midmorning prayer—what I suppose used to be called Terce, since they suppressed Prime—anyway, it's a minor hour, but it's still an hour. If Pete and Neila caught them at just the wrong moment, they might not have been able to get Reverend Mother General's attention."

"They should have stood up in the middle of the room and shouted and howled until they did."

"You were going to ask me something else?" Scholastica said.

Gregor turned his mind back to the problem at hand. "You said something about the literacy program at St. Andrew's. Don Bollander did the grub work for the literacy program at St. Andrew's."

"That's right."

"Didn't I read in the Cardinal's report somewhere that Brigit Ann Reilly worked in the literacy program at St. Andrew's?"

Scholastica nodded. "Yes, she did. We make a point of requiring our postulants and novices to do all three kinds of work: intellectual, charitable, and practical. Brigit's practical work was going back and forth to the library every day, among other things. Her charitable work was to teach reading to adults at St. Andrew's."

"Does that mean Don Bollander and Brigit Ann Reilly knew each other?" Gregor asked.

Scholastica considered this. "In a way," she said, "I suppose it does. He would have known her by sight, certainly, even if he didn't know her by name. He spent a fair amount of time on site. I don't think he would have known her well. In fact, I'm sure he didn't."

"Why?"

Scholastica snorted. "Don Bollander was the kind of person who dramatized himself," she said. "He was the kind of person who liked to be near excitement. If he'd known Brigit Ann Reilly well, he'd have told everyone in town about it after she died, just to have an association with the thrill of it. Instead, he was wandering around town telling everybody how he was engaged in a hush-hush project that would ensure the canonization of Margaret Finney and turn Maryville into the new and improved Lourdes."

"New and improved Lourdes," Gregor murmured, and then he straightened up. Now there was noise coming at him, much more noise than he'd thought it possible for nuns to make. First the noise was in the courtyard, a low hum like too many bees near a flower and the stomp of feet on stone. Then the courtyard door opened and Reverend Mother General came in. Behind her, Gregor could see nothing but a sea of black and white head coverings and Pete Donovan's blond thatch. Beside him, Scholastica stood up.

"Reverend Mother," Scholastica said.

"Is there a man dead in here?" Reverend Mother demanded. "In the laundry sink?"

There was more commotion at Reverend Mother's back. Pete Donovan was pushing himself forward, excusing himself to nuns at every turn. He got to the doorway and gave Reverend Mother General a gentle and apologetic nudge to make enough room to get himself inside

"If there's a body in here, I want to see the body in here," he said, and then he pushed Gregor out of the utility room doorway and walked inside. Going in, he was caught in the same cheerful and skeptical mood he had been in talking to Neila outside. No sooner had he got all the way inside than that changed.

"Jesus screaming Christ," he said, in a voice loud enough to carry to every nun in the vicinity—and making them all wince. "She was telling the truth," he bellowed. "There really is a dead man in here."

Gregor already knew there was a dead man in there. That wasn't what he wanted to think about for the moment.

What he wanted to think about was how strangely similar Scholastica's descriptions of the characters of Don Bollander and Brigit Ann Reilly had been.

Two

❖

[1]

Unlike Pete Donovan, Miriam Bailey had never been able to say she knew most of the people in town, by sight or any other way. Her father had been much too strict about the distinctions of class to allow her a latitude like that. To be precise, he had been much too strict about the distinctions of class *for women*. Men were supposed to be able to hold their own in rough company. Miriam's father had divided the world in a great many ways, always marking those divisions by gender. Later, when Miriam went to college and discovered that no one shared his rules and regulations for proper conduct in women and men, she had wondered if he had invented them just for her. Rules for a wayward daughter, she had told herself at the time, and then almost immediately dismissed the thought. There was nothing wayward at all about her at the age of eighteen, at least on the surface—and her father was no mind reader. If he suspected her of subversion, he was experiencing a form of clinical paranoia. Miriam at eighteen was plain and awkward and shy and badly dressed, in spite of a clothes allowance the size of one of her father's bank clerks' salaries. Miriam at eighteen was also polite, courteous, modest, retiring, and deferential to men.

Miriam at sixty-odd was in something of a bind. She might not know everyone in town, but the people she

did know were far too numerous. It was just a little after
noon. Over the last hour, sitting alone in the house on
Huntington Avenue, she had taken at least eleven phone
calls on the subject of Don Bollander—or maybe she
should think of it as "Don Bollander's demise." Whatever it was, she had heard much more of it than she
wanted to. Sheila McRae over at Bell Epoque—Bell
Epoque was a house; the cuteness of its name was
apparently what passed for wit in Sheila's Smith College
graduating class—had wanted to know what Miriam was
going to do about it, with Don lying all bloody in the
convent well. Deborah Martin had been more sensible.
She'd at least known that Don wasn't found bloody or in
the convent well. Her speciality had been sympathy,
sticky and sweet. After a while, Miriam had thought she
could see Deborah's voice, sliding down the wire like
molasses down a string. The phone rang and rang, rang
and rang. Every time Miriam picked it up, she thought
it would be the police, but it never was.

"I'm sure they wouldn't call me if they needed
information about a funeral," she had said to Katherine
Hale, who had set out to be the sensible one. Of course,
there was nothing very sensible about nattering away on
the subject of Don's funeral when he'd just been found
murdered somewhere in town. If that really was what
happened, it might be weeks before the police were
ready to release his body to anyone at all. That was just
like Katherine Hale. Katherine had been with Miriam at
Manhattanville—and if it hadn't been well before the age
of competitive admissions, she wouldn't have been at
Manhattanville at all. Katherine Hale couldn't think her
way out of a paper bag.

It had been just after Katherine called that Miriam
had made her decision. She had no doubt that Don was
dead—too many people had agreed on that point to
make it anything else but true—but she didn't want to
think about it for the moment. She didn't want to be
questioned by the police about it, either. There would
come a time when she could avoid neither of these
things. That time would arrive very soon, accompanied

by unspoken demands on her to produce the appropriate emotion. Miriam hadn't the faintest idea what that emotion could be. For the moment, she simply wanted to disappear.

If she'd had a normal marriage, or even a normal May–December arrangement, she would have relied on Josh to get her away from it all. He could have put her into that car she'd bought him and taken her for a ride. Because she didn't have a normal anything, Josh was not around. He had gotten into that car very early this morning and taken off on his own. Since he couldn't be with Ann-Harriet Severan—Miriam had taken care of that for the weekend by giving Ann-Harriet a great deal of last-minute, must-rush extra work—Miriam hadn't any idea at all where he had gone.

If you want to find a banker on the weekend, the last place you look for him is at the bank. Miriam's father had taught her that. That was why, as the sound of church bells died away in the air over her head, she was standing at the bank's back door, fishing keys out of her purse. It was very cold and very bright, the kind of day that looks warm when you're standing inside. Outside, the wind was high and stiff and rigid and threatening to get worse. Miriam got the key turned and the door open and pressed herself inside.

The back hall was where the rest rooms were, and the storage closets, and the stairs to the basement. Miriam passed through it, listening to the sound of her heels on the hardwood floor and feeling a little foolish. Back at home, she had tried to convince herself that getting dressed to go into the bank on a day it wasn't open was silly. Anyone else who had come in to do some extra work would be lounging around the office floor in jeans. She hadn't been able to convince herself. She'd never come in to the bank on a weekend before. If she had extra work to do, she took it home. Before coming out, she had struggled into yet another Chanel suit and another layer of makeup—and then she had wasted time resenting it all.

She made absolutely sure the back hall was empty—

she even checked the ladies' room, although not the men's; she didn't have the courage to check the men's—and then started up the stairs to the office floor. From up there, the sound of a soft voice talking drifted down at her. It was only one voice, so Miriam assumed it was talking into a phone. She reached the landing, paused to listen, then went up the rest of the flight. She reached the second floor and paused to listen again. The voice was low and humming-bird sweet, but strong. It was the voice of a girl of twenty-two.

The floor of the upstairs office hall was made of checkerboard marble. There was no way Miriam could walk down it without being heard. She didn't bother to try. From where she was standing, she could see the door to Ann-Harriet's office, pulled back and propped open. Every once in a while, she could see Ann-Harriet's arm, drifting gracefully through the area the open door revealed.

"But this is terrible," Ann-Harriet was saying. "How could something like this happen?"

There was a seductive note in that voice, but it wasn't the right seductive note. Whomever Ann-Harriet was talking to, it wasn't Josh. Miriam began to walk down the hall toward the open office, going slowly, thinking herself into an Alfred Hitchcock frame of mind.

"Just a minute," Ann-Harriet said, "someone just came in."

There was the sound of a chair being pushed back and then of heels on carpet. Ann-Harriet's head appeared in the open doorway. She caught sight of Miriam, nodded, and disappeared again.

"It's the boss," Miriam heard her disembodied voice say a moment later. "I don't know if she's heard about this or not. I'll call you back later."

The phone clicked in the receiver, too sharply, too loudly. The wheels on Ann-Harriet's desk chair creaked. Miriam walked the rest of the way to Ann-Harriet's office door and stood in the door frame, checking out a scene she checked out at least once every weekday. Ann-Harriet was the kind of person who cluttered up her desk with personal things: pictures of brothers and sisters and nephews and nieces; the scroll she'd received for being half of the "cutest couple" in high school; her life horoscope engraved in brass. Miriam stared at the life horoscope and frowned—this was a Catholic town, for God's sake—and then wrenched away from it, to look Ann-Harriet in the face instead. Miriam always looked Ann-Harriet in the face. It was one of her operational absolutes. It also raised the tension level of their every encounter by six or seven points on the Richter scale.

Ann-Harriet had stood up when Miriam first walked in. Now she stepped back a little and tried out a smile that didn't quite make it.

"Miss Bailey," she said, "I didn't expect you in."

"You shouldn't have expected me in," Miriam told her. "I never come in on weekends." She nodded toward the phone. "Someone was telling you about Don Bollander being dead."

"Oh," Ann-Harriet said. "Yes. That was Bob Corliss, Miss Bailey, who works at the Chase branch out in Wender. You know."

"No," Miriam said. "I don't know."

"Oh. Well. He was telling me about Don Bollander, or as much as he's heard. He was telling me Don Bollander had been murdered."

"Maybe he has been."

"Oh," Ann-Harriet said again. Her desk was covered with computer sheets, some of them flat and some of them crumpled and still others folded neatly in half. She pushed her hands into them to no purpose and cleared her throat. "I was right in the middle of doing all this stuff," she said, "when the call came, and then I forgot all about it."

"Because Don Bollander had died," Miriam said.

"Because he'd been murdered," Ann-Harriet said. "And that girl was murdered, too."

"So what did you think?" Miriam said. "That you were the most likely candidate for the next one?"

Ann-Harriet flushed. "I didn't think anything, Miss

Bailey. I was just shocked. Do you want to go over these papers? Is that why you came in?"

"It might be."

Miriam was still standing in the doorway. Ann-Harriet looked at her there and seemed to make up her mind about something. Miriam could just guess what. Ann-Harriet shuffled her papers more decisively and sat down in her chair.

"I've been over these several times today," she said, "and I've back-checked them with every confirming report. In my estimation, you were right to be concerned—"

"I'm *always* right to be concerned."

Ann-Harriet flushed. "There's leakage," she said decisively. "Not very much leakage at any one time, but going back at least a year, and it adds up. To the best of my knowledge, after just a few days' investigation, what it's added up to so far is about a hundred thousand dollars. Is that what you wanted to know? Is that what you were looking for?"

"Maybe."

"You need someone better than I am to tell you who's doing it. I don't have the expertise to trace something like this."

"I haven't asked you to."

"What have you asked me to do?" Ann-Harriet demanded, beginning to sound a little wild. "I've been here all afternoon. I was here all night last night and all night the night before that. If I'm not looking for the right thing, you ought to tell me I'm not looking for the right thing."

Outside Ann-Harriet's single office window, the sky was beginning to cloud up again. It reminded Miriam of her last conversation with Josh, and started a whole stream of questions tumbling through her mind—but they were questions about the web of sex, and useless to ask. Besides, she didn't really want to ask them. She just wanted to go on making Ann-Harriet uncomfortable. She had already made Ann-Harriet afraid.

Miriam left the door frame and sat down in Ann-

Harriet's single visitor's chair. She wondered how Ann-Harriet felt about her office. There were secretaries on the first floor with better offices than this.

Miriam bent over Ann-Harriet's papers and said, "I'm going to stay here for a while. I want you to take me through it, step by step, all the paper trail you've managed to find. I want to see what it looks like."

"Now?"

"Of course now."

"It's Saturday afternoon."

"I've worked most of the Saturday afternoons of my life."

That wasn't quite true—but Miriam thought it was more than justified. She hadn't spent any of the Saturday afternoons of her life in bed with somebody else's husband, and that ought to count for something.

[2]

It was one o'clock when Josh Malley showed up at Sam Harrigan's front door, and by then Sam was in a very peculiar mood. On the one hand, he was happy—and happy to a degree he found embarrassing, considering the smallness of the incident that had made him so. At twelve forty-five he had received a phone call from Glinda Daniels. She was calling from the library—if she'd been calling from her little house, he'd have walked down the hill to her as soon as they'd hung up—and the news she had was not good. To Sam, the news didn't much matter. It had been less than twenty-four hours since he had taken Glinda home after buying her dinner. He had spent that short period of time worrying about it. Had she liked him? Had she not liked him? He really was behaving like a fourteen-year-old—and yet, he wasn't. Not exactly. There was something strange about the way Glinda Daniels responded to him. She was too hesitant and too afraid—and God only knew there wasn't a single bloody thing about Sam Harrigan for a woman to be afraid of. One of those movie stars who

periodically flitted through his life, more passionate
about ecology than she was about him, had told him
contemptuously that he was the least sexually aggressive
man she had ever met. What she meant was that he took
no for no whether she wanted him to or not. Sam
Harrigan had made his rule about that long before the
present feminist movement came to flower. He didn't
know enough about women to know if they always
meant no when they said no, but he did know enough
about *people* to understand that any woman who said no
when she meant yes needed to have her head examined.
The movie star had definitely needed to have her head
examined. Aside from her attraction to rape games,
bondage movies, and a host of frighteningly bizarre
sexual devices, she thought the trees were giving her
advice on the best way to murder Dan Quayle.

With Glinda Daniels, though, there should have
been no ambiguity of any kind. One of the other rules
Sam Harrigan had made for himself long ago was never
to try to take a woman to bed on a first date. He'd tried
it a few times and even succeeded a few times, but he
hadn't liked it much. His impression was that the
women hadn't liked it much either. It seemed that in this
late decade of the twentieth century, sex had become
obligatory. Women went through with it for the same
reason they put on makeup in the morning—because it
was expected of them, whether they liked the idea or
not. Sam Harrigan wanted more than that out of his sex
life. He wanted more than that out of himself.

He had taken Glinda out for a steak and bought her
a big piece of triple-chocolate cake and two glasses of
champagne for dessert. He had tried to bring the
conversation around to something personal and had
failed utterly. The whole time they were together, Sam
had had the impression that Glinda was more than a
little annoyed with him, he didn't have any idea why. By
the time he brought her home, he thought he was in for
one of the more spectacular failures of his career. Glinda
wasn't simply not attracted to him. She loathed him. She

wished he wouldn't impose on her time any more. She wished—

Getting up this morning, Sam had changed his mind about all of it—he just wasn't sure to what. He had asked and she had accepted. If she hadn't wanted to accept, she had only had to say no. He hadn't been pushy or crude. He at least ought to give the whole thing another shot, especially because, after several hours in her exclusive company, he was finding her more attractive than ever. It was the "extra" twenty pounds that made all the difference, physically. Sam didn't find them "extra" at all. He found them crucial.

He was on phase three of this mental mess—wondering if Glinda was secretly and perhaps hopelessly, but of course irretrievably, in love with someone else—when the call came. He was also sitting out on his screen porch potting nettles. Potting nettles when your mind is occupied elsewhere is a very bad idea. You forget not to touch the leaves with your bare hands and your fingers begin to sting. When the ringer on the phone went off, his fingers had probably been stinging for some time. He hadn't noticed. He did notice as soon as he had the receiver in his hand, because it stung.

"It was Scholastica who told me about it," Glinda said, after she'd given him the news of Don Bollander's death. Sam didn't think he knew Don Bollander. Once the name was mentioned, he tried and tried to put a face to it, but he couldn't do it. "Scholastica was there," Glinda went on, "so I suppose I have a good chance of having heard the straight story. Within ten minutes after I finished talking to her, four people came into the library with other stories—"

"Oh, no."

"Oh, yes. I don't know what I look like. One of those cork sounding boards or something. Everybody who wants somebody to tell something to tells it to me. And that was what I was thinking about, Sam. People telling me things, I mean. Don Bollander telling me things."

Sam Harrigan considered this information. One of the things he and Glinda had done the night before was to use up a large quantity of cocktail napkins trying to solve their little local murder. They had taken as their starting point the various "sightings" of Brigit Ann Reilly as they had been reported to Glinda over the week since the death. In Sam's mind, this had been his best conversational gambit. It had released Glinda from a tension that had nothing to do with him, but wasn't doing his cause any good. It had also been interesting.

"Don Bollander," he said. "Is that the one who saw her in the bank?"

"That's right. He was Miriam Bailey's assistant at the bank. And he came in on Friday and told me he'd seen her. At eleven thirty."

"Isn't he one of the ones we decided was impossible? I seem to remember our working out a timetable—"

"I know," Glinda said. Then she sighed a little. "Scholastica's half-hysterical, you can just imagine. And she said Pete Donovan's even worse. He was with Gregor Demarkian when Neila showed up talking about a body, and he just didn't believe her. Apparently, he's had his office full of hysterical postulants for days now, and laypeople too, all seeing ghosts and goblins and God only knows what else. He hadn't told Demarkian about it so Demarkian was furious. Scholastica said it was very tense. I keep thinking of what he looked like on television and wondering what he's like when he's furious."

"Gregor Demarkian, you mean."

"Mmm. Sam? We're not really detectives, you know. We could have had it wrong. About Don's information being bogus."

"I suppose we could have, yes. Do you think he was killed for that, because he's seen her in the bank?"

"I don't know. I just know I haven't been feeling very well since that call. And the library is packed."

"Do you have any help?"

"Oh, I have a lot of help. I even have The Library Lady. That's how I've been able to lock myself in here and talk to you."

Sam had more than nettles to pot. He had thistles, too, and wild heather. There were plants and pots of dirt everywhere, and Miracle-Gro and seeds everywhere else. He was sitting in a rocking chair he couldn't rock, because any movement he made tipped something over. He took the pot of nettles he had left in his lap when the phone rang and put it on the floor. He tried to think clearly through the growing excitement of his realization that she had decided to call him first. There were a hundred possible reasons for that that had nothing to do with his sincere hope that she was in the midst of falling in love with him back, but he had no bloody damn intention of considering any of them. Illusions could be a lot of fun.

"Listen," he said to her, "you haven't met this Demarkian yet, have you? He hasn't come to talk to you?"

"Of course not. He just got here—I forget when. Scholastica said, but it slipped my mind. Not very soon before they discovered the body, though."

"When did they discover the body?"

"Around eleven o'clock, I think."

"All right," Sam said. "Right now, for the next couple of hours at least, he's going to be busy over at the convent and Pete Donovan's going to be busy with him. You always take care of the immediate crisis first. So, they'll be there, then—then it depends. He'll probably check in to wherever he's staying—"

"I know where he's staying," Glinda said. "It's the St. Mary's Inn. Edith Jasper told me about it herself. The arrangements were made by the Chancery at absolutely the last minute, but Edith is Edith. She wasn't going to say no to the Cardinal and she wasn't going to give up a chance to make herself sound important, either. This is the biggest thing that's happened to this town since—since I don't know what."

"The beatification of Margaret Finney?"

"Maybe the '53 flood."

"I was just feeling sorry for the Sisters of Divine Grace and for Margaret Finney," Sam said. "Here it is, one of the biggest events in the history of their order, and it's being buried under a lot of melodrama and blood and guts."

"Just a minute," Glinda said.

She must have taken the phone away from her ear, because the next time Sam heard her voice it sounded faint and very far away. "Those go in the science section," she was telling someone he couldn't hear. "They're not fiction, no matter what they look like. Put them there." There was a pause and then, "Yes, I understand that, but I'm busy right now—yes, I'll be out as soon as I'm done—yes, I do understand, I just don't think this is the kind of crisis you seem to. I'll be out in a little while.

"They're going to drive me insane," she said, back into the phone. "I don't know what it is with people these days. They can't do anything you don't tell them to do right down to the last detail. I'm sorry. You've been so patient listening to me and now as soon as you start talking, I'm going to have to get off the phone."

"I forgive you," Sam said magnanimously, "just don't go quite yet. Hear me out. All right?"

"All right."

"Fine. Now, Demarkian will go back to his room and Donovan will go back to his office. You've already talked to Donovan, so I presume you'd prefer to talk to Demarkian from here on out—"

"I don't understand what you mean."

"Well," Sam said, "you never told Donovan what Don Bollander said to you, did you?"

"Of course I didn't," Glinda said. "Why should I? I told you last night how many people came in saying the same sort of thing—"

"Almost as many as came into Donovan's office seeing ghosts," Sam finished for her. "But Don Bollander's dead now. What he said might be important."

"Do you think so?" Glinda sounded doubtful.

"No," Sam told her. "But I do think Demarkian and Donovan will both think it's got to be important, and that's why you've got to tell them. On your own initiative. Right away. Then, if it is important, you don't have to worry about someone murdering you to keep your mouth shut."

"Don't be silly," Glinda said. "Don wasn't the kind of person to keep his mouth shut. He must have told half the town."

"Even so."

"Are you sure?"

"I'm sure," Sam said. "I'm so sure, I'm going to come down and pick you up and take you over there, just so I'm satisfied you're safe. And that you go along and do what I tell you to do. All right?"

"All right," Glinda said. "I get off at three."

"I'll be there at quarter to."

There was a pause on the line that went on so long, Sam almost thought she'd hung up without saying good-bye. Then she cleared her throat and said, "Sam? I had a very good time at dinner last night. I enjoyed myself very much."

This time, she did hang up without saying good-bye. The phone went to dial tone hardly a breath after the last of her words, leaving Sam Harrigan stunned.

He was still stunned fifteen minutes later, when he heard all-too-human rustling in the brush beyond his screens and stood up to see who it was. He was so befuddled he forgot he'd put another pot on his lap just after he'd hung up. The pot crashed to the floor of the porch as soon as he got out of his chair, breaking into six pieces and scattering dirt everywhere.

"Who is it?" he demanded, listening to the shaking and screeching of frozen shrubbery. "This is posted property you're on."

The shrubbery shook and screeched a little longer, and then a man emerged from it, looking cold and petulant and sour. He was one of the few men anywhere that Sam Harrigan had ever disliked on sight. Sam had had several sights of him before this one, and what he had picked up from those told him his dislike was justified. The man was a gigolo—but that could be excused, Sam thought, under the proper conditions. The problem was, this man wasn't even an honest gigolo.

Sam had seen him with his own eyes, putting it to a young lady with nothing in common with his aging wife in the backseat of an expensive car he couldn't have bought with his own money.

"What do you want?" Sam asked him. "Why didn't you come to the front door and ring?"

The man had fought himself free of clinging branches at last. He was standing right in front of Sam's screen, with his arms at his sides and the wind in his hair. Sam, protected by a roof and half-walls on all sides, was wearing a hat with earflaps and keeping his toes next to an electric space heater. It was some kind of lethal vanity that was willing to risk a frostbitten head to preserve itself from wearing something so unfashionable as a hat.

"I did come to the front door and ring," Josh Malley said. "You didn't answer."

"I'm not going to answer now," Sam told him. "Go away."

Josh Malley looked up at the sky above his head and sighed. "I can't go away, Mr. Harrigan," he said. "I have something I have to talk to you about. Something that has to do with snakes."

"I'm a herpetologist," Sam said. "I don't have to talk to anybody about snakes."

"You have to talk to somebody about these snakes," Josh said.

Then he moved very close to the screen, as close as he could get considering the fact that it was elevated, and smiled.

It was the coldest smile Sam Harrigan had ever seen on a human face, and it made him want to run. He'd met cannibals with better arrangements of facial muscles.

Three

❖

[1]

When Gregor Demarkian had still been with the Federal Bureau of Investigation, he had never been called in to a crime scene that was still a scene. No matter how vitally involved the Bureau was supposed to be in any subsequent investigation, they left the bottom-line work of discovery and classification to the locals. Since Gregor had retired, he had been at a number of crime scenes, but he hadn't made up his mind about them. He was always happy for the chance to see a body before anybody else touched it. Once the photographers and the forensics team and the lab men came, it was touch and go. Of course, Pete Donovan and Maryville hardly had that sort of sophisticated assault at their disposal. What showed up in response to Pete Donovan's radioed message for help with a homicide, was a small pack of young-looking, scared-looking, suspicious-looking boys who looked too small for their uniforms. Gregor got a strong impression that they hadn't counted on things like this when they'd signed up for the force. He wondered what they had counted on. Since he'd been in Maryville, he'd heard about slums and dope and he didn't know what else. Surely that meant that there had to be violence in these people's lives every once in a while. Maybe Pete Donovan only hired the naive, and then the naive quit on him as soon as they saw a little action.

It was now half past one in the afternoon, and the naive young men were finished with what Pete Donovan had asked them to do. They had taken the body out of the laundry sink and bagged it. There was only one ambulance in Maryville, and it was delivering a burst appendix to the county hospital. There was a funeral van, but it was picking up a paying customer in the Adirondack Mountains and the roads were bad. Since there was nothing anyone would ever be able to do for Don Bollander ever again, there was no hurry about getting him moved to the county morgue. Gregor had watched the young men lift the body out of the sink and try to lay it down on the floor. The body was curled, stiff and unyielding. Every time they tried to move one of its limbs, it resisted. Gregor wanted to tell them they had no choice. They were going to have to break something. He didn't say it. He could just imagine what kind of reaction it would have gotten. Instead, he stepped back a few paces until he was even with Pete Donovan and said,

"Look, the body was here before rigor set in."

Pete Donovan cleared his throat. He had been clearing his throat a great deal since he had walked in to find an actual body. He had been explaining a great deal, too. Gregor understood the explanation—although he still couldn't forgive Donovan his behavior—and was even interested in it. There were a million small things like that in this case, bits and pieces, confetti evidence. Logically, most or all of these things were going to turn out to be nothing. From experience, Gregor knew that one or two of them might turn out to be important. Which one or two couldn't be established in advance, or even by decree. The confetti had to be sifted through and examined. Gregor fully intended to examine it, but he didn't want to do that now. He also didn't want to listen to any more of Donovan's embarrassed blithering.

"Look," he said again, to forestall what he was sure was looming apology number sixty-seven, "it's not just that the body was moved before rigor, it's that it was moved before death. Of course, we need the forensic report to be sure—"

"Don't we always?"

"—but all the signs are there. Or all the signs are not there. There's nothing on his clothes."

Pete Donovan shot Gregor a skeptical look, no apology in it at all. "You don't know what's on his clothes," he said. "Most of the stuff labs find is microscopic."

"I know," Gregor told him, "but look at his suit."

"What about his suit?"

"It's wool."

"So?"

"You ever see wool with a major water stain that hasn't been treated? It puckers and it darkens. I just took a long look at that suit while your boys were getting the body to the floor. There isn't a water stain on it."

Pete Donovan frowned, working his way through it. "That doesn't make sense, does it?" he asked. "That's a sink he was in. He should at least have been wet from the sink."

"I thought of that," Gregor said. "I asked Sister Scholastica. She says the sink gets wiped down after every use, the faucet has never been known to leak, and this particular sink probably hasn't been used for a week or two. There hasn't been anyone sick or in the infirmary in that time, and this utility room isn't convenient to much of anything else. It's perfectly possible that that sink was bone dry when the body was put into it. And when I looked in for the first time, the faucet was turned away, over by the backboard instead of over the well. It wasn't available to drip on the body even if it did drip. I don't think Neila Connelly moved it."

"You think we should ask Neila Connelly if she moved it," Pete Donovan said. "I still don't see your point. How does a lack of water stains on the suit translate into Bollander being alive when he got to the utility room?"

"Not necessarily the utility room," Gregor said,

"just the convent. And not just alive, either. Walking under his own power."

"What?"

"Look at this."

Gregor grabbed Donovan by the wrist and led him across the hall to the doorway that led outside, directly across from the one that led into the courtyard. It opened onto a narrow path bordered on each side by tall evergreen bushes. Beneath the evergreen bushes were evergreen ferns. Above them were the bare, spreading branches of trees reaching out from farther back on the lawn. Everything was crusted with snow, three or four inches thick.

"I dare you," Gregor said, "to carry anything down that path without getting snow on it—a lot of snow on it. Those branches stick right out over the path. Anybody who tried to carry Don Bollander up this path dead or unconscious would have ended up with Don Bollander coated in white. Look at that out there. Nobody has so much as walked that way, single and alone and alive, since the last good fall."

Donovan shook his head. "Maybe they brought him in by another door," he said. Maybe they brought him in by the front door. I don't see how you can tell."

"What about the other doors?" Gregor asked him. "Are they close to here?"

"I don't know."

"Are they kept open? Do the nuns lock up at night?"

"I don't know that either."

"I know something," Gregor said. "To bring a dead body into this building and walk it through the halls to get to this particular utility room would have been crazy."

"The nuns do go to bed early," Donovan pointed out.

"The nuns are human beings like anybody else," Gregor told him. "They get restless. They have insomnia. You couldn't count on them staying in their beds. You couldn't count on them all being heavy sleepers.

You couldn't count on not being heard. It would be much too risky, and what would you be taking the risk for?"

"Murderers," Donovan started.

Gregor waved it away. "Murderers are always consistent," he insisted, "internally consistent. They aren't always rational—they're almost never that—but they are always logical. There is only one logical reason why Don Bollander's body should have ended up in that sink, and that was that was the most convenient place to put it. There is only one logical way for Don Bollander's body to have been where it would have had to be to make putting it in that sink convenient, and that is if Don Bollander was already here while he was still alive. There is only one logical way that Don Bollander could have been here while he was still alive without any of the nuns knowing, and that is if he was being very careful to stay quiet. And that means—"

"I know what that means," Donovan said. "Either Bollander came here to meet someone out of normal visiting hours, which would have been clandestine. Or Bollander came up on his own with the intention of breaking in—which would have to mean that one of the nuns was Bollander's murderer. Or Bollander came to meet a third party, and the third party convinced him that they had legitimate reason for doing what they were doing—"

"Or the third party was part of a break in," Gregor said. "Yes."

"Do you have logical reasons like this for why Brigit Ann Reilly ended up covered with snakes?"

"The snakes aren't part of it," Gregor said. "It's that storeroom that counts. There's Sister Scholastica."

"I know that's Sister Scholastica."

"I'm going to get her."

Donovan was startled and more than a little put out. Gregor picked up on the signs. He didn't do anything about it. He didn't want to talk about Brigit Ann Reilly right now. Ever since he had first begun to examine the body of Don Bollander, his mind had been working overtime—but it needed to work some more. He could almost see the bare bones outline, the structure of the crime. That wasn't enough. He needed to fill in the details, to color by the numbers. He needed to understand the personalities. Right now, he needed to know how a convent really worked.

Scholastica had come out of the corridor door closest to the utility room and was hurrying across the hall in the direction of Reverend Mother General. Gregor forced his way through a small knot of policemen into the only open space in that hall and shot out his arm to catch her.

[2]

Gregor Demarkian and Pete Donovan had been so intent on bodies and sinks and body bags and evidence, they had been oblivious to everything else that was going on around them. Gregor especially had forgotten that he wasn't in the midst of what he still thought of as the "normal" venue for a homicide, the scene most often chosen by the serial killers he had spent so much of his professional life tracking. He was in a living, breathing, functioning institution, not an abandoned building or a vacant lot. While his mind had been elsewhere, great changes had been taking place around him. The nuns who had crowded the door to the courtyard and the space just beyond it were gone, he didn't know where. Reverend Mother General was still holding the fort in an unobtrusive corner, watching the naive young men with a frankly contemptuous eye, but she was so silent she could have been invisible. Gregor saw her see him catch Scholastica's arm and nod, as if she had been expecting something of the sort to happen soon. He was getting that feeling he always got with old-fashioned nuns, that he got with the Cardinal's secretary: The feeling that wheels upon wheels were turning in a mind much more intelligent and much more disciplined than his own.

"He wants to know how a convent runs," Scholastica told Reverend Mother General, after she had heard

Gregor out and dragged him across the room to her superior. "He says it makes a difference to how the body got into the utility room."

Reverend Mother considered this. "Tell me you've done what I asked you to," she said to Scholastica. "Spell it out."

"Yes, Reverend Mother, of course. The postulants are darning socks. Sister Gabriel is with them and she's enforcing silence. The novices are in chapel with Sister Agnes Bernadine, praying for the repose of Don Bollander's soul and the quick apprehension of his killer. They aren't silent, but they won't be getting a chance to talk about this for at least an hour. Sister Alice Marie has taken over portress duty so she can answer the phones. If parents call up being hysterical, she'll calm them down. As for the Sisters—"

Reverend Mother General waved away the Sisters. "They'll be all right," she said. "I can trust most of them in a real emergency, even Peter Rose." Then Reverend Mother General turned to Gregor Demarkian and smiled. "I know what you're getting at," she said. "You think this man was alive and well when he got here."

"Not necessarily alive and *well*," Gregor said cautiously, "but alive. It can take quite a long time for coniine to work, especially on a large man like Don Bollander. He could have swallowed the poison any time up to an hour before he arrived at the convent and still have been moving under his own power."

"Are you sure it was coniine?" Reverend Mother General wanted to know.

"No," Gregor admitted. "It will take forsenics to tell me that for sure."

"You think they will tell you that for sure?"

"Don't you?"

Reverend Mother General smiled, much more broadly this time. "Of course I do. We all do. Every Sister in the house. We'd rather not, but we do. All right, Mr. Demarkian. You want to know how a convent runs, I'll show you how a convent runs. I'll show you how this one runs, at any rate. There are a great many variations these days."

"Is Mr. Donovan going to go with us?" Scholastica asked.

"Mr. Donovan has to stay and supervise his men," Gregor said.

"You're not going with us either," Reverend Mother told Scholastica. "I want you to call the Chancery and make a report. Not to the Cardinal, mind you, and not to one of his assistants, either. I'm not ready to talk to John O'Bannion and I won't be for several hours."

"He'll be ready to talk to you," Scholastica said drily.

"Yes, he will," Reverend Mother General said, "and it'll be the first time in years, too. Alice Marie can talk to him. Alice Marie is so feminine she confuses him, and then he hangs up and has to call back again."

"Right," Scholastica said.

Reverend Mother General unhooked her keys from her belt and turned to Gregor Demarkian. "Come along," she said. "This is a very modern house built to accommodate a lot of very old-fashioned customs. It gets confusing sometimes."

[3]

"The first thing you have to realize," Reverend Mother General told him, after she had led him away from the crime scene and its craziness, across the courtyard and through a door he hadn't noticed before. The courtyard was full of doors he hadn't noticed before, and windows, too, as fully open to the first-floor rooms that lined it as it could have been as long as that floor had walls. That the courtyard was lined mostly with rooms was confirmed by the fact that it was a room Reverend Mother General had shooed him into. Going inside, Gregor had looked back over his shoulder and done a quick count. There were two sets of four doors. One set opened into each of the corners, presumably into halls like the one where they had just been. The other four were near the center of each courtyard wall, and presumably opened into rooms. Reverend Mother General caught Gregor's distracted stare and said, "Yes?"

"I'm sorry," Gregor said. "It was the doors. Do you lock those doors?"

"We never lock the doors to the courtyard," Reverend Mother General told him. "There's no reason to. They go from one part of the convent to the other. They don't go outside."

"They'd make it easier for someone coming in from the outside to get around the convent without being heard," Gregor said. Then he shook it off. "I'm sorry, Reverend Mother. I didn't mean to interrupt you."

"That's quite all right, Mr. Demarkian. I was saying that the first thing you have to realize is that the women in this house are not, canonically, nuns. According to canon law, a nun is a woman religious who has taken solemn vows. All true nuns in the Catholic Church are now contemplatives, women who live by and large in cloister and whose apostolate it is to pray rather than to teach or nurse or run consciousness-raising centers in California. The women in this house have taken simple vows and they are, therefore, technically religious Sisters."

"Does that mean I should stop calling them nuns?"

"Not at all. The names business is really the result of a lot of wrangling in the late seventeenth and early eighteenth century, when the first active orders—that's what we call an order like ours, Mr. Demarkian, that does work in the world, active or mixed—at any rate, those first orders had their trouble getting permission from Rome to establish themselves, and some of the objections were finally got round by calling the women who joined them 'religious sisters' instead of 'nuns.' The distinction really doesn't exist much of anywhere anymore except in official Church documents. People call us nuns and we call ourselves nuns. The distinction, however, does make a difference in how this house is run. Do you know anything about cloistered nuns?"

"No."

"Well, there are variations in that area these days, too," Reverend Mother General said. They had gone through the small room—which had been empty, but possessed of a blackboard at one end, as if it had once served as a classroom and since been abandoned—and across a narrow hall. Then there had been another that opened onto another hall, a long one this time, with a crucifix at the far end and a door under that. Gregor followed Reverend Mother moving through it. Reverend Mother walked unnaturally close to the wall.

"Basically," Reverend Mother said, "a cloistered or contemplative order will have a much stricter constitution than an active or mixed one. Rome keeps a much closer watch on the Holy Rules of orders like those. A Holy Rule is a set of regulations and principles by which a congregation lives. The active and mixed orders have been allowed a great deal of latitude in their constitutions, and they've taken advantage of it. We've taken advantage of it. We've been experimenting. Thirty years ago, no Sister would ever have left convent grounds except in the company of a companion Sister. Now we enforce that rule only in the worst neighborhoods of large cities, and it has nothing to do with religious obedience. It's purely practical. Then there are restaurants. Thirty years ago, no Sister was allowed to eat in the presence of a secular. That was a rule first established in the Counter-Reformation, in an attempt to stem the tide of abuses in religious orders that had led to scandal. Now Sisters can eat in public all they like and in restaurants, too, if their families pay for it. Their families often do. We have a retired Sister here named Sister Rosita whose granddaughter sends her fifty dollars every month to take herself and the other four retired Sisters to McDonald's. During Lent they put the money in the poor box with the granddaughter's blessing. Do you see what I mean?"

"You mean you don't have any idea where anybody was last night," Gregor sighed. "I was afraid of that."

"I mean nothing of the sort," Reverend Mother

General said. "What I'm trying to get at is why I think you must be wrong. I don't think Mr. Don Bollander could have gotten into this convent last night. I don't think he could have gotten into it until this morning—"

"Reverend Mother, rigor mortis—"

"Hear me out," Reverend Mother General said. They had gotten to the end of the corridor, to a point nearly underneath the crucifix. Reverend Mother General turned to her left, looked through her keys, and fitted one into the lock of the door. When the door opened she put her hand around and flicked a light switch. Gregor saw fluorescents flicker and then beam into a strong glow. Underneath them and over Reverend Mother General's shoulder he saw what looked like a room full of drafting tables.

"Come in here," Reverend Mother General told him. "This is the plans room. I don't know what it was planned for originally, but a couple of years ago we had to have some rewiring done and it was empty, so I had our blueprints and floor plans set up here. Come and take a look at this one in the middle. It's the easiest one to read."

Gregor stepped into the room and up to the large drafting table set up in its center. He looked down on what seemed to be a gigantic cross with a square shaped hole cut out of its middle where the sections overlapped.

Reverend Mother pointed to the short end—the head—and said, "That's the front door. It faces the front gate and Delaney Street." She pointed to the short arm to its right. "That's where we are now, or near enough. The crucifix we were just looking at is at this end, and as you undoubtedly noticed, the door is underneath it. That is a door to the outside. There is one in a similar position in the other arm and the foot."

"Are they kept locked?" Gregor asked.

"Oh, yes," Reverend Mother said. "They're plugged into an automatic security system, too. That's why we had the house rewired. If you try to open one of those doors, or even to unlock it, without neutralizing the security system first, you will set off the alarms."

"Is the security system ever off?" Gregor asked her. "Are those doors ever *unlocked*?"

"During the daytime, yes, Mr. Demarkian. But we lock up here at six o'clock. Before six o'clock, this house is a very busy place indeed. Do you really think Mr. Bollander could have come in through one of these four doors and wandered around for I don't know how long—or even just walked down one of these corridors. These are the main arteries of the house. Before six o'clock they would have been full of people."

"This one isn't full of people," Gregor pointed out. "Not now."

Reverend Mother General made a short jabbing gesture with her hand, impatient. "That's because I've got everybody up front, trying to keep them busy enough so they don't brood. On a normal day the room across the hall from this one would have had Raphael and John Damascene in it, packaging catechisms to be sent out to our outreach missions. And three doors down you would have had Sister Clare, answering letters about the beatification and sending out brochures to girls who have expressed interest in joining the order."

"What about the other doors?" Gregor asked. "There was a door off that hall that led outside."

"Yes, there was. And there are four of them, too, in the corners on the outside perimeter of the center of the cross. And yes, they're unlocked and not connected to the alarms in the daytime. But it is the daytime, Mr. Demarkian. And those doors are locked just like everything else at six. They're on a central switch. That switch is in my office."

"Someone could have gotten into your office."

"True," Reverend Mother General said. "They could have walked in any time they liked. *That* is never locked. They couldn't have tampered with the switch, however, because to work it you have to have the key, and the only key there is in this house is right here on my key ring. It was there when I locked up last night. It was there when I unlocked this morning. It was hanging on my belt in my cell all last night and I know that perfectly well because I am a very light sleeper. Of course, there is an override."

"An override?"

"On the front door there is a special lock that takes a special key that overrides the system, for emergencies. That key is also on my key ring. It has not left it."

"What about other people," Gregor asked desperately. "You can't have the only emergency—"

"I don't. The bank made us put the system in. We had some very bad vandalism in our chapel about three years ago and it played havoc with our insurance. They have a key. The security company has a key. That's in case everybody loses theirs. Do you really think Mr. Bollander was killed by an employee of the security company—"

"No," Gregor said. This recital had been depressing, although not for the reasons Reverend Mother General had thought it was. She didn't seem to realize that if nobody could have gotten in from the outside, suspicion would have to fall on one of her nuns. Especially because the first death had been one of her postulants. But Reverend Mother General was plowing remorselessly on, getting grim satisfaction out of every word.

"Remember what I was telling you about the latitude Rome shows us in our Rules? Well, Mr. Demarkian, we've taken less advantage of it than some, but we have taken advantage of it. Before the changes, every nun's day was regulated almost down to the second. We went to sleep together. We got up together. We went to chapel together. We went to meals together. Well, we gave that up. We still do some things as a group. That's why I said he could have been gotten in here this morning. We would have been in chapel en masse, for Mass and Divine Office. It's the only time of day we are together en masse at all anymore. At any other hour, and that includes four in the morning and during Compline, there are always one or two Sisters doing something on their own, taking care of emergencies, just getting extra work done. With the beatification and the Cardinal coming for St. Patrick's Day and the murder—the first murder—there's been a lot of extra work to get done. So, Mr. Demarkian, it's just possible that if Don Bollander entered this house through the front door on his own two feet last night, he could have been careful enough so that we didn't see him. But trust me, he wasn't carted around this house dead as a doornail and dumped in the utility room and he didn't come in through any of the side doors. The alarms would have gone off and whoever was carting him around would have been caught in the act. There were a lot of Sisters awake last night. We were having a Forty Hours Devotion in the chapel."

Four

❖

[1]

Gregor Demarkian didn't believe in locked-room mysteries. He didn't believe in poisons that leave no trace, identical twins who successfully switch identities, or the silent menace that walks the dark, either. Back on Cavanaugh Street, Bennis Hannaford fed him detective stories the way some mothers feed their children hard candies, as a pacifier. Sometimes she hits a real clinker, a resurrected unknown "classic" of the thirties. Gregor always ended up wondering what those authors had been thinking of. Mothers who didn't know their own children. Brothers who didn't know their own sisters. And locked rooms. Always locked rooms. There was a man, John Dickson Carr, who specialized in locked rooms. It made Gregor feel a little better about being called "the Armenian-American Hercule Poirot." If there was one thing Mrs. Christie had had the good sense never to indulge in, it was locked rooms.

No matter how he felt about it, though, what he seemed to have was a locked room. He went over and over it with Reverend Mother. He established the obvious. Either Don Bollander was dead at the time he arrived at St. Mary of the Hill, which meant he would have to have come in by the outside door in the hall where the utility room was. If he had come in at any other place he and his murderer—or he and his

179

transporter—would most likely have been discovered. Besides, there were dozens of other hiding places for a body on the first floor of the Motherhouse. There were room closets and storage bins, ordinary closets, and half-filled packing crates stuck in out-of-the-way rooms. The only sensible reason for Bollander to have ended up in the laundry sink was that it was convenient, and the only thing it was convenient to—assuming someone was carting around a corpse—was that door.

If Don Bollander had been alive when he came to St. Mary of the Hill, he could have come in almost anywhere, although the two best bets would have been the same (impossible) side door from the first scenario or the front door. Most of the other side doors opened onto staircases that opened onto dormitory floors at least on the second story. The front door had the advantage of having access to a wide variety of corridors all at once. It would still have been risky, creeping through the Motherhouse halls in the dead of night, but as an explanation it was more likely than the one Reverend Mother favored, which was that Bollander, dead or alive, had arrived around six o'clock this morning. Gregor didn't believe it. He didn't believe Bollander had been moved to the Motherhouse after his death. He had only been able to examine small stretches of bare skin—it wouldn't have been polite, or politic, to start ripping away at the man's clothes—he hadn't seen the kind of markings he would have needed to believe that. Then, too, both the visible skin and the clothes were too clean. If a corpse had been carried all over hell and gone, there should be something on it that would look out of place if that corpse came back to life and started back working in his office. As for Reverend Mother's favorite scenario, Gregor knew it was absurd. The body could not have arrived alive at St. Mary of the Hill at six o'clock this morning and been in the state of rigor in which they found it at eleven. It could not have arrived already in rigor and been stuffed in the laundry sink without something breaking. Gregor had watched Pete Donovan's men pull Bollander out, and they were the ones who'd had to do the breaking. And that meant—

Gregor didn't know what that meant. He supposed that—barring some real absurdity like a secret plot being carried out by an employee of the company that had installed the security locks—it meant he was stuck with a locked-room murder whether he liked it or not. It made his head reel. It put him in a particularly bad mood. Murderers were logical, he'd told Pete Donovan earlier. Well, Gregor Demarkian was logical, too. He didn't like Alice in Wonderland cases. He didn't like to be confused. Most of all, he didn't like to feel as if he were missing something very blatant and very simple— which was exactly what he did feel like.

In the end, he looked Reverend Mother over once or twice—she was launched on a discourse on the depredations of religious superiors in the United States since the close of Vatican II—and made up his mind to strike out on his own. It might be hours before Pete Donovan and his men were finished, or minutes, but Gregor didn't care. He wanted to get out in the air and think for himself. When Sister Scholastica passed the plans room for the fourth or fifth time, he stopped her and asked for his coat. When she brought his coat he thanked her, shrugged it on and said, "Well, Reverend Mother, it's been very interesting talking with you. I have to thank you for your cooperation."

"I wasn't cooperating," Reverend Mother said. "I was monopolizing the discussion."

Actually, she hadn't been. Gregor had asked too many questions for that. He smiled at her anyway, thanked her again, and asked to be directed to the front door.

[2]

It was a clear day but a frigid one, a deceptive day offering sunshine but no warmth. Gregor set out through the propped-open leaves of the Motherhouse's wrought-iron gate with half a purpose in mind. The Cardinal had shown him a map of Maryville that seemed to indicate that the street that dead-ended at the Motherhouse gate on this end dead-ended at the library on the other. In between was practically everything of importance in town, except Sam Harrigan's house and the town's minuscule barrio. This was the walk Brigit Ann Reilly had taken on the day she died and on every day before that for two months, excepting Sundays. Gregor wanted to walk it himself, at least as far as his hotel, which so far he hadn't seen. After leaving Gregor off at the Mother-house gate, the Cardinal's driver had been deputed to drop his luggage at the St. Mary's Inn. According to the Cardinal, the inn was on the corner of Delaney and Londonderry streets, "right across from the bank." Whether that made its location a good one or a bad one, Gregor didn't know. He had his mind on other things. What he definitely did not have it on was locked-room mysteries, but before he left the Motherhouse he checked out the front door lock anyway. It was just as Reverend Mother General said it was. There were a series of dead bolts that seemed to have nothing with which they could be closed. There was a conventional lock under the doorknob and a much smaller one higher up. Gregor recognized the brand name etched into its polished brass front and was impressed. The security company had given the Sisters a top-of-the-line job. He wondered whose doing that was, the Cardinal's or the bank's. He supposed it might have been both.

Whosever it was, contemplation of it was definitely not good for Gregor's mood. That lock was just one more argument in favor of a locked-room puzzle and against Gregor's most fervently held conviction, which was that the whole thing was going to turn out to have been a mistake, or gross stupidity on his part. He got himself away from it by moving as quickly as possible into town. He wanted to get a feel for Maryville. He wanted to feel what Brigit Ann Reilly had felt. He could get to Don Bollander later.

Whether any of this made any sense, he never

knew. The only feel he got from Maryville concerned its commitment to St. Patrick's Day and its own Irish-American heritage, which was extreme but rather endearing. He passed a cluster of buildings calling themselves St. Ignatius Loyola Catholic Church and St. Ignatius Loyola Parochial School and marveled at the variety and extent of the decorations scattered through the branches of their trees and across their doors and windows. He passed a hole-in-the-wall store whose narrow plate glass window was so crowded it was impossible to see through it to the room inside. It had gold letters painted across it that said, MARYVILLE CATHOLIC CENTER. RELIGIOUS ARTICLES. It had a hundred tiny green-and-white shamrocks growing like mad vines into every available space. Gregor thought it was all very nice, but he couldn't see what good it was doing him. Irish pride and bitter cold. It seemed like a strange combination.

He was just about to give it up, find a phone booth and call a taxi, when the doors of one of the stores he was passing opened and a small man stepped out. The man was elderly but not ancient and very sharp. Gregor picked that up from the man's eyes behind his thick glasses. He was also wearing nothing to protect himself from the cold, as if he were just coming out to do something that wouldn't take much time and would be going right back in again. Gregor couldn't imagine what that would be. He couldn't imagine how the man was able to stand in the wind like that without shivering, either.

Gregor was stretching his mouth into a quick perfunctory smile and getting ready to pass by—not only was that the right thing to do but he didn't like looking at this man; it made him feel as if frostbite might be contagious—when the man stepped forward, rearranged his glasses, touched Gregor on the arm and frowned.

"Excuse me," he said, as Gregor stopped dead in his tracks, startled. "Are you that man I saw on TV? The one the Cardinal sent out to find whoever killed Brigit?"

Gregor had made it a point never to answer ques-

tions like this directly, at least when they were put to
him by people he'd never seen before who'd accosted
him in the street. Today, he forgot all about that. He was
that surprised.

"Yes," he said. "Yes, I am. I'm Gregor Demarkian."

"Gregor Demarkian," the man repeated. "I'm Jack
O'Brien."

For a second, Gregor thought the name Jack
O'Brien was familiar only because it was so common.
There had to be thousands of Jack O'Briens across the
United States. There had been three in the Federal
Bureau of Investigation alone during Gregor's time
there. Then he remembered: Jack O'Brien was one of
the names on the Cardinal's list. He was one of the
people who had seen Brigit Ann Reilly on the day she
died. In fact, he was the first. Gregor took the hand Jack
O'Brien was holding out to him and shook it.

"We could go in the store," Jack O'Brien said, "if
you've got a minute."

"I've got a minute," Gregor said.

"Good," O'Brien said. "It's getting cold out here."

[3]

The store, as Jack O'Brien called it, turned out to be
an old-fashioned shoe store. The left half of it was taken
up with displays of solid-looking work boots and excru-
ciatingly stiff wing-tip formals. The right half of it held
seats and supplies like laces and removable inner soles.
At the back, behind a half-wall with a counter nailed to
its top, was where the real money was made: the
cobbler's machine shop with its black oily equipment
and uneasy air of being covered with fine leather dust.
The equipment looked well used and permanently settled in. It was part of what gave the shop the air of having
been here "forever." The other part of that was the plate
glass window at the front. It said O'BRIEN'S in large
black letters, but nothing else. If you didn't already

know what this shop did, you weren't going to learn it on a quick pass through town in your car.

There was an electric percolator plugged into the wall near what Gregor thought might be the lathe—he really wasn't very good at machines—and as soon as they came in from the cold, O'Brien headed straight for it.

"You want some coffee?" he asked, while he was in the midst of pouring a cup.

Gregor said yes, even though the coffee looked black and muddy and suspiciously like Father Tibor's. He was cold.

"I had intended to come down here and talk to you," Gregor said. "You were one of the people on my list."

"Because I'd seen Brigit that morning?" O'Brien brought the cups—white plastic foam cups, the kind that imparted to coffee a taste all their own—and handed one to Gregor. "There's really not much of anything in that," he said. "I saw Brigit every day except Sunday. That day was no different from any other."

Gregor took a sip of his coffee. It was exactly like Father Tibor's, and undrinkable. He sat down in one of the chairs set out for shoe-buying customers and put the cup on the floor beside his legs.

"Are you sure?" he said. "I was talking to Sister Scholastica and she mentioned something about Brigit having been—strange, most of that week."

"Not strange," O'Brien said. "Brigit was having one of her het-ups, that was all."

"Het-ups?"

"Brigit got excited about people," O'Brien explained. "Especially people who were different than she was. I guess she must have grown up in one of those suburbs where everybody is supposed to be alike. I've never been to a place like that myself. But I heard her talking about me to that Neila Connelly once and she said, 'He's so wonderful. I never knew old people could be so wonderful.'"

"It must have been nice to be called wonderful."

"It would have been nicer not to have been called

old," O'Brien said. "Anyway, it was like that. I could tell. She had somebody new she was excited about."

"Did she tell you who?"

"Nope. I had a feeling it might be Sam Harrigan."

"Why Sam Harrigan?"

Jack O'Brien took an enormous swig of coffee and got up to get some more. Gregor could only admire the strength of his stomach lining.

"It was a couple of things," O'Brien said. "First place, it had to be someone she looked up to and not someone her own age. I'd seen her get worked up with both kinds of people and the way she got worked up was different. With people her own age she got happy. With older people she got awed. You get the difference."

"I think so."

"Only other person I ever saw her that awed about was Reverend Mother General. Even Sister Scholastica came a bad second. Oh, well. Then there was all that stuff about the eye of the needle."

"What?"

"You know," O'Brien said. Having filled his coffee cup until it was nearly erupting from its plastic foam cell, he came back into the center of the room and sat down. "The camel passing through the eye of the needle. Father Fitzsimmons does that one every time he gets up to speak at the opening of parish fund-raising drives. Not that I'm in Father Fitzsimmons's parish. He has Iggy Loy right up the street here. I live over on the other side of town."

"I still don't see—"

"About rich people," O'Brien said patiently. "There's two ways to read that passage, and one is that it says that if you're rich you can't go to Heaven no matter what, and the other is that it's another example of God's being able to do what he wants to do. Anyway, lately Brigit was very intense about how the rich could really be noble souls, look at all the aristocratic people who had ended up as saints. I think that means that whoever it was she was in awe of was probably well heeled."

"And Sam Harrigan is well heeled?"

"Sam's about as rich as you get around these parts," O'Brien said. "The only person who comes close is Miriam Bailey over at the bank, and maybe Josh. Josh is Miriam's new husband. He doesn't have a dime, but Brigit might not have known that. I don't think Brigit knew much about anything."

"There isn't anybody else?"

"Who's rich, you mean?" O'Brien was surprised. "I guess there's Father Doherty down at St. Andrew's. I don't think he's rich now, but I know he used to be. Or maybe I should say his people were."

"Is he from around here?" Gregor asked.

"No," O'Brien said, "but he doesn't have to be. Doherty Lumber, that's where the Father's from. His brother still runs the business. Comes up here once a year around Thanksgiving in a big black car and drives right through the slum down there in it, you know Father Doherty's parishioners really like him because after the first year nobody has ever broken the brother's windows. You know about St. Andrew's?"

Gregor knew about St. Andrew's. That had been in the Cardinal's report, too. The Cardinal could be faulted on some things, but not on the extent and precision of his knowledge of the parishes in his Archdiocese. "St. Andrew's is the parish where Brigit Ann Reilly went to teach reading to adults," Gregor said. "Is it a very bad slum? Is this Father Doherty some kind of martyr?"

"Father Doherty is a doctor," O'Brien said, "and for a slum it's not too bad. Some drugs, some violence—but if you ask me, the drugs and the violence aren't always the fault of the people who live there, if you know what I mean. Good, hardworking Catholic people from South America, most of them are. Half the time, there's trouble down there, it's the spoiled brats from the better parts of town who're causing it."

"Mmm," Gregor said. To his mind, Father Doherty fit O'Brien's description of the kind of person Brigit would be in awe of—and Sister Scholastica's, too—far better than Sam Harrigan. Father Doherty, after all, had Given It All Up to work with the poor. Gregor reached down, picked up his cup, and absentmindedly took another sip of Jack O'Brien's coffee. The shock to his system was enough to keep him from ever doing anything absentmindedly again.

"Well," he said. "That's all very interesting. It's very hard to investigate these things when you haven't known the victim. And you almost never have."

"Around here you would have," Jack O'Brien said. "But that wasn't what I called you in here to talk about. It was about something else, something you might have missed."

"What?" Gregor knew himself capable of missing a great deal, but he didn't believe the Cardinal was capable of it. "The reports I got were very complete. I know they won't be perfect until I've had a chance to look around for myself, but I still—"

"The reports you got were from the Cardinal, weren't they?"

"That's right."

"Well, the Cardinal's a good man and a thorough one, but he knows us out here all too well. He's made up his mind about what kind of people we are. He knows who he trusts and who he doesn't."

"And?"

Jack O'Brien finished off his second cup of coffee. "And he judges and he sifts and he brings in only the wheat, except this time he might have been mistaken about something. I don't know that he was. I haven't seen your reports. I just think that he might be. He tell you anything about a woman named Mrs. Barbara Keel?"

"Yes," Gregor said slowly. "She was with Glinda Daniels when Glinda Daniels found the body."

Jack O'Brien smiled. "And the Cardinal basically told you Barbara Keel was a nut, right?"

"No," Gregor said, glad he could be truthful about this. "Not exactly. Why? Did she see something when the body was found that might be important?"

"Not when the body was found," Jack O'Brien said,

"earlier. At the Immigrants National Bank. You know the Immigrants National Bank?"

"By reputation."

"Yeah, well, I know Barbara Keel. She's a snoop and a gossip and more than a little of an airhead and she's always been all three, but she doesn't make things up. She was in the bank before she went to the library—she volunteers at the library, puts away books—and it was a crazy day, the day before they ship the old money out to the Federal Reserve, you know about that?"

"Yes. They exchange old and damaged bills for new ones and the old ones are sent somewhere to be burned."

"Well," Jack said, "from what Barbara says they were in the middle of getting ready for the transfer and they were setting up their decorations for St. Pat's at the same time and she just happened to wander down a hall where she didn't belong and knew she didn't belong, but being dithery and old and a woman goes a long way. If she'd got caught, she'd just have said she was lost."

"She didn't get caught?"

"No, she didn't. She did see something, though. Something I think you ought to know about."

"And you won't tell me?"

"I don't think I should," Jack O'Brien said. "It's not my story and I might get some of it wrong. I'd definitely miss parts. Barbara's got a right to tell it, do you know what I mean?"

"You mean Barbara's a very lonely woman."

"That, too."

Jack O'Brien got out of his chair and went to the electric percolator for the third time. Gregor saw and Gregor marveled. The man had to have something better than a stomach made of cast iron. He had to have a stomach that produced death rays that acted only on coffee.

"You want to find Barbara Keel," Jack O'Brien told him, "what you do is, you go talk to Glinda Daniels at the library."

Jack O'Brien said this quite seriously, as if Glinda Daniels were the last person Gregor was likely to see.

[4]

Half an hour later, having been drawn into an extended discussion of last year's case in Colchester and the Cardinal Archbishop's chances of being elected Pope, Gregor walked swiftly down the short stretch of Delaney Street that led to the intersection with Londonderry and stopped for the Don't Walk light. On his right was the bank, an imposing building whose second-floor window boxes did indeed seem to be filled with hemlock. The dwarf plants were sharply green against the snow. Right in front of him, on the other side of the street, was a somewhat less imposing building with a discreet sign on its Londonderry side door that said, "St. Mary's Inn." It looked very much like a bed and breakfast he and Elizabeth had once stayed in while on vacation in Scotland. Gregor was in the midst of allowing himself to sink into that memory when a door on the side of the bank flew open and a woman came out, followed closely by a young man in Ralph Lauren jeans and four hundred dollars worth of blue cashmere sweater.

"I don't see what you're so upset about," the young man was saying, "you didn't die. You didn't even get sick."

"I could have died," the woman told him. "I could have been a good deal more than sick. It was right there in my box of tea bags."

"It didn't even look like a tea bag. You wouldn't have been fooled."

"I might not have been looking."

"You're not upset about this at all," the young man said. "You're not even upset about Don and for God's sake, Miriam, the man's dead. You're just upset because I let Ann-Harriet drive the car."

"I'm never upset about Ann-Harriet," the woman said. "I wouldn't waste my time."

The Don't Walk light had turned to Walk, but Gregor wasn't paying any attention to it. The names he had just heard seemed to be still floating in the air. Ann-Harriet. Don. Miriam. The woman and the young man were heading up Londonderry Street away from him. As he watched, they turned to jaywalk across the middle of the block. He caught a better look at the woman then. She was tall and spare and old—in her sixties and looking it. So this was the famous Miriam Bailey, and that was her famous Josh. They weren't the way Gregor had expected them, somehow. Maybe it was just that Gregor had known a number of old women who married much younger men, and those women had always been desperate, striving, insecure types. Miriam Bailey had been angry, not desperate, and she had been secure enough to be wearing her own face. Then there had been the last of the things she'd said—"I'm never upset about Ann-Harriet. I wouldn't waste my time." Ann-Harriet, Gregor assumed, was Josh Malley's fancy piece, as Scholastica had put it. If Miriam Bailey knew her name, she probably at least suspected the woman's connection to her husband. And yet, hearing the words he'd heard, Gregor had believed them absolutely. Miriam Bailey was never upset about Ann-Harriet. She wouldn't waste her time.

Queer, Gregor thought. Almost as queer as what they were actually talking about, which had sounded very much like an attempt on Miriam Bailey's life. This time, when the light changed to Walk, Gregor obeyed. He crossed the street with his hands in the pockets of his coat and his head bent against the wind, working it out. The wind in Maryville was pernicious. It seemed to come at you from every direction.

The St. Mary's Inn had a revolving glass door framed in bronze. Gregor pushed his way through it, walked up to the ornately carved antique registration desk and rang the hand bell positioned to the left of the lined guest book. Then he told himself that he would go upstairs, unpack, and lie down for a while. He'd even leave instructions that he was not to be disturbed. It would be time enough to get back to Pete Donovan when he'd had a little chance to rest.

Rest, however, was something he was not destined to get. He rang the bell a second time because no one had appeared to help him. As soon as he had, a door behind the registration desk opened and a small plump woman with a head of frizzy gray hair hurried out. She headed toward him with the determined hostility of someone who was about to deliver a lecture on the evils of impatience, stopped halfway to him, and let her jaw drop open. A second later, she was squealing in a high, sharp wail that was exactly like a pig's.

"Oh, my goodness," she was saying. "Oh, my goodness. Heavens to Betsy. I can't believe this. It's Gregor Demarkian himself."

"Yes," Gregor said, alarmed. "It is—"

"And I just hung up on her. I just can't believe it."

"You just hung up on who?"

"On your agent, of course," the woman said. "She had to be your agent. She was definitely a woman, and she kept insisting that her name was Dennis!"

Five

❖

[1]

In towns like Maryville there are two systems of communication—official and unofficial—and the unofficial one is often the most efficient. When Pete Donovan's force was calling Don Bollander's family and Don Bollander's boss, someone else—no one was ever able to pinpoint who—was calling someone else, who in turn was calling someone else, who in turn was having a bridge party. By three o'clock in the afternoon, everyone in town knew that Don Bollander's body had been found at the Motherhouse in a utility room sink. Half the town had their theories about who had done it and how. The other half were holding out for the kind of crazed serial killer that had made other places famous. It was almost as if they thought a Son of Sam or a Hillside Strangler would do the town's image good, at least after he was caught. Glinda Daniels didn't know what they thought. She had started getting the calls at just around noon. She had started getting the walk-ins fifteen minutes later. Now she didn't know what to do with herself. If she barricaded herself in her office, the phone rang. If she stood out at the check-out desk, people walked up to her and expected her to gossip. She didn't know what to do. The only safe spot in the library was in the stacks over near that door, and she certainly didn't want to go there.

She was standing on a stepladder, rearranging a

display of children's classics on the broad-based revolving wooden pyramid Miriam Bailey had given to the library on the fifth anniversary of its new building, when Sam walked in. He was wearing his big shaggy coat, as always, and attracting attention to himself, as always, and getting waylaid by old ladies, as always. One of them had him in her grip as soon as he came through the door, but she was very short and he was able to wave to Glinda over her head. Glinda waved back and started down the ladder. The ladder was close up against the shelving for children's science books, and Shelley and Cory must have been on the other side. Glinda hadn't noticed them because she couldn't see them. She couldn't see them now, but she could hear them whispering.

"There he is again," Shelley was saying. "I'm telling you, I'm not crazy. There's something going on."

"What could be going on?" Cory asked her. "Sam Harrigan and the old maid librarian?"

"Glinda Daniels is a very attractive woman. And she's hardly an old maid yet. She's only about forty."

"She's fat."

"She's not fat." Shelley sounded exasperated. "For God's sake, Cory, not everybody has to have anorexia nervosa to look good."

"I'm not talking about anorexia nervosa," Cory said stubbornly. "I'm talking about Glinda Daniels."

"Oh, for God's sake," Shelley said.

"Sam Harrigan and the old maid librarian," Cory said again. "It's gross. I mean, it pains me just to think about it."

It was very hard to move the ladder without making any noise, but Glinda did it, millimeter by millimeter, pulling it across the carpet. From the corner of her eye, she could see Sam on the other side of the room, disentangling himself from the old lady. In the back of her mind, she could hear the voice of Donna Leary, a girl she had known in high school and considered to be her friend. "I like Glinda a lot but I wouldn't want to be that intellectual. Boys don't like you and it makes you fat." Fat. Fat, fat, fat. Glinda got the ladder out of the children's section and began to fold it up. It made a clatter as its parts came together.

"Cory?" she said, much too loudly for a library. "This ladder has to go back in the storeroom."

Then she walked into her office and shut the door.

"Fat," she said to herself.

She looked through the window wall at Sam, still caught by the old lady, being polite and impatient at the same time. She had noticed his ability to do that and marveled at it, but now she didn't want to notice anything about him at all. She didn't want to notice anything about anybody. She picked up a stack of clippings from *Librarian's Day* magazine, all on things to do for children that would encourage them to read. Glinda knew it was very, very important to encourage children to read. She took the clippings and dumped them in the wastepaper basket. Then she thought about setting fire to them. She might have done it except for the window wall. She was afraid people on the other side of it would see the flames and panic. Instead, she took her thin file of newspaper clippings on the progress of the state library budget in Albany and ripped it in two.

She had just started turning her computer-printed annual report into confetti when Sam opened the door, looked at the mess she was making on the floor, and said, "Didn't quite meet your standards, did it?"

"Go to Hell," Glinda told him.

"Right," Sam said. Then he shut the door behind him.

Glinda had finished with the report and gone on to her four-color copies of the last ALA convention booklet. She had six of those in the office, because she had been president of the New York State chapter last year and her picture was on page thirty-six. The annual report would be replaceable by merely pushing the right buttons and running a copy off the printer, but these wouldn't be replaceable at all. They never ran enough of them for people who wanted extras and nobody would be willing to give up what they had. Glinda ripped them in half and then in quarters and dumped them on the floor with the rest of the mess.

Sam Harrigan cleared his throat. "Glinda?"

"What?" Glinda said.

"Is it my fault? Have I given you reason to be angry with me?"

"No."

"Fine. That's a relief. Do you want to tell me who has got you angry with him? Or it?"

"No."

"Would you like me to find you something else to tear up?"

Glinda had finished with the booklets. She picked up the latest copy of the *Library Journal* and started thinking about fire again. Ripping things up was fine but fire would be perfect.

"Do you know what?" she said. "When I went to college—I went to Bryn Mawr—when I went to college, I studied archaeology. Do you know why?"

"It interested you?"

"I wanted to go to Egypt," Glinda said. "I've still never been to Egypt. Later on I went to graduate school and got a degree in French. I've never been to France. I've never been anywhere but one school or another and Maryville, New York, and let me tell you, I'm sick of it. I am sick of the library, I am sick of my house, I am sick of my life, and most of all, Mr. Harrigan, I am sick of myself. I have half a mind to chuck my job right here, check into someplace like the Golden Door, lose twenty pounds and start living."

"Chuck your job," Sam said quickly, "but for Christ's sake don't lose twenty pounds. I'll take you to Tahiti."

"Don't be facetious."

"I'm not being facetious. Tahiti's very nice. If you're conventional, we can make it a honeymoon."

"These days, if I were conventional we'd have to make it an affair. Look, um, I know, we're supposed to go over to find Mr. Demarkian. I called you. You're doing me a favor. I can't stop talking fast. Give me a minute, all right? I'll calm down."

"I don't want you to calm down," Sam said seriously. "I will take you to Tahiti. It is nice. You could even use your French."

"Why not?" Glinda said. "I have very good French. I can listen to people saying 'How is it possible, Sam Harrigan and the old maid librarian' in a different language."

She hadn't meant to say it—she really hadn't meant to say it. She'd had a lot of experience being the fat, intelligent one. She knew better. It was just that she was holding the *Library Journal* in her hands, looking at the drawing of a frazzled librarian on the cover and thinking she didn't even like libraries, when she wanted a book she bought one—and it just came out. A second after it did, the office was so quiet it felt like the inside of a vacuum jar. Even the sounds coming from outside the office seemed to have been cut off, the people in the library rendered mute.

"I'm sorry," Glinda said, and thought: They're probably all out there staring through the glass at me, wondering if I'm having a nervous breakdown or what. She put the *Library Journal* back down on the desk very softly and refused to look through the glass. If they were staring at her, she didn't want to stare back. "If the ALA heard me talking, they'd probably have me arrested for egregious stereotyping. We're not supposed to say things like 'old maid librarian' these days."

"Did somebody call you that? Did they say that to you? 'Sam Harrigan and the old maid librarian.'"

"It was something I overheard."

"Were you meant to overhear it?"

"No."

Sam had been standing against the door. Now he came across and sat down on the edge of the desk, as close to her as he could come, so that Glinda could feel the heat of him.

"I'm sorry," he said.

"For what?"

"For your having had to hear that. It was my position that did it, after all, and maybe the way I've gone about all this. I mean, without the show, what am I? A shaggy old fart with gray hair who smokes cigars and hasn't bothered to keep himself in shape."

"You're Sam Harrigan." Glinda smiled. And then she laughed. "And I'm an old maid librarian."

"Are you?" Sam asked her. "An old maid, I mean."

Glinda blushed. "No."

"Well, that's good, anyway. But you've got to stop thinking of yourself this way, Glinda, it's imperative. Old maid librarian. Lose twenty pounds and start living. I've been driving myself crazy all morning trying to figure out what was wrong between us last night and it turns out to have been your insecurity complex. Bloody Hell. It just won't do. You've got to give it up."

"Why?"

"Because it's making it damned hard to seduce you."

Glinda had gone down to the floor in the middle of Sam's speech, starting to pick up the mess she had made and feeling a little stupid. Now she shot up and grinned. It had been a long time since she'd talked this sort of nonsense with anyone. She'd forgotten how much fun it was.

"Is that what you've been trying to do," she asked him, "seduce me?"

"It depends."

"On what?"

"On whether or not you want to be seduced."

And that, Glinda realized later, was when it happened. One second everything was light and teasing. The next it was different, shifted, so that when she came out with the first thing that had come into her head, it sounded much more significant than she had meant it to be.

"Do I?" she asked him.

There was still that window wall, looking out on the check-out desk, making them available for view to a good cross-section of a very small town. Sam seemed to have forgotten about it and Glinda decided that she just didn't care. He put a hand in the hair at the back of her neck and pulled her close to him. She wrapped her arms around his chest and felt him slide off the edge of the desk and up against her. After what seemed like minutes, they came up for air and Sam answered her last question, courteous to a fault.

"Yes," he said.

It was then that the first of the growing sounds from the other side of the window wall penetrated to them. It was a measure of their distraction that that sound was a piercing shriek.

"See?" Shelley was screeching. "See? I told you so! I told you something was going on!"

[2]

Sister Mary Scholastica had been present at the scene of a murder before. She knew how long it took for the police to get organized, for the evidence to be collected, for the discussions to take place that would provide the foundation for the investigation to come after. Most of all, she knew how boring it was for the bystanders, innocent or otherwise. There was nothing any of them could do but sit and wait—and it wasn't like a hospital wait, either. Nobody was hovering in the background, promising to provide them with information as soon as it was available. Nobody thought they had any right to any information at all. They were supposed to keep their mouths shut and their bodies out of the way, until they were called. Then they were supposed to answer questions, not ask them.

That nobody else at the Motherhouse understood these simple rules of procedure was obvious from the way they were behaving. Reverend Mother General had put Scholastica in charge of "keeping order for this unusual day" because she'd had experience—Reverend Mother General herself was going to be busy on the phone to the Chancery, making arrangements for one thing and another with the Archdiocese—but the result of it was that the Sisters were taking their frustrations out on Scholastica instead of on the police. They wanted to know what was going on and were angry with Scholastica because she wouldn't tell them. They wanted to understand how Don Bollander's death connected to Brigit Ann Reilly's and were angry with Scholastica when she didn't know. Maybe *angry* was too strong a word. Nuns trained under the old dispensation—and most of the nuns at the Motherhouse had been trained under the old dispensation—had their emotions well under control. Not one of them would have dreamed of shouting or making a scene. They were just all putting out little electric charges of tension into the air. Scholastica felt it as a sharp stinging on her skin, a sure sign that she was under too much stress. She used to feel the same thing when she'd had to take math tests in high school, and all day every day during her postulant year.

Directly after lunch, Scholastica had put her postulants to work folding form letters and stuffing them into envelopes. The form letters were requests for help in establishing a case for the canonization of Margaret Finney, and were going out to the Motherhouse's entire mailing list, a group of nearly 15,000 people. Major benefactors and small donors, women who had once been members of the order, women who had come for formation but left before taking vows, women who had written with interest but decided not to come or been turned down, former students, former lay teachers, former employees, women who had come on retreat or for the special seminars the order held twice a year on women and theology—it was incredible how many different categories of people were connected to a Motherhouse, or how much work it took to contact them all at once. Scholastica thought she'd given her girls enough to do to last them for the rest of the day, and when she looked in on them at three fifteen she saw she had been right. She had put them in the big sewing room. In the old days, when the Sisters had worn a distinctive long habit that had to be made by hand and there had been 3,000 Sisters who needed two habits each, this room had served the Sister Seamstress and her assistants. Now, with the dress of their modified habit bought from a supply house and only their veils made on the premises, it was mostly empty. Scholastica found it cheered her up enormously to see the room full and busy again. She counted heads and came up with one missing. She searched faces and saw that Neila Connelly was not in the room. Then she made herself calm down. She couldn't panic like this every time she couldn't lay eyes at will on one of her postulants. She'd go crazy. They had to visit the bathroom in peace periodically.

She went back into the corridor and walked west toward her office and Alice Marie's. Alice Marie's door was open and she was sitting at her desk. Scholastica stuck her head in, looked at the phone and winced.

"Has it been bad?" she asked. "I heard you when I came through a few minutes ago. You were using that tone of voice you have that sounds like you're trying to explain nuclear physics to a five-year-old."

"I was talking to Thoma Andreotti's mother." Alice Marie sighed. "I can tell you when the news hit the network television stations," she said. "At the one fifteen news break. How do they get on to these things so fast?"

"They were already on to it," Scholastica said. "I mean, they were looking out for any more news about Brigit. They saw the name of the town, they saw the name of the convent, they saw it was a murder—"

"I see what you mean. Well, however it works, it certainly was fast. And I don't know what to say to these people. I don't feel right telling them their daughters are perfectly safe. I don't know what's going on."

"I don't either," Scholastica said quickly.

"I know you don't. You know Gregor Demarkian, though. Maybe you could get him to tell you something."

Scholastica didn't think it was possible to get Gregor Demarkian to say anything he didn't want to say, and she didn't think she knew him all that well. She fiddled with the rosary at her belt and said, "He's gone home. To the inn, I mean. At least, that's what he told Reverend

Mother. The police have locked up the stairwell and gone home, too."

"And I'm left here fielding phone calls."

"Do they want to take their daughters home?"

"Yes, to put it bluntly. Of course, their daughters are eighteen years old and legal adults in New York State, but you know how these things are. I'm not too worried about the novices. Once the girls get into habit, the parents tend to calm down a little. But the postulants—"

"Sheila Cormier and Martha Eggars," Scholastica said. "They're both on the brink of leaving anyway. I'm on the brink of throwing Martha out."

"Martha," Alice Marie said thoughtfully. "The sexual hysteric?"

"Classic case," Scholastica agreed.

"I know how it is. You want to give everybody the benefit of the doubt and you end up putting up with much more than you have to. You can ask Martha Eggars to leave. Count yourself lucky to have such a large class of normal ones to go on."

"I will."

The phone on Alice Marie's desk rang. She picked it up, said hello, and stretched her mouth into a placating smile. Then she looked up at Scholastica and shrugged.

"Yes, of course," she said into the phone. "You're Sister Beata's mother and I met you at the memorial Mass for the Vietnam War dead. I remember you very well."

It wasn't, Scholastica thought, a pleasant memory. She mouthed "see you later" at the top of Alice Marie's head and went back into the corridor, heading again for her own office. She tried to remember Sister Beata and couldn't. A canonical novice, probably. The canonical novices spent a lot of time on their own, practicing silence and trying to get their religious lives into shape. After all, that was supposed to be the point. It wasn't the teaching or the nursing or the missionary work that you did that mattered. It was your relationship with God.

Scholastica's office was at the end of the corridor

with the door in it. She made a slight bow to the crucifix and turned in at her own door. Her desk was clean of all papers. Her visitor's chair was placed three-quarters of the way along the front of the desk from the door side of the room. The statue of the Blessed Virgin Mary was at the very center of the top of her filing cabinet and hadn't been moved at all. To Scholastica, it was painfully obvious that she had spent very little of this day in this room.

She went in, sat down at her desk, and opened up the center drawer. There were pens and pencils in there, good cheap sensible Bics and Eagles. There were paper clips in there, too, and a small squeeze bottle of glue. There was a little stack of holy cards bound together by a rubber band and a small box with three plastic rosaries in it. The plastic rosaries were the kind the parish used to give out to children making their first Holy Communion when she was principal at St. Agnes's. She closed the drawer again and sighed.

She was being an idiot. Old Sister Jerome had been right. If you're worried about something you can't do anything about, you've got to go out and find something to take your mind off it. Scholastica didn't know what. Saturday was always a dead day at the Motherhouse, especially in Lent. There were things to be done for St. Patrick's Day and the Cardinal's visit, but she was too distracted to do them. She heard a knock on the frame of her door and looked up.

"Yes?" she said.

A head peeked through, Neila Connelly's head, looking worried.

"Sister?" she said.

"Come in, Neila. I'm glad to see you. I looked into the sewing room a few minutes ago and you weren't there. I was worried. I suppose I'm getting hypersensitive with all this business."

"Yes, Sister."

"Come in."

Neila finally made up her mind and came in. She looked even more tired than Alice Marie had, and a good deal more worried. Scholastica thought she was still grieving for Brigit and had a right to a few sleepless nights. Now she probably wants to talk it all out, Scholastica thought, and that made sense, too. Scholastica had been expecting Neila to show up at her office door to have it out for days now.

"Sit down," Scholastica said.

Neila had made it halfway across the office from the door. Now she scurried the rest of the way to the chair and sat. She folded her hands in her lap and looked down at them. She crossed her feet at the ankles and hunched her shoulders. She looked thoroughly miserable.

"Sister," she said, "do you know all that stuff you were telling us the other day, about religious obedience? And how Christ was obedient to God unto death?"

"Yes, Neila, but I think I also said that none of you were likely to be called on to be obedient unto death. This order doesn't send Sisters into Communist China."

"I know. What I want to know is, how can you tell if God's asking you to do something?"

Oh, no, Scholastica thought. Not this. Not from Neila. Neila was her best hope in the whole postulant class. It wasn't that Scholastica didn't think it was a sensible question. It was a much better question than that. It was just that she knew what it usually meant when it was asked by postulants, and that wasn't sensible at all.

"Neila," she said carefully, "if you think God has been talking to you—"

Neila's head shot up. "It's not me," she said desperately. "I went to confession and I tried to explain it to Father Fitzsimmons and he just didn't understand. Nobody understands. It's not me I'm talking about."

"Who are you talking about?" Scholastica was bewildered.

"Brigit, of course. Brigit said that it was all right, doing what she did, because she went to God and he told her—I don't remember how it worked. It was crazy. But she said it was God and I didn't like to tattle and then she was dead and I didn't know what—"

"Stop," Scholastica said. "Go back to the beginning. What did Brigit do?"

Neila stared at her hands. "She stole one of the postulants' dresses, the extra ones we keep for emergencies—I guess I don't mean stole it. She took it."

"But why? If she needed a new dress we'd just—"

"It wasn't for her," Neila said. "It was a different size. I don't know what size but bigger than hers because she was saying she couldn't use one of her own because it would never fit. And she took it with her the day she died wrapped up under her own clothes and she was supposed to deliver it to somebody down on Diamond Place or Clare Avenue and when I heard that on the news about Sam Harrigan saying he'd seen her there I thought it was right and then I was sure, I really am sure, that that was why she ended up being killed and now there's been another one and where's the extra postulant's dress? Where is it?"

"Calm down," Scholastica said. "Calm down."

"I can't calm down."

"You have to calm down," Scholastica told her. "I'm going to call Mr. Demarkian back here and you're going to tell him everything you told me. Everything."

As far as Scholastica was concerned, Neila was going to tell Demarkian a good deal more than that. She was going to tell everybody a good deal more than that. It was vital.

For the first time since the day Brigit Ann Reilly died, Scholastica felt she was finally doing something.

Six

[1]

"I called you," Bennis Hannaford said, after Gregor had managed to detach himself from the clutches of the woman at the desk, get up to his room, and get through to Cavanaugh Street on AT&T, "because Lida called old George Tekamanian, and old George Tekamanian called Father Tibor, and Father Tibor called me. And even then I would have left you alone, except that Father Tibor said he was going to call me back."

Gregor's room was on the second floor and large, a big square wood-paneled space with a fireplace. There was an oversize closet and a bathroom with too much equipment in it. The tub was some kind of a whirlpool and the stall shower had knobs and hoses and spouts for functions Gregor couldn't begin to imagine. The phone was a Princess, which always made Gregor feel as if he were being asked to talk into a child's toy version of a boomerang. He shrugged off his jacket and tucked the receiver between his ear and his shirt. Then he went to work on his tie.

"I take it Lida heard the news on television," he said. "Would you mind telling me which news?"

"It was some kind of press conference. Cardinal O'Bannion—"

"Oh."

"Oh?"

"Well, it could have been worse."

"If you mean she could have seen the reports of a second murder in Maryville, she did," Bennis said. "So did I. It made the newsbreak at one. Even you don't manage to get instant publicity, Gregor. It's very curious. Do you want me to come up?"

"No."

"Be glad I'm working. If I weren't, I'd hop in my car and come up anyway."

She probably would have, too. Gregor threw his tie on the bed, realized it seemed to have unraveled itself into threads, and threw it in the wastebasket. Then he said "just a minute," put the phone down on the bed, and took off his shirt. As soon as Bennis got off the phone, he wanted to take a shower, to help himself think. Not that there was much to think about—he was fairly sure he had figured out everything he could figure out from what he had so far. The problem was to discover how he could find out the rest of what he needed to know. In the cases he had handled since his retirement, he had always been faced with inverted pyramid investigations, situations in which he knew the people first and only then worked his way down to the hard small core of the murder. This case was more like real police work. Here was the murder. The people, with the exception of Sister Scholastica, were just so many names on a list of possibilities.

He picked up the phone again, kicked off his shoes, wedged the receiver between his ear and his arm, and went to work on his socks.

"It really is very strange," Bennis was saying again, "about all this publicity. I mean, even when you were up at my mother's house, investigating a lot of rich people on the Main Line, you didn't get this kind of play, and I thought the media liked rich people."

"They like bizarre death even better," Gregor pointed out. "And these deaths were certainly bizarre. At least, they looked bizarre. All those snakes."

"That sounds bizarre enough to me," Bennis said drily.

"I know, but it's the simplest thing. I figured that out before O'Bannion ever got in touch with me. Standing in the lobby of the Hilton Hotel in Manhattan, looking at Schatzy's copy of *People* magazine. Body heat."

"What?"

"Body heat," Gregor repeated. "Snakes don't make their own. In cold weather they hibernate. In warm weather they like to stay in the sun as much as possible. These snakes had been wandering around in a false spring and it was suddenly beginning to get cold again, so they—"

"Wait a minute," Bennis said. "Are you telling me she was *alive*? That girl? While the snakes were—crawling on her?"

"When they first crawled on her, yes," Gregor said. "She would have had to have been, I'd think. Or at least not very long dead, not more than say half an hour or so. I don't think she was conscious, though."

"Wonderful."

"It's the only way it makes sense." Gregor had his socks off and his belt unbuckled. He let his pants fall to the floor. Sitting on top of the rest of his clothes in his suitcase was a yellow terry cloth robe Bennis had bought him for his birthday, bringing it all the way from Paris after she'd paid a flying visit to France to—as she put it—"get her head together and drink." Gregor put this on, admired the thickness of the terry cloth and the textured smoothness of the hand-embroidered initial on the front pocket, and sat down on the edge of the bed.

"The problem with pieces of business like the snakes," he said, "is that they look strange and creative, but they're really very restrictive. You're stuck with two possible explanations. Either they were so necessary to whatever the murderer wanted to do, they amounted to the *only* way the murderer could get it done, and that wouldn't apply in this case—"

"Why not?"

"Because I don't know of any way on earth anyone could have made that happen," Gregor said. "Maybe there is a way. There's a man up here who used to be a herpetologist, Sam Harrigan—"

"Sam Harrigan the Fearless Epicure? I *know* Sam Harrigan the Fearless Epicure."

"You would. Anyway, I'll ask him, but I don't expect any surprises. Nobody could have made that happen. Therefore, it happened by accident and there must be a natural explanation for it. Therefore—"

"Body heat," Bennis said. She paused. "I see," she said slowly. "And where the snakes came from isn't so mysterious either, is it? From what I remember, Sam Harrigan likes to keep snakes and other animals around."

"He isn't the only one. The snakes, by the way, had been depoisoned or whatever you do to them to make them harmless without taking out their fangs. So. According to the Cardinal, Mr. Harrigan keeps snakes. And according to Sister Scholastica, a woman named Miriam Bailey who owns the local bank also owns a very young husband, and one of the toys she's bought him is a menagerie. Sister Scholastica has never seen it, but I think I can reasonably suppose that some of the animals it might contain might be snakes. I'm putting that badly, but you see what I mean."

"I see what you mean. How old is this Miriam Bailey to make you sound so much like a Puritan when you mention her husband? How old is her husband? What are they like?"

When are you going to get your mind off sex? Gregor wondered. He said, "Miriam Bailey is in her sixties, I think. Her husband is twenty-five. At least three people have told me that. I don't know what either one of them is like. I haven't met them."

"You haven't met them?"

"I haven't met anybody." Gregor sighed. "I got here. I went up to the Motherhouse—before even checking into this hotel, mind you; the Cardinal's driver did that for me—and there was another body on my doorstep. I feel like I'm doing one of those mystery jigsaw puzzles where they don't give you a picture of what the puzzle is supposed to end up looking like."

"Well, if I were you, I'd put this Miriam Bailey at the top of your suspect list, even if you haven't met her." Bennis laughed. "Old woman. Young man. Small local bank. It sounds like exactly the kind of thing that gives Federal regulators attacks of apoplexy."

"I agree. Unfortunately, I do not as yet know of any reason for that to lead to the death of Brigit Ann Reilly. The second victim was an employee of the bank—"

"Was he?"

"Oh, yes. In fact, someone—I think it was Pete Donovan, the local cop—told me he was Ms. Bailey's personal assistant. I've thought about it, Bennis, I truly have. If Miriam Bailey wanted to kill her own assistant, she had a hundred ways to do it that didn't involve sticking him in a laundry sink in the local convent—a difficult and risky thing to do, by the way."

"She might have been trying to direct attention away from herself."

"Sure," Gregor said, "but since she runs this bank, we have to assume that she is reasonably intelligent, and if she is reasonably intelligent, she has to realize that the attention would be right back on her in about three minutes, which it was. And that still leaves Brigit Ann Reilly, and the flood."

"What flood?"

Gregor sighed. "Go back to work, Bennis. You know more about trolls than you do about life. There was a flood up here the day Brigit Ann Reilly was killed, not a huge one, but substantial. There was enough warning for the town to get organized for evacuations and emergency services. If we assume Brigit Ann Reilly was alive either when or shortly before she was found—"

"Wait a minute," Bennis said. "What did she die from?"

"Coniine," Gregor told her, "hemlock. She was a small girl, according to my reports, and she wouldn't have eaten much that morning, so say it took about half an hour to start feeling sick, two hours to pass out and two and a half hours to die, that would mean she would have had to have been fed hemlock somewhere between ten and ten thirty, by which time everyone already knew the flood was coming—"

"Maybe our murderer thought the flood would cover it," Bennis said. "Maybe he thought the body would be found and everybody would think she'd been drowned."

"Maybe," Gregor said, "but I don't think so. I think Brigit Ann Reilly was killed that day because she had to be killed that day and no later. Don't ask me why. That's what it feels like."

"Mmm," Bennis said. There was the sound of a match popping into flame, and Gregor realized she was lighting a cigarette. He thought about giving her another lecture about how bad that was for her health and bit his tongue instead. Every time he lectured, she told him, "That argument only works on people who think the most important thing in life is health."

Gregor heard her take a drag and then blow out a stream of air. She always did that through pursed lips, as if she were trying to whistle. Sometimes she did whistle. It was odd, because she could never whistle when she wanted to.

"Well," she said, "you're right about one thing. I do know more about trolls than anything else, at least at the moment. I ought to go back to knowing about trolls, too. This manuscript is already overdue. I miss you."

"I miss you, too," Gregor said.

"I wish everybody would come back from vacation and liven the place up a little. It's spooky. I'm the only one of us in this building in residence, and I go look out my front window and Lida's house is all closed up. Can you imagine that? Lida's house all closed up. I keep expecting Zeus to fall from the Heavens."

"He won't," Gregor said. "Lida has all the windows open in her house down in Florida and by now she knows who in the neighborhood's having a baby and who's having an affair and she's taught Donna's Tommy at least fifteen new words, half of them in Armenian and—"

"Don't," Bennis said. "Just come back soon. I think

I'm going to call the rest of them up and tell them to come back soon, too. I'm getting lonely."

"You can't ask them to come back and keep you company when you're still refusing to leave your apartment," Gregor said reasonably.

"Yes, I can," Bennis told him. "Stop it with this. Finish up up there and come home. I'll talk to you later."

There was a click in his ear, and the phone went to dial tone. Gregor replaced the receiver in the cradle and looked at his bedspread, really an antiquey-looking quilt that was probably made of polyester and sprayed with Scotchgard to prevent stains. It was pretty anyway, but not as pretty as his quilt back home, which Elizabeth had made herself in the year before the year in which she died.

Gregor got up, went to the bathroom, and looked into the stall shower at all the knobs and hoses. He tried a couple of the knobs and found the one that operated the plain shower with no trouble at all. He took off his robe and threw it over the edge of the sink.

Maybe, he thought, he should have told Bennis about the locked-room problem, even though he didn't think it was going to turn out to be a locked-room problem, in the long run. Bennis was good at things like that. He often picked her brains when he was having trouble with his cases, in spite of the fact that he worked overtime to keep her physically out of the cases themselves. As Father Tibor Kasparian was always saying, nobody with any brains wanted to put Bennis near any real danger. She'd open her arms and embrace it. She had no sense of self-preservation whatsoever. On the other hand—

He was just taking off his watch and laying it on the little glass shelf above the toilet when the phone rang again. He grabbed for his robe—he was of a generation that had been taught to be modest even in private—and headed back for the main room, where the Princess phone sat looking ridiculous on an oversize mahogany bedside table. He picked up and said, "Yes?"—causing himself to be immediately subjected to a high excited voice delivering a monologue that was half message and half stream-of-consciousness narrative. He knew that voice and that monologue very well, even though he had heard it for the first time less than half an hour ago. They belonged to Mrs. Edith—Gregor couldn't remember Mrs. Edith what. He didn't know if he'd ever known it. He only knew that for the next few days, she was his landlady. He'd never had a better reason to finish a case and finish it fast.

"Oh, Mr. Demarkian," Edith was screeching. "I'm so glad I found you, you have no idea, I get so nervous being handed these important responsibilities but, of course, that doesn't matter, I want to do the best I can for the Cardinal, the Cardinal only has to ask and now there's a visitor for you down in the lobby and I need to know if you're supposed to see him at all although, of course, I'd think you are, since it's Father Doherty and Father Doherty—"

Gregor didn't wait to find out if Father Doherty was a saint or a sinner, the Cardinal's right-hand man or the local leader of the forces of the Antichrist. It would have taken too much time. He interrupted Edith, told her to ask Father Doherty to wait downstairs for ten or fifteen minutes, and hung up. Then he headed back for the shower.

[2]

For some reason, Gregor had not expected Father Michael Doherty—it was Michael; Edith had managed to get that in at the end—to be a serious man. Maybe he had heard too much the last couple of days about false reports and Brigit sightings, about the localized panic and hysteria that ripples through any small town in the wake of a violent death. Maybe he was still too much a creature of Washington and cities like it, caught in the (false) assumption that real heavyweights do not "bury" themselves in the backwaters. As soon as he saw Michael Doherty, Gregor knew he had a heavyweight. It was all over the man's face, and especially his eyes. Here was a man who had not only "seen something of the world"—any damn fool could do that for the price of a plane ticket—but who had seen into it. Here was a man Father Tibor Kasparian would like.

Michael Doherty was sitting under an amber- and yellow-shaded, mock-Tiffany reading lamp in an equally mock-leather armchair across from the reception desk, reading a copy of *Time*. When the elevator doors opened to let Gregor out, he looked up and smiled. Then his smile grew wider, and Gregor understood why at once. Father Michael Doherty was dressed in a pair of twill pants, a button-down shirt left open at the neck to reveal a Roman collar and a good wool sweater. Except for the Roman collar, Gregor was dressed in exactly the same way. It was a style of dress adopted universally by a certain class of American middle-aged male, what Bennis always called "the Harrison Ford look." They both seemed to have declared themselves members of that class with a vengeance.

Gregor walked out of the elevator and across the reception room floor. Michael Doherty stood up and held out his hand.

"Mr. Demarkian," he said. "I'm sorry to bother you. I'm Father Michael Doherty."

"You call yourself Father," Gregor said.

"I've never really understood the men who don't," Doherty answered. "You do all that work to get through the seminary, all that work to get ordained. Well, maybe that's because I came to it late. I think we'd better go into the lounge, if you don't mind. I could use a beer and we could both use a place where Edith can't eavesdrop."

"Is there such a place?"

"Several. But don't count on the rooms. I think they're bugged." Doherty walked toward the reception desk, toward the left of which was a frosted glass door. "It's right through here," he said. "It's very nice, really, and I almost never get a chance for a beer and a talk away from work anymore. Come along with me."

Gregor came along with him, a little apprehensive

that what he was going to find behind the frosted glass
was a hoked-up replica of an Irish saloon or a New York
City Irish neighborhood bar. He found instead a plain
place with a large fireplace in it, too many scarred
wooden tables, and a scattering of the same St. Patrick's
Day decorations that had infested the rest of Maryville.
Gregor was getting so used to those, he hardly noticed
them. There was a candle in the shape of a leprechaun
on their table and a tiny basket full of silk shamrocks.
Gregor pushed them out of the way as soon as he sat
down and asked the waitress who seemed to be hovering
just over his head for a glass of red wine. Father Doherty
asked not simply for a beer, but for a St. Pauli Girl.
Gregor thought about what Jack O'Brien had said, about
Father Doherty and Doherty Lumber.

The waitress brought their drinks, smiled at Gregor
and told Michael Doherty to have a good day, and
disappeared in haste. Doherty watched her go and said,
"It's one of the great advantages of being a Catholic
priest in a town like this. The service is always outstand-
ing. Of course, if you don't watch yourself, you could end
up thinking you were one step better than God."

Gregor shook his head. "According to the Cardinal,
that's not really true. According to the Cardinal, there's
been more than a little trouble on the religious front up
here in the last few years."

"If you mean garden-variety anti-Catholicism,
there's been some," Doherty admitted, "but not in town.
You get that mostly from the region around us, the small
farming communities with heavy enrollments in scattershot fundamentalist sects. And I do mean scattershot.
This is not the Southern Baptist Convention we're
talking about here. This is single churches with no
connections to any organized denomination, run by
pastors who've ordained themselves because that's the
best way they can think of to make a little bit better
living than they could have doing factory work in
Colchester. Their parishioners are poor and scared and
undereducated and probably on the whole not very
bright, and they have been known to get both nasty and

violent—but on the whole I don't worry about them. Quite frankly, on the whole I think they're sad but harmless."

Gregor took a sip of wine. "Tell me," he said thoughtfully, "do you think the rest of the Catholics in Maryville would agree with you? What about the rest of the priests? What about Father—is it Fitzsimmons?"

"Barry Fitzsimmons at Iggy Loy?" Doherty grinned. "Let's just say if he held any other opinion on this one, I would have heard about it. Everybody would have heard about it. That's what Barry's like."

"And the rest?"

Doherty took a long draft of beer and poured some more from the bottle into his glass. "There are two more," he said, "and we all see each other fairly regularly. I haven't heard anything about any anti-Catholic activity of any kind, serious or not, from any of them. Why? Did you have a reason for thinking there would be?"

Gregor thought of the letters the Cardinal had received and the letter—as well as the snake—that had been delivered to Reverend Mother this morning. He said, "There's a young girl dead and she was training to join a religious order. There's a man dead, too, and he was found in that religious order's utility room. Those two things seem to me to be enough reason to at least consider the possibility that what we have here is some kind of antireligious mania."

"I suppose they are," Doherty said. "All I can tell you is, I haven't seen anything of the kind. To tell you the truth, it's been quiet on every front I can think of over the last few months. I work down in a parish called St. Andrew's—"

"I know about St. Andrew's," Gregor told him. "Sister Scholastica was explaining it to me. Poor parish, mostly Hispanic immigrant population. Lots of programs, literacy classes, and a clinic."

"That's right. Also citizenship classes and, believe it or not, a parish school. Don't ask me how we keep it running, because I don't know. Bless those nuns. From time to time we get some know-nothing activity, anti-immigrant, antiforeigner stuff, but not recently. Recently, even the dope sales have been down."

"Hmm," Gregor said.

Doherty shifted a little in his chair. The lights in the lounge were so dim, and the windows so carefully tinted, it felt like the middle of the night instead of the middle of the afternoon. Doherty coughed into the side of his fist and said, "Mr. Demarkian, I came here because—no, let me put it another way. I know, because I read my local newspaper and because I spend a good deal of my time talking to Glinda Daniels, who's been a friend of mine for years, anyway, I know all about the people who have come forward to say they saw Brigit Ann Reilly on the day she died. I know that most of them are fantasizing. I know that, from your perspective, reports of that kind are probably less than worthless, but I really did have to come—"

"You mean you saw Brigit Ann Reilly too?" Gregor wanted to add that if Father Doherty said he'd seen her, Gregor would believe he'd seen her. Father Doherty was a believable man.

Father Doherty was shaking his head. "Not exactly," he told Gregor. "Hear me out. St. Andrew's parish is down near the river. All the really bad parts of town are. On the day of the flood, I got worried early. I started packing us up well before noon. I didn't want to take any chances. We have a lot of old people in our parish. You know how it is. The young men come here and work until they can bring their parents over and then their brothers and sisters and then their aunts and uncles and then their grandparents. The Irish did it and the Armenians did it and I suppose other people than these will do it in the future. You end up with a lot of old people being supported by fewer younger ones and everybody living in a small space, and the old people aren't like the people here who live to be old. They're feeble and they're sick. That makes them hard to move. So, around about eleven thirty or so, when the rain was coming down in torrents, I made a few phone calls and got ready to evacuate. I got a bunch of the boys together and Sister Gabriel—she's a nurse. She's between assignments and the Motherhouse loans her out to me for the clinic—anyway, I got us all together, told Barry Fitzsimmons to get ready for us in the auditorium at Iggy Loy, and sent the boys out to search the apartments in the buildings around us and make sure we didn't forget anyone. Then I had to wait for a phone call, so I stayed in my office, just sort of standing there, and that was when I saw the nun."

"Nun?"

Michael Doherty took a deep breath. "Postulant. Whatever. I recognized the dress. She came down Beckner Street, straight at me as if she were headed for the church, and she made me very nervous. I mean, what was she doing down there, in that weather? What could she be doing? So I left my office and went out to intercept her. I got to the front door of the church and she was gone, except that I thought I saw a piece of black cloth disappearing through the door of Number Thirty-seven."

"I see," Gregor said slowly. "And you think this figure in black may have been Brigit Ann Reilly."

"No," Father Doherty said.

"What?" Gregor asked him.

Doherty took a long draft on his beer and slammed the glass onto the table in front of him. "I'm away on most program nights, visiting the prison. There are half a dozen postulants who volunteer in the programs at St. Andrew's that I've never seen. Brigit Ann Reilly was something else again. Brigit Ann Reilly didn't volunteer in the literacy program last month. She worked on my liturgical committee. She would have been on my liturgical committee this month, too, because she was good at it, except that she developed a violent crush on me and I had to cool it off. I knew Brigit Ann Reilly very well. And let me tell you, Mr. Demarkian, whoever that postulant was, walking down Beckner Street just after eleven thirty on the morning Brigit Ann Reilly died, it wasn't Brigit Ann Reilly."

Part Three

One

❖

[1]

If Edith had been a different kind of woman, Gregor Demarkian would have gone back to his room by crossing in front of the reception desk and taking the elevator. If he had, he would have been handed the messages waiting for him in his box. One of those messages was from Sister Mary Scholastica. It asked him to come to the convent and gave him a sketch of what the schedule was like there. In spite of the relatively relaxed atmosphere at the Motherhouse in these days following Vatican II, there was a religious schedule there and it did have to be followed. The other messages were mostly from people whose names he wouldn't have recognized. Since the Cardinal's press conference—why the Cardinal always had to hold a press conference, no matter what, was beyond Gregor's power to understand—the full force of Maryville's fantasies of conspiracy and violence had been turned in his direction. The St. Mary's Inn was the only decent place to stay in town. If you wanted something else and weren't interested in drunks or squalor, you had to go out to the Ramada Inn on the other side of the highway. It had taken no time at all for Maryville's most determined conspiracy theorists to find out where Gregor was staying.

Because Edith was the kind of woman she was and because Gregor couldn't stand the idea of being screeched at one more time, however, he took the back stairs both going back up and coming back down, avoiding reception altogether. One of the things the Bureau had taught him was to find secondary exits immediately. He had noticed the fire door at the back of the hall on his room floor when he had first been brought upstairs by Edith and the fire door at the end of the hall leading to the downstairs men's room when he'd been saying good-bye to Father Doherty. Fire doors almost always meant stairs. Gregor was always surprised with what had stayed with him. "Always find a secondary exit" was a rule for a field agent, and he hadn't been a field agent for ten years before his retirement. "Always organize your complaints on paper" was a rule for administrators, and he had forgotten how to carry out that one on the day he handed in his resignation.

After he left Father Doherty, he ran up to his room, grabbed the heavy brown leather jacket Lida Arkmajian had given him for his birthday, and ran down again. Then he left the St. Mary's Inn and started heading even farther down the slope of Delaney Street. Eventually he wanted to head up and back to the Motherhouse, but not yet. All he needed to do up there was to check his suppositions. Right now he wanted to go to the library, where he might actually find out something new.

It wasn't a very long walk. In fact, in Gregor's estimation, the entire stretch from the Motherhouse gate to the library's main doors was barely twelve full city blocks. It was a short enough distance to travel, and it made the "sightings" a little more forgivable. There was something eerie about a girl disappearing along a walk as short as that and showing up dead. It wasn't a deserted walk, either. Gregor tried to think of Brigit walking—staggering, really—anywhere on Delaney Street after she had been poisoned, close to the end. He couldn't do it. Even in the flood, somebody would have been around to see her. Delaney Street was lined with public buildings and small stores with apartments above them. Glinda Daniels had just been closing up the library when she found the body. Surely somebody would have been around on the street in the half hour or so before that, when Brigit must have been on her way to the storeroom, by one means or another. No, either Brigit Ann Reilly walked to her place of dying on a road other than this one, or she was brought there in a vehicle and dumped. Gregor was a little shocked to realize that the problem he was considering now was essentially the same one he had been considering earlier this afternoon, when he had been talking to Pete Donovan about the death of Don Bollander. In each case, he had a body dumped someplace where, on reflection, it couldn't be. With Bollander, that had been all too obvious. With Brigit Ann Reilly, it hadn't even been considered, because there had been too much else to think about. The snakes, the flood—Gregor was nearly at the library doors now and he shuddered. Where was the storeroom door? If it was anywhere in sight of these doors he was headed for now, getting Brigit Ann Reilly through it, conscious or unconscious, would have been damn near impossible. If it was around the back—he would have to go around the back.

He stepped up to the main doors and let them slide open in front of him, gliding smoothly in their tracks. He watched with his mind half on something else as the smoked glass gave way to a typical small-town scene, with children sitting in a ring around a reader in the children's section and two teenagers fumbling with the card catalog and a middle-aged woman with a stack of romance novels checking out at the desk. The Norman Rockwell picture was entrancing, and for a moment it obscured what else was going on in the Maryville Public Library. Gregor Demarkian was not one of those people who believed that Norman Rockwell had painted a false-faced, cotton candy, never-existing world. He had known dozens of Norman Rockwell families and Norman Rockwell towns in his career. This just didn't happen to be one of either.

The disturbance was being caused by a very small woman with bright red hair. When the main doors had opened for Gregor, she had been momentarily silent. By the time he stepped inside, she was being silent no longer. She was standing at the check-out desk in a bright green toggle-fronted cashmere car coat, pounding her fist against the desk's blond wood. Since every one of her fingers had rings on them, every pound she made gave off metallic echoes.

"I don't care where she is or what she's doing," she was shouting, "I want to talk to that little bitch right now!"

It should have ended right there, because the girl behind the check-out desk was being stubborn. Gregor could see the lines of mulishness in her young, plain face and a secret satisfaction. In some way Gregor couldn't understand yet, these roles were being reversed. In most encounters between these two, it was the red-haired woman who would be winning. The girl at the desk crossed her arms over her chest and said,

"Miss Daniels is out. I don't know where she is. I don't know how to get in touch with her."

"This is Maryville," the red-haired woman screeched, "not New York. There aren't all that many places she could be."

"Maybe she isn't even in Maryville."

"Maybe's she's gone off to have hormone injections," the red-haired woman said. "That's the only thing I can think of that would turn that desiccated old bitch into a woman."

"No she's not," the girl behind the counter said in a kind of hysterical triumphancy. "No, she's not, she's—"

There was an office behind the check-out desk with a window wall in it. Gregor had noticed it when he first walked in. Now he saw a door at the back of it open and a woman come through. She was only five feet four and solidly built, but there was a magnificence about her that caught at Gregor immediately. It caught at the red-haired woman, too. Finally, even the girl at the check-out desk felt it. She turned her back to the red-haired woman and stared.

"Well," the red-haired woman said finally. "There she is. Maryville's answer to Liz Smith."

"Oh, Miss Daniels," the girl at the check-out desk said. "I didn't mean you to overhear. I was just going to send her right out of here."

Glinda Daniels passed through the office door into the library proper, walked up to the check-out desk, patted the girl there on the shoulder ("That's all right, Shelley, I'll take it from here") and surveyed the room over the red-haired woman's head. She paused when she came to Gregor and when she came to the older woman standing a few feet from him. She didn't pause long enough in either case to make Gregor feel he should speak. Then she turned her attention to her assailant and sighed.

"For God's sake, Ann-Harriet," she said, "what do you think you're doing? You know it's just Miriam getting you all worked up again."

[2]

"Her name is Ann-Harriet Severan," Glinda Daniels told Gregor twenty minutes later, when she had the library calmed down, Ann-Harriet off the premises and the patrons back to looking through the books. She'd even managed to get Shelley at the desk to calm down and go back to work. That was a good thing, because there was no place in the library for a private talk but that office with the window wall in it and they needed Shelley to run interference. Otherwise, half the people in town were going to want to have their own personal private conversation with Glinda Daniels, just as they had all week. Along with Gregor, Glinda had brought in the old woman Gregor had noticed outside, introducing her as "Mrs. Barbara Keel." Mrs. Barbara Keel had told Gregor to call her "The Library Lady." "Mrs. Keel was with me when I found Brigit's body," Glinda explained. "She was supposed to be in the rest home getting over it for at least another week, but here she is."

"I get bored," Mrs. Keel said.

"I would too," Gregor told her.

Glinda had been making coffee in one of those Dripmaster automatic coffee makers. Now she picked up the glass pitcher, poured coffee into a plastic foam cup and two stout mugs, and handed them out. Gregor got the plastic foam cup. Mrs. Keel got the mug with the teddy bear on it. Glinda got the red mug with a picture of a lizard etched in gold on one side and "The Fearless Gourmet" etched in gold on the other. When she put it down on her desk she said, "Sam brought it in for me when I broke my old one last week," and shook her head in wonder. Mrs. Keel ignored her and put a quarter cup of milk and ten packets of sugar in her coffee.

"Anyway," Glinda said finally, "as I was saying. Her name is Ann-Harriet Severan and she's one side of our local triangle. I don't know if you've heard anything about this—"

"I think I have," Gregor told her. "A woman named Miriam Bailey, who owns the local bank and is in her sixties, married a much younger man named—I can't remember what he's named—"

"Joshua Malley," Mrs. Keel said brightly.

"Thank you. Miss Bailey married Mr. Malley and Mr. Malley proceeded to behave like a normal young man and took up with a young lady. That, I take it, was the young lady."

"Ann-Harriet Severan," Glinda repeated. "Right. When the police let it out that Brigit had probably been murdered, a lot of people in town said it was the wrong murder. None of us would have been surprised to wake up one morning and find Miriam dead and Ann Harriet standing over the body with a knife in her hand. Maybe it will happen yet."

"Why would Ann-Harriet be the one with the knife in her hand?" Gregor asked. "Wouldn't it be more to the point if it was Mr. Malley?"

Glinda waved this away. "Josh would never have the stomach for it. I don't know if you've met him—"

"I saw him when I was walking on Delaney Street earlier. He was with a woman I think was Miss Bailey. He was whining."

"You mean you haven't met Miriam Bailey yet?" Glinda was surprised. "Maybe she's more worried about her marriage than I thought. Usually when the Cardinal sends someone into town, she has them stay at her house and chauffeurs them all over town."

"Maybe I'm not famous."

"You're famous enough. Good Lord. The woman must be off her feed."

"What did you mean when you said she must be more worried about her marriage than you thought?" Gregor asked. "I'd think that if her husband is having an affair with a younger woman, she was bound to be worried."

"Why?" Mrs. Keel demanded. "She's the one with the money, you know. He doesn't have any."

Glinda Daniels laughed. "Barbara's right. Miriam found Josh in Greece somewhere, looking pretty and hanging around. She married him out there and brought him home from vacation, just like that. It was so unlike her, the whole town was in shock for a month. Then Josh took up with Ann-Harriet, and we all held our breaths, but Miriam just went right back to being Miriam. The only thing she does is goad Ann-Harriet the way she did today, put the pressure on. Did you know that Ann-Harriet works for Miriam's bank?"

"No."

"Well," Glinda said, "it's the only bank to work for around here, really, unless you want to go to a branch of Citibank or Chase. And Ann-Harriet can't afford to quit because her credit cards are all charged into the stratosphere and if she went without a job for a week she'd be bankrupt and jobs aren't that easy to come by around here. Anyway, Miriam drives Ann-Harriet nuts and Ann-Harriet runs around town driving everybody else nuts, and we're all just waiting for it. Not that Ann-Harriet would be the least bit interested in Josh if he wasn't due to come into Miriam's money—"

"Is he?"

"Who knows?" Glinda shrugged. "Somebody has to, and Miriam doesn't have any relations. She'll probably give a lot of it to the Church. You still have to expect she's left Josh some of it."

"They talk about it," Mrs. Keel said confidently. "That Joshua Malley and Ann-Harriet Severan. They talk about all the wonderful things they could do if Miriam was dead."

"Barbara hears things," Glinda said neutrally. Then she saw that her coffee cup was empty and got up to get herself some more. Gregor wondered what it was, that he always seemed to be attracted to people who drank too much coffee.

Glinda took hers black. She poured out and leaned against the cabinet where the coffee maker was. "I don't suppose all this is what you came here to talk to me about," she said. "I know you've been asked to investigate Brigit's death. I didn't see the press conference, but Sam told me about it."

"It looks like I'm also going to be investigating the death of Don Bollander," Gregor said. "Do you have any idea how those two deaths might link together?"

"Not the slightest. I can think of a couple of people who might like to have killed Don, including Ann-Harriet, by the way. Don served as Miriam's spy now and then. I can't think of anyone who would want to kill Brigit."

"He wasn't there the day of the flood," Mrs. Keel butted in. "In the back hall where I was, I mean. There was just Mr. Malley and Miss Severan and Miss Bailey. The other two didn't know Miss Bailey was there."

"Barbara was at the bank before she came to the library on the day Brigit died," Glinda said.

"I went to the ladies' room," Mrs. Keel said. "It's in a back hall there that goes behind the tellers. It was all a big mess because of the decorations for St. Patrick's Day and moving the money. And there they were."

"Necking in a packing crate," Glinda said.

"And there she was," Mrs. Keel said, "standing in the door that goes to the steps that go to the basement and the vault, looking at them going at it and laughing up her sleeve."

"She wasn't laughing," Glinda said. "She couldn't have been."

"She wanted to be," Mrs. Keel said. "Oh, you young people think you know everything. You think they're giving her a pain. Well, they make her laugh and that's the truth."

"She makes Ann-Harriet spit," Glinda said. "Never mind. Mr. Demarkian wants to know about Brigit."

Actually, although Gregor had every intention of going through the motions of asking Glinda Daniels all the proper questions about how and when and in what condition she had found the body, he didn't really need the answers she could give him. That was routine police work, and it was something Pete Donovan did well. He had fifteen solid pages of Glinda Daniels talking to Pete and other police officers about the snakes, the storeroom, and the body. There were other, more esoteric things he needed to know.

"What I want you to tell me," he said, "is how the storeroom works. How it's situated. What it opens onto. From what I remember, in the report I got it said the storeroom opened both into the main room of the library and onto the outside."

"That's right."

"Where on the outside?"

"To the back parking lot," Glinda said. "Some of the other people on staff—Cory especially—used to go right through there to their cars. Just lock up behind themselves, if you see what I mean. I always went through the front, no matter what the weather was like. Going through the back never seemed right to me somehow."

"A parking lot," Gregor said. "A parking lot is almost too convenient. It wouldn't happen to be shaded by evergreen trees, by any chance?"

"No. We have the lawn in the front and the hedge—a hemlock hedge, I'm told now—but in the back we have nothing. The parking lot takes up all the land the library has between the building and the street on that side, and on the other side the building comes right up to the sidewalk."

"What's out there? Stores? Houses?"

"There's a triple-decker house split into three apartments and a line of single-family row houses right across from the parking lot."

"Were they inhabited on the day Brigit Ann Reilly died? Had they been evacuated?"

"They were being evacuated just around the time Pete Donovan showed up to look at Brigit's body," Glinda told him. "I remember standing at the window in the ladies' room off my office, trying to stop heaving and watching the cars come down. We're in a deep hollow here, but we're well inland. I don't think anybody thought of the necessity of clearing us out until the last minute. Then the cars must have been freed up because everybody else was at Iggy Loy or the Motherhouse, and they came here."

"What cars?"

"All sorts of cars," Glinda said. "The Motherhouse sent vans. The bank sent half a dozen vehicles, including Miriam's Mercedes. Josh and Ann-Harriet were nowhere to be seen, by the way. And Sam sent his four-wheel drive. There were cars all over the place that day."

Gregor considered it. It was impossible to tell if this made his problem easier or harder. If the area was being evacuated *after* Pete Donovan arrived at the scene, then it had probably been full of people before Glinda discovered Brigit's body—and with the weather the way it was, those people had probably been spending a decent amount of time staring anxiously out their windows. It was almost like a dress rehearsal for the Bollander situation, full of the danger of sudden discovery, defined by heavy risks.

Gregor finished the coffee Glinda had given him and put down his cup. "All right," he said. "Let's move on to what you were going to tell me. You said something a little while ago about Don Bollander claiming to have seen Brigit Ann Reilly on the day she died."

Glinda sat up a little straighter. Gregor got the impression that this was the speech she had been steeling herself to give all day. "Half of everybody in town has been saying they saw Brigit on the day she died," she said, "so I didn't pay any attention to it at the time. Don was one of those people who love to think of themselves as insiders, but never quite are. But he came into the library a couple of days ago and said so. The problem was, it was the way I worked it out with Sam, he must have been making it up."

"Why?" Gregor asked her.

"He made up a lot of things," Barbara Keel said. She had been so quiet for so long, both Gregor and Glinda jumped. "He was a liar, that man was. A bad liar. He'd lie and then forget he'd lied."

"He did like stories," Glinda said, sounding a little doubtful. "Anyway, he said he saw her at quarter of one, coming out of the ladies' room in that hall at the bank where Barbara saw Josh and Ann-Harriet necking. But he couldn't have, could he? It was one o'clock when I found her. She had to have been already in the storeroom by quarter to."

"Not necessarily already in the storeroom," Gregor said slowly, "but already unconscious, I would think. She was dead when Pete Donovan got here. That was in the report."

"Oh, yes." Glinda shuddered. "Of course, that was before we knew the snakes belonged to Sam and weren't dangerous. It was terrible."

"I'm sure it was."

"She did have to be already in the storeroom by quarter to one," Glinda said. "She had to have time to get the snakes on her. Oh, I don't know. It's just the way I told you. Sam and I talked about it. The story is impossible. I can't see how he could have been killed for telling a story that wasn't true."

"Miss Daniels and Mr. Harrigan discuss a lot of things together," Mrs. Keel said blandly. "In private."

Glinda Daniels shot her an outraged look, but Barbara Keel didn't notice. She was busy searching through her handbag for nobody knew what.

"I think it's a very good idea, myself," she said,

"Miss Daniels and Mr. Harrigan. I think it's about time Miss Daniels got out and saw a little bit more of what there is in the world to make a happy life. And Mr. Harrigan is such a good man for the job, too, you know, so rich and so nice and so single and so Catholic."

"*Barbara,*" Glinda Daniels said.

"Well," Barbara Keel said, "you were the one who was kissing him in full view of half the town not four hours ago. I can't see why you'd mind us talking about it now."

"That's Sam coming in right now." Glinda Daniels sounded desperate. "And please, Barbara, try to remember that that scene you witnessed was his idea, not mine."

"It might have been his idea to start with," Barbara said imperturbably, "but it was yours by the time it was finished. You better go out and rescue him. That's Millie Verminck that's got hold of him and you know what she's like. By the time she's done with him, he'll be booked into giving speeches at women's clubs for a month."

"Oh, dear," Glinda Daniels said.

Gregor watched with some amusement as Glinda shot out of the office and through the gate in the reception desk, heading for Sam Harrigan and the round vigorous woman who had attached herself to him like a barnacle. Sam Harrigan would have been easy to recognize as a personage, even if Gregor hadn't found his face familiar from magazines and TV. He had that kind of presence. Gregor turned to Mrs. Keel and lifted his eyebrows.

"Did you just do that for fun," he asked her, "or did you have something you wanted to say to me in private?"

Barbara Keel was still hunting through her handbag. "Mr. Harrigan's going to come and tell you all about how Josh came to his house this morning. Joshua Malley, that is. I always call him Josh or Joshua Malley. I don't call him mister the way I might with anybody else."

"You don't like him?"

"I don't think Glinda is right," Mrs. Keel said,

"acting like Joshua isn't important. I don't think it's true. I think he's very important."

"To the women in his life."

"To one of the women in his life." She lifted her head and gave Gregor a fishy stare. "Are you one of those people who believe that people will kill for love?"

"What?"

"Are you one of those people who believe that people will kill for love," she repeated insistently. "I'm not. I believe people only kill for money. It really is true."

Glinda Daniels had managed to get Sam Harrigan separated from his tormentor. Now she brought him to the office door, shoved him inside, came in after him and closed the door behind her.

"Thank Heavens," she said. "That woman is some kind of vampire."

Sam Harrigan had his hand stuck out and a smile on his face. "Gregor Demarkian, I presume," he said, in a thick Scots burr that seemed to be getting thicker with every word.

Gregor decided the man was ill at ease and tried to change that. "I hear we have a mutual friend," he said. "Bennis Day Hannaford."

It worked. The smile on Sam Harrigan's face changed its character. His eyes lit up.

"Oh, that's wonderful," he said. "You know Bennis the Menace!"

Two

❖

[1]

To Sam Harrigan, anything that came between him and Glinda Daniels was a bad idea. Gregor Demarkian wasn't exactly coming between them, but he was there, a big tall bulk of a man standing in the middle of Glinda's office and reading the titles on the spines of the books she kept on the shelf behind her desk. When Sam had first walked into the library and seen him standing there, he had been a little alarmed. There was no way to determine anyone's size on television, not really. Sam had met Mr. T once and been disappointed. In the case of Gregor Demarkian, he had merely expected to be. Next to him, Glinda looked so damned small. Caught out there by Millie Verminck's chatter, Sam had been ready to rip up the carpet to protect her. Then she had come out of the office and rescued him. Now they were all back inside and Sam didn't know what to think.

Glinda was drinking down a cup of coffee as if it were a glass of orange juice and she had just run the Boston marathon. She had very bad habits like that with coffee and Sam intended to do something about them. Gregor Demarkian was leaning with one crooked arm against Glinda's filing cabinet, staring at The Library Lady with a very odd look on his face. Sam had heard that a lot of people dismissed him as stodgy or stupid or not very sophisticated. Sam was not about to make the

same mistake. Sam had spent too much of his life with
media people. Publicly funded media people were the
worst. Then there was Mrs. Barbara Keel, also known as
The Library Lady and one of the banes of Sam's existence. He kept tripping over her, and she never made
any sense. Now she was huddled in a chair, looking
lumpy and inert. From the look on Demarkian's face,
she had just told him something either important or
intrinsically fascinating. From the look on her own, it
was impossible to guess what.

Sam decided he was having stage fright and he had
to do something about it. He had laughed too hard and
boomed too loud at the mention of Bennis Hannaford's
name. Now he looked sideways at Glinda. She looked all
right, but he had no way of knowing what Demarkian
had been doing to her while he had been away, running
down to the store for a minute to get her a pack of cough
drops. He would have felt much better if they had
advanced on Demarkian on their own initiative, but he
couldn't see what they could have done beyond what
they had done. They'd called the St. Mary's Inn and
asked Edith if Demarkian was around. Edith being
Edith, she would know.

Of course, they had also spent half an hour in the
parking lot in the backseat of his Jeep Wagoneer,
necking like a pair of sixteen-year-olds, but there was
only so much Sam Harrigan intended to feel guilty about
not giving up in the pursuit of scientific solutions to local
murders. He grabbed one of Glinda's small metal chairs,
dragged it across the carpet to Gregor, and sat down on
it backwards, with his chin resting on the vinyl-covered
curve of its back.

"Well," he said.

"Well," Demarkian answered pleasantly.

This was not what Sam was looking for. He cleared
his throat. "Well," he said again, "has Glinda already told
you about her talk with Don Bollander? We were going
to come right over and tell you about it this afternoon,
but when we called the inn, you were gone."

"You could have been anyplace you wanted to be,"

Mrs. Barbara Keel said blandly. "They were too busy making whoopie in the backseat of a car."

"*Barbara,*" Glinda said.

"You ought to be glad you aren't in high school any more and old Father Corrigan is dead," Mrs. Keel said. "Oh, the lectures he used to give when he caught the teenagers in their cars, in this day and age it's hard to believe."

"You make me sound a hundred and four," Glinda protested.

"Oh, no I don't," Mrs. Keel said. "I make you sound hardly old enough to know better."

Gregor Demarkian bit his lip.

It was time to put a stop to this. Sam snaked out an arm to grab Glinda by the wrist and cleared his throat again.

"So," he said, sure he had started off that way in his unsuccessful attempt just a moment ago. "*Did* she tell you what Don Bollander told you?"

"Yes."

"Oh."

"It was very interesting information," Gregor said. "And, of course, he was telling the truth. He wouldn't have been killed if he hadn't been telling the truth."

Glinda jumped, shuddering under his hand. Sam held on tight. "But I thought we just agreed," she said. "He couldn't have been telling the truth. There wasn't enough time."

"He was mistaken on a couple of points," Demarkian said, "but he was telling the truth as he knew it. I wish it wasn't Saturday. I'd like to go over and take a look at that bank." He considered it. "Not that it would make any difference, of course."

Glinda took Sam's hand off her wrist and moved in closer to him, so that she could whisper. "I read about this in *People* magazine," she said. "They say he just suddenly knows everything and it just strikes him mute."

"It probably just strikes him mute in front of *People*

magazine," Sam told her. "I'm struck mute in front of those people at least once a year."

"I don't know everything," Gregor said suddenly. "I just know the structure of it."

Sam watched in fascination as Demarkian pushed himself off the filing cabinet, found his coat lying across Glinda's desk and shrugged it on. He seemed to be moving in a trance, his head shaking back and forth in rhythmic little arcs. He put Sam in mind of the old women in the village he had been born in back in Scotland, clucking their tongues and muttering "what a shame." Demarkian got his gloves out of his coat pocket and put them on. Then he got his scarf untangled from his collar and began to wind it around his neck.

"I should have made the time to buy a hat," he said absently.

Sam cleared his throat for the third time. "There's something else," he said. "Something that happened while I was waiting around at my place until it was time to come get Glinda. Josh Malley came to see me. Do you know who Josh Malley is?"

For some reason, this stopped Demarkian in his tracks. "Yes," he said. "I know who Josh Malley is. What did he come to see you about?"

"Snakes," Sam said triumphantly.

"I forgot about the snakes," Glinda said. "It really was very odd. Josh had never been out to visit Sam before. Josh has snakes."

"Black snakes," Sam Harrigan said. "Harmless. Keeps them out there with a lot of other miserable animals in cages. What anyone sees in zoos is beyond me. Anyway, that woman bought him a goddamned collection. Had a lion out there until the town complained."

"He still has an ocelot," Glinda said. "And the town only complained because you did."

"I had the right idea, too," Sam said. "Josh came out today to ask me if I'd tampered with his snake cages. Can you imagine that? His snake cages."

"They were your snakes, weren't they?" Demarkian

asked him. "The ones that were found on Brigit Ann Reilly's body?"

"That's right," Sam said, "but I didn't keep them in cages. I had a nice warm burrow for them and they were hibernating before the thaw hit. Then the thaw did hit and they woke up and got out. It wouldn't have been too hard for them to get out. I don't know how they ended up here."

"Fate," Glinda said.

Sam squirmed. Demarkian was no longer in a hurry to get out the door, but his attention was wandering again. He was rubbing the side of his face and muttering to himself.

"What Josh was all worked up about," Sam said, "was that one of his black snakes was missing. They were sleeping away like all good snakes in the winter and then when he went there this morning one of them was gone. I don't know why he thought I might have it. Maybe he believes all herpetologists collect snakes."

"You do collect snakes," Glinda said, "Josh probably thought you wanted to eat one."

"You don't eat black snakes," Sam said. "They taste terrible. If you want to eat a snake—"

"I don't," Glinda told him.

"Good thing, too," Sam said. "I only eat the damned things on television. Did I tell you I have a beautiful pair of T-bone steaks sitting in the freezer at my house, all ready to be thawed out in the microwave?"

"Yes," Glinda said, "you did."

"Did you say you'd come home and let me cook you dinner?"

"Well," Glinda said, with a determined gleam in her eye, "I said I'd come home and let you do something for me."

"Dear sweet Jesus Christ," Sam said. "You're making me blush. You're even making Demarkian blush."

But Demarkian wasn't blushing. He was looking at the two of them as if they were extraordinarily bright two-year-olds he was too fond of to spank. Sam wanted to bury his own head in the sand.

"Two more questions," Demarkian said. "In the first place, Mr. Harrigan, do you think Josh Malley was telling you the truth? Had one of his snakes gone missing? Or was that just an excuse he had for coming up to your place?"

"Oh, one of his snakes was missing, all right," Sam said. "Josh is no mental giant. He barely qualifies as a mental midget. He's no actor, either. He just kept repeating it. He used to have six and now he has five."

"Fine," Demarkian said, "that's perfect. Now, Miss Daniels. Brigit Ann Reilly came to the library every weekday and Saturday just after ten o'clock, correct?"

"Correct," Glinda said. Sam was all ready to jump to her rescue, but she didn't seem to need rescuing.

"Wonderful," Demarkian said again. "Now, a number of the people I've talked to have said that in that last week before she died, Brigit Ann Reilly had developed an odd sort of crush on someone—"

"And you want to know if I know who it was?" Glinda said. She shook her head. "It had been going on longer than a week, though. Brigit was always doing that kind of thing. Falling in love with people's souls. Or what she wanted to think were people's souls. My personal opinion is that most people's souls are sewers. At any rate, all I can tell you for sure is that whoever it was was connected to the work she did at St. Andrew's."

"You're positive?"

"Oh, yes. She actually said so one day—that someone she'd met at St. Andrew's had changed her entire perspective on life. Except that she didn't say perspective. I don't remember what she did say. Perspective is what she meant."

"Are you sure?"

"I'm sure. She said her whole idea of what a vocation was and how it happened and when it happened and who it happened to had been turned right around and transformed—and transformed *was* the word she used. Then she asked me if I didn't think it would be noble work, helping people who were confused about it realize that they'd been called by God." Glinda sighed.

"Brigit was always saying things like that. What's worse, Brigit was always believing it."

"She gave you no indication at all who it might be?"

"I asked Glinda the same question," Sam said. "I had exactly the same idea. We worked on it for hours."

"We got nowhere," Glinda said. She made a futile gesture in the air. "Brigit was always keeping secrets, always hinting around, always so full of—I don't know. If she hadn't been so basically sane and viscerally optimistic, she would probably have gone in for conspiracy theories. And she was so reflexively *nice* about people. Even about Ann-Harriet."

"Ann-Harriet." Sam swore to himself he could see Demarkian's antennae go up.

"Ann-Harriet was a perfect little bitch to all the postulants," Glinda said, "as if the only reason anyone would decide to become a nun was if she were stone ugly and rock stupid and didn't have any other prospects at all. Ann-Harriet would needle them. She reduced that little Neila Connelly to tears right in this library one day. But Brigit was always saying there had to be a reason, or something. I'm sorry. I didn't always listen to her."

"Redemption," Gregor Demarkian said. Then he buttoned up the rest of his coat. "I've got to go up to the Motherhouse now," he told them. "If anyone's looking for me, tell them they can find me there for the next half hour or so."

"Of course," Glinda said.

"Is that all?" Sam asked him.

"What else could there be?"

Demarkian turned on his heel and walked out the office door, with Glinda and Sam staring after him. Sam especially felt disoriented and—yes, and let down. He hardly wanted to admit it, but he had been half looking forward to the third degree. He'd heard so much about it from hard-boiled mystery fiction.

It was too embarrassing an emotion to admit. Sam turned to Glinda, who was looking thoughtful but hardly raked over the coals, and said, "You are off duty. And we

have seen Demarkian. And it is getting dark. Let's go up
the hill and have a deeply meaningful discussion about
the nature and purpose of life."

"Deeply meaningful discussion my foot," Mrs. Barbara Keel said. "Well, I just hope you two have your
brains in the right place. If you can't be good, at least be
careful."

And with that, Mrs. Barbara Keel sailed through
the door Gregor Demarkian had left open and on into
the library proper, looking for all the world like a proud
old ship gliding into the sunset at the end of a long and
distinguished career. She couldn't have looked any more
like the Queen Mum if she'd had plastic surgery. Sam
stared after her in astonishment. Glinda stared after her
in astonishment. Then they each looked at the other and
burst out laughing.

[2]

It got dark early in Maryville in March—not as early
as it got in February, but early enough. On bright days,
the Motherhouse turned its lights on at three thirty
in the afternoon. On overcast ones, it turned them on at
three. By quarter after four it was almost always pitch
black out and threatening to get blacker. Sister Mary
Scholastica had been born and brought up in the region,
so it didn't bother her, but it often bothered both
postulants and novices who came from farther south.
Scholastica didn't know how long it took to get used to it.
It was now five o'clock on Saturday night. Standing at
the side of the Motherhouse's open front doors, Scholastica found it easy to imagine she was looking out on
midnight. She tried to concentrate on Gregor Demarkian instead. He was coming up from the gate,
walking carefully on pavement that was icing over in the
increasing cold that came with the absence of the sun.
He looked as thoroughly tired as his voice had sounded
not ten minutes ago on the phone. Scholastica stepped
into the doorway and waved him a greeting.

"You ought to move faster," she said. "It keeps you warmer in the cold. What an odd thing for you to call up and ask me, under the circumstances."

"Mmm," Gregor said. He had reached the door. He slipped into the foyer and closed it after him, with a click, as if doing something definitive. "Well, there I was, standing outside my own hotel, and it hit me I could ask you what I had to ask you on the phone as well as in person. It wasn't as if there was anything else I needed up here."

"Except there was," Scholastica said.

"Well, that depends on what Neila Connelly has to say. Have you done the checking I asked you to?"

Scholastica nodded. "When you called we were just going into chapel. Most of the Sisters are there now. Reverend Mother stood up and asked the congregation right out before prayers started. It's the most efficient way to get anything done around here."

"Reverend Mother was telling me all about it earlier," Gregor said. "Nobody came forward? Nobody admitted to even knowing that somebody else had been in town on the day Brigit died?"

"No," Scholastica said, "and quite frankly, I didn't expect them to. I really do think Neila's explanation is the right one. I realize that was the day of the flood and things were a little less organized around here than they usually are." Scholastica looked to see if Gregor seemed to be thinking that that wasn't very organized at all, but she couldn't tell. "Anyway," she went on, "it's still not 1966. There aren't two or three hundred women in the house. There are only about sixty."

"Meaning you would have noticed."

"Meaning Reverend Mother would have noticed," Scholastica said. "And I know there weren't any postulants missing, because right before we started working on the evacuation I counted them. Brigit was gone. The rest of them were sitting in my classroom, listening to me make a hash out of the theology of Thomas Aquinas. Or somebody."

Gregor Demarkian was getting that glazed look on

his face Scholastica remembered from the first time she had led him through these halls. She was so used to the Motherhouse after seventeen years of long and short visits to its halls, it didn't faze her any more. She did remember what it had been like in the beginning, though, and decided to help him out.

"Through here we have the office corridor," she said, opening a fire door and shoving him through. "And that door second from the end on the right is Reverend Mother's. It's open. Go right in. Reverend Mother and Neila are waiting for us."

Reverend Mother General and Neila Connelly were indeed waiting for them. In fact, they were sitting right where Scholastica had left them, Reverend Mother General in the chair behind her desk, Neila on a small folding chair Scholastica had had to bring in from outside during their first discussion. That had been hours ago, and the strain was telling on Neila's face. It had that glassy, rough-shined look of skin that has recently been bathed in tears. Still, Scholastica thought, it was better than she had been expecting. She was sure that as soon as she was out of sight, Reverend Mother General was going to take the opportunity to take Neila Connelly apart. It didn't seem to have happened. In fact, Reverend Mother General and Neila Connelly seemed to be sitting quite companionably, as if they'd come to a new understanding of each other while Scholastica had been away.

I'm making that up, Scholastica told herself, shooing Gregor in ahead of her. Then she put a big smile on her face and said in her perkiest voice, "Well. Here's Mr. Demarkian. We all know Mr. Demarkian."

The rest of them looked at her as if she'd gone insane.

Reverend Mother General rose up from behind her desk and motioned Gregor Demarkian to a seat. When he declined, she sat down again and spread her hands. Scholastica breathed a sigh of relief. It was always easier when Reverend Mother General took charge.

"Now," Reverend Mother General said, "it seems to

me we have two issues to consider in this present matter. One is the matter of a postulant not Brigit Ann Reilly having been seen by Father Doherty on Beckner Street on the day of the flood—"

"Also by Don Bollander at the bank about fifteen minutes before Glinda Daniels found Brigit's body in the library."

"Is that true?" Scholastica asked.

"Of course, it's true," Reverend Mother General snapped. "Why would he say so if it weren't true? It does make our conclusions even more—conclusive. From what I remember about the police reports, Glinda found the body at approximately one o'clock?"

"That's right," Gregor said.

"Well, by quarter to one we'd all been organized in teams to help Father Doherty and the other people who had come up to Iggy Loy to get out of the wet, and if anybody else had been missing, I would have noticed."

"If it had been a postulant, I would have noticed," Neila Connelly put in. "We were all very nervous with the weather and Brigit missing. We were all packing boxes in a big room and we kept counting ourselves over and over to make sure."

"I didn't think any of you were missing," Gregor said, "but I had to be sure. You have no idea how many great ideas have foundered on the rocks of not making sure."

"I think I have," Reverend Mother said. "I once spent ten years teaching English composition in a high school. Now. The other matter is the witness of Neila Connelly here, and I use the word *witness* advisedly. I have talked the matter over with her and I believe her. I think it would be a good idea if you believed her, too."

"I intend to," Gregor said.

Neila Connelly had gone very pale. Scholastica knelt down next to the girl's chair and touched her arm. "Neila, if you can't go on with this I'll send you straight to the infirmary, no matter what Mr. Demarkian wants to know. Brigit and Mr. Bollander are dead. There's no reason on earth why you should kill yourself."

"I'm all right, Sister." Neila started to cry, a squeezed outcry that dripped tears from the corners of her eyes like the tail end of a tube of toothpaste coming out onto a brush. Neila didn't notice that the tears were there and let them run down the sides of her face. "The thing is," she said, "I don't really know much of anything at all." She turned to Gregor pleadingly. "I told Sister Scholastica everything I could think of the first three minutes after I started talking. I was supposed to be Brigit's best friend, but I didn't get to know much more than anybody else did."

"But you did know about this—uniform, or whatever it is," Gregor said gently.

"Oh, yes." Neila nodded vigorously. "Brigit took it out of the habits room the night before she died. After Compline. We're supposed to observe Grand Silence after Compline, but Brigit had been getting worse and worse at that over the last few weeks, so she was talking away. And I was scared to death, because during Grand Silence you can hear a butterfly flap its wings in this place, I'm not kidding. So I thought we were going to get caught."

"Stealing this postulant's dress?"

"Talking," Neila said. "And she didn't just take a dress. She took a veil and stockings and shoes, too."

Scholastica watched Gregor consider this. "They wouldn't have been missed?" he asked finally. "A set like that can go out of the convent without anyone noticing?"

"Not forever," Reverend Mother General told him, "but for a while, yes. We don't have the staff we used to. We can't spend time checking for things every day. We do inventory every month on the fifteenth unless the fifteenth is a Sunday. Then we do it on the following Monday. Until then, no one would necessarily know where anything was."

"Oh," Scholastica said, "I wouldn't put it that strongly."

"I would," Reverend Mother General said.

"She thought she'd get them back long before they were missed," Neila told them. "She hid them under her

mattress that night and then just before she was supposed to leave for the library she came up here and
stuffed them all under her skirts. The way this skirt is
made, we've got a kind of extra belt under there, a rope
thing that goes around the waist to keep the top part in
place—I'd have to show you and I don't think I should."

"That's all right," Gregor said.

"Well. She tied everything to that. It would never
have worked if she'd had to go down to chapel that way,
because it was noticeable. Not as noticeable as you'd
think, though. I had no idea there was so much material
in these skirts. Anyway, after she tied the things to
herself, she wrapped herself up in a shawl, and the
shawls we use cover everything. I mean they're enormous. If you wrapped one the right way, you could
probably cover a ninth-month preg—I'm sorry, Reverend Mother."

"That's quite all right, Neila. Of course, in my day
there were girls who entered the convent without ever
once having heard that word spoken in their lives, but
there were others who knew a few you probably don't.
Including myself. Mr. Demarkian, as far as I know, this
is all the information Miss Connelly has."

"It is," Neila Connelly said. "It's all I ever knew.
Brigit didn't tell me anything."

"Did she tell you what she was going to do with the
outfit?" Gregor asked.

"Oh, that," Neila said. "Yes. She told me what she
was going to do with that. She was going to give it to a
friend of hers, a new and special friend and that friend
had a friend who had just begun to realize she might have
a vocation—I got the impression that Brigit thought this
friend of a friend business was all made up. That whoever
had asked her for the dress was the one who was going to
wear it around and see if she liked the feel of it."

"What size was this dress?" Gregor asked.

"Twelve," Neila said. "The shoes were tens but I
wouldn't put too much into that. Brigit didn't know the
right shoe size. She kept saying that whoever this was
had bigger feet than she did and then she got the biggest

because you could stuff them, you know, and still wear them, but if the shoes were too small there was nothing you could do with them at all."

"I wonder who's size twelve," Gregor said.

"I am," Scholastica told him. "So are half the women I know, in the convent and out. Alice Marie. Ann-Harriet Severan and Miriam Bailey both, that's a joke. Glinda Daniels. We've all got big feet, too."

"Miriam's feet aren't big," Reverend Mother General said. "I don't think they're even sevens."

Scholastica turned to Gregor. She had meant to make some passing comment about the shoes not counting, but she didn't. The look on his face was very familiar. She remembered it from Colchester, and it frightened her.

"Oh," she said. "You know?"

"What?" Gregor looked up at her. "No. I don't know. I almost know. Are you acquainted with a woman named Barbara Keel?"

"Senile," Reverend Mother General said.

"Well, she may or may not be, but she said something very intelligent to me tonight. I knew there was no such thing as a locked-room mystery."

"What?" Scholastica said.

The phone on Reverend Mother General's desk rang and she leaned over to pick it up, barked hello into the receiver, and listened. A few seconds later, she handed the receiver across the desk.

"It's for you," she told Gregor Demarkian. "It's Pete Donovan and he sounds half out of his mind."

Three

❖

[1]

Gregor Demarkian had a driver's license, but he did not drive. According to Bennis Hannaford—and to everyone else who had ever had the misfortune of spending time with him when he was behind the wheel—he was a world-class menace on four tires, especially to the car. He was bad even with small machines. Blenders and electric pencil-sharpening machines seemed to come apart in his hands. Cars seemed to blow up. Once he had set a brand new 1979 Honda Civic on fire in the parking lot of a Stop & Shop in Brookfield, Connecticut, nobody ever knew how. Fortunately, he wasn't a man with much of a yen for high-speed car chases—just a little one. Mostly he considered all that sort of thing silly and beneath his dignity. Sometimes, watching *Bullit* late at night on television, he wondered what it would feel like. If he was ever going to get the chance to know which he was sure he wasn't—this call from Pete Donovan would have been it. Reverend Mother had understated the case. Pete Donovan wasn't half out of his mind. He was all the way out of it and on his way to becoming a form of free-floating electricity. Gregor knew that tone of voice all too well. Here was a man who kept watch over a small town. Small towns were warm places, full of routine and predictability. Now the routine was in ruins and the predictability had been shot to hell. Sanity did not look likely to make a reappearance soon. The world was a mess and getting messier by the minute. No wonder Pete sounded as if he wanted to strangle somebody, preferably God.

"It's Miriam Bailey," he said, when Gregor had taken the phone from Reverend Mother General. "Dead as a doornail and—never mind and. You can see for yourself. I'm coming to get you."

"Shouldn't you stay at the scene?" Gregor asked him.

"I've got half the local state police barracks at the scene, and they're not going to do any more good than I would. I'll be there in five minutes."

"Five minutes," Gregor repeated dutifully.

"I've got Josh Malley here and when I get the other one, I'm going to strangle her with my bare hands. Just for the aggravation."

Pete Donovan slammed the phone in Gregor's ear and Gregor handed the receiver back to Reverend Mother General.

"I've got to go," he said.

[2]

Five minutes later, Gregor was standing on the stone steps outside the front door to the Motherhouse with Scholastica beside him, feeling the wind under the collar of his coat. Pete Donovan turned in at the gate with a squeal of tires, rolled up to the steps and popped the passenger door open with the motor still running. How he managed it, Gregor never knew.

"Get in," he said.

Gregor said something reasonably polite to Sister Scholastica and got in. He slammed the passenger door after him and looked expectantly at Donovan. Donovan was in no mood to satisfy expectations. He gunned the motor, popped it into gear and slammed his foot on the gas pedal. Unfortunately, he slowed to make the turn that led to the gate. Otherwise, Gregor thought, his performance would have been perfect.

Gregor waited until they were out on the main streets of Maryville before he started talking. Then he went about it in as careful and uncontentious a manner as possible.

"So," he said in a neutral voice, "where are we going?"

"Huntington Avenue," Pete told him, running a red light at Delaney and Sands. "Miriam has a house up there. I should say the Baileys have a house. Miriam's grandfather built it."

"Miriam's grandfather who founded the bank?"

"That may have been her great-grandfather," Pete said. "I can never remember those things."

"It comes down to the same thing," Gregor said dismissively. "The family. Always the family. How did you find Miss Bailey dead?"

"We didn't." They were now at Delaney and Londonderry. A right turn would have taken them to Diamond Place and Clare Avenue and Beckner, an area of town which Gregor had never seen but of which he had heard in detail. They turned left instead, up another hill, but a more gentle one than the slope of Delaney Street itself.

"Josh Malley found Miriam," Pete Donovan said, "or at least that's what he's telling us at the moment. He's the one who called."

"Are you sure?"

"Positive. I took the call myself. I've been thinking about it ever since. He must have called me just before he called the fire department."

"The *fire* department?"

"The house has had a nice little job of arson done on it," Pete Donovan said. "Kerosene splashed all over the floor of the conservatory and lit. It caught the conservatory windows just as we got there, but it had been going a good long time before that."

"Hmm," Gregor said. "What about the body?"

"The body is the kicker," Donovan told him. "The

conservatory leads to a greenhouse kind of thing. It's where Josh keeps that menagerie of his. The only way you can get to it is through the conservatory. The body is on a second-level ledge in the greenhouse."

"Can't you come at it from outside?"

"According to the fire department, no. The trees are too thick and too close. Also too old. By the time you hacked through them the house would have burned to the ground. If she was alive in there—" Donovan shrugged.

"You're sure she's not?" Gregor asked him.

"Positive. I can use a pair of binoculars as well as anyone else. You can see the body, Gregor, you just can't touch it."

"Hmm," Gregor said again.

Pete turned the car off Londonderry Street and onto something called Farrow. Farrow wound around the base of a small hill and turned into something called Fox. From Fox, Gregor could finally see it: first a glow on the horizon, then the pulsing red of fire about to go out of control. The car spun off Fox onto Huntington and he was faced with what could only be the very best part of town. It was a street of graceful brick two-stories on graceful wide lawns, a uniformity broken only by the great stone pile with the fire engines and police cars parked in front of it: Miriam Bailey's Huntington Avenue house. The neighbors on either side of it and across the street were out on their front steps, watching the action. Pete Donovan skidded by them with a shudder of disgust.

"You'd think people like this would know better," he said. "My mother always told me it wasn't good manners at all to chase fires."

Gregor had known a president of the United States who liked to chase fires. "Maybe they're chasing a murder," he told Pete Donovan.

They turned into the Bailey house's drive and went up as close as the knot of vehicles there would allow them.

"Come out to the back and see it while you still

can," Donovan said. "By now the kerosene fumes ought to be mostly cleared out. They were so strong when I got here, I almost vomited."

"Really," Gregor said.

Pete hopped out onto the drive and waited for Gregor to follow him. "We go this way around back. It gets you the closest you can be. God only knows what's left of her now."

The import of that statement became clear almost as soon as Gregor got out of the car. Because of the way the house was built, it was difficult to see anything of what was going on at the back. Gregor discovered later that the floor plan was a fat tee, with the short wide end at the front. It was possible, however, to feel what was going on. Now that it was full dark, the air was hard and cold. The stars above their heads looked like chips of mica against black velvet. The wind was cold, too, but it brought with it intimations of something else, short gusts of heat that came and went so quickly, they might have been fantasy. That they weren't was attested to by the glow of red and the spirals of black smoke rising up from the back. Pete Donovan got Gregor by the wrist and pulled him along.

"Move," Donovan said. "We really don't have much time."

Gregor moved as fast as he was able, and in no time at all he could see what Donovan was getting at, about everything. Donovan had been wrong about the kerosene. The smell of it was thick in the air. Gregor found himself thinking that she must have poured it on in buckets. God only knew where she'd gotten hold of all of it. Then there was the position of the conservatory, and the greenhouse. Donovan had brought Gregor around the building to the right. Farther to the right were broad lawns covered with untouched carpets of snow. To the left were trees, ancient and massive. Up from the middle of them rose the glass panes of the roof of what must have been a three-story greenhouse. Just behind those panes, just where the trees cleared, the house was in flames.

"You've got to climb the wall," Donovan told him. "I

mean, you're supposed to climb the wall. It's got a ladder built into it. Miriam's father built it as an observation post for sky watching. He used to have the local Boy Scouts out here. You just—"

But Gregor shook his head. There was indeed a ladder in the wall Pete Donovan was talking about. The wall itself created a division between the property's front and back yards. Gregor and Donovan had had to walk through the gap between it and the house to get to where they were now. The wall was made of stone and the "ladder" was made of the lack of stones, here and there, in a hand-over-hand pattern that made Gregor seasick just to look at. It went up three stories and ended in a little square roofless turret.

"I don't think so," Gregor told Donovan. "I don't think it's my kind of thing. Is this as close as you've been able to get?"

"Hell, no," Donovan said. "When we first got here I walked right up under her practically. I put on one of those asbestos suits they've got and went right through the fire until I was standing in the middle of all those animals. I broke a couple of windows and let the animals out."

"Good idea."

"I wanted to get her out," Pete Donovan went on, "but the fireman said there wasn't enough time. The conservatory was going up really fast and you can't get to the greenhouse any other way. It's like I told you. With those trees you're stuck going in through the conservatory or not at all."

"You said she was on a ledge?"

"Like a shelf," Pete Donovan said. "The greenhouse has got these glass shelves, or clear shelves anyway—"

"Could they have been some kind of plastic?"

"I guess. Do you need that for something?"

"No," Gregor sighed, "not exactly. Go back to telling me about this shelf. How far off the ground was it?"

"Ceiling of a room second story up," Donovan said promptly. "I could reach it without a ladder, and there wasn't a ladder."

"In a greenhouse? In a greenhouse where they keep animals?"

"I thought that was fishy, too," Donovan said. "The way I look at it is, we were never supposed to find her—Miriam, I mean—but she took the ladder away just in case. Ann-Harriet I'm talking about now."

"Yes," Gregor said, "I thought you were."

"Yeah," Pete Donovan said. "Well, Ann-Harriet killed Miriam, stuffed her up there on that shelf by carrying her up a ladder and dumping her in a heap, doused the conservatory in kerosene and lit a match."

"Why the conservatory?"

"Closest thing that would light. It's got wood floors. The greenhouse has tile floors. Maybe she doused the body, too, to be safe. It's a good plan, Demarkian, much better than I would have expected from Ann-Harriet. It has all the elements. If Josh hadn't panicked and called us, the place would have burned down and the body would have been reduced to ash before we ever saw it. We'd never have been able to prove that Miriam hadn't burned to death."

"Hmm," Gregor said for the third time. Then he left Donovan's side at the edge of the wall and advanced across the lawn in the direction of the fire. He supposed it was just possible that it had happened the way Donovan said it had, that she had killed and then transported the body up a high stepladder to that shelf. In fact, it must have. Gregor had worked the whole thing out over the last few hours, the who, what, when, where, how, and why. He knew he couldn't be wrong, because there was no other possible explanation that fit all the facts. Even this fact—this body left in an inaccessible place to be destroyed—could be accounted for in no other way. Still, he was even more impressed with her than he had been. It couldn't have been easy. She had more determination than any other murderer he had ever met.

He got as close to the fire as he could, right up to the point where the heat began to make his face feel ready to blister. He was held back at that point by a frightened looking boy in a yellow slicker. The slicker had a shield with "Maryville Volunteer Fire Department" written into its borders.

"Can't go past here," the boy said. "It's dangerous."

"I won't go past," Gregor told him. "I was looking for someone who might have seen the body. Someone might be able to answer a few questions."

"I saw the body," the boy said. His face went green and he turned away, to look at the flames. "Only for a minute, though. I threw up."

"Was it that bad?"

The boy heaved. "It was the back of her legs," he said. "She was all curled up there on her side with her legs sticking out into the room and they had bubbles on them. You could just see the bubbles. It was—"

"Never mind," Gregor said. "I know what it was. Do you know someone named Josh Malley?"

"Oh. Oh, yes. I do."

"Is he around here somewhere?"

"He'd be a good person to ask about the body," the boy said. "He saw it before it was—before the heat got to it. I heard Pete Donovan tell my chief. I heard Pete Donovan tell my chief Miss Bailey was murdered, too."

"Does that make it worse," Gregor asked him, "that she was murdered?"

"Just so long as she was dead before the heat got to her." The boy turned and looked around, into the arch lights, into the flame light. The lawn was becoming more and more of a mess by the minute. The hose trucks and the hooks and ladders were parked around to the other side. It had been easier to get them there, with no star-gazing wall to get in their way. The activity on this side was heavy even without them. The boy peered at one face after the other and shook his head.

"I don't see him," he said. "He was talking to Pete Donovan for a while, though. And then he was talking to Harry Demos from the state police. He'll be around here somewhere. All right?"

"All right."

"I don't mind anything as long as she was dead when the heat got to her," the boy said again. "That's all I could think of when I saw her, with those shoes with the high spiky heels and the heels were starting to melt it was so hot in there and then the skin—"

"She was dead long before the heat got to her," Gregor said.

"That's all I wanted to know."

There was what felt like a gust of hot wind but was instead a puff of heated air breaking through a window. Shouts went up from the other side of the house, followed by banging that must have been axes against wood. Gregor looked up to see that the conservatory had lost the integrity of its shape. There was nothing left of it now but charred broken rafters and fire. The rafters were black and growing smaller by the minute. The fire was triumphant and swelling. Gregor couldn't see any stars in the sky at all anymore. Instead, even the puffs of breath that hung in the air every time he exhaled were tinged with red.

He backed up, away from the boy, and looked around. Pete Donovan was in the middle of a cluster of policemen, state and local, talking earnestly to a tall man in a Smokey the Bear hat and riding boots. Gregor had never understood why state police everywhere went in for riding boots. He walked over to the group and pulled at Donovan's sleeve.

"There's one more thing I have to check out and then I think we'd better hurry," he said. "I know this is the middle of nowhere, but I can't believe we'll have much time."

"Time for what?"

"Time to pick her up."

"What are you talking about?" Donovan demanded. "She isn't going anyplace. Why would she bother? She thinks she's got it made. Miriam dead, Josh ripe for the plucking, a ton of money in Bailey bank accounts or whatever it is that Josh inherits."

"We don't know that he inherits anything," Gregor said irritably. "And not one of these three people was killed because Ann-Harriet Severan wanted Miriam Bailey's money."

"They weren't." Pete Donovan was stupefied. "Well tell me," he exploded, "why were they killed? Why else could they have been killed? Do you think I've got two or three murderers running around town? Why kill Miriam Bailey at all if you aren't after her money?"

"Exactly," Gregor said. "Why kill Miriam Bailey at all? Brigit Ann Reilly was killed because she stole a postulant's habit and brought it to a building down on Diamond Place to be picked up by someone she liked and trusted. She was killed on the day she was killed because that was the day the bank packaged up the old money to be sent to the Federal Reserve for new bills—"

"You mean Ann-Harriet stole the old bills?"

"If she had, Maryville would have been invaded by federal marshals long before now," Gregor said. "It wasn't old bills that were stolen. It was new ones. If you check the bank's computer system I think you'll find evidence of a fraud, a very small and confusing fraud, going back some months. That's what would have been used to cover the missing cash, at least temporarily. It would have to be very temporarily."

"You've gotten yourself into the bank's computer?" Donovan demanded. "How?"

"I didn't get myself into anything, Mr. Donovan. I'm extrapolating. You'll find that fraud because it has to be there. Go looking for it. Don Bollander was killed because he saw what he thought was Brigit Ann Reilly wandering around in the bank a quarter of an hour before Brigit was found dead."

"Right," Donovan said.

"It's a good thing we're dealing with such monumental arrogance," Gregor said. "If we weren't, she'd have had time to get all the way out of the state by now. She might have had time to get out of the country. Do you know where Josh Malley is?"

"Yes."

"Good," Gregor said, "let's go talk to him. Just in case there's even the slightest chance I might be wrong, let's make absolutely sure."

Donovan looked like he was about to make a protest, stopped himself and turned. Then he marched into the crowd with no attempt whatsoever to make sure Gregor could keep up with him.

[3]

They found Josh Malley sitting by himself, alone
and ignored and dressed only in a heavy sweater, against
the end of the stone wall closest to the house. There was
a lot of activity going on around him. Men and women
walked in and out through the gap, carrying equipment
and notebooks and talking to each other in loud voices
meant to carry through the shouts of firefighters still
battling away at the house. They ignored Josh and Josh
ignored them. Gregor thought he had never seen a more
thoroughly dejected man, or a more ineffectual one. Josh
at this meeting was just as Josh had been this afternoon
outside the bank. Most of the boys who sold themselves
for money—to men and women both—were psycho-
paths. They had neither scruples nor emotions and
weren't interested in acquiring either. Josh was just a
floater, a perfectly harmless type but lacking in organization and purpose and especially in intelligence. He
went from one thing to another without knowing why or
where or what it all meant. If it turned out badly he was
upset. If it turned out well, he was surprised. Gregor
almost felt sorry for him.

When Gregor and Donovan reached him, Josh
looked up, blinked, and tried a smile. Then he slumped
down again and shrugged.

"Nothing," he said. "I've been sitting here for half
an hour now and I still have absolutely nothing."

Pete Donovan cleared his throat. "Never mind what
you have, for the moment," he said, displaying what
Gregor thought was a commendable lack of concern
about what Josh Malley had actually meant. "Mr. Demarkian here wants to ask you a few questions. Mr.
Demarkian is the man—"

"I know who he is," Josh said. "I was going to talk to
him, but Miriam didn't want me to. I was going to talk
to him about how I saw Brigit down on the levy on the
day of the flood."

"Did you?" Gregor asked him.

"No." Josh flushed. "I made it up. Because it made Miriam crazy when I said things like that. Miriam always hated publicity. And she was making me crazy lately. Watching me."

"From what I hear, you could have used watching," Gregor said.

"You mean because of Ann-Harriet?" Josh shrugged. "It's the kind of thing Miriam got upset about. I never did understand why. I mean, sex is sex, you get my drift?"

"No," Pete Donovan said.

"Talk to me about tonight," Gregor said. "How did you happen to find the body? Somebody said the greenhouse was where you kept your animals. Were you going in to look at them?"

"We only kept the animals in the greenhouse in the winter," Josh said. "In the summer they had a place outside. The greenhouse got too warm. I wasn't visiting the animals. I never do that at night."

"Then why were you there?" Gregor persisted.

"Because I was asked to go," Josh said. "We were supposed to go out to dinner, Miriam and I, and we came back from town and went puttering around doing our own stuff and then it got to be about four o'clock and I wanted to know what I was supposed to be doing. Maybe it was four thirty—"

"It was close on five," Donovan said.

"He should know. He wears a watch." Josh shrugged again. "If I called him at five, it probably was about four thirty. Anyway, I went wandering around, looking for Miriam and the house was empty because it's Saturday night and the help all has the night off, they always have Saturday nights off, Miriam says in the old days you could get them where they would stay on duty for the weekends but now you can't. Anyway, I went down to the kitchen and there was a note on the refrigerator saying she was in the greenhouse, if I wanted her I should look for her there."

"Did she often leave notes for you on the refrigerator?" Gregor asked.

"All the time."

"Are you sure this note was from Miriam?"

"Absolutely. I'd know her handwriting anywhere. Anyway. I found the note and then I started from the back of the house, and when I got there I found her. Just like that. She was just sort of scrunched up there on that shelf, out of reach, with her ass sticking into the air over my head. I wanted to get her down, but I couldn't find the ladder we keep in there. It was just plain gone. And then I thought I shouldn't get her down. She had to be dead, the way she was lying. The fact that she was there at all. She had to be dead and dumped there. I know you're not supposed to touch anything. So I started to go call Donovan here. And that's when I smelled it. The smoke."

"Just smoke?" Gregor asked. "Not kerosene?"

Josh Malley thought about it. "Smoke and kerosene," he said finally. "I was still in the greenhouse. You know that funny smell greenhouses get. That was all I could smell at first. And then there was the smoke and I went out into the conservatory to see what was going on and I smelled the kerosene. I told him about the kerosene when I called." Josh jerked his head in Donovan's direction.

"Did you call immediately?" Gregor asked him. "Right then?"

"Yes," Josh said.

"It was five oh one exactly," Donovan said.

"Fine." Gregor didn't wear a watch. He grabbed Donovan's wrist and checked his instead. It was five twenty-two. "She was still here at five oh one," he said, "that means she's had twenty-one minutes to get where she wants to go. Is there a local airport?"

"Yes, there is. Shuttle flights to New York City and into Canada."

"Exactly." Gregor nodded. "That's where we're going to go. Go tell your state police people to put out an all-points for a nun."

Four

❖

[1]

It was called Maryville International Airport and it sat on the flats east of town, a meager collection of hangars and lights that never handled anything bigger than a twenty-passenger shuttle. The *international* came from its ties to Canada, which were both numerous and strong. Up here, there was a lot of traffic back and forth. Americans went to Canada for the entertainment. Canadians came to America to buy cigarettes at less than five dollars a pack. Gregor thought it was Canada that changed Pete Donovan's mind about the urgency of what they were doing. At first, although he had made the calls and contacted the authorities Gregor asked him to, he was inclined to go about his part in this adventure with due deliberation. Waiting around for him to get into the car and get the motor started and stop talking to everybody north of Albany on his two-way radio drove Gregor to distraction. Then the dispatcher said something about how lonely she was this weekend, her son had gone off to spend some time with his girlfriend in Canada, and Pete Donovan said, "Shit."

"Excuse me," Gregor asked him.

They were still sitting in the driveway of Miriam Bailey's Huntington Avenue house. The great arc of the drive was still clogged with police cars and fire engines. The drive behind Pete's car was blessedly still clear, but not by much. The state police had sent for a mobile crime unit and it was pulled up half onto the drive's center lawn. Pete Donovan gunned his engine, slammed his gears into reverse and hit the gas pedal—much harder, this time, than he had back on the road when he had been bringing Gregor in. The car kicked. The car skidded. The car steadied itself on the gravel of the drive and shot off onto the street. Moments later they were barreling into the center of town again, running red lights and causing havoc. Gregor closed his eyes and asked himself what he could have been thinking of, wishing for a chance to take part in a high-speed car chase. He didn't know what they were chasing but they were certainly going at high speed. He didn't like it a bit. Pete Donovan seemed to like it just fine, and after a while he did what Gregor had expected him to do at the beginning: he turned on his siren. Gregor had never been in a police car with the siren going before. The Federal Bureau of Investigation didn't have police cars with sirens, and the local police who sometimes called them in on serial murder and kidnapping cases didn't invite them to go tearing over the countryside in black-and-whites with the whoopy whistle blasting. Gregor had had no idea that the damn things were so loud.

"Can't you turn that thing off?" he asked Pete Donovan.

"Soon as we get out of town," Donovan said. "Don't want to cause a traffic accident."

"Why not? You've already caused three heart attacks."

"I want you to tell me the whole story from the beginning," Donovan said. "Then I'm going to read you chapter and verse about what I'm going to do to you if you're wrong."

"I can't tell you anything with that noise going on over my head."

"That's Delaney Street coming up," Donovan said.

That was, indeed, Delaney Street coming up. They jumped the red light and bolted into it, turned right up the hill toward the motherhouse, and turned off to the right again onto a gentle fork. Commercial buildings began to shade into two-story hybrids and then into small houses with small yards, but the St. Patrick's Day decorations didn't shade into anything. Gregor saw all the same leprechauns, pots of gold, and shamrocks he had on Delaney and at the St. Mary's Inn. Out here, some of the houses even had their lawns and porches decorated in a way that was more usual for Christmas. There were green and white lights and big fat leprechauns sitting on pots of gold and lit up from inside. Pete Donovan saw Gregor staring at it all and said, "They import 'em from the city. You can get anything from New York City."

"Right," Gregor said.

"Tell me a story," Donovan said.

Gregor pointed to the roof.

Donovan leaned over to the dashboard and shut the siren off.

[2]

"So," Gregor said a couple of minutes later, while they were winding their way through small and narrow roads that inevitably slowed them down. They weren't as slowed as Gregor would have liked to be, but it wasn't much use talking to Donovan about his driving. He wouldn't listen. "So," Gregor said again, "if you're going to go back to the day the first of the murders happened—"

"I like that day," Donovan said.

"Yes. Well. If you're going to start there, you've got this. Brigit Ann Reilly was a girl who may or may not have had a vocation as a nun, but who very definitely had an avocation as a conspirator. She also had a strong sentimental streak. She was the kind of girl who liked stories about lost puppies saved from drowning and who imagined herself in the starring role in all the most affecting stories of the ancient saints. She had also been very sheltered, so that she knew very little of people who were not like herself. When the Sisters sent her down to work at St. Andrew's, she had her eyes opened—but not just to poverty, the way the Sisters wanted her to be. St. Andrew's is Maryville's favorite local charity—"

"Of course it is," Donovan said. "It's easy to help those people. They work their butts off—"

"That's hardly the point," Gregor told him. "The point is, Brigit didn't meet only poor people at St. Andrew's. She met rich and exotic ones, too. She met Miriam Bailey, for instance, because Miriam and the bank funded a lot of programs and Miriam liked to keep an eye on them. She met Ann-Harriet Severan and Don Bollander, because Miriam Bailey insisted on her employees' involvement in charitable work. She met Father Michael Doherty, the ultimate sentimental hero, a man who had left a rich family to live with the poor. If Father Doherty hadn't been so conscientious, Brigit Ann Reilly might never have died. Her first inclination, I think, was to develop a roaring crush on *him*."

"Father Doherty would never have put up with that sort of thing," Donovan said.

"He didn't. He told me about it earlier this afternoon. Brigit got silly, Father Doherty got stern. As I said, in a way it was too bad, because Brigit didn't just give up her romantic fantasies, she transferred them. And this time she transferred them to the wrong person."

"I'd say that was putting it mildly."

"Mmm, yes. Well. This person had a problem she had not been able to solve. She wanted to steal a great deal of money from the bank and she'd more or less figured out how to do it, but it had a couple of snags. What she wanted was to go into the vault on the day the old-new money transfer occurred and take not the old money—as I told you before, that would be too quickly discovered—but a large chunk of the new money. Not as large a chunk as you might think, by the way. She'd already been stealing the bank blind for close to two years. *That* money is probably salted away in the

Cayman Islands. What she wanted now was about fifty or sixty thousand dollars, enough to get out of the country and lie low until she was sure nobody had discovered the bank accounts. She was going to get that information rather quickly because on the fifth of March, the bank auditors were going to come in. No fewer than three people mentioned that to me over the last two days—including John Cardinal O'Bannion. It went right past me."

"Why shouldn't it?" Pete Donovan said. "There's been that S and L disaster. And there's been rumbles about something just as bad in banking."

"Yes, of course," Gregor told him. "It's in the atmosphere. Now, the problem was, no matter how well all this had been planned out, a bank audit was going to blow it and bank audits are not announced well in advance. She was lucky to get the month or so she got. In that time she had to get done the rest of what she needed to get done and she had to get out of the country. She didn't have much time. Brigit Ann Reilly's romantic infatuation with saving her soul came as a godsend. She had to get down to the vault and move a fair amount of money at a time when dozens of people would be around to see her go in and out. Fine. She wouldn't go in and out. A nun would go in and out. A little makeup, a little care to keep her face turned away from people—if she'd had to come face-to-face with anyone who knew her, it wouldn't have worked, but most of the people she ran into were absolute strangers. They saw a nun, generic. People don't really look at nuns in habit, even modified habits. And of the two people who did know her and saw her in that habit, only one recognized her. The other one—and I'm talking about Don Bollander now—simply saw "a nun" and later convinced himself that he'd seen Brigit Ann Reilly."

"Don always was a jerk," Donovan said.

"Maybe so." Gregor sighed. "What she did was, she told Brigit that she was thinking of devoting herself to the religious life, that she'd thought about it for a long time, that these days there were ways of doing that no matter what your life had been like. At any rate, she told Brigit something to make Brigit think that it would be a good idea to give her a chance to walk around in a habit for a day or two. She needed that habit on the morning of the day the money was exchanged and no later. She got Brigit to steal it for her and bring it down to an abandoned building on Diamond Place to hand it over in private. While Brigit was there, she fed her coniine—in tea or coffee or orange juice, I don't know, but my guess would be tea. It's easy to carry around a thermos of tea and it's easy to distill coniine from hemlock in tea, too, if you know what you're doing. This was at about ten thirty, by the way, before Sam Harrigan saw Brigit wandering around down there. My guess is that she— our murderer, not Brigit—wanted to be sure the coniine would do its work. The one thing she couldn't have was Brigit telling Sister Scholastica or Reverend Mother General what she'd done, and there was no way to ensure that except to make Brigit dead. Brigit liked to keep secrets, but she was only capable of keeping them for so long. Anyway, my guess is that our murderer gave Brigit a few extra errands to do in the low-rent district, got her moving around a little. That helped the coniine to work faster—it wouldn't have taken long with Brigit, but our murderer didn't necessarily know that—anyway, it got Brigit's blood moving and the coniine working as fast as possible, and it did something else. It muddied the waters unbelievably, because while Brigit was running around doing errands, our murderer was just running around. That was why you had so many 'sightings' after the body was found. That was suspicious on the face of it. Of course, you always get sightings and hysteria in small towns after particularly bizarre violence. The sort of people who report that kind of thing, though, are of a type. Here, you had bank officials, nuns, schoolteachers, doctors—you had everybody. And the only conclusion I was able to draw from that was that people had seen her, or had seen someone they later thought was her, someone in a habit. Because our friend did a little walking around on her own. She went up to

Beckner near St. Andrew's parish church. Father Doherty saw her, well enough to know she wasn't Brigit but not well enough to know who she was—"

"Is that likely?" Donovan asked. "Father Doherty knows Ann-Harriet very well."

Gregor rubbed the leg of his trousers. "If you're not expecting to see a woman dressed up as a nun, you don't see a woman dressed up as a nun, you see a nun. If you understand me. At any rate, the two of them went wandering all over the place. Finally, Brigit went up to the library, probably already feeling sick. Our murderer went back to the bank and down to the vault, picked up a few stacks of new bills, stashed them where they would be convenient and then went to fiddle with the computer again. She's been doing a lot of fiddling with the computer. At any rate, at that point she was fine. All she had to do was spend a couple of days getting her frame in place—because she wanted someone else suspected of that theft, someone she hated—and then she was free to take off. By the time the bank auditors showed up on March fifth, she was going to be long gone. And then things started to go wrong."

"Explain the snakes," Donovan said. They were past the houses now and out on the open road. Gregor kept expecting to see airport lights, but he was always foiled by trees and hills. He shifted in his seat and wished that Donovan hadn't picked up so much speed.

"The snakes," Gregor told Donovan, "were her first piece of bad luck. The snakes belonged to Sam Harrigan and they'd gotten out of the caves he'd made for them. They were a little mixed up because of the false spring and logy. They ended up at the library, I'd say, purely by accident. Brigit ended up there because that was where she was going, and coming up from Diamond Place the shortest way to get there was from the back. By the time she reached the parking lot and the storeroom door— which was kept unlocked, by the way, because some of the staff used it to get to and from their cars—by the time she got there she was very sick indeed, probably staggering and close to dead. You ought to check through your sightings material to see if any of the people who live on that block made one. They might not have. They might have been at work or glued to the television set for the weather news, but it's a chance."

"I'll do it."

"Brigit went in through the storeroom door and collapsed," Gregor said, "and her body was still warm, so the snakes swarmed over it, trying to keep their own body heat up. Then Glinda opened the door, and found the body and the snakes, and with the media already in force in Maryville and the surrounding towns because of the flood, the thing became an instant sensation. That was exactly what she didn't want. Brigit might still have been alive if Michael Doherty had been a less conscientious man, Don Bollander might still have been alive if there hadn't been so much publicity about Brigit Ann Reilly's death. The nuts would have come out of the woodwork no matter how Brigit died. A man like Don Bollander would have needed a solid inducement to get involved."

"I don't know," Donovan said. "Bollander was—you know. He was a whisperer."

"You mean he liked to pretend he was an insider," Gregor said. "Yes. People have told me that. But I still say that an executive of a local bank doesn't get mixed up in police business if he doesn't absolutely have to. If Brigit had been found in an ordinary way and attracted little or no national press, Don Bollander either wouldn't have said he saw her at all or wouldn't have said so to so many people."

"I still don't see why Ann-Harriet had to kill him," Donovan said. "Why not let him go on blithering like everybody else in town?"

"Our murderer couldn't let him do that," Gregor said, "because the times were wrong. Don Bollander saw his nun in the back hall at the bank at quarter to one that afternoon. Since he didn't say otherwise, we have to assume that nun was on her feet and moving normally. Brigit couldn't have been either at that point. She was unconscious and at least close to dead fifteen minutes later, and three blocks away. Eventually, somebody had to tumble to that. Eventually, I did."

"So why did he end up in the convent?"

"Sleight of hand," Gregor said firmly.

"What?"

"Sleight of hand," Gregor repeated. "A couple of weeks ago, John Cardinal O'Bannion started to get very strange and pointed hate mail, postmarked at Maryville and hinting not so subtly at murder. Reverend Mother General got one, too, on the day we found Don Bollander's body. She may have gotten more. Our murderer expected those letters to be reported, I think. Given the character of John Cardinal O'Bannion, she at least expected them to be mentioned. She didn't realize how much of that kind of thing rolls into a Chancery. She didn't understand that the hierarchy and even the nuns are very used to dealing with it in their own way. At any rate, she wanted attention focused on the convent and not on the bank for as long as possible, and there she was, stuck with Don Bollander, who had 'bank' written all over him. She did the only thing it made any sense to do. She fed him coniine at the bank—that was the easiest place to do it; they were both there; she had all her things there—and then she took him up to the Mother-house and waited for him to die. She probably told him they were doing something for the Sisters. That's not farfetched. The bank and its employees were always doing something for the Sisters, and the bank held the mortgage on the Motherhouse. There were business and charitable and personal reasons for the two of them to be there. I've been wondering if she didn't tell Don Bollander they were hatching a surprise—a name day party for Reverend Mother General, maybe, or something else that had to be prepared for in secret. Given what I've heard of Don Bollander's character, something like that would have been perfect."

"Why'd she stuff him in a laundry sink?"

"Because it was there," Gregor said. "It was convenient. It was probably close to where he collapsed."

Donovan rubbed the side of his face, thinking it

over. "What about this last one?" he said. "Why did she bother to do that? All this planning you're talking about, this last one was bound to get us onto her. I mean, it couldn't have helped."

"Oh, it might have," Gregor said, "if we hadn't worked all of this out. Even if it couldn't have helped under any circumstances, though, I think she would have done it anyway. It was her worst mistake. Hate is always a mistake. She had the frame all set up. She should have left it there."

"Left it where?" Donovan asked.

"There's something going on up ahead of us," Gregor said. "I think that's a state police officer."

It was a state police officer. The road they were traveling on had given up its bends and curves over the last five miles or so. It now proclaimed itself to be Route 896 and lay flat and straight in a line to the arc lights of the airport. The state police car had been traveling just ahead of them on the two-lane blacktop, doing a leisurely pace. Gregor had noticed Pete Donovan growing frustrated and his fingers itching to get to the siren switch. Then the state police car had bucked, jumped, and taken off, its own siren screaming. Pete Donovan stared after it in amazement for a moment or two and hit the gas.

"Turn on the radio," he said to Gregor, and they shot down the road. "I turned it off so I could hear the great detective give his explanation."

"If you weren't already chief of police, you could get fired for that, Gregor shouted back.

He turned the radio on and heard the voice of Pete Donovan's dispatcher, putting out a stream of letters and numbers that even Gregor found easy to translate, in spite of the fact that he had never been part of an investigation in Maryville before.

"They've got her," he said.

"Either that or they've got some poor nun on her way to visit her sister in Akron, and there's going to be hell to pay from the Cardinal."

Actually, Gregor had never had any trouble of that

kind from the Cardinal. There were a lot of things O'Bannion did and didn't like—and a lot of areas where even Father Tibor Kasparian would have to admit that the Cardinal's personality could stand improvement— but he was better than fair about the glitches that occurred whenever people tried to do a good job. Gregor pulled his seat belt a little tighter around his waist and wished for an airbag that came out of the glove compartment. Pete Donovan pushed his car up to eighty and then to eighty-five, and didn't come close to catching up to the statey.

"There's the gate," he said, "here we go."

It was a small airport. There was the one small parking lot and the three small runways. There was the one small waiting building with its one small baggage carousel. Gregor could see a pair of men in overalls pushing baggage through a flap in the wall of the building. He was paying no attention at all to the state police cars crowded together in a knot just beside him, or to the state police officers in their Smokey the Bear hats, or to the nun in abbreviated habit in the middle of them. Pete Donovan braked and cut his engine and jumped out, and Gregor jumped out after him. This was an interview he did not want to miss.

It was not, of course, an interview with Ann-Harriet Severan. Ann-Harriet Severan was not the woman with her hands in her pockets and her feet placed wide apart, looking like she was ready to bolt and make a foot-race run to the Canadian border.

Miriam Bailey was.

Five

❖

Twenty-five miles away, back in the middle of Maryville, Father Michael Doherty was standing on the front steps of St. Mary of the Hill, ringing the doorbell and feeling inexpressibly tired. It was Saturday night and still early, but he had already been out to the county hospital twice. His head was full of the screaming of a woman whose child had just died from drinking a bottle of ammonia. The bottle of ammonia had been left under the main hall staircase by the janitor that served that woman's apartment building and four others. The janitor drank and Michael Doherty had been trying to get him fired for the last four months. Sometimes it seemed to him that nothing was worth anything, that nothing he did ever did any good. Sometimes he felt he spent his time patching holes in a beach ball that sprung six more leaks every time he got one fixed. The analogy reminded him of the seminary, where it had been used to warn him about what would now be called "parish burnout." For once in his life, Michael Doherty didn't care if he was being trite. There were footsteps behind the door and then the sound of the elaborate ritual the Sisters had to go through to get the door opened from the inside without setting off the alarm. Michael sometimes joked to Reverend Mother that she ought to give him the security key, because it was a hundred times easier. The door opened and Sister Gabriel was standing there, smiling. She had checked him out in the peephole.

"I just came to use the chapel," Michael Doherty said, stepping inside. "I'll only be about half an hour. I need to get out of the fray for a little while."

Sister Gabriel smiled and nodded. Michael Doherty did this every once in a while. They were used to him. He was used to them, too, and wouldn't try to make them talk when he knew they weren't supposed to. He followed Sister Gabriel down the hall to the center section and bid her good night as she turned to the right to go to her cell. He turned to the left and made his way to the chapel.

Usually, when Michael Doherty went to this chapel, he sat front and center so that he could look at the wall-size stained-glass window that had been given to the order by a benefactor in 1987. It was one of the most powerful depictions of the resurrection he had ever seen—not good art so much as effective art—and it always made him feel lifted up. Tonight, he moved instead to the side, where a large picture of the Blessed Margaret Finney had been set up under a small crucifix. He sat down in a pew at the front and rubbed at the little finger of his right hand. He had cut it trying to do something to save the child, grabbing for something on a tray, he couldn't remember what. The cut was long and thin and hurt like Hell. He stretched out his legs and looked the Blessed Margaret Finney straight in the eye.

"Margaret," he said, "sometimes I wish I wasn't so educated. Sometimes I wish I could be like that woman who came to my office this morning and believe in physical miracles. Sometimes I just wish I didn't have to spend nights like tonight."

He closed his eyes and put back his head and thought about it all, the way he had thought about it when he first decided to enter the seminary, the things that had convinced him. The lame will walk and the blind will see, he thought, and it was true. It just wasn't true the way they wanted it to be, the skeptics and believers both. Nothing went *poof*. No instant cures rained down from the sky or blossomed out of pairs of praying hands. The blind will see and the lame will walk and they did—because in every place Christian civilization had touched, the progress of medical technology had been startling. It was nice to say that medical science had done it only in rebellion against Christianity, as a friend of his had told him when he'd tried to explain all this, but the fact was that a hundred years ago, most of the world had been made up of societies hostile to science. Why had it all happened here? It was a weak argument and he knew it. It didn't begin to answer the questions he asked on nights like tonight. It was still the only argument he had and he held to it, because it was the only way he could explain the emotional part. The emotional part was solid. It harbored no doubts at all.

It was cold in the chapel and he was feeling sleepy. He had a parish to look out for and a few dozen parishioners who were going to need his help. He had only so much time to spend hiding from the world like this. He opened his eyes and said, "Well, Margaret, I'm going to go back to work. That's why I'm so in favor of having you declared a saint. You were always going back to work."

He grabbed ahold of the kneeler rail in front of him and started to stand up, and that was when he noticed it. Actually, that was when he didn't notice it, the pain in the little finger of his right hand. The pain had been there, a sharp stabbing thing, since he knew the fight for the child was lost. It had probably been there before that, but unnoticed. He looked down at his hand and blinked.

There was nothing there.

No line of red.

No blood smeared against the skin.

No ridge of skin jutting up from the cut.

Nothing.

Father Michael Doherty looked back up at the picture of the Blessed Margaret Finney and then to the crucified Christ above her and started to smile.

He could have been mistaken.

He might never have had a cut at all.

He could have imagined the whole thing.

Imagined or not, he was never going to tell a single soul on earth what had just happened to him.

They would never believe him.

Epilogue

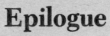

me we have two issues to consider in this present matter.

[1]

At ten o'clock on the morning of Sunday, March 17, just as the Maryville St. Patrick's Day Parade was beginning its march from the Maryville Public Library to the steps of St. Mary of the Hill, Gregor Demarkian and Bennis Hannaford decided to remove themselves from the festivities for a while and get to someplace warm. Because it was Sunday and all the stores on the street were closed, this amounted to finding a handy doorway to stand in out of the wind, where Bennis could get a cigarette lit and Gregor could feel safe about taking off his hat. When they'd decided to take the Cardinal and Reverend Mother General up on their invitation and come to Maryville for St. Pat's, Gregor had gone out and purchased a hat with ear flaps especially. It looked ridiculous worn with his citified winter coat and good leather gloves, but it kept his ears from freezing. Bennis, as usual, was dressed in jeans and an assortment of wrapped garments Gregor had no way of identifying. The top half of her looked a little like the drawings of children in the wind in Evelyn Nisbett books. The doorway they found was close to the Motherhouse, just south of Iggy Loy. Gregor chose it for both its practical and sentimental values. It was the doorway of the shoe repair shop owned by Jack O'Brien.

Bennis got her cigarettes out and got one lit and blew a stream of smoke into the air. Gregor thought about giving her another lecture on how she had to give up smoking and decided against it. He was sure the lectures goaded her into smoking more. Bennis was like that. She blew another stream of smoke into the air and Gregor found himself wondering if it was smoke at all. It was cold enough to turn their breath to mist.

Bennis took off something that looked like a large scarf and dropped it on the concrete step beneath her. Then she sat down on the scarf and stretched her legs.

"What I don't understand," she said, "is when you knew it was Ann-Harriet who was dead in the greenhouse and not Miriam Bailey. I mean, you didn't even see her."

"I didn't have to see her," Gregor said. "Pete Donovan told me Miriam Bailey had died and he was convinced Ann-Harriet Severan had killed her. Well, I tried to work the whole thing out as Ann-Harriet's doing and it wouldn't go. There were too many conditions she couldn't meet. There was the key to the Motherhouse's front door, for one thing. Without that, I had Don Bollander trapped in a locked-room puzzle, and there just isn't any such thing as a locked-room puzzle. People don't do things like that. Then there was the timing of Brigit Ann Reilly's murder—the murder, not her death. Brigit had to have taken that poison during the half hour that nobody saw her that morning, and that was between ten thirty and eleven. She had to have taken it down by the river, too, because that's where she was the last time anyone had seen her. That meant that Ann-Harriet would have had to have gone down to the river, administered the poison and got hold of the extra postulant's habit, and got back to her desk—it would have taken a good hour if not more. Here's a woman working for a hostile boss. Do you think she would have been able to take an hour away from her desk in the middle of the morning without causing a stink?"

"And you'd have heard about a stink," Bennis said slowly.

"In a town this size, with a woman as universally disliked as Ann-Harriet Severan, the news would have been all over the place in ten minutes. Then there's Josh Malley to consider. Everybody said Ann-Harriet was sleeping with Josh Malley, and I'm sure it was true. But so what? Look at what Miriam was doing with Josh Malley."

"I really don't get all this business about Josh Malley."

"It's simple," Gregor said. Out on the street, some band had just struck up "The Wearing of the Green." "Miriam Bailey went to Corfu and picked up Josh Malley and brought him home and married him, or married him and brought him home, it doesn't matter which. It surprised everybody, not just because it wasn't like her—older women and older men have crises of that kind all the time—but because she didn't change in any other way. She should have been going in for silly clothes or spending too much money on cosmetics or something. That's how women usually act when they discover sex in their late middle age, but Miriam Bailey didn't. She spent money on Josh Malley. She spent an ostentatious amount of money on Josh Malley. Otherwise, she went on just as before. And that figures, you see, because she hadn't discovered sex in late middle age. She'd discovered a scapegoat."

"She went in for scapegoats, didn't she?" Bennis said. "Sending fake hate mail to the Cardinal and the convent on a computer that could have belonged to anybody—"

"Pete Donovan told me about that. Miriam gave the library a new computer system last year. It's compatible to the one used at the bank. That tied in with the little game she played with Ann-Harriet just before she killed her. Miriam told Ann-Harriet that Glinda had told Miriam about Ann-Harriet and Josh. Ann-Harriet did what she always did when Miriam goaded her, went off half-cocked and staged a very public confrontation. Of course, as soon as Glinda told her she'd been tricked, Ann-Harriet knew it was true, so she went barreling off again to have another confrontation, this time with Miriam. Miriam, in the meantime, was sitting calmly at home, knowing perfectly well that Ann-Harriet would show up on her doorstep eventually. And in the meantime—"

"In the meantime, it looked like Glinda and Ann-Harriet had had a fight, so if Ann-Harriet showed up dead and was identified, the first person the police would want to talk to would be Glinda."

"Maybe the second one," Gregor said.

"Well," Bennis told him, "I just met your Glinda about ten minutes ago. I was talking to Sister Scholastica and she came by with Sam Harrigan, and, of course, I've met Sam on and off the talk show circuit, that happens, I told you. Anyway, he says he's been in love for two weeks and he's going to marry her."

"Good," Gregor says.

"She said he had to give up cigarettes because she isn't running away to Tahiti with anybody who's trying to commit suicide, and as soon as she said that he threw his cigarette on the ground and put it out. It was the strangest thing. He looks very happy. I always had the feeling he was an enormously lonely man."

"He's an enormously outrageous man," Gregor said, "and she's probably one out of three women on earth who could put up with him. *I* talked to Cardinal O'Bannion. *He* says she's bringing him back to the Church."

"I'll bet he's talked her into premarital sexual intercourse anyway," Bennis said.

"Stop thinking about sex," Gregor said. "Think about food. Glinda looks very nice, you know, and she's just your height. *She* doesn't look as if she hasn't been able to afford a decent lunch since 1964."

"Never mind," Bennis said. "Get back to the point. Miriam picked up Josh Bailey meaning to use him as a scapegoat and a blind while she stole a lot of money from the bank—"

"Exactly." Gregor was engaged immediately. He didn't want to discuss anybody's life anyway. "Miriam went to Corfu looking for a young man for just that purpose," he said, "because it was just the kind of thing that would divert attention from anything and everything else she was doing. And the money she spent on him was a good diversion, too. There was a lot of outgo and activity in her accounts because of it. It was a lot easier to move around the money she was embezzling when she was moving a lot of money around anyway. Everybody thought she was doing her usual thing to keep on pampering Josh. I'm expressing myself badly."

"Tibor would understand you with no problem at all."

"Tibor's in the parade. Can you imagine John O'Bannion insisting on that?"

"They're old friends."

"Never mind that," Gregor said. "The thing is, it was a perfect plan. She got Josh. She had all the time in the world. Eventually, she was going to be free and on her own and seriously rich. You know, everybody kept saying how rich she was, and in relation to ordinary people she was rich. But she was Maryville rich, not New York City rich. And she was greedy."

"Isn't everybody?"

"No," Gregor said. "Anyway, I don't think she meant it all to come to a head so quickly. I think she meant to take her time, two or three more years, but then the Feds announced their audit and there she was. She, of course, had the fake computer fiddle, all set up to incriminate Ann-Harriet Severan. The Feds would find that first. The problem was, the Feds would find the rest of it in no time at all. The only chance she had was to get out before the fifth of March, and she had to pick up some serious cash in the meantime. You know, for a last minute bail-out plan, the one she came up with was very good."

"A little bloody, wouldn't you say?"

"There was no blood, Bennis. There was only poison. And yes, there was too much, but it's the way I told Pete Donovan. The last one was for hate. She brought Josh Malley back here and she expected him to keep up his half of their bargain. She paid for a very nice life for him and he pretended to be devoted to her instead. If she'd known more about people, she'd have realized that that was unlikely to be the way it worked out. I've met half a dozen women in my life who've married boys like Josh Malley. Not one of those boys was faithful."

"But," Bennis said, "she didn't care at all for Josh Malley. Why did it matter if he wasn't faithful?"

"Vanity." Gregor shrugged. "She's an arrogant woman and a conceited one, too. That love affair infuriated her. In the beginning I think she'd only meant to make Josh look foolish, to use him as a cover and then discard him. In the end, just to get back at him and Ann-Harriet for their extracurricular sex, she not only killed Ann-Harriet, she set up her murder to look as if Josh had committed it. Pete Donovan and his boys found a jar—a jar, mind you—of distilled coniine in Josh's gym bag. They also found kerosene. If Miriam didn't get him one way, she was going to get him another."

"But how did you know it wasn't Miriam dead in the greenhouse?" Bennis asked again. "How could you have?"

"I told you," Gregor said, "logically it couldn't have been. Then I started to ask around, and it was immediately apparent that nobody had actually seen her face. They'd seen her clothes. And then there were the shoes."

"The shoes?"

"Miriam Bailey was wearing stack-heeled shoes when I saw her outside the bank earlier that day. From the way the corpse was described to me by various people, it was wearing the same clothes Miriam had been wearing then, but spike heels. I'd also seen Ann-Harriet Severan earlier that day. She'd been wearing spike heels."

"Why do I feel," Bennis asked him, "that you're making this all up? That you made a lucky guess and it worked out and now you're taking credit for it."

"I'm not taking credit for anything," Gregor said. "Believe me, I've never felt so stupid in all my life."

"*Time* called it your most brilliant piece of deduction so far."

Gregor fixed Bennis with a stern look. "It is not a

brilliant piece of deduction," he said, "to drive yourself crazy for two hours trying to figure out how a corpse came to be in a locked building to which your chief suspect happens to have a key. It is not even common stupidity."

Bennis giggled. "Oh, dear. Was it that bad?"

"I was standing with Reverend Mother General in a room full of floor plans listening to her tell me that the only people who had a key to the front door that could circumvent the security system from the outside were herself, the security company that had installed the system, and the bank that held their mortgage and insisted on the system. I don't know how many times I'd been told by how many people that the Immigrants National Bank always held the mortgages on the Motherhouse when the Motherhouse needed them."

"It was that bad," Bennis said. "I'll have to get you something really nice to make up for it."

"Don't get me something really nice. Every time you get me something really nice, I feel like I ought to get it insured."

"It's silly to get things insured," Bennis said, "unless you're talking about houses or cars or something. Things are just things."

"Whatever that's supposed to mean."

"That's the float," Bennis said. "There's Tibor in a chair right behind Cardinal O'Bannion, next to the guest rabbi or whatever he is. At least Tibor's face is green."

[2]

Bennis had stood up and gone out to the sidewalk. Now Gregor went out after her, marveling again at how small she was. She had a great deal of force of personality. He often forgot that she was only five feet four. He stood behind her and looked out on Delaney Street, at the Cardinal in full regalia and his priests in fairly impressive costume as well. Behind them sat what Father Tibor had earlier that morning called "the ecumenical contingent." "It is a show of solidarity, Krekor, but it is silly. Between John and me there is solidarity. Between John and Reverend Marshall from the Baptists there is at this moment war." Gregor watched Tibor sitting bolt upright and staring straight ahead and smiled. It was going to be good to get back to Cavanaugh Street, even if it was going to be a few months before Tibor was finished with his teaching and in residence full-time. Bennis, at least, had finished the first draft of her book—if she hadn't, she wouldn't be here—and would be available for lunch and conversation.

"Bennis?" he asked. "When are the rest of them coming home?"

"The rest of who? Oh. Well. Old George Tekemanian is home."

"I thought he wasn't due back until the first of April."

"He wasn't. He got thrown out of Nassau."

"What?"

Bennis whirled around. "Now, Gregor," she said, "don't get upset. I mean, you know George, he's eighty-something, he couldn't really have been smoking marijuana, he says he was just trying to talk this boy he met out of smoking it and I believe him and as to the pinching women, well you know how he gets and he doesn't mean any harm by it—"

"Whom did he pinch?" Gregor demanded.

"Well, it was the governor's wife or the somebody's wife at any rate and you know he didn't mean—"

Out on Delaney Street, a new band had struck up "Danny Boy" in a distinctly marchlike, unsentimental way. Gregor took a deep breath and did his best to keep his face as stern as it ought to be. After all, he was the designated purveyor of Right Thinking and Common Sense on Cavanaugh Street. He couldn't have them thinking he liked all the nutsy things they did.

Stern or not, though, he was going to be glad to eat his way through this celebration and get himself home.

THE WORLD OF GREGOR DEMARKIAN

If you enjoyed *A GREAT DAY FOR THE DEADLY*, you will want to read Jane Haddam's other award-winning holiday mysteries!

Gregor Demarkian can't seem to take a holiday from crime.

At the age of 55, with a master's from Harvard and a 20-year-stint in the FBI, he finds himself retired, a widower, and an unofficial crime consultant. And in Gregor's neighborhood at holiday time, the death toll seems to climb. . . .

Not a Creature Was Stirring

❖

In the following excerpt from Jane Haddam's first Gregor Demarkian mystery, our hero is telling his old friend and neighbor George about a mysterious dinner invitation for Christmas Eve.

"Do you know a man named Robert Hannaford?" he asked.

"The robber baron?" George brightened.

"The great-grandson of the robber baron," Gregor said. "The one who's alive now."

George frowned. "Robert Hannaford can't have a great-grandson," he said. "He's only—forty something. I read it in the paper."

"Forty something?"

"In *The Inquirer*," George said.

"This Robert Hannaford who was in *The Inquirer*," Gregor said, "was he in a wheelchair?"

"Oh, no. He'd just won—a tennis championship, I think. It was in the paper, Krekor. I read it."

Gregor thought it over. "That's probably the son," he said finally. "The son of the Robert Hannaford who came to see Father Tibor. Tibor said he, this Robert Hannaford, had seven children—"

"Then he's not my Robert Hannaford," George said. "They called this one an eligible bachelor. You know what that means. Not married and making whoopie with every girl he meets."

"Yes," Gregor said. "But a robber baron?"

"A corporate raider," George said helpfully.

"Ah," Gregor said. "This is getting interesting.

Seven children, one of them a—robber baron. One of them a famous novelist—"

"Bennis Hannaford," George said, excited. "Father Tibor gave me her books. She's very good, Krekor. Very exciting."

"Does everybody around here read those things?" Gregor asked. It was remarkable what cultural climate could do. He had no interest whatsoever in fantasy fiction, or in fiction of any kind, but he was getting the urge to read Bennis Hannaford's books. He took another sip from his cup. "Mr. Hannaford asked Father Tibor to get in touch with me. He wants me to go out to his house and have dinner there on Christmas Eve."

"That was it? Just that you should have dinner there?"

"That was it for the request. He gave Father Tibor his card, and Father Tibor gave the card to me. I'm supposed to make a phone call. But Tibor said Hannaford insisted, and he stressed the 'insisted,' that there was nothing more to it but one dinner on the Main Line."

"Maybe it's because you're famous," George said, repeating the inaccuracy that was apparently believed by every resident of Cavanaugh Street. "Maybe he wants to impress his friends by bringing you out to dinner."

"Maybe."

George threw up his hands. "So what is it? It has to be something. What did he do, threaten Tibor with a gun?"

Gregor sat back, stretched out his legs, and told George all about the briefcase, the money, and the deal. His powers of narration seemed to have increased since he left the FBI. He'd never claimed quite that degree of attention from his listeners before.

By the time Gregor was finished, George was up on his feet and pacing—something, given arthritis and the general creakiness of old age, he never did. "But Krekor," he said. "That's crazy. That's the craziest thing I've ever heard."

"It's even crazier than you think it is," Gregor said.

"I don't see how it could be. It's crazy enough to start."

Gregor held up his glass and let George take it from

him. He wasn't in need of another drink, but watching George pace that way, in such obvious pain, made him feel terrible.

"Listen," he said. "If Robert Hannaford had been a self-made man, I might have looked at this thing and decided it was crazy but not impossible. But Robert Hannaford is not a self-made man. Do you see what I mean?"

"No," George said.

"Self-made men sometimes think anything can be solved by money. Their whole lives have been motivated by money. A man I knew, a congressman, told me once it was true that anyone can get rich in America—as long as that was all he wanted to do. That's the kind of commitment it takes, to be Carl Icahn, say. But the hereditary rich are different. They have money."

"So?"

"So they learn early that there are a hundred better ways of getting what they want than shelling out cash. They have family connections—in Washington, in New York, in government and industry and the security services. If Hannaford wants me out at Engine House for Christmas Eve dinner, why not just call somebody who knows somebody at the Bureau? The Bureau knows where to find me. What's more, anybody with any sense has to realize I owe those people."

George nodded. "All right. So why?"

"My considered judgment?"

"Yes, of course."

"Gossip," Gregor said definitely. "Whatever's going on with Robert Hannaford has to be sensitive enough so that he doesn't want any gossip. Which means it's probably actionable. You know what I'd do, if this had happened when I was still working?"

"Send Mr. J. Edgar Hoover after them?"

"J. Edgar," Gregor said, "is blessedly dead. Blessedly for the rest of us, I mean. No, what I'd have done is go straight to the senator I thought I could trust most. And I do mean straight."

George had settled himself in his chair again. The part of him moving now was his head. It was going back and forth like a door swinging on its hinge in a stiff wind. "Krekor, you're talking as if this is about spies."

"Spies is one of the things that might explain it. I can think of two others."

"What?"

"That one of his children is involved in a plot to kill the president. Or that one of his children is involved in major fraud."

This time it was George who took a long pull on his drink. He looked like he thought he needed it. "Krekor, in your voice I can hear it. You don't believe any of those things. I don't believe any of those things, either. They sound like science fiction. Miss Hannaford's unicorns are for me more real."

"Well," Gregor said, "that sort of thing is real enough for me. I've spent most of my life living with it in one way or another. What bothers me is that I don't think any of it is real in this case."

"Why not?"

Gregor waved a hand in the air. "For serious espionage, you need access. From what I've been able to figure out so far, neither Hannaford himself nor any of his children have it. As for the other things—Tibor thinks this man is, I wouldn't say an agent of the devil, but close. He didn't like Hannaford at all."

"Then there's probably nothing to like," George said. "Tibor isn't a practical man, but I would listen to him about people."

"So would I," Gregor said. "Tibor thinks Hannaford hates his children. Hates them unreservedly."

"And?"

"And a man who hates his children doesn't throw a hundred thousand dollars in cash around to get them out of trouble."

"Ah," George said.

"Exactly," Gregor said. "I thought about the wife, but Tibor says she's some kind of invalid. Very social and very involved in good works, but basically domestic and too ill to get around and do things. I think she gets written up on the society pages a lot."

George sighed. "So," he said. "Here we are. Maybe

the man is just crazy in the real way. Maybe he belongs in an institution."

"I don't know, George. I just know I don't like this thing. I don't like him involving Tibor, and I don't like—well, what it feels like."

"Do you know what you're going to do about it?"

"No."

"I don't know what you're going to do about it, either. Have a little more rum, Krekor. It's good for the brain."

Gregor doubted it, but he knew it was good for the nerves. He needed something for those.

Precious Blood

❖

In this Gregor Demarkian mystery, Eastertime is the time for crime. In the sample that follows, Gregor talks to the irrepressible Father Tibor Kasparian about the curious demise of Cheryl Cass.

Gregor eyed the coffee warily, picked it up, took a sip, and put it down again. Why were the only people he knew who could make palatable coffee women? Especially since women didn't want to make it any more. For reasons Gregor had to admit were totally justified.

"Several weeks ago," he told Tibor, "some time between Ash Wednesday and the end of that week, there was a death."

"A death?"

"The woman who died had been a classmate of Andy Walsh's in parochial school and a student at the sister school of the boys' school he attended for high school. Her name was Cheryl Cass. She'd moved out of the parish, out of Colchester in fact, before she ever graduated. As far as anybody knows, she'd never been back."

"As far as anyone knows?"

Gregor shifted uncomfortably. "You have to understand, Tibor. I've got all my information on this thing over the phone—"

"And from John O'Bannion?" Tibor smiled.

"I'm not an idiot, Father. No, I've talked to the Colchester police more than once. There's a lot about this that's very fishy. It's just not fishy the way the Cardinal wants it to be."

"What way is that?"

"Let me explain. Cheryl Cass was dying. She'd had a double mastectomy, and the cancer, according to the coroner, had not been caught in time. She was riddled with it. In all likelihood, she had only months to live. The Colchester police are fairly certain she hadn't been living in town for any length of time before she was found. She wasn't known at any of the hospitals and they haven't turned up a local doctor who'd been treating her, although somebody had been. The body showed signs of extensive radiation therapy."

"Where had she been?" Tibor asked.

"They don't know. She wasn't carrying a driver's license—"

"Isn't that very unusual? I thought I was the only person in America without one."

"She'd been on radiation therapy, remember. And she'd probably been taking painkillers. She probably hadn't been able to drive for a long time. Unfortunately, without the driver's license, there's no way to know where she'd been living."

"Credit cards?"

"She didn't have any Maveronski at Colchester Homicide said she didn't look like she could have gotten them. Her wardrobe was definitely low rent."

"A poor woman, then," Tibor said. "This is very sad."

"It gets sadder. As far as anyone knows, Cheryl Cass showed up in Colchester on Ash Wednesday and immediately got in contact with several people. Andy Walsh was one of them. So was O'Bannion's chief aide, Father Tom Dolan. So was the principal at St. Agnes Parochial School, Sister Mary Scholastica, once known as Kathleen

Burke. Cheryl went to visit all these people over the course of the day—"

"Did she know them, Krekor?"

"Oh, yes," Gregor said. "They'd all been at those brother-and-sister schools I told you about. Cathedral Girls' High and Cathedral Boys'. They were either all in the same year or close to it."

"That's very clear, then, Krekor. This is a poor woman who is dying. She goes back to the town of her childhood and visits her old friends. Just one more time. That is understandable."

"I agree with you. So, by the way, do the Colchester police. They think she went to visit all these people and then walked around town some, maybe disoriented. There were no traces of painkillers in her body and none on her person. They think she may have run out and been wandering around in pain. Anyway, wander she did, clear across town to the hotel district."

"And?"

Gregor sighed. "Common sense says she should have rented a room, but she might not have been able to afford one. There wasn't any money found on the body, either, but that doesn't mean anything. It could have been taken off her where she lay."

"Krekor, I don't understand. She was outside?"

"In an alley that connects Schrencker Street with Maydown Avenue, between two of the most expensive hotels in the city, the Lombard and the Maverick. Those, she couldn't have afforded. The man I talked to in the Colchester Homicide Department says it looked like she'd just lain down on the ground and let herself die."

"From the cancer?"

"No," Gregor said explosively. "This is where it gets fishy. From nicotine poisoning."

Act of Darkness

❖

The Fourth of July finds Gregor playing sleuth at the lush seaside estate of the wealthy and eccentric Victoria Harte. The following section describes his arrival.

Out on the drive, Bennis Hannaford and Victoria Harte were standing together, not so much making small talk as trading monosyllables. Neither of them was looking at the other. Gregor got the distinct impression that they'd each decided to loathe the other on sight.

Gregor brushed the wrinkles out of his trousers and came around the car to the two women, feeling like a ball of wax melting under the heat of a flame. It was quarter after nine, and the temperature had to be well above the seventy-eight degrees it had been at eight o'clock. It might even be over eighty-eight. The air felt as thick as half-set Jell-O.

He held his hand out to Victoria Harte and said, "What kind of gate-crashers?"

Victoria Harte smiled. "It's only on holiday weekends," she told him. "They know Stephen and Janet will be here, and probably bringing a pile of friends, and they think with the confusion—"

"The gate-crashers are looking for Senator Fox?"

"No, no." Victoria Harte waved this away. "They're looking for me, naturally. Women my own age mostly, I'm sorry to say. I don't seem to go over big with the present generation, except with homosexuals, of course. Sometimes I wonder what women my age would do without homosexuals. Are you a supporter of the civil rights of gays?"

"Excuse me?" Gregor said.

"I was a supporter of gay rights long before any of these people thought of it," Victoria Harte said. "Years ago, even back in the fifties. And of course, I've done a great deal of work collecting money for research into AIDS."

"Mmm," Gregor said.

"I'd heard about it," Bennis said.

Victoria Harte shot Bennis a look and went on. "My son-in-law," she said, "is not what I'd call staunch in the struggle. Not staunch in any struggle for anything, if you want to know the truth. But Miss Hannaford probably told you that. She used to be a—great supporter of the senator's." Victoria smiled carefully.

"I met him a couple of times when I was living in Washington," Bennis said tightly. "Ten years ago. At least."

"Not all that much changes in ten years," Victoria said. "Especially not with Stephen. I've known him for twenty, and I don't think he's had a single new idea in all that time. I don't think he's had a single old one, either. May I ask you a question, Mr. Demarkian?"

"Of course." Actually, what Gregor really wanted was for Victoria to go on talking, babbling bitchiness, just as she had been doing. It would have given him time to collect himself, and he needed it. The heat was getting to him. He was feeling a little sick.

Victoria must have noticed it. She was moving away from the car, toward the shade of the portico, talking all the way. They both followed her as if drawn, because there was nothing else to do.

"You may have noticed I'm being very patriotic this weekend," she was saying. "Flags. Red, white, and blue." She gestured at the decorations on the lawn, which were limp. "Of course, I'm not patriotic in the vulgar sense at any time. The Vietnam War took care of all that for me. All waving the flag around ever does is give governments an excuse to kill a lot of innocent people. Especially this government. But—"

"But?" Gregor said. Then he thought, This would make more sense if she sounded like she meant it, which she doesn't.

"But," Victoria Harte went on, "the fact is, I probably wouldn't have shown the colors this weekend, even for Stephen and Janet's sake, if it wasn't for just one thing."

"What thing?"

"You," Victoria said.

They were now comfortably under the portico, out of the sun but not out of the heat. Gregor could feel a river of sweat rolling down his spine. Great Expectations had to have central air conditioning. It was the kind of house that was built for it. He desperately wanted to get inside.

Victoria stopped at the doors and turned back to them. "Remember how I said I wanted to ask you a question?"

"Yes, I do." He bit back the rest of what he wanted to say, which was, Get on with it.

"It's actually a series of questions. It starts with an easy one. Are you the man who helped John Cardinal O'Bannion with his little problem up in Colchester a few months ago?"

"Whoosh," Bennis whispered in his ear. "There goes our cover."

"Are you?" Victoria insisted.

"Yes," Gregor said.

"Fine. Then I take it you are also the man who founded the serial murderers division at the Federal Bureau of Investigation."

"It's called the Behavioral Sciences Department, Miss Harte. And I didn't found it. It was founded by an Act of Congress and the then-director of the Bureau. All I did was the day-to-day dirty work."

"I don't think that's quite honest," Victoria said. "But we'll let it go. It comes down to the same thing, no matter how you phrase it. You're a specialist in murder."

"I'm not a specialist in anything, Miss Harte. I'm retired. I'm not a private investigator. I have no license. I have never taken money, as a private citizen, for investigating anything at all."

"After you left Colchester, Cardinal O'Bannion paid twenty-five thousand dollars into the Armenian Refugees Relief Fund in the name of Father Tibor Kasparian. Father Kasparian is your parish priest."

"Father Tibor," Bennis said automatically.

"Father Tibor and the cardinal," Gregor said, "have been close friends for several years."

"Really. I suppose it's even true. But I'll tell you something that isn't true, Mr. Demarkian. You, as a campaign contributor. Especially as a campaign contributor to Stephen Whistler Fox. You're much too intelligent for that. Do you want to know what else isn't true?"

"What?"

"You, as the fat, middle-aged lover of this wayward debutante here."

"Ah," Gregor said.

"I am not a wayward debutante," Bennis said.

Victoria pulled open the great front double doors of her house, stepped into the foyer, and told them, "If the two of you were lovers, she'd be wearing a great deal less underwear."

Quoth the Raven

❖

QUOTH THE RAVEN is Jane Haddam's Halloween treat for Gregor Demarkian fans. The next passage sums up Gregor's feelings about the spookiest night of the year.

The problem, he decided later, as he climbed the marble steps to that crazily covered door, was in his history. It was nice to pretend that Halloween was nothing but a holiday for children, that nothing went on under the cover of it but the benign fantasies of little boys who wanted to grow up to be superheroes. It was even nice when grown-up people, who ought to know better, worked overtime to make sure their children got a cozy, unthreatening picture of the dead of night. It was not so nice when the grown-up people began to believe their own propaganda. Gregor Demarkian had not only spent twenty years of his life in the FBI. He had spent ten of those twenty years—the whole second half of his career, from the day the states of Washington and

Oregon had requested federal help in catching a killer called "Ted" to the day his wife Elizabeth, ill with cancer, had entered her final crisis—chasing serial murderers. He knew far too much about the things people did to each other and more than far too much about Halloween. Halloween was, as a colleague of his had once said, the night of the werewolf. For 364 days out of every year, things went along more or less as they could be expected to go along. Even the Green River Killers, the Ten Bundys, the Sons of Sam, had their routines. On the 365th day, all hell broke loose. The rabbity serial killer you had been tracing for six months suddenly took his knife and cut fifteen people in half an hour. The teenage boy who had always seemed only to want to look like James Dean suddenly decided to ram himself and six of his friends off the edge of lover's lane. The nicest little old lady in the neighborhood suddenly made up her mind to put cyanide into the caramel apples she passed out to the children who came to her door. *Suddenly* was definitely the best word for Halloween. *Unexpectedly* was the second-best one.

Jane Haddam's Gregor Demarkian Holiday Mysteries are spellbinding. Don't be surprised when you get a *sudden* and *unexpected* urge to read the next one . . . *A FEAST OF MURDER*, available from your local bookseller in time for Thanksgiving, October 1992.